Three Great
Nancy Drew®
Mysteries

Nancy Drew®
in

The Twin Dilemma

The Captive Witness

The Mystery of the
Winged Lion

by Carolyn Keene

illustrated by Paul Frame

This *Nancy Drew* Three-in-One
was first published in the UK in 1987.
This edition published in 1994 by Diamond Books,
77–85 Fulham Palace Road, Hammersmith,
London W6 8JB.

Published pursuant to agreement with Grosset & Dunlap, Inc.,
New York, NY, USA.

Nancy Drew® in

The Twin Dilemma

The Twin Dilemma was
first published in the U.K. in a single volume in Armada in 1982

Contents

1

The Missing Model

"Nancy!" Eloise Drew exclaimed happily as she opened the door of her apartment. "Am I glad you're here!"

"That makes two of us, Aunt Eloise," the eighteen-year-old said. "I mean, four of us!"

The young detective gestured toward her friends, Bess Marvin and George Fayne, who were dragging large suitcases down the carpeted hallway.

"You didn't know we planned to stay in New York forever," Nancy said teasingly as the girls set the luggage down in the apartment.

Aunt Eloise laughed. "I hope you're as well prepared for the assignment I have for you as you seem to be with all that luggage you brought along. It's a model mystery."

9

There was a glint of mischief in her doe-brown eyes as she noticed her niece's bewilderment. Nancy was the daughter of Carson Drew, Aunt Eloise's brother, a well-known attorney in River Heights. Nancy had frequently assisted him on cases and had gained a substantial reputation for herself as an amateur detective.

Bess and George looked surprised as well. "I thought we were here to see a benefit fashion show and have a fun vacation," Bess said, poking a strand of blond hair behind her ear.

"Is that where the model mystery is?" George asked. Unlike her plump cousin, Bess, she was tall and slim with dark hair cropped fairly short.

"Yes and no," Aunt Eloise replied. "Remember, I told you I'm involved in running a benefit fashion show? Well, one of our models has disappeared. She wasn't at the rehearsal today, and she isn't at home. Nobody seems to know where she went. Jacqueline Henri is her name. Perhaps you've heard of her."

"Oh, she's gorgeous," Bess swooned. "Bony thin with fabulous black hair and violet eyes. She's been on the covers of lots of magazines. I'd love to meet her!"

"I was planning to introduce you tonight—"

"What if we can't find her before the show starts?" Nancy said, assuming that the search was the assignment her aunt had mentioned.

"You'll be stuck without a model," George said to Nancy's aunt.

"No, I won't," Eloise Drew said. "If you promise not to disappear on me, too, Nancy, I'd like you to stand in for Jacqueline."

"Me? Oh, I couldn't!" the girl protested.

"Sure you could," Bess spoke up. "You've done modeling before."

"But only at the Woman's Club," Nancy said. "Besides, how could I possibly wear clothes meant for Jacqueline Henri? She must be thinner than I am, and we don't have the same coloring."

"Not much thinner," Aunt Eloise said, stepping back to look at the girl. "And your coloring is fine, too. You'll see."

"But what about Jacqueline?" Nancy asked.

Her aunt pursed her lips. "I don't know what to think. Marjorie Tyson, my co-chairman, has been trying to track her down ever since this morning."

"Maybe something happened to her," Bess commented.

"Or maybe she's just unreliable," her cousin added.

"Well, I don't want you girls to trouble your-selves about her until after the show," Aunt Eloise said. "We expect to have more than five hundred people in the audience and we can't disappoint them."

Although the program was still several hours away, the visitors quickly freshened up and changed. Aunt Eloise made a number of tele-phone calls, and when she finally laid down the receiver, she sighed happily.

"It's all arranged. We have to get over to the hotel as soon as possible," the woman said, ducking her head into the girls' room. "Mr. Reese—"

"Richard Reese, the famous designer?" Bess interrupted.

Aunt Eloise nodded. "He needs to see you for a fitting, Nancy."

"I'm almost ready," the young detective said, fumbling nervously with the zipper of a long, emerald-green taffeta skirt.

"Very pretty, dear," her aunt replied, "but why not carry it with you? You can change for the party after the show."

"Oh, you're right," Nancy said while Bess and George helped each other fasten tiny hooks on their gowns.

"Come on, slowpoke," George teased Nancy

as she slipped out of the skirt into another and kicked off her satin shoes in favor of leather heels.

She put everything into a garment bag with pockets for accessories, then joined the others in the living room. Bess giggled while George stepped toward Nancy, her eyes clearly fixed on the girl's titian head.

"What's so funny?" Nancy asked.

George removed a hairclip that had pinned back an unruly curl.

"The stylist will fix your hair," Aunt Eloise assured her niece as they left.

The girls didn't discuss the model again until their cab cut across Fifth Avenue toward Rockefeller Center. It came to a halt for a few moments while two limousines merged into the line of traffic, giving Nancy and the others a chance to study the crowd who watched the skaters in the rink below. They were gliding in tempo to a familiar melody.

As the cab started to move again, Nancy and Bess, who was nearest the window, noticed an attractive young woman among the pedestrians on Fifth Avenue. She wore a dappled fur coat and a hat to match that barely covered a thick mane of ebony hair.

"It's Jacqueline Henri!" Bess cried, as the

model darted to the corner of the block behind them.

"Are you sure?" Nancy asked.

"Positive."

Instantly, Aunt Eloise, who was squeezed tightly between the girls, reached for the cab door.

"Please stop," she told the driver, but retracted the request when she observed Jacqueline stepping into a cab that was evidently headed downtown, away from their destination.

"We couldn't catch her if we tried," she concluded.

"Does Jacqueline live around here?" Nancy inquired.

"On the other side of Rockefeller Center, near Broadway, I think," Aunt Eloise answered. "Perhaps she had trouble getting a taxi up there and decided to walk until she found one."

"At least we know she's all right," Bess said.

"Aunt Eloise, you said people were trying to track her down all day," Nancy commented. "Did anyone actually go to her apartment?"

"Probably not. Everybody's been terribly busy at the hotel ballroom."

"Does Miss Henri have an answering service?" Nancy went on.

"Oh, yes. I'd venture to say every working model does."

"But she didn't leave a message?" George put in.

"No. There was no explanation for her absence whatsoever."

"That's strange," Nancy said. "Seems to me that she didn't become a top model by being irresponsible. And yet, she's obviously in town. She could have called."

They rode in silence until they reached the hotel. By now the last glimmer of sun had faded between the tall buildings, and there was only a residue of dusky glow when the girls got out of the cab and smiled at the doorman under the gold canopy.

Nancy took a deep breath as he opened the door, admitting the visitors to an elegant, wood-paneled lobby. Aunt Eloise led the way past velvet ottomans to a room adjacent to the dining area. It was filled with clothing racks.

"I can't wait to see everything," Bess sighed, watching a girl pull a soft coral-colored pants suit off one of the racks. "Which outfits will Nancy be wearing?"

George noticed a sheer turquoise dress on the same rack marked REESE. "That one, maybe?" she said.

"No," Aunt Eloise replied. "Because of the switch in models, Mr. Reese has made a few changes in his selection. Follow me, everybody."

"Suppose Jacqueline shows up in time?" Nancy asked.

"She'll be out of luck," Aunt Eloise said firmly. "We won't rearrange everything again at the last minute."

She stepped across the room and introduced the girls to Marjorie Tyson, a petite woman with short, gray hair that framed her thin, lively face.

"Am I glad you're here!" she greeted Nancy, causing the girls to laugh.

"That's what Aunt Eloise said, Miss Tyson," Nancy explained. Then she told the woman about the model they had spotted at Rockefeller Center.

"Well, if she comes now, she'll be too late," Miss Tyson said, agreeing with Aunt Eloise's decision. "And please call me Marjorie. Nancy, the dresses you'll be modeling are over there. Bess and George, do you mind waiting while I take Nancy to a dressing alcove? There's a bench for you in the corner."

"Of course not," Bess replied and Marjorie

16

strode toward the rack of clothes. Then she gaped in shock.

"There are only a few outfits left! I wonder what happened to the rest."

Suddenly, a man in a turtleneck sweater and jeans appeared from behind a screen carrying an empty box. He dumped it on the floor, his face a contortion of rage.

"They're gone! Every last one gone!" he shouted angrily.

"But what about these?" Marjorie said, touching one of the pastel gowns on the rack.

"Never mind these," he roared. "They're the ones the thief left!" With that, he snapped them off the metal hanger and stormed past the two women.

"Mr. Reese!" Majorie pleaded. "Please tell us what's going to happen. This is Nancy Drew, Jackie's replacement. She's all ready to—"

"Forget it!" the designer snapped. "I don't care who she is. All I know is that my clothes are gone!

2

Design Scoop!

The force of his words made Nancy flinch. She knew it was futile to try to stop the man. He had already ignored Marjorie Tyson and was marching forward, blinded by the puffed sleeves of an organza dress he was clutching tightly.

"Out of my way!" he bellowed at no one in particular.

But it was too late! Bess and George, who had left their seats to talk with Aunt Eloise, were just crossing the room in front of him. He crashed into them, causing them to stumble in different directions. Mr. Reese himself tripped over the metal foot of the rack, and fell headlong into the clothes that hung on it, ripping them off hangers.

"Oh, Mr. Reese!" Marjorie squealed, running to help the man up.

Aunt Eloise and the girls joined her, but he refused their assistance. He sputtered as he tried to get to his feet, then slipped on the hem of a satin skirt and wound up on the floor again.

The young detectives tried to keep from laughing, but the designer heard Bess's giggle and gritted his teeth. He flung the satin skirt aside, clearing his path at last. When he stood up to face Miss Tyson and Aunt Eloise, he glared at them.

"I should never have listened to Sheila," he complained.

"Who's Sheila?" George whispered.

"Maybe his wife?" Bess guessed, as the girls picked up the fallen clothes and hung them on the rack.

"Those don't belong there," Mr. Reese snarled, pointing to the four outfits he had held in his arms before he fell. "Can't you read?"

The sign on the rack said STEINER, referring to another designer in the fashion show.

"Did you want to leave your things on the floor?" a voice from behind them asked.

It belonged to a woman who wore a smock and a pincushion on her wrist that contained plenty of needles.

"And you're fired, Rosalind!" he growled back, sending the woman into a flood of tears.

"You can't walk out on us now," Aunt Eloise begged him.

"What do you mean I can't? I can and I am."

"Mr. Reese," Nancy interrupted in the sweetest tone she could muster, "perhaps I can be of help. I'm a detective."

He looked at the girl, his expression changing dramatically. He gave a war whoop and laughed loudly.

"Sure. And I'm the Emperor of China!"

Bess and George bit their lips to keep from saying something they might regret later.

"Nancy *is* a detective." Aunt Eloise defended her niece.

"Of course, maybe Mr. Reese doesn't need a detective," Nancy challenged. "He hasn't told us yet what his problem is!"

"I'll tell you what I need—a bodyguard for my clothes!" he stated flatly. "The ones I selected for you, Miss Drew, were taken."

"Stolen?" George asked.

"Exactly."

"What makes you so positive they were stolen?" Nancy inquired. Then, seeing the irritation grow in his face, she quickly changed the question. "Might they have been misplaced?"

"No. I personally rode over here with everything, and up until an hour ago when I had to make a phone call, I did not leave this room."

As he talked, Nancy walked toward two chairs, leaving her friends to discuss the situation among themselves. By now, the man's temper had subsided and he followed her, anxious to know her thoughts on the situation.

"It was all Sheila's idea—my wife's," he said. "She's involved in practically every charity in New York, including this one. She asked me if I'd mind showing a few of the new spring designs before their official debut. Well, I said I would look over the lot and pull what I could for this show."

"How many outfits in all?" Nancy questioned.

"In the spring collection or for this show only?"

"For this show."

"Seven."

"There were four in the alcove," Nancy muttered, "so three are missing."

"That's right."

"I still don't understand, though, how they could've disappeared without someone seeing the thief."

"I can't figure it out, either." The designer

moaned. "I'll have to leave that mystery up to you."

The girl detective had only been in New York a short time and already she had encountered two mysteries—Jacqueline Henri's strange behavior and the theft of the Reese creations.

Out of the corner of her eye she noticed Aunt Eloise checking her watch. The fashion show was scheduled to begin in fewer than forty-five minutes, and Nancy wondered how they would compensate for the missing portion of the program.

Richard Reese saw the anxiety in her eyes, cleared his throat several times, and finally spoke. "You're not Jacqueline, but you'll do."

"You mean it?" Nancy gasped in excitement. "You'll let me model your clothes?"

He nodded, somewhat embarrassed, then regained his composure and ordered her into the dressing alcove.

"Rosalind?" he called out, but there was no response. "Where is she?" he asked Marjorie Tyson.

"You fired her, remember?"

"Oh, that's ridiculous," Mr. Reese said. "She knows I have a bad temper."

Even so, his assistant did not return and another young woman was asked to help out.

"This is Yolanda. She's one of our stylists and she will help you dress," the designer announced. "We don't have much time left and I must fit you before you go onstage."

It was decided that instead of introducing the program, Nancy would be third.

"Good luck—I mean, break a leg," George told her friend as she and Bess excused themselves to find their table in the ballroom.

Nancy, however, was busy listening to instructions from the designer and did not hear the girls say good-bye. She was quickly hurried behind the screen in the dressing room and handed a softly ruffled, blue silk blouse and a matching skirt with a short linen jacket.

I hope it fits, she murmured to herself, fastening the skirt waist. It was snug, but not uncomfortable. Then came the jacket over the blouse. The sleeves slid over her arms easily and, to her relief, the cuff length was perfect. She stepped out in front of the mirror, letting Yolanda tug and smooth the clothes until they hung neatly.

"Now the hair," the stylist said. She pulled a brush out of a pocket and swept it through Nancy's titian waves. "We want a natural look," she said as she finished, and then led her to Mr. Reese.

"Wonderful!" he exclaimed, then asked Nancy to walk the length of the room. "Just relax," he told her. "Now turn and come back."

The grin on his face proved that he was pleased with her performance. A few moments later, he escorted her to the stage, leaving her to wait for her cue.

"The spring season would not be complete . . ." Nancy heard the hostess say into the microphone, and she felt someone nudge her onto the runway.

Lights flashed around the ballroom as the girl detective posed in front of the curtain for a few seconds. The hostess, a striking woman in a glittering sequined gown, smiled at Nancy, motioning her to move forward.

"The jacket is reversible," she told the audience, something Nancy had not even noticed. The girl opened the jacket to reveal the lining and was about to remove it when Mr. Reese suddenly bolted toward the microphone.

"Leave, Miss Drew!" he shouted. "Get off the stage—now!"

Nancy blinked her eyes, momentarily stunned. Surely he wasn't serious, she thought, and remaining poised, she turned on her heels and walked back to the curtain.

"I am very sorry about this, ladies and gentlemen," he said, "but I must remove my designs from this program! I have been robbed!"

The hostess quickly cupped her hand over the microphone, begging him to say no more. He shrugged, then grabbed Nancy's arm and pulled her offstage. "I should never have listened to you," he snapped.

Nancy stared at him, openmouthed. "What happened?"

Mr. Reese hurried her back to the dressing room and pointed to a large catalog that bore the name Millington.

"Look at it," he told the girl.

Nancy leafed through the book, unsure of what she was supposed to find. It contained a variety of items, mostly clothing.

"Stop there," Mr. Reese said as she turned to a page near the end.

By now Bess and George had made their way into the dressing room, wondering anxiously what had caused the latest disruption. Aunt Eloise and Marjorie Tyson, on the other hand, had darted behind the stage to soothe the nerves of the next model.

"I think Reese is a bit daffy," Marjorie confided to Aunt Eloise. "The way he blows hot and cold, why, it's enough to drive anyone crazy!"

3

Stranger's Story

"But how could anyone get hold of your designs?" George asked Mr. Reese.

He had collapsed into a chair and buried his face in his hands. "I don't know, I don't know," he kept repeating. "We have very tight security in the office."

"Maybe that's part of the answer," Nancy said.

She was about to inquire into his staff but realized she ought to wait until after the fashion show. The sponsors had lost a precious contribution when the designer pulled out so abruptly, and she was determined to do all she could to reverse the effect.

"Please let me go on," Nancy begged the man.

"And have these clothes photographed for the Millington catalog, too? Never!"

"But the damage has already been done," Nancy said. She thrust the catalog under the man's nose and pointed to a picture of a skirt and jacket that closely resembled the one she wore.

"That's right," Aunt Eloise, who was standing in the doorway, chimed in. "Our patrons have paid a lot of money for their tickets, Mr. Reese, and to disrupt every—"

Her voice broke off as tears welled up in her eyes. She started to walk away when Marjorie Tyson strode past her, carrying a message.

"Maybe this will change your mind," she said confidently.

Mr. Reese glanced at the folded paper with disinterest.

"Please—read this," the woman persisted.

As he opened it, Nancy could not help seeing that it was a request to buy the same outfit she had modeled only a short while ago.

"Zoe Babbitt is an old customer of mine," the man mumbled, referring to the signature on the note.

"Then—" Nancy said hopefully.

"Yolanda, get the organza!" Mr. Reese demanded, and the stylist hurried off.

Instantly, Aunt Eloise threw her arms around his shoulders and planted a kiss on his cheek. "You're wonderful," she said gaily.

"Oh, stop it," he replied in embarrassment. "And hurry up!"

"Thank you," Aunt Eloise said quietly. She and Marjorie followed Bess and George back to the ballroom, leaving Nancy to attend to the next change of clothing.

As before, the second outfit fit almost perfectly. This time, however, Nancy winced as Yolanda drew the long zipper over her waist and up the back.

"Can you breathe?" Yolanda teased, noting the pinch in the midriff.

"Barely," Nancy replied hoarsely. She didn't dare relax for fear she would split a seam!

"What do you think, Mr. Reese?" Yolanda asked when the girl stood before him at last.

Instantly, he noticed the thin crease in the waistline, but a glance at his watch made him admit, "I'm afraid we haven't time to fix it." Then, as if a bolt of lightning had struck, he snapped his fingers. "Wait a minute," he said, and dived into a nearby box filled with assorted buttons and ribbons. He pulled out a long, wide band of grosgrain that was the same shade of lilac as the gown.

31

"Perfect," Yolanda said. She tied it into a pretty bow around the girl's waist, then quickly pinned Nancy's hair back, letting only a few wisps play against her cheekbones.

It was no surprise to either Mr. Reese or his assistant that the young model was greeted with loud applause. Nancy was stunning and sailed down the runway as if she had done it many times. The remaining two outfits, a tailored white suit and a silk hostess gown, were equally popular.

When Nancy stood at the end of the platform for the last time, a camera flashed in the back of the room, drawing her attention there. Not far from where the flash had come stood a woman in a dappled fur coat thrown casually over her shoulders.

That looks like Jacqueline Henri, Nancy thought. She was tempted to stare, but forced herself to turn instead and walk slowly toward the curtain where she posed once more before exiting.

"Wasn't she marvelous?" the hostess said to the audience over the microphone, bringing another round of applause for Nancy.

But the girl detective heard only an echo of it as she rushed back to the dressing room to change into her own skirt and blouse. She wondered if Bess and George had spotted the model, too. However, before she could consider the possibility further, she found herself surrounded by Mr. Reese and several young women. All of them complimented her profusely.

"Miss Drew," Mr. Reese said with an air of formality, "will you help me find the thieves?"

"I was just about to ask you for your business card," Nancy replied, smiling.

She pulled away long enough to slip into the clothes she had brought from Aunt Eloise's, then emerged to face Mr. Reese once again.

"Where are you running to, Nancy?" he asked inquisitively, adding, "I'd like to talk with you if you can spare a minute."

Nancy glanced past the man in preoccupation. She was eager to find Jacqueline Henri but decided not to mention anything to Mr. Reese.

"Perhaps we could discuss the theft tomorrow," she suggested, smiling politely.

"I may have to leave on business," was the reply. "Can't we—"

The girl detective broke in gently. "On second thought," she said, "I wonder if you would draw me some rough sketches of the dresses that were stolen tonight."

"Of course, I'd be glad to, but—"

"And jot down the type of material you used for each one," Nancy concluded. "Now, I really must get back to the ballroom."

As she hurried toward the corridor, Mr. Reese told her he would have the sketches ready by morning.

"Great," Nancy called back. Her feet picked up speed as the sound of music drifted into the lobby, but when she stepped into the ballroom, she halted immediately.

What if Jacqueline had left? She trained her vision on the couples who were dancing, then shifted it to the tables. Bess and George waved to her, but Nancy did not see them. Instead, she was struck by the sight of a dappled fur coat on a nearby chair.

That's Jacquel—Nancy gasped to herself when the young woman seemed to appear from nowhere.

"Miss Henri!" Nancy exclaimed, running to her. "We've been worried sick about you."

The puzzled expression that greeted her prompted Nancy to explain the comment. She introduced herself as Eloise Drew's niece.

"I tried to be here on time for the show," Jacqueline said, "but couldn't make it. I phoned your aunt, but she had already left."

"I'm sure she'd like to talk to you now," Nancy said. "She—" Her sentence was interrupted by an announcement over the loudspeaker.

"Will Jacqueline Henri please come to the desk."

The young woman looked worried and tense. "That's for me," she said. "I'll have to go now."

"Is something the matter?" Nancy asked, sensing that there was.

"No—I'll call your aunt tomorrow." But before the model was able to excuse herself, Bess and George had joined the two.

"Oh, Miss Henri! It's a pleasure to meet you!" Bess called out, extending her hand at the same time. Jacqueline's was cold and clammy. "Wasn't Nancy wonderful?" Bess rambled on until her cousin spoke.

"We wondered what had happened to you," George said. "Why didn't you come to work?"

"I—I couldn't," Jacqueline said. "Something terrible happened and—" She broke off and started to turn away from the trio.

Nancy gently put her hand on the model's arm. "Maybe we can help?"

Jackie shook her head. "No, you can't," she answered. "It's about my brother. He may have been kidnapped!"

4

Studio Clue

"Kidnapped! Are you sure?" Nancy asked.

Again the call came over the loudspeaker, interrupting the model before she could reply.

"Miss Jacqueline Henri, will Miss Jacqueline Henri please come to the desk," the voice repeated.

"I'll be back," she told the girls abruptly and walked away.

"If she believes her brother was kidnapped," George said, "what's she doing here?"

"Maybe *he* was supposed to be here," Nancy suggested, glancing in the direction of the lobby.

The hotel desk was not visible from where the girls stood and Nancy wondered how much longer it would be before the young woman returned.

"Maybe she said that only to keep us from following her," George remarked after several minutes.

"Come on," Nancy said, leading the two cousins across the corridor. "Let's see if we can find her."

As they stepped into the main lobby, they were astonished by the number of people with suitcases crowding the registration area.

"They must've come in on a late plane," Nancy observed.

"Or a bus," George said, directing everyone's attention to a man in a driver's uniform.

He pushed his way through the crowd, waving his hands and talking at the same time. The hubbub dissipated as the group huddled around him.

"I don't see Jacqueline anywhere," Bess commented.

"She could've met someone and left," Nancy said, and hurried toward one of the desk clerks, asking if he knew where the stunning, black-haired woman had gone.

"I haven't seen her at all," the young man replied, "and from your description, I'm sure I'd remember her."

Then, on a sudden thought, she approached the bus driver. He had been outside the hotel when Jacqueline left, if, in fact, she had. But to Nancy's chagrin, the man said he had not seen her, either.

"Let's go back to the ballroom," Nancy said. "I'm sure Aunt Eloise is wondering what has happened to us."

As the trio weaved between tables, several patrons stopped Nancy, complimenting her performance and the gowns she had worn.

"Absolutely exquisite," someone said from behind, causing Nancy to turn toward the dance floor. "Miss Drew?" The young man who spoke stepped closer, aligning himself under the soft light of a chandelier.

Nancy judged him to be in his thirties, despite the deep lines under his gray eyes. "Did you say something?" Nancy asked.

"I was just about to invite you to dance," came the unexpected reply.

The orchestra was switching tempos and Nancy nodded. She followed the stranger to the center of the floor where several other couples were trying unsuccessfully to keep from bumping into each other.

"I don't know your name," the young detective said as the two began to dance.

"It's Chris," he said. "Chris Chavez. You took

Jacqueline Henri's place on the program, didn't you?"

"Mm-hmm," Nancy replied casually. "Do you know her?"

"Doesn't everyone?"

"I guess so."

Chris swirled her away from him, but held her hand firmly, drawing her back.

"Do you do a lot of modeling?" he inquired.

"As a matter of fact," Nancy said, "this is the first time I've done anything like this. I've modeled before, but not on this scale."

"That's really hard to believe. You looked so professional up on that runway," Chris went on. Despite the dim light, he could see the blush in Nancy's cheeks. "I hope I'm not embarrassing you," he said.

"Oh, no," the girl said, starting to giggle. "I was just thinking how happy it would make our housekeeper if I changed careers."

Her dance partner appeared bewildered. "What's your current occupation?" he asked as the music finished at last.

"I'm a detective," Nancy said. Now it was her turn to watch for a change of expression, but to her surprise, there was none. Chris made no comment. Instead, he trailed her to the table where Bess and George sat with Aunt Eloise and Marjorie Tyson, and Nancy introduced him to her friends.

"Not *the* Chris Chavez." Marjorie grinned. "The photographer?"

Chris nodded. "And I'd like to take a picture of Nancy in that gorgeous gown she wore earlier."

"Well, I'm sure that can be arranged," Aunt Eloise said enthusiastically.

Bess, meanwhile, tugged on Nancy's arm. "George and I were wondering where you went," she whispered. "We didn't realize you had met such a handsome man. Does he have a couple of friends?"

"I don't know. Shall I ask?" Nancy replied.

The blond girl giggled while the young photographer jotted down his phone number and handed it to Nancy. "I'll be at the studio tomorrow, so let me know if you can come by," he said, then walked off quickly.

"What will Ned think when he sees you on the cover of some famous magazine—and photographed by the world-famous Chris Chavez?" George teased Nancy.

"Ned Nickerson," Nancy replied, referring to her boyfriend from Emerson College, "won't think anything because he won't see any such thing."

"Want to bet?" Bess winked.

"It's not so farfetched, Nancy," her aunt said instantly. "You could become a top model like Jacqueline."

"But I don't want to be," Nancy declared. "I'm very happy doing what I do. Which reminds me—what do you know about Jacqueline Henri? I assume Bess and George told you about our encounter with her."

"Yes, they did," Marjorie said. "I really don't know very much about her. You should have asked Chris."

Chris! Nancy thought, irritated that she had literally let him slip through her fingers.

"I'm going to call him in a little while," she declared.

"You are?" Bess repeated. "But it's after midnight."

"He only left a few minutes ago, so I'll try his house in half an hour," Nancy decided.

The ballroom had begun to empty as Nancy made her way down the quiet hallway to a phone booth not far from the dressing room. The overhead lights had been turned off, but

41

the sconces on the wall were still lit.

Nancy gasped as the silhouette of a man played across a distant, smoke-colored mirror. She ducked into the booth, waiting for the stranger to show himself.

Where's the security guard? Nancy wondered, suddenly aware that the precious designer clothes had been left unprotected. Although chains had been strung through the garments and locked, the girl detective knew that a professional thief wouldn't be easily discouraged.

Now the mysterious figure hurried across the room to the door, as if he suddenly realized he had left it open by accident. Nancy stuck her head out at the same moment, linking eyes with him!

He had small, even features, and despite the streak of gray in his hair, he looked fairly young. He also wore a tuxedo, causing Nancy to assume that he had attended the fashion show.

"Who are you and what are you doing in here?" she asked boldly.

The intruder responded with a cold, angry stare. He strode past the girl, not saying a word. She decided to postpone her phone call to Chris, and dashed quickly into the dressing

42

room. So far as she could tell, nothing had been disturbed, but before she returned to her table, she reported the incident to the hotel desk.

"Perhaps the man was just an interested admirer," Aunt Eloise told Nancy when she related the story. "It doesn't pay to be too suspicious, dear."

The young detective would have been the first to agree under other circumstances, but she did not argue the point. As it was, she barely could keep her eyes open on the way back to the apartment.

In spite of her exhaustion, however, Nancy tossed restlessly. Who was Jacqueline's brother and why did the young model imagine he had been kidnapped? The same questions rose in her mind as she awoke the next morning.

Before I do anything, though, I'm going to call Dad, Nancy decided.

She dressed quickly and joined her aunt and the other girls at the breakfast table, where they planned the itinerary for the day, beginning with phone calls home and one to Chris Chavez, who invited them to come to his studio later that morning.

Then, leaving Aunt Eloise, who was to meet Marjorie Tyson at the hotel office, the young detectives headed for Mr. Reese's. Nancy was not entirely surprised to learn that he wasn't there.

"He is flying to Palm Beach today," the receptionist said, "but he left this envelope for you, Miss Drew."

Nancy opened it immediately, discovering several sketches of the missing gowns, along with other pertinent information.

"When will he be back?" Nancy inquired.

"Tomorrow, perhaps."

"There are too many disappearing acts around here to suit me," Bess whispered to George.

"You can say that again," her cousin replied. "I think—"

"Let's go," Nancy interrupted, and turned to leave. "Our next stop is the studio of Chris Chavez!"

On the way, she studied Mr. Reese's sketches, almost memorizing them, and advised Bess and George to do the same.

"If only one of these gowns turned up in my closet, I'd be thrilled!" Bess said, as their taxi halted in front of a seemingly deserted store. "Is this the studio?"

"Guess so," Nancy said as they stepped out.

The chill in the air had left a thin layer of frost

on the window, so the visitors could not see inside. The door was open, though, and they entered.

"Anybody home?" Nancy called out across the empty foyer.

No one answered.

At the end of the hall was another door and an unshaded lamp shone brightly.

"Somebody must be here," Bess commented, walking forward. Nancy and George followed.

Suddenly, two voices rose in argument and the hall door slammed shut!

5

The Lion's Message

Nancy and the cousins listened to the angry voices behind the closed door.

"Ted Henri can take care of himself," the man, apparently Chris, was saying to someone.

He must be talking about Jacqueline's brother! Nancy thought, and knocked on the door.

Bess was apprehensive. "Shall we wait for you outside?" she whispered to her friend, not wishing to get caught in the middle of the strangers' argument.

To her chagrin, however, Nancy shook her head. "I might need your help."

"But—" Bess mumbled as the voices subsided and the door opened, revealing an unexpected surprise. A young woman stood before them with Chris Chavez, who was looking over her shoulder.

"Jacqueline!" Nancy exclaimed.

"Oh, so you know each other," Chris interposed.

"We met last evening," Nancy said, adding pointedly, "When you didn't come back, Jackie, we were worried."

"I'm terribly sorry," the model apologized. "I was so tired that I left the hotel after I took my message." She paused, turning to Chris. "Nancy is a detective, you know."

"Yes, I do," the photographer said. He kept his eyes evenly fixed on Nancy. "I imagine Jackie has told you about her brother."

"Not really," Nancy said. "Who *is* your brother?" the girl detective went on.

"Ted's a journalist—an investigative reporter," Jacqueline said, then stopped as if wondering how much to reveal.

"Go ahead," Chris urged her. "Tell Nancy everything. She may be able to help you."

The young woman's cheeks flushed. "I don't really know where to begin," she said. "As I told you last night, I believe my brother may have been kidnapped."

"But you're not sure," Nancy said.

"I'm almost sure. It's not the first time he's

been threatened. In the course of his job, he has exposed numerous undercover schemes and stepped on lots of toes."

"But what makes you think he was kidnapped?" Nancy questioned.

"For one thing, he was supposed to arrive on a charter flight from Singapore yesterday evening. I got a cable to meet him at Kennedy Airport. That's why I couldn't be in the fashion show. Anyway, when I reached the airport, I couldn't find him."

"Was he on the passenger list?" Nancy asked.

"As far as I know."

"Then, are you suggesting he may have been abducted from the airport?"

Jacqueline shook her head. "I don't know what to think," she said. "When I went home, I found this in my mailbox." She dug into her purse and produced a piece of paper.

On it was written a message with some scribbling at the bottom that resembled a lion's crest. Nancy read the message aloud:

IF YOU DON'T HEAR FROM ME IN A FEW DAYS, CALL THE POLICE. DON'T TRY TO CONTACT ME BEFORE THEN.   T.

The girl glanced at Jacqueline. "Is this your brother's handwriting?"

"I'm not sure. It may be a good imitation. That's why I'm so afraid he might have been kidnapped."

"Suppose he did write the note," Nancy said. "I assume the 'T' stands for Ted. But what's this funny symbol next to it? It looks like the head of a lion."

"I don't know," Jackie said.

"You see," Chris spoke up, "Ted's been working on an important expose about a fake operation at an auction house."

"I don't think we should talk about that," Jacqueline interrupted. "I'm sure Ted wouldn't appreciate it."

"Why not? If Nancy is to help you, she has to know what's going on." The young man paused a moment, then continued. "It seems that some auction house here in Manhattan has sold spurious reproductions of antique jewelry to a number of people, including dealers."

"But surely they would know the real stuff from the fake," Nancy commented.

"That's what makes the case so interesting," Chris remarked. "Obviously, there must be a very talented artisan involved in the scheme—"

"Or an agile assistant who substitutes the fake items for the real ones after the customers' bids are in," Nancy concluded.

"Very astute," Chris complimented her. "Maybe you ought to work with Ted."

"Except that he prefers to work alone," Jacqueline added.

"As it is," Nancy smiled pleasantly, "I already have my own mystery to solve."

The curiosity in the faces of her listeners encouraged the young detective to explain.

"You see, Mr. Reese, the designer, has asked me to help him find a thief."

"Really?" Jacqueline asked, throwing a quick glance at Chris.

"In fact," Nancy continued, "several gowns, which you were to have modeled last night, Jackie, disappeared from the hotel."

"How terrible!" Chris exclaimed. "Do you have any leads yet?"

"Nothing definite," Nancy said vaguely. She decided not to mention the stranger she had discovered in the dressing room.

"Forgive me for saying this," Chris went on, "but I think you ought to leave that sort of investigation up to someone with experience."

"Like Ted Henri?" Nancy replied, her mouth becoming a thin line.

"Nancy has had a lot of experience as a detective," Bess defended her friend.

"Oh, I'm sure she has," Chris answered. "It's just that you never know how tough things might get, and I wouldn't want anything to happen to her, or you, for that matter."

"Well, nothing has so far," George spoke up.

"Even so," Jacqueline commented, "Chris is right."

"And to think we were going to offer to look for your brother—undercover, of course," Nancy said quickly.

"We were?" George raised her eyes with uncertainty.

Jacqueline looked at Chris with an urgent, almost pleading expression and fidgeted with the handle of her bag.

"What do you think?" the model asked him.

"It's up to you," he sighed.

"We wouldn't do anything to mess up Ted's investigation," Bess put in.

"I imagine he's trying to gather as much evidence as he can against the auction house," Nancy said. "I'm sure he doesn't want police interference, so we'd have to keep a low profile."

"It's a good idea, isn't it, Chris?" Jacqueline pressed.

"Yes, so long as these young ladies think

51

they're able to handle it," the photographer replied. "Tell me, Nancy, how do you plan to start your search for Ted?"

Nancy was thoughtful for a moment, then smiled. "Well, first we have to find the lion's crest!"

6

Medallion Mystery

"I wonder what the lion's crest means," Bess said, pondering Ted Henri's message.

Nancy was thinking about the variety of architecture she had seen throughout the city, especially the pair of stone lions that flanked the entrance to the New York Public Library. Was it possible that a lion's crest existed somewhere on a building where Ted might be hiding out?

"How about the auction houses?" George put in. "Do any of them have a lion's crest on the canopy?"

"Not to my knowledge," Chris said, "but it's possible."

As he spoke, Bess picked up a thick telephone directory and began to scan the classified section.

"Look at all the auction houses!" she exclaimed in discouragement. "There must be a hundred of them!"

"Not quite that many," Nancy said, snatching a glance at the list.

"Even so," George said, "it will take more than a few days to visit all of them."

Nancy noticed a newspaper lying on a desk. "Chris, may I look at that?" she asked.

"Of course," he replied, sensing what was on her mind. "Maybe you'll find something under 'galleries.' I was just about to suggest it myself."

Nancy quickly located the page filled with announcements about various auctions. One in particular drew her attention.

"There's an interesting sale scheduled tonight at Speers, Limited," she pointed out, adding that among the items being auctioned off were heraldic shields and medallions. "Maybe we'll find something bearing a lion's crest among them!"

"And perhaps Ted!" Jacqueline added excitedly.

"It's a shame we missed the preview exhibition," Nancy said. "That was this morning. But if we try, we can make the auction at 8 P.M."

"By the way," George said to Jacqueline,

"what does your brother look like? In case he happens to be there, we'd like to tell you."

"Oh, well, he's taller than I am and he has dark wavy hair and hazel eyes. His face is rounder than mine. It's ruddier, too."

"Do you have a picture of him?" Bess asked.

"No, unfortunately—only a childhood photograph, and I assure you we both have changed a lot since then." The model laughed, tossing back her mane of hair, letting the lamplight pick up highlights.

Before the girls left, Bess whispered to Jackie out of earshot of her friends and then jotted something on a piece of paper.

"What's up?" George asked her cousin when they stood on the sidewalk again.

"You'll see," Bess replied, mysteriously. "I have to run now. See you back at the apartment. 'Bye."

Like a bolt of lightning, she flashed down the street and disappeared into a taxi that had stopped to let off a passenger.

Nancy and George gaped at each other, breaking into giggles as they realized that Bess's admiration for the glamorous model was probably at the root of her latest adventure. The afternoon passed quickly at Aunt Eloise's and when the doorbell finally rang, Nancy and

George ran to answer the door together!

"Bess, is that you?" Nancy asked, gaping at her friend, while George put a hand over her mouth, biting her lips to keep from laughing out loud.

Bess looked hurt. "What do you think? Of course, it's me!"

She had obviously gone to a hair and makeup artist who had changed everything except the color of her eyes. Her hair was swept upward in small fine ringlets, a few of which dangled over her ears and around the base of her neck.

"Well?" Bess said, noting that her friends had fallen into total silence.

"The hair isn't bad," George said, "but those eyes! Wow!"

Nancy, too, was spellbound by the transformation. False eyelashes, curled thickly over Bess's own, appeared to be half an inch long! One had loosened and Bess had carelessly stuck it back above the lid, making her look like a Paul Klee painting.

"Did Jacqueline recommend this?" Nancy inquired.

"Not *this*. Him," Bess said. "He's a wonderful hair stylist and makeup man. All the models go to him."

She marched to a mirror in the living room,

quickly observing the lopsided eyelash. Embarrassed, she hurried to adjust it, but it drooped down over the lower lid and came loose, leaving her with one set on and the other off.

George roared as Bess turned around. She grimaced angrily at her cousin.

"You're just jealous!" Bess charged.

"Jealous!" George laughed, and grabbed her camera which she had left on a small table in the foyer. "I can't miss this one. Dave will love it!"

"Don't you dare!" Bess cried, tearing off the other set of lashes.

But it was too late. Her cousin had already snapped a picture. "Here she is, folks. The new model of the year!" George said gleefully, taking the finished print out of the camera.

All through supper neither of the cousins spoke to each other, which made Nancy and her aunt feel uncomfortable.

"I like your hair, dear," Aunt Eloise complimented Bess, causing her to smile briefly.

"Thank you very much," she said. "Please pass the salt, Nancy."

That was the extent of Bess's conversation until they reached the auction house of Speers, Limited. They noticed that most of the audience were holding catalogs, and Nancy hurried to a desk to purchase one.

"Ooh, there are some gorgeous things in that book!" Bess said to the others, after glancing at someone else's brochure.

Nancy quickly leafed through hers, pausing now and then to look at stunning color photographs of Old English silver and Oriental porcelain.

"Go back a few pages," George said shortly.

Nancy did so and, to her amazement, discovered the entry of a medallion that bore the head of a lion! It had belonged to a man named Galen Kaiser.

Was this what Ted Henri was referring to in the mysterious message he sent to his sister?

The girl detectives were careful not to discuss their find openly. Instead, they scanned the audience, looking for someone who matched Ted's description. A couple of men came close to it, but one had a bulbous nose and the other a ring of pock marks under his eyes. Jackie had not mentioned either of those characteristics.

Then the auction started and the girls' attention was drawn to a number of fine gold teacups. They were displayed on a velvet table that swung into view on a moving platform.

"Shall we bid?" George asked teasingly as the auctioneer called out successive bids.

"I have five hundred dollars. Do I hear more?" he said.

"Well, I'm not really looking for gold teacups," Nancy responded lightly.

One after the other, items from the estates of several wealthy people passed in and out of sight. Nancy and the cousins eagerly awaited the medallion.

"Here it comes!" Bess murmured as it appeared on the table, glittering under the spotlight.

From where the young detectives sat, they could not see it fully. Then, the auctioneer covered the microphone with his hand and turned sideways to speak to his assistant, completely obscuring the table from the girls' view. When he addressed the audience again, the young detectives were surprised to see that the medallion was gone. A small gold dish with a stand-up rim stood in its place!

"Do you suppose the medallion was stolen?" Bess whispered to her friends, who did not reply.

The auctioneer soon announced that the order of entries had been changed and the medallion would go up for bid shortly.

"Maybe somebody is switching the real one for a fake," Bess continued.

"That would be too obvious," George declared.

When the medallion came into view again, Nancy leaned forward. She didn't want to miss anything that was about to happen!

The bidding started. One hundred, two hundred, up to five hundred dollars!

"It's only estimated at one hundred fifty," Nancy informed the cousins. She held up her hand, signaling an offer.

"Are you crazy?" Bess cried under her breath, as the auctioneer announced Nancy's bid of five hundred fifty.

"I'm just curious," the young detective replied, waiting for one of two other bidders to respond.

Both of them had seemed unusually eager to buy the piece, but now they were silent.

"Going once, twice," the auctioneer said slowly. He held his mallet ready to pound on a desk.

Panic-stricken, Nancy realized that she was about to become the proud owner of something she really didn't want. Not only that, she would have to drain her savings account to pay for it!

7

The Fake Bidder

The auctioneer held the mallet a moment longer, glancing at the men who had bid first on the medallion. Nancy's heart pounded as she prayed that one of them would raise his hand.

She didn't see the signal, but the auctioneer suddenly said, "Six hundred dollars. I have a bid of six hundred. Do I hear more?"

"Whew!" Bess exclaimed, echoing Nancy's own relief. "What would you have done?"

"I'd probably have to scrub Dad's office for the rest of my life!" Nancy said.

"Why did you bid on that thing, anyway?" George inquired.

Nancy shrugged. "I did it on the spur of the moment, thinking perhaps I'd get some reaction from those men by starting to compete with them."

Nancy paused a moment, then added, "And I was hoping that if I entered the bidding, I might pick up a clue as to why they both wanted the medallion."

"Well, it didn't happen," George said.

Nancy nodded. She wondered if the men would challenge each other further, but the medallion went to the one who had offered six hundred dollars.

Eagerly the girls watched the rest of the auction. A set of Meissen dinnerware was sold to a woman. Georgian candlesticks went to someone else and an unusual array of dinner bells to a third person. The men who had bid for the medallion remained silent throughout the balance of the sale.

When it was over, Nancy rose to her feet. "I'd like to congratulate the winner," she told her friends.

"We're sticking with you," Bess said, following her cousin and Nancy through the crowd.

The man who had bought the medallion was short, with a bald head that shone like a billiard ball, and Nancy was able to keep him in sight easily. He went to a counter already filled with winning bidders who wished to claim their prizes. When one woman stepped away with a small carton, he quickly took her place.

Nancy and her friends moved behind him, noticing the name stamped on the check he signed. It was Russell Kaiser!

Was he related to Galen Kaiser? the girls wondered. If so, why would he have bid on something that belonged to the Kaiser family in the first place?

"Mr. Kaiser," Nancy said as a clerk handed him the medallion, "I wanted to—"

"Aren't you the person who forced the bid to six hundred?" he grumbled.

"Yes, I am," Nancy replied, somewhat embarrassed.

"Humph."

"May I ask you a couple of questions?" she went on boldly.

"What about?"

"The medallion, of course."

"I'm sorry, miss. I have a dinner party to go too and I'm late already. Excuse me."

He brushed past her, muttering under his breath, and hurried toward an exit sign.

"He certainly wasn't very friendly," George said. "I wonder why that medallion is so important."

"I guess we'll never know," Bess commented with disappointment.

Just then a voice behind them stopped the conversation. "Miss Nancy Drew?" a man asked, causing the girls to face the other bidder on the medallion.

He was blond, about forty, and had thick, straight eyebrows that lay close together over a long and rather slim nose.

"I'm Nancy Drew," the young detective spoke up, surprised that he knew her name.

"I'm Russell Kaiser."

"Huh?" Bess replied, incredulous.

"No, *that* was—" Nancy started to say, quickly catching herself. She let the man continue.

"I recognized you from a newspaper article that covered a recent mystery you solved," he went on.

"Which one?" Nancy replied.

"I'm sorry to say I really don't remember," he said, blushing.

"Are you sure your name is Kaiser?" George asked, unable to restrain herself any longer.

"Of course."

"We don't mean to sound presumptuous," Bess said, "but the gentleman who just bought that medallion claimed *he* was Russell Kaiser."

"What? That's impossible."

"His name was on the check he signed."

Immediately, their listener pulled out a checkbook, then other identification cards, glancing through them rapidly.

"Everything's here," he said, slipping them back into his coat pocket. "But I've got to stop payment on that man's check in case he's trying to draw money out of my bank account!"

He hurried to the desk clerk, spoke to him briefly, then returned to the girls.

"Mr. Kaiser—" Nancy began.

"Call me Russell."

"Okay, Russell. If you don't mind my asking, I'd like to know why two men would bid three times the estimated value of that medallion."

Her listener hesitated a moment before speaking. "I just returned from a business trip and found a letter from an old friend of my uncle's," he began.

"Your uncle was Galen Kaiser?" Nancy inquired.

"Yes. His friend indicated that he wished to have the medallion for sentimental reasons. Everything, though, had been shipped to the auction house already, and there was no way to get hold of the medallion before the bidding started. So the only thing I could do was bid on it myself."

"What a shame," Bess commented, thinking

the man had not only lost out on the piece for his uncle's friend but an impostor had walked away with it!

"Are you sure your uncle's friend only wanted the medallion for sentimental reasons?" Nancy inquired.

Russell seemed puzzled by the question. "What do you mean?"

"Well," Nancy went on, "isn't it strange that someone else would have bid so much for the piece?"

"Nancy's right," Bess said. "There must be something about the medallion that none of us realizes."

"I certainly don't know what it is," he said. "I bid as much as I could possibly afford, but then—" His voice trailed off and he looked as if he were about to cry. "My uncle was a fine man—good to his friends, and they loved him. I happen to know that the man who wrote to me helped my uncle at a time when he needed it."

Although the girls knew nothing about the Kaiser family, they were overwhelmed by the nephew's obvious sensitivity. If only they could capture the stranger and rescue the medallion!

"Will you help me find the impostor?" the man pleaded.

"Definitely," Bess replied.

"I'll give a complete description of him to the police," Nancy volunteered and stood up to go to the nearest telephone.

"Wait!" Russell said. "I'd rather postpone that for the time being. You see, my family is well-known, and I'd like to avoid any publicity about this. If you don't track the man down on your own, we can call the police then."

Nancy hesitated a moment, but then acceded to the man's wishes. "We'll see what we can come up with," she promised. "Where can we reach you?"

"Here," he replied, handing her a printed card. "I work out of my home," he added.

The address, to Nancy's surprise, was not in a chic East Side neighborhood. It was in the heart of midtown, west of Fifth Avenue.

"We'll be in touch as soon as we have something to report," she said.

On the way back to Aunt Eloise's apartment, the girls discussed the strange events of the evening.

"It's really peculiar," George commented. "We go to an auction looking for Ted Henri and wind up hunting for Russell Kaiser's impersonator."

Nancy nodded thoughtfully. "I guess we've stumbled on a completely new mystery!"

8

A Precious Secret

The next morning, the girls were up early. "What's our program for today?" Bess asked when they all were seated around the breakfast table.

"I think we should go the police station and take a look at the mug shots. Perhaps we can find a lead to the identity of the fake Russell Kaiser," Nancy declared.

"Good idea," George declared.

"I also want to call Jackie, just to make sure that neither of the two men we saw last night was Ted."

As soon as Nancy swallowed her last mouthful of scrambled eggs, she contacted the model. Jacqueline confirmed that her brother did not have a bulbous nose or any pock marks under his eyes.

"I'm sorry you weren't successful," she added.

"Well, we've come upon another interesting mystery in the interim," Nancy said, and told the young woman about the medallion with the lion's head on top and the two Russell Kaisers. "I don't know if there's a connection between the symbol on your brother's note and the figure on the medallion, but we're following it all up. I am leaving for the police station now."

"My, you are a busy detective." The model laughed into the phone.

Nancy smiled. "My stockpile of mysteries is getting a little heavy," she admitted. "After we finish talking to the police, I'll have to stop by Mr. Reese's office."

"He happens to be near a wonderful little dress shop, which you all must see," Jackie said. "Promise me you'll go." She gave Nancy the address.

The girl detective chuckled, secretly wondering if the dresses would be as outlandish as the makeup results on Bess.

"We'll let you know if we buy anything," she concluded the conversation.

Bess and George had already slipped into their coats and waited impatiently for Nancy to put hers on. Then they said good-bye to Aunt

Eloise, who was also preparing to leave.

"Marjorie and I have to tally the proceeds of the show this morning," she informed her niece.

"Well, I hope you made a whole bucket full of money and—" Nancy said when the ring of the telephone interrupted her.

"You take it, dear," Aunt Eloise said.

To Nancy's surprise, it was a telegram from her father! She listened intently to the message which the operator read:

COULD NOT REACH YOU BY PHONE. SENDING IMPORTANT PAPERS TODAY. PLEASE WAIT FOR THEM.

"How strange!" Nancy said to her friends as she hung up the receiver.

"Who was it?" Bess asked.

"Dad—I mean a telegram from Dad."

"That *is* odd," George remarked. "Of course, we came in late last night, but he could have called this morning. Maybe you ought to try phoning him."

The same thought had occurred to Nancy. She made two telephone calls, one to the house where Hannah told her that her father had already left for the office, and the other to the office where his secretary informed her that Mr. Drew was off on an all-day business appointment.

"Well, I can't chance it," Nancy told the other girls. "If Dad wants me to wait for documents, I'd better do it."

She took off the coat that hung loosely on her shoulders and returned it to the closet.

"Of course, this doesn't mean you girls have to stick around," she added.

Bess and George looked at each other undecidedly. George finally suggested that they could save some time if she and Bess checked out the police mug shots.

"Good idea," Nancy concurred. "By the time you get back, I ought to have the papers, and then we can head for Mr. Reese's."

"Are you sure you don't mind?" Bess said, knowing that Nancy would have liked to review the police pictures herself.

"I'm positive," Nancy said. "You saw the same man I did at the auction."

That was reassurance enough to send the girls on their way.

"Oh, wait a minute," Nancy said. "Here, take this. It's the address of a dress shop Jacqueline told me about. Since we're running short on time, maybe you ought to stop there before you come back."

"Great!" Bess exclaimed.

Nancy handed each of the girls an umbrella from the closet. To Bess she said, "It's supposed to rain today. I'm sure you don't want those new curls to come undone." The tiny curls that had framed her face the day before had begun to sag a bit, but Bess was determined to keep the hairdo.

In reply, Bess merely rolled her eyes and said, "Be back soon."

Leaving Nancy to wait for the mysterious documents, Aunt Eloise followed the cousins out the door. When they arrived at the police station after a circuitous ride in a taxicab that had deposited Eloise Drew en route, George introduced herself and Bess.

"We're friends of Nancy Drew, the amateur detective."

The sergeant on duty had heard of Nancy and smiled. "Are you helping her on a case?" he inquired.

George nodded. "That's why we're here. We'd like to take a look at mug shots, if you don't mind. We're searching for a man whose name we don't know."

"What'd he do?" the sergeant asked.

"Impersonated a client of ours who doesn't want any publicity about it. We promised to try finding the man on our own."

"I see. Well, go ahead. Take a look at our file."

He led them into a room and provided the photographs they had requested.

"Thanks," the girls chorused almost in unison.

"Let me know if you recognize the guy!" The sergeant grinned.

For several minutes, the young detectives pored over the pictures, stopping once in a while to stare at a face that seemed familiar. A couple of the men bore similar features to the impostor—a bald head, for instance, but the shape of the eyes or nose was different.

"Hey!" Bess said suddenly as they reached the bottom of the pile. "Look at this!"

The girls stared at a photograph of a man in his late thirties, maybe early forties, whose eyes were pinched together under thick, straight brows. His nose was long and slim, the mouth full, and the face was framed by blondish hair.

"It's Russell Kaiser!" George gasped. "Not the bald man who bought the medallion and who we assumed to be the impostor. It's the man who approached Nancy and asked us to help him!"

"His real name is Pete Grover, and he's wanted for check forgery in the State of California," Bess added. "It says so right here under the picture."

"Maybe the sergeant has more information about him. Let's ask," George suggested.

The officer was very interested when he heard that they found a man in the mug shots who resembled someone they had met the night before.

"Now, you say you saw him at an auction," the sergeant asked. "Did he buy anything?"

"No," George replied, "but he bid on a medallion. He didn't get it, though."

The policeman nodded. "We'll look into it."

"What do you think is going on?" Bess asked her cousin on the way out.

"Beats me, but I have a hunch we'll have to do a little more investigating before we find out. Pete Grover's hair was a little different, but I'm sure he was the man we met last night."

The girls headed for the dress shop on East 67th Street. It was small and stocked with expensive, imported clothes.

"No wonder Jacqueline comes here," Bess commented. She thumbed through the hangers, pausing to look at a gold lamé jumpsuit. "These pants are meant for sticks to wear."

George laughed. "Well, that lets you out!"

"Very funny," said Bess, who was used to

being teased by George about her waistline. She shoved the suit along the rack. "Now, here's something. Oh, I want to try it on."

Before George could get a close look at what it was, Bess dashed into a dressing room in the back of the store. Within a few minutes, a clerk went after her, then returned to the rack for a larger size.

George sat down on a velvet cushion, preparing for Bess's entrance. She heard peculiar noises from the dressing room—sighs, and then giggles.

"Ready or not," Bess called out at last.

She stepped into view, watching the frozen look in her cousin's eyes.

"Like it?" she asked gaily.

George gulped.

The one-piece pants suit was a shimmer of silver and black that ballooned over Bess's figure, ending in a tight hug over her ankles. Bess turned in front of a mirror and grinned at George.

"Cat got your tongue?" she asked.

"Mm-hmm," George said. "You're a true vision."

"Thanks," Bess replied, evidently pleased. "How much is it?" she asked the clerk.

"Only four twenty-five."

"Four hundred and twenty-five dollars?" Bess gasped. "Oh, and I do love it!"

"Well, maybe you can find a dressmaker in River Heights to sew something like it," George consoled her.

"These are one of a kind," the clerk insisted haughtily.

"I'm sure," George replied. "Let's go."

"I'm so disappointed," Bess said when they were outside again.

"Just think of it this way. If you had bought that outfit, Dave would have thought something had happened to the good old Bess he once knew! Besides, it would have looked better on a thinner girl."

"Good old Bess. That's me," Bess sighed. "I guess I'm just never going to be very sophisticated."

When they reached the apartment again, they were still talking about their excursion. George described the silver-black creation Bess had wanted to purchase, then they discussed the visit to the police station. Nancy was flabbergasted when she heard about the photograph they had seen.

George mentioned something that had been on her mind. "If Pete Grover is the impostor, though, why would he have deliberately intro-

77

duced himself to you?" she asked Nancy.

"I have no idea."

"What about the papers your father sent? Did they come?" Bess inquired.

"No. A few letters arrived for Aunt Eloise. That was all. But I figure Dad must've mailed everything by special delivery, which means it could turn up here almost any time today."

The girls prepared a light lunch, and when they were done, it was almost two o'clock.

"I really ought to go to Mr. Reese's office," Nancy decided.

"If you want us to wait here, we will," George offered.

"But suppose the papers come and Nancy has to do something with them right away?" Bess objected. "No, I think she'd better stick around."

"I agree," Nancy said, "but I'd hate to spend the entire day cooped up in Aunt Eloise's apartment waiting for something that might never arrive. Maybe Dad's secretary can tell me where he is. I don't like to disturb him during a business meeting, but what else can I do?"

She called the attorney's office once more and, to her delight, discovered that her father had returned earlier than expected.

"What's up, dear?" Carson Drew asked pleasantly.

"Did you send me a telegram today?"

"No."

"And some important papers?"

"Papers? Why, no!"

As quickly as she could, Nancy gave an account of recent events, ending with the mysterious message.

"It was a phony, Nancy," her father said gravely. "Someone obviously didn't want you to leave the apartment for a reason!"

9

Fashion Accusation

But who? And why would anyone play such a mean trick on me? Nancy wondered.

When Mr. Drew heard about the events at the fashion show, he sounded even grimmer. "It seems to me that someone thinks you're getting too close for comfort."

"Thanks for the compliment, Dad, but I don't feel very close to anything."

"Maybe you just can't see the forest for the trees," the lawyer said. "And before you get lost in the wilderness, I want you to promise to call me every day!"

"I will, Dad. And I won't get lost. You'll see."

His deep, reassuring voice was enough to bolster Nancy's confidence. "We have a lot to do," she told her friends. "I've been thinking about my conversation with Jacqueline this morning."

"And?" George prompted.

"And I wonder if she has passed information along to the fashion thief who figured he'd keep me from going to Reese Associates today."

"You think Jacqueline is an accomplice in some way?" Bess asked in disbelief.

"No, but she could be an innocent conduit."

Her listeners pondered the idea for a moment.

"She and Chris are the only people who know you're trying to help Mr. Reese," George said.

"Also, it was only moments after I talked to her that the telegram came," Nancy added.

"Maybe we ought to talk to her again," George suggested.

"She's probably working now," Bess said. "A model who's as popular as Jacqueline would be in great demand."

"I'd like to visit Mr. Reese first, anyway," Nancy stated. "I don't want to give away my schedule again—"

"Especially to a thief!" Bess interrupted.

When the girls arrived at the designer's office, Nancy was pleased to learn that he had returned from the business trip he had been on the day before, and was out doing some investigating on his own!

"Did he leave a message for me?" she asked the receptionist, whose long, polished fingernails sifted through a basket of papers on her desk. "I'm afraid I don't see anything marked for Nancy Drew," she said, lifting her head in a smile. "Perhaps you ought to speak with Mr. Reese directly. He's at Zanzibar's."

The name didn't sound familiar to the girls.

"It's a photographic studio," the receptionist went on. "They do a lot of catalog work for major department stores."

"Okay," Nancy said. "If by any chance Mr. Reese should return before we get there, will you tell him I'm looking for him?"

"Will do."

The receptionist jotted down the address of the studio, which was located in the heart of the garment district. The buildings were gray and, apart from a sign that said Zanzibar's, the young detectives might have passed by without realizing what it was. The entrance was small, too. There were a few color advertisements from old store catalogs that hung on the wall, but no evidence of what lay beyond.

Nancy led the way to a desk at the end of the hall, where a stubby woman was seated. She greeted the visitors pleasantly, but when Nancy mentioned the name Reese, the woman stiffened.

"He is talking with one of our photographers," she said, "and I'm sure they don't wish to be disturbed."

"But Nancy is trying to help him investigate the thefts from the hotel last night," Bess blurted out.

The woman stared at Nancy. "You hardly look like a detective," she said, as shouting voices broke through a far door.

Nancy recognized Mr. Reese's instantly. She strode past the receptionist with Bess and George close at her heels.

"You can't go in there!" the stubby woman cried, but the girls had already opened the door.

"My models are getting paid plenty by the hour," the photographer was barking at Mr. Reese, "and you're taking both *my* time and theirs!"

A young brunette, who was standing in front of a long sheet of seamless blue paper, moved out of the strong light that poured over her.

"It's getting too hot for me," the detectives overheard her remark. The men, however, had missed the comment.

"I am going to have you arrested, Mr. Vinton!" the fashion designer yelled.

"Fine! Go ahead!"

"Oh, Nancy, let's get out of here," Bess whispered.

"And that includes your assistant!" Reese was pointing a threatening finger at a woman in slacks and a smock who was standing near the model. He charged angrily toward her. "What's your name?" he growled, pushing aside one of the tall lights.

It teetered, then crashed to the floor in splinters of glass!

"Oh!" the woman cried as a chunk slid close to her foot. "You're a madman! That's what you are!"

Reese boiled at the remark. "You haven't seen anything yet!" he fired at her, shoving the young model out of the way and tearing the paper off a metal bar.

"Mr. Reese! Please, Mr. Reese!" Nancy called from the doorway.

But the man paid no attention. His face and neck were a blaze of red as he turned back to the photographer, who grabbed him firmly by the shoulders.

"I am going to throw you out personally!" Vinton roared.

"Stop him, somebody!" Bess trembled as

Reese swung a fist at the man, just missing him.

By now the noise had traveled through the whole studio, where, behind several closed doors, other photo sessions were being conducted. One after another, people infiltrated Mr. Vinton's room and, at last, two men tackled Reese before he could land another swing.

"I'll send you a bill for this mess!" Mr. Vinton rasped loudly.

"And I'll see to it that you pay for every dress you filched!" the designer snapped, as Nancy stepped closer to interrupt.

"Mr. Reese," she said firmly, catching his attention at last.

"What do you want?" he grumbled.

"You should be careful about making accusations you can't back up."

Now the man laughed hard. He flexed his arms, seeking to be free of the tightening hold.

"That's very funny. Are you a lawyer, too?"

Nancy took a deep breath and Bess and George pulled behind her.

"No, I'm not a lawyer," the girl replied calmly. "But I do know that you can get into an awful lot of trouble if you can't support your charges."

"Well, I can support them," he snarled. "These men are nothing more than cheap crooks, and if I ever find out who commissioned them to photograph my clothes, I will sue them!"

The girls wondered if Zanzibar's had, in fact, photographed the copies of Mr. Reese's original designs that had appeared in the Millington catalog. Nancy noticed the torn page of one sticking out of his coat pocket.

"Is that from the Millington book?" she asked.

"No. This is from the Chalmers catalog," the designer replied, referring to an expensive department store.

He whipped out the page and waved it under Nancy's nose, his hand still trembling in rage. "Here, look for yourself. See these two gowns? High-priced merchandise, wouldn't you say? Not at all like the stuff Millington manufactures. But they're my designs, too!"

"What makes you think the photographer had something to do with the theft?" Nancy inquired.

"Because he wouldn't tell me who gave him the assignment! He's covering up for someone, I'm sure of it!"

10

A New Discovery

Nancy stared at the pictures in the Chalmers catalog. The two beautiful gowns Reese had indicated were, in fact, credited to Arnaud Hans, a competing designer!

The girl's mind was racing with questions, but she decided to wait until they had left the studio before asking them.

"I think we should go," she said to Mr. Reese. "There's nothing more we can accomplish here."

Apparently the temperamental designer agreed, because he walked to the door. "You'll hear from my lawyer!" he called back to Vinton.

"And you from *ours!*" the photographer replied coldly as the girls followed Reese out the door.

The young detectives trooped after him to his office past the receptionist and into an oak-paneled room where he gestured for them to sit.

"Mr. Reese, who saw your spring collection before all of these terrible things began to happen to you?" Nancy asked.

"Very few people," he replied.

"Would you mind giving me their names?"

"Chris Chavez is one."

"Chris Chavez, the photographer?" Nancy was aghast. "I thought a collection wasn't supposed to be photographed before it was shown in public."

"Well, Chris didn't shoot anything, but he's a good friend, and I showed him a few things."

"Who else had access to the designs?" George inquired.

"Only three, maybe four other people on my staff, and they're all trustworthy. Now, if you will excuse me, I have some important appointments."

He led the girls to the door, indicating that he didn't wish to continue the discussion.

"I think he was insulted when you asked him about the people he had shown his collection to," George said to Nancy on the way out.

"I think he's just upset about everything that happened," Bess declared.

"Well, he isn't helping his own case very much," Nancy remarked, "which means we'll have to put on two thinking caps apiece!"

"I can easily wear two, but I doubt that Bess can!" George laughed. She eyed the mountain of curls her cousin had coaxed back into place after trying on clothes that morning.

Bess tugged on a few stray wisps, saying, "I'm going to pretend you never said that, George Fayne."

Another round of teasing was brewing, which Nancy decided to cut short. "I have a choice," she said.

"A choice?" Bess replied.

"Yes, I can either try to get a job with the Millington Company or with Chalmers."

"Are you kidding?" George said. "You've never worked for anybody in your whole life—other than your father, of course."

"I know," Nancy said, "but there's always a first time. Besides, how else am I going to get any inside information?"

The cousins had to admit Nancy was making good sense.

"Can you type?" Bess asked.

"Some."

"Take shorthand?" George inquired.

Nancy shook her head. "But I can scrub floors

if I have to." She giggled. "What about you?"

"You mean we have to get jobs also?" Bess asked.

"Well, I won't be able to work in two places at the same time," Nancy persisted.

"Okay, okay," Bess said. "I'll sure try. But how about a snack first? I'm starved!"

The girls went into a nearby restaurant where Nancy found a Manhattan telephone directory on a back table. She quickly located addresses for Millington and Chalmers, noted them on a pad, then headed into the dining room where Bess and George were already seated behind menus.

"Lunch was only three hours ago," Nancy said.

"So we'll have some dessert," Bess remarked. "I can't work on an empty stomach."

"That's assuming we get jobs," George said. "What if we don't?"

"And what if no one will interview us?" Bess added.

"Then I'd like you to track down Jacqueline and find out whom she may have talked to about the Reese investigation."

The cousins agreed and Bess shut her menu as if she had reached a decision.

"On second thought," she sighed, "I've been

thinking about that gorgeous silver and black pants suit. If I lose a few pounds—"

"And find four hundred and twenty-five dollars," George put in.

"I might be able to get into a smaller size and buy it when it goes on sale," Bess finished.

"By that time," Nancy said, "the suit will be out of style. Come on, let's go."

She rose to lead the way past the cashier when someone opened the restaurant door and held it for a woman in a wheelchair.

Through the open door, Nancy heard a man in the street greet another. "Well, if it isn't Chris Chavez. How've you been, buddy?"

"Oh, just fine, Sam," the other man replied. "Sorry I can't stop to talk to you, but I'm in a hurry."

Nancy stared at him in surprise. He had a short, sculpted haircut, and a pencil-thin mustache. Certainly he was not the photographer she had met!

The man waved to his friend and hailed a taxi. The door, meanwhile, was still blocked by the wheelchair and the girls had to wait. Nancy bit her lip, hoping she would get out in time to talk to the man. Was he really Chris Chavez? And if so, who was the man who had pretended to be the photographer?

Bess and George had witnessed the conversation, too, and now George tugged on Nancy's arm. "Do you believe this!" she whispered. "Now there are two impostors in our case!"

Nancy nodded. "I wish I knew how to solve this dilemma," she murmured, "or rather this *twin dilemma!*"

Finally the woman in the wheelchair was through the door. The girls rushed outside, but at the same moment, Chavez climbed into a cab that had pulled to the curb. Before the girls could reach him, however, the taxi pulled away!

"What are we going to do now?" Bess wailed.

"Proceed with our original plan," Nancy said. "Let's flip a coin. Heads, you take Chalmers, tails, I do."

A moment later, while Nancy went off by herself to tackle the Millington Company, Bess and George caught a bus to the Chalmers building. When the cousins reached it, they couldn't help comparing the lobby with that of the Zanzibar studio. Catalog covers in beautiful, gilt-edge frames hung low over spotlights, and the walls were papered in rich, brown suede that created an aura of luxury.

"I'm nervous," Bess admitted as she and George went to the personnel office.

An attractive woman wearing gold-rimmed

eyeglasses greeted them with a smile. "Are you applying for the secretarial jobs?" she asked.

"Were they the ones advertised in the paper?" George replied with an air of confidence.

"Yes."

"Then those are the ones we're interested in," George said, causing Bess to gulp.

"Fine. Please follow me, if you will," the woman responded.

She motioned them toward a table and asked them to fill out applications. Then, with only a brief glance at the forms, led them toward a room with a desk and typewriter.

"I have some material for you to type," she said. "I can see from your applications that you don't have much prior experience."

"None," Bess murmured to herself.

"Even so, I don't mind giving young talent a chance," the interviewer went on. "If you pass this test, we'll move on to the next one."

Next one! The cousins moaned. How many hurdles would they have to overcome before the company would hire them?

"Now, who wants to go first?" the woman inquired.

George offered instantly, but the confidence she exuded was short-lived as she stared at a mass of information she was instructed to type in orderly fashion.

"I'll shut the door," the woman told her, "so no one will disturb you."

For a moment, George froze in front of the typewriter. Then she set her fingers on the keys, pressing out a few words slowly and carefully until she was able to pick up speed. But as the words fell on the paper in rapid succession, she stopped paying close attention. It wasn't until she had finished one page of work that she realized what she had done! By mistake, she had typed most of it in capital letters and put in wrong punctuation!

"Oh, no!" She gasped in horror. "I've ruined it!"

She tore out the paper, slipping another one in place, racing to make up for lost time. But the keys jammed.

"It's no use!" George cried aloud, as the door opened.

"How are you doing?" the personnel manager inquired pleasantly.

"I'm not doing well at all," the girl admitted, pushing back her chair.

"You're not giving up, are you?"

George never liked being called a quitter, but she realized that she wasn't qualified for a secretarial job. Neither was Bess, who, meanwhile, had looked at magazines, including the current Chalmers catalog.

Remembering the page Mr. Reese had taken from another copy, she hunted for it and again studied the lovely gowns. When she saw the personnel manager coming out of the room with George, she had a sudden inspiration.

"These pictures are just beautiful," she said to the woman. "Do you know who photographed those gowns?"

The woman looked at the catalog. "Most of this collection, including those dresses, were done by Chris Chavez," she responded. "Doesn't he have a terrific flair?"

Bess nodded. She was as flabbergasted as George. Was Chris Chavez, Mr. Reese's personal friend, an accomplice to the thefts?

11

Puzzling Information

Meanwhile, Nancy had filled out an application at Millington. When the manager, whose name according to a sign on his desk was T. Iannone, reviewed it, he looked at her closely.

"So you want a job, eh? I think, Miss Drew, it's more likely you're here to snoop!"

His biting remark hit Nancy unexpectedly, and she decided to tell him the truth. "Could we speak privately?" she suggested, glancing at a nearby secretary who was pretending not to listen, but Nancy could see she was interested in the conversation.

"This way," the manager said, leading Nancy into an inner office. "I happen to know that you were Jacqueline Henri's replacement in the fashion show the other night—and that Richard

Reese has asked you to help track down a dress thief. News travels fast in this business."

"Yes, I can see that." The girl detective knew it wouldn't help to disguise her motive for being at Millington's and went straight to the point. "How do you explain the fact that copies of Mr. Reese's original dresses turned up in your spring catalog before the originals were made public?" Nancy asked.

"I have no idea."

"But you admit the Millington dresses are copies of Mr. Reese's," the girl reiterated.

"I'm not admitting anything. We run a very clean business here. Anyway, the Reese name doesn't appear with any of our merchandise, so obviously we're not making extra money off it."

That was an interesting clue, Nancy thought. Without the name of the designer attached to the clothes, they wouldn't be so valuable. So perhaps the thief cared less about the designs themselves and more about destroying Mr. Reese's business!

"Mr. Reese is very upset," the girl continued. "He's determined to get to the bottom of this and to sue whoever is involved in the matter."

The man yielded reluctantly. "What do you want me to do about it?" he asked.

"I want you to hire me so I can get to know a

few of the people who work around here."

Again there was a long pause.

"Tell me what kind of work you're capable of doing," Mr. Iannone sighed.

As he spoke, Nancy was aware of someone eavesdropping outside the door, but the person moved away upon realizing the manager was in conference.

"I'll gladly take any job that will provide contact with your staff."

"In that case, I suggest you help out as a stylist," he said, "You can begin tomorrow. In the meantime, I'll introduce you to someone who'll show you what to do."

He led the girl to a windowless workroom filled with a large table, dressing mirrors, an ironing board, and racks on which hung dresses with tags. In one corner stood a small desk.

"Now wait here," the manager said, closing the door.

"Thank you," Nancy said.

She peeked at the dresses, which were made of a rough cotton material, and noted the uneven stitching along the seams. Unlike the apparel in the Chalmers book, these clothes were cheap-looking.

Nancy went to a chair at the far end of the room and sat down. Suddenly, the lights went out, throwing her into total darkness!

A moment later, she heard shouts in the hall-way. Doors were slamming, people were yelling, and it seemed to Nancy that a general panic had broken out.

The electricity must have gone off in all the offices, the girl said to herself. I'd better get out of here!

She groped her way through the room, careful to avoid the clothing racks, but then grazed against the corner of the table.

"Ouch!" Nancy winced and rubbed her hip. "That hurt!" From then on, she hesitated before every step. Finally, she made it to the door and fumbled for the knob. When she turned it, a flash of fear stabbed through her. The door was locked!

The young detective paused a moment, her mind whirling. Did someone lock her in on purpose? Mr. Iannone, perhaps? It must have happened after the lights went out, when all the noise started, she reasoned. Otherwise, she would have heard the click.

Who else knew I was in here? Did Mr. Iannone tell the person who was to train me? Nancy asked herself.

She banged her fist against the door and called out, but no one came.

Bess, in the meantime, was struggling through her own typing test. She went along more slowly than George, careful not to make any mistakes. But she had finished only half the assignment when the personnel manager stopped her.

"Time's up, dear," she said. "Now let me see what you've done."

Her smile faded rapidly when she realized that Bess had filled less than a page.

"It's very neat," she said, "but you'll have to build up your speed if you want to work here."

"Yes, ma'am," Bess replied, adding hopefully, "Is there something else I could try?" George had raised the same question.

"I don't think so," the woman said. "Let me check my files, though."

She disappeared briefly, letting the girls chat during her absence. Bess quickly told George that Chris Chavez had done the photos for the store catalog.

Soon the personnel manager returned with a folder. "Have either of you had any bookkeeping experience?" she asked.

"Not a bit," Bess said promptly.

"Well, I'm sorry, but I've nothing for you."

Before the cousins left, however, George decided to ask about Chris Chavez. "We met him at a benefit fashion show the other evening," she explained.

"Here in New York?" the woman replied in bewilderment. "Are you sure it was Chris?"

"Yes, why?"

"Because he's been on assignments for us in Europe. He only flew back to New York yesterday!"

The girls were surprised, but did not press the conversation further. Their job applications had just been turned down and they didn't wish to create undue suspicion about themselves. So, after thanking the woman for her evident kindness to them, they said good-bye and headed for Jacqueline Henri's apartment.

"Too bad we didn't get jobs at Chalmers," George said.

"I feel terrible," her cousin mumbled as their cab came to a halt in front of a building marked "15."

"Well, don't. Look at it this way," George said. "We picked up that great piece of information about Chris Chavez."

"Doesn't prove anything."

"Even so, it adds another intriguing aspect."

The girls stopped speaking as they opened the door of the apartment building. To their right was a bank of mailboxes and a small television screen. Ahead was another door that was locked.

"They sure believe in security, don't they?" Bess commented, pressing a button next to the name Henri.

A few minutes passed. Nothing happened and the girls concluded that the model was not at home.

"Let me try again," Bess said. This time she held the buzzer half a second more and a voice responded.

"Who is it?" The voice was distorted by the loudspeaker.

"Jacqueline, is that you?" Bess replied.

"Who?"

"I'm looking for Jacqueline Henri," Bess continued.

"There's no one here by that name," the voice said and clicked off.

George rechecked the address. It was correct! They scanned the names on the wall directory, discovering there was only one Henri listed.

"Maybe there's something wrong with the buzzer system," Bess said.

George tended to doubt that, but she was determined not to leave the building without visiting 3-C. As a couple came out through the locked doors, she quickly stepped up and held them open for Bess.

They rode the elevator to the third floor and turned left around a corner. There were no names on the apartment doors, only brass knockers. George was about to lift the one on 3-C when they heard a man's voice filter through.

"It's your job to keep Nancy occupied," he said, as he was walking toward the door.

"He's leaving!" George whispered. "Let's get out of here!"

Quickly, the girls scooted back toward the elevator. They heard the apartment door slam, and Bess grabbed George's hand. "He'll see us once he comes around the corner. What'll we do?"

"Let's hide on the other side," George gasped, and pulled her cousin in the opposite direction from apartment 3-C. They rounded another corner and pressed themselves closely against the wall.

The man's footsteps could be heard approaching the elevator. "I'm going to take a look," George declared boldly, and, for a second, she stuck her head around the corner. Then she pulled back with a little gasp, covering her mouth at the same time to stifle the sound.

Bess tugged impatiently on her cousin's hand. "Well, who is it?"

"Chris Chavez!"

"The first one or the second one?"

"The first one!"

They heard the elevator doors open. The man entered, and soon all was quiet as the elevator descended.

"Oh, I wish we could follow him!" Bess murmured.

"We can. Come on, down the stairs!"

George led the way to the stairwell. The girls flew down, taking two steps at a time, hoping the elevator would stop on another floor to delay Chavez. However, when they reached the lobby, the elevator was there, empty, and there was no sign of the photographer. Quickly, the young detectives hurried out into the street and looked in both directions. Nothing!

12

The Culprit

"We lost him!" George exclaimed angrily between gasps for air.

Bess shrugged. "Well, we tried. Let's go back to Aunt Eloise's and tell Nancy about this."

George nodded. "There's a bus pulling up on the corner. We'll have to run to catch it."

Bess groaned. "I'll never make it! I'm out of breath as it is!"

But George wasn't listening. She was already running toward the bus, with Bess trailing behind. They just managed to squeeze through the door before it closed.

"How do you know this is the right bus?" Bess panted.

"I don't, but let's hope so."

To the girls' chagrin, however, they soon discovered that they were heading away from Aunt Eloise's apartment. It was getting dark, too, and a damp chill had seeped into the bus.

"We'll get off the next stop," George said, but it proved to be a desolate corner, causing the two passengers to debark at the following one which seemed livelier.

There they caught a taxi and were home in less than fifteen minutes. Surprisingly, they discovered that Nancy had not yet returned.

"Where is she?" Aunt Eloise questioned when she saw that her niece wasn't with Bess and George. "She ought not to wander around the city alone at night."

Bess explained how they had tossed a coin which had sent Nancy to the Millington Company.

"Well, I'm sure they're closed now," Aunt Eloise said fearfully. "George, will you call their number?"

George complied at once, but there was no answer.

"The switchboard operator must have gone home," she said.

"Did you dial the right number?" Bess asked, observing the worrisome look on Eloise Drew's face.

"Of course, I did," the girl said. She dialed

again, however, to satisfy everyone, and again all she heard was a steady ring.

Nancy had been beating her fists on the workroom door in the Millington office, hoping someone would come to free her. But in the general confusion outside, no one seemed to hear. After a while, the shouts and footsteps died down as the office emptied out, and Nancy was left in the room all alone.

She stumbled through the darkness, bruising herself on the leg of an ironing board as she searched for the desk.

I have to find something flat, a letter opener perhaps, that I can use to force the lock! she said to herself.

She opened a side drawer and her fingers ran over pencils and paper clips before coming to rest on a slim cardboard box that contained filing tabs of some sort. Nancy took one, then went back to the door, shoving the tough sliver into the crack between the door panel and the frame. She pushed it down slowly, trying to slide it over the tumbler. But it jammed. Desperately she tried again. This time, the lock slipped and released.

Dropping the tab, Nancy opened the door

and felt her way into the adjoining stock room, where she groped for a light switch. She found one finally and pushed it, but nothing happened. Through the window she noticed that lights were on in the surrounding buildings. Their glow filtered dimly through the dusty glass.

Apparently, the blackout is restricted to this building, Nancy thought. Well, I'd better call Aunt Eloise.

She made her way slowly to the main office, letting her hands trail over a desk top until they settled on a telephone. To her dismay, however, she couldn't make a connection. All calls were apparently controlled by a switchboard that was closed.

Trying to remain calm, Nancy headed for the door that led to the reception area. To her relief, it was open!

The elevator is right across the hall from here, she thought. I hope it works!

When her outstretched hands made contact with the metal doors after she had crossed the corridor, she fumbled for the button and punched it. A slight hum indicated that the elevator was indeed operating!

"Thank goodness," the girl detective murmured, and stepped inside the car.

When she arrived on the ground floor, she found the main entrance unlocked. Instantly, she rushed outside to hail a taxi. The driver gabbed cheerfully, trying to engage her in conversation, but Nancy felt so tired all of a sudden she could only raise enough energy to suppress a series of yawns. By the time she reached the apartment, she was ready to fall asleep.

"Nancy!" Aunt Eloise cried upon seeing her. "Where have you been?"

The torrent of questions that followed from Bess and George woke the girl up immediately.

"We were just about to call the police!" George exclaimed.

"Oh, I'm glad you didn't," Nancy said, dropping into a chair.

She spun out her story as fast as she could, then listened to the others. Bess and George had made phenomenal discoveries, she told them.

"So it seems that the guy we saw in the restaurant today is the real Chris Chavez," Bess said.

"And the one who introduced himself to me at the party is someone else," Nancy put in. "Just who is he?"

"Well, we know he's a friend of Jacqueline's and he knows her brother," George commented.

"If I'd never heard about Ted Henri, investigative reporter," Nancy said, "I'd wonder if he weren't a figment of her imagination."

"Maybe Jacqueline's involved in the design thefts and when she heard you were coming to town, figured she had to cover up somehow," Bess suggested.

"But taking off the way she did before the fashion show and leaving Aunt Eloise in the lurch only drew attention to herself," Nancy replied.

"That's for sure," George said. "It made everybody suspicious."

"Us in particular," Bess concurred. She grappled with her bewilderment. "Jackie's behavior doesn't make any sense at all."

"Precisely," Nancy responded, "and I'm too tired to worry about it tonight. Let's try to figure out things tomorrow."

Before going to bed, however, Aunt Eloise spoke to Nancy alone.

"What are you going to do about that job you supposedly have at Millington?"

"Oh, I'm going back there tomorrow morning."

"After all that's happened to you? I don't

think it's a good idea," Aunt Eloise objected. "Of course, you realize you were locked in that workroom on purpose."

Nancy nodded. "But I want to find out who did it and why!"

Aunt Eloise still looked doubtful. "At least promise me you'll discuss it with your father first."

"I'll call Dad in the morning. And please don't worry, Aunt Eloise."

In spite of her exhaustion, the young detective slept fitfully that night. When she awoke the next morning, her eyelids were puffy and she had trouble keeping them open.

"Didn't you sleep?" George asked Nancy.

"Not very well." She yawned.

"This will wake you up," Bess said, putting a glass of grapefruit juice and the morning newspaper in front of her.

Nancy sipped the juice, allowing her eyes to fall on a small headline. Bess and George watched them pop.

According to the newspaper, Russell Kaiser's co-op apartment had been burglarized the night before! No mention was made about the nature of missing items, but Nancy wondered about the medallion. Had it been stolen and was there a connection between Kaiser's impostor and the robbery?

"I'd say it's a good thing we came along on this visit," George said. "Otherwise, Nancy, you'd be working forty-eight hours a day on these mysteries!"

Nancy laughed, dropping a piece of bread in the toaster. "You're absolutely right," she said, "and I have a hunch I'm going to need lots of energy again today!"

"Are you heading back to Millington?" Bess inquired.

"Definitely. I want to see Mr. Iannone first thing."

"What should we do?" George asked.

"How about visiting Russell Kaiser?" Nancy said.

"Which one?" Bess giggled.

"That's for you to figure out. Maybe you ought to stop by the apartment mentioned in this article."

Aunt Eloise, who had slept later than usual, stood in the doorway. Her presence reminded Nancy of their conversation the night before, and she quickly telephoned her father. Mr. Drew agreed that she should go back to Millington, but warned her to be careful.

"I will be," she promised, then invited Bess and George to meet her for lunch near the Millington office. "That way we can keep check on each other," Nancy said, raising a smile from her aunt.

Half an hour later, she was at Millington's reception desk. When she asked for Mr. Iannone, however, she was told he wasn't in.

"But he hired me yesterday," Nancy said to the receptionist.

Out of the corner of her eye, she noticed a brown-haired woman pass hurriedly through a door. Nancy turned her head, catching the face before she disappeared. The young detective was positive that it was Rosalind, the stylist whom Mr. Reese had hastily fired the night of the fashion show!

The girl at the desk now pressed a buzzer, calling someone to come out for a moment.

Soon, an officious woman in a green wool suit appeared. "This is Nancy Drew," the receptionist introduced the visitor.

Again Nancy asked for Mr. Iannone.

"He doesn't work here any longer," the woman informed her. "He quit yesterday."

Nancy gulped. "Quit!"

"Yes. Are you a personal friend of his, may I ask?"

"No, but he offered me a job here."

"Well, he had no authority to do so. I'm in charge now."

The steely tone in the woman's voice told the girl it would be tough to persuade her to go along with Mr. Iannone's decision. So Nancy took a different tack. She related her unpleasant experience in the workroom and her suspicions that it was somehow connected to the recent thefts from the Reese collection.

"My, you do have an active imagination," the woman said. "I'm quite positive that your trouble yesterday was an accident. I'm sorry about it, but I'm not going to hire you because of it!"

There was nothing left to say, so Nancy departed. Disappointed, she took the elevator to the lobby, not paying much attention to anyone until her eyes settled on the revolving doors ahead of her, and the man approaching them.

He looked familiar, but his head was bent low in a long, plaid scarf wrapped thickly around his neck. Nancy ducked into a magazine booth as he came forward, then watched as he loosened his scarf while he waited for an elevator.

Nancy had picked up a magazine, burying her face in it until she heard the door slide open. Then, as the stranger and several other people stepped inside, and turned to face the corridor, the girl lifted her eyes. The man was Jacqueline's friend who claimed to be Chris Chavez!

She dived back out of sight as the door hung open an extra second for a last-minute passenger. Then it closed and Nancy watched the bank of numbered lights as the elevator moved up slowly. It made two stops, one of which was Millington's floor!

If the man wasn't the real fashion photographer, what was he doing there? Was he the thief who had stolen the designs?

13

Baffling Trail

While Nancy's discovery had stunned her momentarily, Bess and George were preparing themselves for their own investigation.

"It's a good thing that the two impostors believe they've duped us totally!" Bess told her cousin.

"And we have to make sure they don't find out anything to the contrary," George said.

When the girls arrived at the apartment listed for Russell Kaiser in the news article, the doorman said he had strict instructions not to admit anyone while the police were still there.

"Have they been here a long time already?" George inquired.

The doorman glanced at his watch. "About thirty minutes," he said, "but they could be around the whole day, for all I know."

"Let's go," George said, and pulled Bess out the door.

"Where are we going?" her cousin inquired.

"Some place where we can stake out the building," George suggested.

The girls headed across the street toward a small coffee shop. Bess giggled. "If I have to stake out anything, there's no place I'd rather do it from than a coffee shop!"

"I bet," George answered. She carefully avoided patches of ice forming on the sidewalk and tried to scrape the icy granules that drizzled relentlessly out of the sky onto her coat sleeve. "This weather is terrible," she complained. "How can we investigate efficiently if we have to slip and slide everywhere we go?"

"Don't worry, we might have to sit here all day," Bess said, as they entered the restaurant.

George shook her head. "I wonder if Mr. Kaiser is even home. I think I'll call the apartment to see what I can find out."

She left Bess in a booth by the window and returned a few minutes later in a flurry of excitement. "The maid answered," George said. "Mr. Kaiser is leaving right now."

The girls dropped coins on the counter and dashed outside. The sidewalk was treacherous, slowing them to a snail's pace. Bess crept close to the shops, looking for iceless patches.

"Hurry!" George called back as she cut across the street.

Bess tried to, but felt the soles of her leather shoes skid forward. "You go ahead!" she cried.

The traffic light changed and she halted, watching George almost slide into the corner of Kaiser's apartment house.

She managed not to fall, however, and walked to the entrance where a bald-headed man was stepping into a patrol car that was parked in front.

He's the one who bought the medallion! she almost blurted.

Bess caught up to her as the car door closed, and George turned to her cousin excitedly. "That clinches it!" she exclaimed. "The second Russell Kaiser who asked Nancy to help is definitely the impostor! And even though his hair is different from that of the man we saw in the police picture, I'm sure he's Pete Grover!"

"He was bidding on that medallion like crazy," Bess said. "He must've really wanted it."

"But if he's a crook, why did he introduce himself to us?" George asked.

Bess had no answer, and no matter how much

they talked about the odd twists in the growing mystery, nothing satisfied them.

Nancy, at the same time, had gone into the restaurant across the street from the Millington office. It was still too early to expect Bess and George, Nancy realized, but she waited, wondering if Jacqueline's friend, whom she had spotted in the elevator, would come out again.

Traffic dragged on the ice-covered street, and a bus now blocked the girl's view of the revolving doors.

What if I miss him? Nancy worried, as the bus inched away.

She pressed closer to the window to look down the sidewalk, but saw no one who resembled the phony Chris Chavez. Minutes went by slowly, it seemed, but suddenly the man appeared! He paused outside the building and turned his head in both directions, apparently looking for someone.

I wonder if it's Jacqueline, Nancy thought. Just then, another bus pulled up right in front of her.

Oh, please move! she begged silently. I can't lose him now!

The vehicle moved along shortly and, to Nancy's relief, the man in the plaid scarf was still there talking to another man. Nancy gasped as she recognized him.

"That's Grover, the guy who told me he was Russell Kaiser," she said under her breath. "Where are they going?"

Figuring that Bess and George might be delayed by the bad weather, she decided to leave a message for them with the restaurant hostess and follow the two men.

"Please ask my friends to wait for me," Nancy told the young woman. Then she pulled up her coat collar and stepped cautiously onto the frozen sidewalk. She followed the men around the block, where they hurried into a fabric shop called Belini's, which boasted a variety of materials and sewing goods.

Through the window, the girl detective saw the men descend a flight of steps in the rear. She entered the store, taking quick note of the colorful polyester and cotton fabrics that were shelved in bolts.

A sign in the back indicated that the sewing supplies and offices were downstairs. Nancy followed the arrow, glancing down at the customers as she went below. The men were not in sight. Apparently, they had stepped into the office.

Nancy headed for a table with large pattern

books on it. She leafed through one, glancing up periodically to look for the two impostors.

"Excuse me, please," a woman said suddenly. Nancy had not been aware of the customer standing next to her, eager to look at the pattern book she was holding. "Are you finished with that?"

"Oh, yes," the girl replied as men's voices suddenly drifted over the sound of file drawers opening and closing.

The office, Nancy soon discovered, was located around a bend in the wall. Next to it was a tall column of narrow metal cabinets that contained all kinds of buttons. Without seeming too obvious, the girl secreted herself behind them. Now she was within better hearing range of the conversation.

"Mr. Belini," Nancy overheard Jacqueline's friend say, "I have only a few questions."

The young detective leaned forward eagerly, but someone approached the cabinets and opened a drawer, digging noisily through the buttons. Nancy quickly busied herself with swatches of material that hung behind her. Then, when the metal drawer slammed shut, she took her place again.

This time the other man was talking, and it seemed to Nancy that she heard the name

123

Rosalind. But his voice fell away in a drone of unintelligible words.

It's so frustrating, Nancy said to herself. She was tempted to leave her hiding place and move closer to the doorway, but what if she were caught? I can't take the chance, she decided.

She rested her hands on the stack of metal and dipped her head to one side. The pressure of her grip pitched the fragile cabinet forward and several drawers slid open, emitting hundreds of buttons!

They poured out in a steady stream despite the girl's attempt to right the cabinet quickly. Then her fingers slipped, and the whole structure crashed to the floor!

14

A Developing Pattern

As hundreds of buttons swirled out, Nancy hurried to the other side of the wall. She felt a lump harden in her throat as the three men ran out of the office.

"Again someone knocked over this cabinet," Belini complained. "Why don't people watch where they're walking?"

Two assistants seemed to appear from nowhere. "That whole setup is just terrible," one said. "We'll have to get a different type of cabinet. This one is so wobbly it falls at least once a week!"

While Belini mumbled something, they scooped up the buttons, separating them into their respective drawers. The three men, meanwhile, went back into Belini's office.

When the clerks finished with the cabinet, they hurried upstairs, allowing Nancy to position herself behind it once more. This time she carefully avoided touching it.

"How well do you know Mrs. Jenner?" she heard the phony Chris Chavez ask.

Belini said something in reply, which Nancy could not understand. Then his voice rose as he added, "Mrs. Jenner has a reputation for being abrasive. But she was a good worker, Mr. Henri, the best stylist around!"

Henri! Nancy couldn't believe her ears. Could it be that the phony Chris Chavez was really the reporter, Ted Henri?

A jumble of thoughts raced through the girl's mind. Why all the pretense? she wondered. And what was Ted Henri's affiliation with the phony Russell Kaiser, alias Pete Grover?

Was Henri investigating the same design thefts that Nancy was? Did they relate at all to the fake auction scheme he, as Chris Chavez, had revealed to Nancy?

Or maybe he trumped up the auction story for my benefit, hoping to sidetrack me onto another mystery! Nancy concluded.

As she continued listening, more questions came from the two men. They wanted to know what Belini's association with Millington was!

The young detective missed hearing Belini's answer as several customers entered the room from the stairway. They were chattering about a choice of colors, but then paused long enough for the girl to hear a few more remarks pass between the men.

"Do you supply fabric to Millington?" Henri questioned.

Belini grumbled something unintelligible.

Then Nancy heard Henri ask if Belini had sold material to Mrs. Jenner.

"Sure. So what? She likes to sew."

Clearly, the man was on the defensive, but before any more was said, the reporter and Grover strode out of the room. Nancy remained out of sight until they went up the stairway and she heard Mr. Belini's voice again.

"Henri will be at the Crystal Party tomorrow night," the man said. Then there was a click as he put down the telephone.

Obviously, he had called someone. Nancy stood stock-still, hoping to hear more, but the man made no other calls. She decided it would be better for her to try and follow the two men, rather than eavesdrop on Belini, so she hurried up the stairs and out the door.

Her eyes roamed the street, but the pair was nowhere in sight! They couldn't have gone too far on the ice, Nancy reasoned. They must have taken a taxi.

Disappointed, she headed back to the restaurant, digging in her rubberized heels to avoid slipping. On the way, she picked up a newspaper. When she arrived, Bess and George were not there.

After the two girls had seen Russell Kaiser leave in the police car, they assumed that he was on his way to the local precinct.

"Let's go there," George suggested. "Maybe we'll get a chance to talk to him."

The girls asked the doorman for the address. He gave it to them but said, "I wouldn't recommend bothering poor Mr. Kaiser now. He's very upset, as you can well imagine."

"Don't worry," George said. "We only want to talk to him because we might be able to help him."

The doorman raised his eyebrows and was about to ask them how, but the girls just smiled sweetly and left.

When they arrived at the police station, they did not see the bald-headed man. Upon asking at the desk, they learned he was talking to the captain, but would be done in a few minutes. Bess and George sat down to wait.

"I bet Nancy has eaten our lunch as well as hers by now," Bess murmured to her cousin.

"I just hope she's still there," George said. "Of course, Millington may only give her a half hour off, in which case she's probably left."

The cousins' conversation ended abruptly as Mr. Kaiser appeared. The girls stood up quickly.

"Mr. Kaiser," George said when he strode toward them.

He paused.

"Remember us? We met you at the Speers' auction the other evening," Bess continued.

"Oh, yes," he said now. "You were with the young lady who bid on the medallion."

"Yes. We saw the news item about the burglary and wondered if the medallion had been stolen, too."

"You followed me here to ask me that?" he replied, incredulous.

"We're detectives," Bess said.

"Amateur detectives," George added. "May we speak to you a moment? We have some information that might be of interest to you."

Kaiser shrugged. "Why not?"

Without revealing too much about the mysteries they were working on with their friend, Nancy Drew, George explained their special concern for the distinctive medallion.

"It's very possible," she declared, "that the man who was bidding on it is the burglar you're looking for. He told us he was you."

"Not only that," Bess spoke up, "but he seemed to want that medallion an awful lot."

"Enough to steal it, I suppose," Mr. Kaiser said with a glint of mischief.

"Exactly," Bess said.

"Well, girls, I appreciate the clues, but I'm afraid you're on the wrong track. You see, the robber wasn't the least bit interested in the medallion. I had put it in the safe with some other things that he took. He left the medallion, though, probably thinking it was a valueless trinket."

The girls were disappointed. "Then obviously the burglar wasn't the man who competed with you at the auction," George said. "But why did he introduce himself to us as Russell Kaiser?"

Mr. Kaiser shrugged. "I have no idea, and to be quite honest, I don't really care. Now, I have other matters to take care of. If you will excuse me, please."

He hurried off, and the young detectives left the precinct and headed for the restaurant. To their relief, they found Nancy still there, dallying over a salad.

"We thought for sure you'd be gone by now," Bess said as she and George sat down. "What happened to your job at Millington?"

"I have no job," Nancy replied, spearing a piece of lettuce with her fork, "but I do have lots of other news."

She told about her encounters, the conversations she had overheard, and her current suspicions.

"I'm convinced Ted Henri deliberately tried to send me off on another mystery—" Nancy said.

"The auction scheme," George put in.

"Right—because he didn't want me near the case involving Mr. Reese."

"And Jacqueline's been helping her brother," Bess remarked.

"Then her story about the kidnapping was phony," George added.

"I'm not positive about that," Nancy said. "Maybe she really did believe her brother was missing. Otherwise, why didn't she appear for the fashion show? What makes less sense is that she turned up at the hotel later."

"Also, we never did see her and Ted together

at any time that evening," George added.

"Exactly. So it's possible that someone wanted her to believe Ted had been kidnapped," Nancy concluded. "Someone who was determined to keep her away long enough to steal those expensive gowns!"

After the young detective's idea took root in everyone's mind, the other girls related their experiences of the morning.

"I'm glad the medallion wasn't stolen, for Mr. Kaiser's sake," Nancy said. "And it proves that Pete Grover wasn't the thief."

George nodded. "If Grover is working with Ted Henri, and now we have ample proof that he is, I'm sure he's not a burglar. Yet, he has a criminal record—he's wanted for check forgery. I can't figure it out."

"Neither can I," Nancy admitted.

"And why would he pretend to be Russell Kaiser?" Bess asked.

"Well, if his job at the auction was to set us up for a fake mystery, maybe he'd done some research. Found out about the Kaisers, their family's lion crest, and the names of surviving members he gleaned from Galen Kaiser's recent obituary," Nancy said.

"Then he and Henri wrote the note to Jacqueline, using the crest as a symbol," Bess added.

"But what was all that business about a crooked auction?" George put in.

"Just a ploy to make the newspaper announcement about the sale of the Kaiser estate even more tantalizing," Nancy replied.

"And all of this to keep us away from their case," George sighed. "I bet if we had combined forces we'd have solved it by now!"

"Whatever we do," Nancy said, "I don't think we should let on to Jacqueline or Ted that we know what's going on."

"Three can play pretend as easily as two," George said, trying to sound less anxious than she was.

"And tomorrow night we're going to get our chance," Nancy replied.

15

Stylist Trouble

Nancy's announcement made both George and Bess stare at her in surprise.

"What do you mean?" Bess asked.

"We're going to the Crystal Party," Nancy replied.

"The what?"

Nancy laughed, then repeated Mr. Belini's telephone conversation. "Ted Henri will be there, and it must have some significance. I think we'll be able to pick up a clue there."

"Where is it?" George inquired.

"I bought a newspaper on the way back from the fabric store, figuring there might be an announcement about it." Nancy turned to a page listing future social events and handed it to her friends.

" 'The Crystal Party,' " Bess read aloud.
" 'Highlight of the fashion year. Every major
designer represented. Tickets two hundred and
fifty dollars. Advance reservations only.'"

"Well, that lets me out," George mumbled.
"Who can afford it, anyway?"

Nancy giggled. "Lots of people," she said.

"Only the crème de la crème," Bess said,
adding, "and Miss Nancy Drew, perhaps."

"Now, now," the young detective said, "I
have a hunch we can go to the party without
paying a penny."

"Sure, if we sneak in," Bess said. "I could
disguise myself as Lady Macaroni and you
could be Baroness von Hootenanny!"

"Even if we could wangle invitations, we'd
have to wear the same things we wore to the
benefit," George put in, "and I spilled salad
dressing on my gown."

"See, it's hopeless," Bess insisted.

"On the contrary." Nancy smiled. "We are
going to be the three most eligible young ladies
there and in the three most beautiful gowns!
C'mon!"

The girls paid the bill and trailed outside,
letting Nancy lead the way. Salt trucks had
spread the melting grains on the street and a

similar layer covered the sidewalk, so Bess was able to keep pace as the trio walked up the street.

"Where are we going?" she asked Nancy.

"To Reese Associates, of course."

"Oh, boy. I hope Mr. Reese is in a better mood than the one we left him in," George commented.

"I hope so, too, because I'd like to persuade him to take us to the Crystal Party."

To the girls' relief, the man's temper had subsided. He even seemed unusually happy, judging by his enthusiastic welcome.

"I just received some very exciting news! Come into my office," he said, adding as they took seats. "Zoe Babbitt has decided to buy everything you modeled the other night, Nancy. Can you imagine? Everything!"

"Congratulations," the visitors chimed in together.

"She said it didn't matter one bit that most of the designs might have been scooped by another dress house," the man went on. "There's nothing like a Reese original, she told me."

"So you were worrying unnecessarily," George said.

"Well, I still don't know how my other clients

will feel, but it's nice to know I haven't lost Mrs. Babbitt."

"Will she be at the Crystal Party?" Nancy inquired.

"Most certainly, and wearing one of my winter creations, I suspect."

"Speaking of winter creations," Nancy continued, "we came by today for a reason."

The man perked up his ears. "Is it my turn to ask what *you've* discovered?"

Nancy smiled. "Well, we've discovered some facts, but it's really too early to discuss them." She was worried that the temperamental designer might inadvertently slip something to the wrong people.

But Reese's curiosity was aroused. "Well, what exactly *did* you find out?" he pressed the girl.

"As I said, I can't tell you yet."

"Can't tell me?" he bristled. "But *I'm* the man who—"

"Mr. Reese," George interposed, "it's important to keep things confidential—for now."

"Tomorrow night could produce the final chapter," Bess added.

Seizing the chance, Nancy quickly expressed how crucial it was for the young detectives to attend the Crystal Party.

"I can arrange that easily. On one condition, though," Mr. Reese bargained. "That you tell me everything."

"I promise," Nancy smiled. "After the party."

The man grumbled in annoyance, but finally agreed to obtain invitations. "And what are you planning to wear?" he inquired.

"I suppose my old green skirt and blouse," Nancy said.

George mentioned her dress with the oily stains on it and Bess shrugged helplessly.

"Well, you can't go to the Crystal Party looking like Cinderellas before the ball," Mr. Reese said. He strode to the doorway, addressing a secretary. "Find Rosalind for me."

Nancy was surprised to hear that Rosalind had been rehired by Mr. Reese after he fired her and she went to work for Millington. Now the young detective was doubly happy she hadn't revealed her discoveries to Reese!

Soon Rosalind appeared. She returned the girls' hellos with a silent nod, then glanced at the designer. "Yes, Mr. Reese?"

"You remember Miss Drew?" the designer said to her.

"Of course," she murmured.

Nancy tried not to seem too obvious about her examination of the woman's face, which contained thin lines and shadows under the small eyes. The skin was paste white, giving her a sickly appearance.

Mr. Reese instructed Rosalind to bring in several gowns. "One for each of the girls," he told her.

Without inquiring about size, she looked at them from head to toe, then hurried out of the room.

"She's a whiz," the designer commented.

"I thought you fired her," Nancy couldn't resist saying.

"I did, but she came back."

"On her own volition?" Nancy asked.

"Well, I didn't get down on my hands and knees, if that's what you're insinuating."

Nancy ignored the comment as Rosalind reappeared with a variety of silks, taffetas, and velvets.

"Those are fine," Mr. Reese said to the assistant. "Now help them make selections."

"That one's gorgeous!" Bess exclaimed, eyeing a royal-blue taffeta dress with a broad ruffle around the bodice. "May I try it on?"

Rosalind was already leading the girls to a cubby of dressing rooms. "You can't leave here unless you do," she said.

While Nancy and George settled on their

choices, Bess was trying to zip up the narrow waist.

"I was almost positive this would fit you," the stylist said to her.

"I'm flattered—really flattered," Bess squeaked as the woman forced the zipper to close. "Only problem is, I can't breathe!"

"I can fix that," Rosalind said, tapping her fingers on her chin.

"You can?" Bess said hoarsely. "Right away?"

Instantly, the woman pulled the zipper down and the girl let out a heavy sigh. "How are you both doing?" she called out cheerfully to her friends.

"Fine," Nancy and George replied, but in fact they were having similar difficulties.

All the clothes were much too tight, George's more so than anyone's. The narrow silk skirt she had chosen hugged her ankles, forcing her to take birdlike steps.

"I'd never catch a thief in this thing!" she laughed, poking her head into Nancy's cubicle.

"Me neither!" Nancy giggled. She gazed at her elegant ivory gown with a skirt that fell in a mass of folds.

"Everything needs work," Rosalind admitted, looking at each girl in turn.

One by one, she fitted them, sticking pins along seams.

"Ouch!" Bess cried as a pin slipped through the zipper into her skin.

"Be careful, Rosalind," Mr. Reese told her from the other room. "After all, these young ladies are my personal detectives!"

With that, the woman overturned a box of pins on the floor. She fumbled, and nervously put them back. When she finished her work, she announced that the dresses would be delivered to the girls the next afternoon.

"I will give your names to the chairperson so you won't have to buy tickets," Mr. Reese said. "I assume you know where the party is being held. I will meet you there—if that's all right."

"Great," Nancy said gaily. "Thanks for everything!"

"I'm just sorry we can't invite Dave, Burt, and Ned," Bess said when they reached Aunt Eloise's apartment house.

"Next time," Nancy remarked.

"Humph—next time," Bess pouted.

But as morning came and the sun shone over a glaze of snow that had fallen during the night, she regained her old enthusiasm.

"I'm really going to pamper myself today," Bess declared, fluffing her curls.

"Considering it could be a long evening," Nancy said, "I think that's a terrific idea—for all of us!"

Despite the fact the threesome chose to stay inside all day, the hours flew quickly. When Aunt Eloise arrived home from shopping, it was already late afternoon and the altered dresses had not yet arrived!

"Maybe we should call Mr. Reese's office," Bess suggested.

Nancy dialed the number, but a voice told her that the designer had left early.

"Is Rosalind there?" the girl inquired.

"Just a minute, please."

After a long pause, the voice returned.

"No, I'm sorry. She isn't here, either."

George spoke as Nancy hung up the receiver. "Well, it's back to salad stains," she said. But a few minutes later, the buzzer from downstairs signaled the delivery.

"Thank goodness!" Bess said, when she saw the gowns in plastic bags.

The girls immediately removed them and disappeared into the bedroom to change. But as they pulled on the small metal tabs to open the long zippers, they discovered tiny stitches around the teeth.

The dresses had been sewn up tight!

16

Undercover Disguise

The three girls stared at the gowns in horror.

"What are we going to do?" Bess gasped.

Nancy quickly asked her aunt if she had a pair of small scissors.

"Or three pairs?" George added.

"All I have are these," the woman replied, removing tiny shears from a sewing basket and large ones from a desk drawer, "and I'm afraid you might cut a hole in the material, if you use the big pair."

"We don't have much time," Nancy said, "so I'll have to take the chance."

While the cousins went to work with the small blades, Nancy slipped the longer ones under the top threads that held the zipper of her dress. She cut through stitch after stitch until she reached the metal base that seemed miles from where she had started. It was only after the threesome had finished the arduous job that they took a moment to talk.

"Who would do such a thing?" Bess said as she hurried to change. "Not Rosalind, I'm sure."

"You never know," Nancy said thoughtfully, remembering Rosalind's connection with Millington. But since the alterations turned out to be done properly, she concluded that Bess was probably right.

"Well, somebody didn't want us to go to the Crystal Party tonight," George said, combing her hair as quickly as she could.

"But whoever it was didn't count on three fine seamstresses." Aunt Eloise laughed.

The girls paraded in front of her, bringing a sigh of contentment from the woman.

"Now that's how I like to see you all—going off to a lovely party," she said. "No dangerous mission, I hope." There was a tone of uncertainty in her voice.

"As long as we stick together," Nancy assured her, "we'll be okay."

"Uh-oh," Aunt Eloise said. "Does that mean you do expect trouble?"

"I don't expect anything," the girl detective said, winking. "'Bye."

When the trio arrived at the hall where the

party was being held, they were completely awestruck by the decorations. Fine, dainty snowflakes and crystal stars hung from the ceiling that overlooked an array of birch trees with silvery branches. Mirrors on dinner tables glowed from candlelit centerpieces that carried out the winter theme.

"It's a fairyland," Nancy said, as women in stunning evening clothes and men in tuxedos mingled animatedly.

"There's Mr. Reese," Bess commented, "and that must be his wife. Wow!"

The designer spotted the girls at the same time and came forward, introducing Sheila.

"She left our house in Florida just to come up for this party," he said, explaining the woman's deep tan.

"Richard has told me a lot about you all," she smiled, her teeth as glistening as her sleek, white gown.

But before the conversation could continue, another woman called her away, leaving Mr. Reese with the three girls. He led them through the crowd, pausing to make introductions.

"I know Reese creations when I see them," declared one man, handsome with a long cap of white hair. "Aren't you going to tell me who these mystery ladies are, Richard?"

But the designer pretended not to hear and joined two other men less than a foot away. The girls, however, hung back to talk with the white-haired man. They practically froze when he announced his name.

"I'm Arnaud Hans," he said.

The designer under whose name the Reese gowns had appeared in the Chalmers catalog! No wonder Mr. Reese had ignored him!

When the young detectives finally gave their names, Hans seemed to recognize Nancy's.

"I've been hearing about you, Miss Drew, that you are doing investigative work for Richard. Well, I want to go on record that I didn't steal anything from him. He blasted me on the phone the other day, claiming that I had taken some of his spring designs and sold them to Chalmers. It's not true and I can prove it. I have dated copies of every sketch!"

Nancy was careful not to say too much, but conceded that it was not impossible for the men to have come up with the same ideas.

"Personally, I don't think Millington stole anything from him, either," Hans went on. "Other people simply created similar designs before Reese did and he's angry about it. That's all. His pride and ego are hurt because he knows he's slipping."

"I don't think he's slipping at all," Bess said in Mr. Reese's defense. "I love this dress."

"Yes, well, it is pretty, but I think it's last year's," Hans replied maliciously.

The discussion ended abruptly as Nancy edged the girls away.

"Where are we going?" Bess asked.

"To see Russell Kaiser," Nancy said.

"Mr. Kaiser's here?" the cousins replied in astonishment.

"Not the real one," their friend whispered. "Ted Henri's buddy, Pete Grover. Here he comes."

When he saw the trio, he greeted them with enthusiasm. "What a pleasant surprise," he said.

"We read about the burglary," George put in.

"Burglary?" the man stumbled.

"Yes, in your apartment," Bess said.

"Oh, oh, of course, *that* burglary." He laughed nervously. "Let's not talk about such a dreary subject," he said. "As a matter of fact, Nancy, I had planned to give you a call about the man who bought my uncle's medallion at Speers."

"You have a lead on him?" Nancy inquired.

"No," the man replied. "But I wanted to find out if you knew anything."

"Well, I haven't spoken to him since that evening," Nancy said, "but I think I know where to find him."

"You do? Oh—that's wonderful. You must tell me all about him. But first let me talk to my friend Bob over there. I've been trying to get hold of him all evening. I'll be back in a few minutes."

With that, Grover turned and was quickly swallowed up by the crowd. The girls were convinced he had just used his friend as an excuse and that he would try to avoid them for the rest of the evening.

A moment later Nancy caught sight of Grover behind a silver birch tree again. Another man in a tuxedo was with him. Wondering who he was, Nancy darted away from the cousins, but was stopped short by Sheila Reese's long, braceleted arm.

"Where are you off to in such a hurry?" the designer's wife asked. "Come, I'd like you to meet some friends of ours."

Nancy did not wish to appear rude, so she followed the woman to a table where her husband and another couple were seated. Bess and George had witnessed the diversion, and to Nancy's relief, went to follow Grover instead. A few moments later, however, they joined the group at the table.

"We lost him," George whispered when they sat down.

"Don't worry," Nancy whispered back. "At least you tried."

Just then her elbow accidentally pushed against a glass of water and it fell.

"Oh!" Nancy cried, quickly righting the glass, but not before several drops had trailed onto her lap. "Excuse me a moment," she said, popping up to go to a powder room, while Mr. Reese stared dishearteningly at the water mark on the precious skirt.

When Nancy emerged from the powder room, she did not return to the table right away. Instead, she wandered around until she finally saw Pete Grover and his companion again. Although their backs were to her, she could see their faces clearly in a panel of mirrors on the wall. The second man was Ted Henri, otherwise known as Chris Chavez! They were looking at their watches as if something were about to happen.

Nancy pulled as close as she could without being observed by either of them, and tried to overhear their conversation. The din of voices in the room, however, seemed louder than ever; and all she was able to catch was Gramercy Park and the number "11." Did it refer to an address or to the time?

No further clarification came as the men were whisked onto the dance floor by two women friends. Nancy hurried back to the Reese table, but no one was there. She scanned the couples who were dancing but saw neither of her friends.

"Where are they?" Nancy murmured, wishing she could tell Bess and George what she had learned.

But they seemed to have disappeared, and in less than twenty minutes it would be eleven o'clock, the hour when Nancy might find the solution to the puzzle. Instantly, she made her decision. She hurried to the check room to get her wrap and left a detailed message for the cousins, then darted out into the street and hailed a taxi.

The snow that had fallen earlier had melted entirely, leaving only a light dampness underfoot, which Nancy appreciated as she reached Gramercy Park. She asked the driver to let her out in front of a building several doors away from Number 11, and stepped toward an opposite canopy.

There, in the glow of a waning moon and a street lamp, she fixed her eyes on Number 11. She noticed a shadowy figure in the second-floor windows. It moved out of sight, emerging shortly in the doorway downstairs.

It was Rosalind, Mr. Reese's stylist!

17

A Four-Handed Ruse

A cold wind penetrated Nancy's cloak as she watched the woman in the doorway, who seemed to be waiting for someone. Then, as if in answer to the girl detective's curiosity, a taxi pulled up to Number 11 and Mr. Belini, the owner of the fabric store, stepped out.

At the same time Nancy noticed a van parked down the street. Its lights flashed on and off and the vehicle crawled toward the building. But the dimness of the street lamps prevented her from seeing the driver and the person sitting next to him.

On a hunch Nancy pulled the collar of her cloak high around her neck and darted to a nearby corner, circling to the back of the van as Belini moved in and out of the doorway. Her heart thumping in panic, the girl dived into the shadow of the adjoining building to watch.

Rosalind seemed to have vanished, but Belini hurried to the vehicle's rear doors. He opened one, revealing a rack of dresses covered in plastic. If only Nancy could get a closer look!

Belini poked his head deeper into the van, running through the dresses as if he were counting them. He shook his head and ran into the building once more, leaving the door ajar.

Nancy instantly raced forward, grabbing a plastic bag and pulling it into the light. As she had suspected, the gown inside was one that had been stolen the night of the benefit fashion show!

Before she could inspect the rest, however, the door opened again and she heard Belini's voice. She leaped into the van, grateful that the engine was running and muffled any noise she made.

Belini walked over to the van, then stopped to talk to the driver. This gave Nancy enough time to hide behind the rack. To her relief, there was a partition between the front and rear of the small vehicle, so no one could see her unless the dresses were removed.

Yet she had little breathing space, and the garments surrounding her created a warmth

that was uncomfortable, almost suffocating.

"Maybe this wasn't such a great idea," Nancy murmured, realizing she was trapped!

But there was no time to change her mind as the wheels of the van began to move under her!

By now Bess and George had met two young men who introduced themselves as Woody Haskins and Frank Vanderveer. Both looked to be in their twenties, and told the girls that their parents were in the clothing business. They had lived in New York City all their lives.

"And where are you two from?" Woody inquired.

"River Heights," Bess replied. "Home of the famous Nancy Drew."

"Oh, yes. She's an amateur detective," Woody said. Then he whirled Bess onto the dance floor.

"Hm-hm. So am I," Bess told him.

"You solve mysteries, too?" Frank asked George. He was tall and seemed reserved like her friend, Burt Eddleton, which made the girl relax almost immediately.

"Oh, we all do," she said brightly, as the music picked up tempo.

The beat was faster now, and the couples fell apart from each other for the duration of the dance. Afterwards, their escorts took the girls to the buffet for a snack. When they returned to their table, Bess and George suddenly realized that Nancy hadn't come back yet.

Vaguely uneasy, they wondered what had happened to her. Bess nudged George. "We've been having such a good time that we forgot all about our best friend!" she whispered. "Where do you think Nancy went?"

"I don't know," George said, "but I think we ought to go looking for her."

The girls excused themselves and moved off, but neither of their escorts was ready to release them so quickly. The music had started again, and Frank and Woody ran after Bess and George, begging for another dance.

"But we can't stay!" Bess insisted as Woody tugged on her hand, pulling her back on the floor.

"Why not? Do you turn into a pumpkin at eleven o'clock?" The young man laughed, causing a tiny grin to wrinkle the girl's face.

"No, but we really do have to leave," Bess declared and motioned to George, who looked forlornly at her date.

When the foursome stood together again, the young men continued to plead. "You came here to enjoy yourselves, didn't you?" Frank asked.

"Why do you want to go home so early?"

"Well, we're not going home," George said. "We're investigating something."

"Tonight?" Woody and Frank chorused.

"We'll go with you," the latter volunteered.

"Oh, no!" Bess exclaimed. "It's nice of you to offer, but—"

"Then it's all settled," Frank put in. "Now tell us, what are you looking for?"

"Our friend Nancy," George said.

"Describe her," Frank went on. "Then we'll fan out and search. Afterwards, we'll meet at your table."

Bess and George were glad to have help, but when they rejoined their dates fifteen minutes later, no one had seen Nancy.

"Maybe she left the party," Woody suggested.

"Let's see if her cloak is still in the checkroom," George replied.

Upon questioning the woman in charge, the girls were given Nancy's message.

"We ought to go there at once," Frank spoke up. "Get a taxi, Woody."

In the cab, Bess whispered to George, "I'm glad we have a couple of strong men with us!"

"Just hope we find Nancy!" George said.

By the time they climbed out of the taxi at

Gramercy Park, most lights had been turned out in the various buildings and Number 11 seemed unoccupied.

"Maybe Nancy gave up on whatever she was looking for and went home," Woody suggested.

"Nancy? Give up? Never!" Bess said.

She and George hurried ahead of the men toward the iron fence that framed the park area itself, thinking they had heard someone crying. But as they drew near, they realized it was only the whine of a small puppy.

"Where could Nancy have gone?" Bess wailed.

She and George roamed close to the fence, peering at the blackness beyond, half wondering if Nancy had been abducted and taken to some forsaken area of the city.

As they returned to their escorts, who had remained near the entrance to Number 11, the cousins glimpsed something shiny in the street.

It was Nancy's earring!

"It's crushed," George said, examining it.

"Maybe a car rolled over it," Frank commented.

"Maybe one that kidnapped her!" Bess exclaimed in fright.

As she spoke, the window above slid open and a woman addressed the foursome. The cousins looked up to see who it was, but the speaker pulled back as a waft of cold air drifted in.

"I believe the girl you are looking for is here," she called out.

"Is that you, Rosalind?" George said, thinking she recognized the voice.

But there was no reply, only a halting cough.

"Should we go up?" Bess asked.

"There's nothing to be afraid of," Woody said.

"Yeah, we're with you," his friend added.

Even so, the girls wondered if the invitation was a sinister ruse. If Nancy were being held captive inside, the cousins might be stepping into the same carefully laid trap!

"Come on," Woody urged, leading the way into the dim corridor. "We have to find Nancy!"

Bess, George, and Frank followed. The sounds of their footsteps on the stairway echoed loudly through the empty building, and the girls shivered when Woody banged his fist on the door. Tensely, they waited for the woman to open it!

18

Escort Accomplices

Almost at once the door swung open, but no one was immediately visible in the plainly furnished room. Bess and George stepped inside, calling, "Nancy?"

"Maybe we're in the wrong—" George started to say when several hands grabbed her and Bess from behind and pushed them toward the opposite wall. Each had a hand clasped over their eyes, so they could not see their attackers.

"Help!" the cousins shrieked as they were shoved into a closet. A moment later, a key turned in the lock.

"Let us out of here!" Bess cried.

"They must have jumped Frank and Woody, too," George said, pressing her ear against the closet door. "I don't hear anything."

Bess listened also, but the room seemed vacant. Had their attackers subdued the two young men and taken them away, leaving the girls trapped in the stuffy closet?

"I think I'm going to faint," Bess murmured, swaying back against George.

"You can't pass out now!" the other girl exclaimed. She was ready to hurl herself full force into the door, but stopped as footsteps echoed outside.

Were their captors returning?

The cousins remained quiet, feeling a sudden fierce shiver pulse up their spines. George quickly squatted to the keyhole. It afforded only a partial view of the room, but enough to establish the identity of those in it.

Woody and Frank! She gasped.

Was it possible that she and Bess had been tricked by the young men? Had they used their charm to imprison the girls?

"What do you see?" Bess whispered.

"Sh—" her cousin said, pressing her ear under the knob to listen to the conversation.

"We'll keep them here until we get rid of the third one," George heard Woody say.

"Where is she?" Frank asked.

"In the van," Woody replied. Apparently,

she found it parked out front and walked right in. They caught her hiding behind the dresses."

Bess tapped on George's shoulder, begging to be told something, but George shook her head. She didn't want to miss anything that was being said.

"Rozzie wants us to meet her at the pier in an hour or so," Frank spoke up again, but the rest of his sentence became unintelligible as he pulled a cellophane wrapper off a cigar and crumpled it.

George was positive that "the third one" referred to Nancy, and that Rozzie was Rosalind, the stylist at Reese Associates. Had she reconciled herself to the designer merely because she needed continuing access to him? That seemed to be the case.

"Reese never should've fired Paula Jenner," Frank said, puffing on the cigar. "Those two sisters are real soul mates."

Now there was a lull as Frank strode toward the closet, letting the pungent smoke clog the keyhole.

"You alive in there?" he called out sarcastically. "Sorry we had to do this, girls."

The cousins did not answer, and George confirmed to Bess that the speaker had been her escort, Frank. The blond girl felt like crying, but George gripped her arm and motioned for her to listen.

The men, however, made only one other vague reference to the last pier at the West Side docks.

"On second thought," Woody's voice came again, "let's take a ride up there now. These two aren't going anywhere."

"They're leaving!" George whispered.

She waited until she was sure the men were out of the building, then leaned her weight against the door and flung herself back and forth several times, hoping to force the lock. It held firm, though, and the searing pain that drove through George's shoulder brought her to a halt.

"I'll do it," Bess said.

With determination, she plunged ahead, hitting the door hard. It didn't open, but it had weakened.

"I knew these few extra pounds would come in handy someday," Bess quipped, crashing forward again.

This time the tumblers snapped.

"You're fabulous!" George complimented her cousin as they raced down the stairs and out into the moistening air.

They dashed to a corner where passing cars

were visible and quickly hailed a taxi.

"Where to?" the driver asked.

"The last pier at the West Side docks," George said.

"The what?" the man gulped. "It's a little late to go swimming, isn't it?"

The cousins were not in the mood for small talk, but listened courteously as the driver continued.

"No boats leaving now, either," he said. "You girls ought to go home."

"I wish we could," Bess murmured, as a chilling breeze swept through the window crack.

"Just be glad we're out of that closet," George whispered.

"And into a frying pan?" her cousin said.

By now, the driver had guided the cab around the park and was heading across town. He kept his pace moderate, giving his passengers time to plot their moves.

"What do we do if one of us gets caught?" Bess asked her cousin.

"You mean by Frank or Woody?"

"Or by anybody else," Bess replied.

"Then the other one hops in this cab and takes off for the police station."

"Maybe we should do that now," Bess said.

"I considered it," George said, "but I really doubt we'd be able to convince an officer to come with us. He'd probably think we're just a couple of kooky teenagers."

"How could he?" Bess said, glancing at the taffeta dress that showed through her coat. "I think we look rather sophisticated."

"Well, that may be so, but New York isn't River Heights where everybody including Chief McGinnis knows us."

George's remark only reinforced her cousin's anxiety as the taxi looped in the direction of the Hudson River.

"It's pitch black out there!" Bess exclaimed.

"Sure you gals really want me to drop you at the pier?" the driver said shortly.

"If you don't mind," George replied, "we'd like you to wait."

"How long?" he asked.

"It depends," Bess put in.

"On what?"

"On what we find, of course."

"Hmm. Maybe you ought to tell me what you're looking for first."

"We're looking for our friend," George revealed. "She was kidnapped and we think she's been taken to this pier."

The man glanced at her sharply for a moment.

"And you're going to play big shots and rescue her, eh? If what you tell me is true, why didn't you call the cops?"

"I'm afraid they wouldn't have believed us," George said lamely.

"Right. They wouldn't, and neither do I."

George and Bess did not comment, and again the driver took his eyes off the street to stare at them. "Where are you from?" he inquired.

"River Heights."

"Just arrived?"

"No. We were at the Crystal Party and that's where our friend disappeared," Bess said.

The driver mumbled something as he drew up closer to the last pier building. It had a bleak, eerie atmosphere. An ice floe rocked against the dock, and except for the hazy glow of the moon, the area lay in frigid darkness.

"I guess I can't really drop you off here and leave you alone," the driver relented finally. "But it'll cost you to keep the meter running."

"That's all right. And thanks," George said, as a chugging sound from the river caused Bess to roll down her window all the way.

"Who'd be out on the river at this time of night?" she asked. The cab moved forward slowly.

"Maybe they're transporting stolen dresses

somewhere," George suggested excitedly, and asked the driver to turn off his headlights.

"Oh, now we're playing cops and robbers in the dark!" he grumbled, but complied with the request.

For a moment, everyone listened as the chugging sound of the boat diminished to a low, even hum.

"It's gone," Bess declared at last. "We'll probably never know what it was here for. Maybe we ought to go back to Aunt Eloise's."

"Good idea," the driver agreed, glancing at the number on his meter. "I can think of better ways to make money!"

He pressed the accelerator lightly and switched on the headlights again. As he swung the cab away from the building, the cousins caught sight of a van parked by a wire fence alongside the pier. A blue car stood behind it.

"Oh, please pull up farther," George begged.

"By that van?" the driver asked.

"Just before it."

He did, and the young detective quickly climbed out of the taxi. Leaving Bess to wait, George raced to the vehicle.

I wonder if this is the one Woody and Frank mentioned, she said to herself, the one in which Nancy was discovered?

Cautiously, George pulled down the handle on the rear door and opened it. A lump formed in her throat as she gazed inside. In the gleam of the taxi's headlights, she saw a heap of black wool. It was Nancy's evening cloak!

She signaled to Bess, then motioned toward the pier building. The entrance bore a sign reading: CLOSED. But a sliver of light was visible underneath the door.

Bess got out of the cab and hurried to join her cousin. "We've got to call the police!" she urged.

"But we don't have time!" George argued.

Bess's heels sank in a layer of gravel and a shiver of fear shot down her spine. "If we go in," she said, "they'll take all of us!"

19

Flaming Rescue

But George paid no attention to her cousin's warning. Instead, with a decisive motion, she slid her hand around the latch and lifted it noiselessly, opening the door a crack.

George peered through, then pulled back with a gulp. "Oh, my goodness!"

"What is it?" Bess whispered.

"Racks of clothes. Here, see for yourself!"

Bess pressed her face against the crack, then said under her breath, "I bet the gang converted this old building into a warehouse, or 'drop' for garments, before distributing them."

"Looks like it," George agreed.

"What are we going to do?" Bess asked.

"We'll have to go in! Nancy might be tied up somewhere!"

"But you know the gang's in there! The

people who came with the van, and I bet Woody and Frank arrived in that car! Also, Rosalind might be around."

"Look, we'll have to take that chance. It's a big place, and if we're careful, they'll never realize we're here." Silently, George crept through the door, not giving Bess another opportunity to object.

Together they ducked behind the nearest rack and listened. Everything was quiet, and after a minute or so, George signaled for her cousin to follow her.

The young detectives tiptoed between racks that contained mostly imported merchandise, searching anxiously for a sign of Nancy or their enemies. But all they found was clothing!

Suddenly, George came to a sudden halt. "Hey!" she called in a whisper, and pointed to a gown that was hanging on a hook without plastic covering. "Isn't that the dress Nancy wore tonight?"

Bess bobbed her head as she noticed a smudge of makeup on the ivory neckline. "It's—"

She was interrupted by the shuffle of feet some distance away.

"Over there!" George said, indicating a stack of cartons along the wall.

The girls edged forward, careful not to clack their heels on the cement floor. Their blood was pumping hard and fast as they heard Frank's voice.

"Hey, Woody! I heard a noise. Someone's in here!"

Another set of footsteps approached, then Woody replied, "Did you see anyone?"

"No, but I heard something rustle."

"All right. You take one side and I'll take the other. We'll check it out."

Bess and George had reached the stack of boxes and squatted down, each girl pulling a large carton over herself.

I hope they don't move any of this stuff, George thought fearfully. Bess almost gasped when one of the men walked past the box she was in, but then the footfalls died away again.

"Must've been a rat," the girls heard Woody say. "Come on, let's finish the inventory and count the stuff that just came in so we can go home."

The two men moved away to another part of the warehouse, and the cousins slowly extricated themselves from their hiding places.

"What'll we do now?" Bess asked. "We can't stay here. Those guys might come back any minute."

George had spotted a door straight ahead. "Maybe Nancy's in there." She surveyed the narrow path between the wall and a pile of paraphernalia lying near it. There was enough room for her to walk through without touching anything, but Bess wore a crinoline under her taffeta skirt, and any contact would make more noise!

"Bess, take your slip off," she advised. "Otherwise you'll hit a million things with your skirt and they'll hear us."

Glancing down the row of boxes, mirrors, and rolls of seamless paper commonly used as backdrops by photography studios like Zanzibar's, the girl knew she had no choice. It was an obstacle course she would have to clear unhindered.

As quickly as she could, she unhooked the waist of her slip and let it fall. Then carefully, she tiptoed after her cousin. George reached for the doorknob and turned it slowly.

To her relief, the door opened without resistance, and they found themselves in a small, windowless room illuminated by a single light bulb hanging from the ceiling. On the floor were more storage cartons and some empty racks. And, beside one of the large boxes lay Nancy Drew, wearing a plain cotton dress. Her hands and feet were bound, and she was gagged!

"Nancy!" Bess cried out, falling to her feet and struggling to free the girl.

George was looking for a pair of scissors to cut Nancy's bonds, when suddenly she heard footsteps again. They sounded like a woman's and were coming closer!

She motioned for Bess to be silent, then flattened herself against the wall, waiting for the door to swing open.

The footsteps stopped in front, as if the person were reluctant to enter. Then the door opened and Rosalind stepped in!

Instantly, the cousins grabbed her, and George clapped a hand over the stylist's mouth before Rosalind could utter a scream. At the same time, she kicked the door shut.

"Let—me—go!" Rosalind managed to whimper through George's hand.

"Not yet!" the girl said, while Bess snatched a wad of material from one of the boxes and stuffed it into the woman's mouth. George removed her rope belt, using it to tie Rosalind's wrists, and forced the stylist to the floor.

Bess sat on her legs, letting George tackle the bindings on Nancy that were only partially loose. George ripped at the thick knot behind the girl's head, splitting a fingernail as the tight loops opened and the gag fell away.

"Thanks!" Nancy said hoarsely. "What happened to the two guys who dumped me here?"

"I don't know," George replied. "All I know is that our ex-dates are here, Woody Haskins and Frank Vanderveer."

"Your ex-dates?" Nancy asked, bewildered.

"And they seemed so nice, too," George grumbled. "Woody was so handsome, with a bit of gray in his hair, even though he was only in his twenties—"

"Was the rest of it dark and did he have small features?" Nancy asked excitedly.

"Why, yes—"

"He must be the guy I saw snooping around the dressing rooms after the fashion show!" Nancy exclaimed. "Apparently, he came back for some reason after the clothes had been stolen. Maybe he lost something. How did you meet these people?"

"I think we should explain later and get out of here as fast as we can," Bess advised.

Rosalind, meanwhile, tried to kick her legs out from under Bess, but to no avail.

"Quit it!" Bess told the woman, who grunted angrily.

By now Nancy was free and she swayed to her feet, still feeling a twinge of pain where the cord had been tightened against her skin.

"Can you walk?" Bess asked anxiously.

"I think so," Nancy replied.

Ted Henri and Pete Grover had left the Crystal Party shortly after Nancy did. On a lead that Mr. Belini had inadvertently revealed to them, they had driven to Gramercy Park. By the time they arrived, however, the small van with Nancy inside had left, and they saw Belini step into a car with another man. Neither Ted nor his associate recognized the stranger.

"Let's see what they're up to," Ted said, putting his car into gear.

The men ahead of them seemed unaware that they were being followed. They moved through the darkened streets, aiming toward an all-night diner on the West Side. As they pulled into the parking lot, Ted let his car hum idly a moment, then swung in behind.

"We'll give them time to sit down before we go in," he told his companion.

"Belini will recognize us," Pete Grover warned.

"Well, I'm hoping he won't see us."

They sat in the car watching the two men slide into a high-backed booth near a window.

"Okay?" Ted said. "Let's go."

He and Pete hurried inside and found a vacant booth behind Belini, where they strained to hear the conversation between Belini and his confederate. "Listen, Iannone, you shouldn't have quit Millington," Belini was saying. "We need you there."

"It wasn't my idea, believe me. It was Rosalind's," Iannone said. "The minute Nancy Drew walked into the place, Rozzie panicked."

"Oh, baloney," Belini grumbled. "Rozzie's just overly worried about getting caught. Now she's back with Reese and you're out of a job."

"Look, it's only temporary. We worked a deal or two with Millington. Once I get situated with a new company, we'll be able to create interest there, too." Iannone paused, letting out a big sigh. "Meantime, I'm available to help you deliver the imported goods. They're down at the pier now, right?"

Belini nodded, then he let his fist fall on the table. "I still can't figure out why you offered that snoopy kid a job to begin with."

"I was trapped, that's all. I tried to dissuade her from working at Millington, but she gave her reasons. They all had to do with collecting inside information, which would ultimately point the finger at someone and free the company from unjust attacks by Reese. What could I say? I was supposed to be a loyal, trustworthy employee!"

Belini snorted.

"Anyhow," Iannone went on, "I figured, with Rosalind's help, we could keep Nancy Drew in check. But Rozzie made a mistake. She rigged a blackout on the floor, and locked Nancy Drew in right after I hired her, hoping to scare her away."

"That was dumb," Belini agreed.

"It was—because it made me look suspicious. I told Rosalind that, and she suggested that we both quit Millington permanently. When everything dies down, I could try to go back, but I don't think it's such a hot idea."

"It isn't," Belini agreed. "Well, let's finish our coffee and get out of here. It's late."

Quickly, Ted and Pete left the diner. They moved the car so it pointed toward the street, shut off the ignition, and waited for the men.

"Nancy Drew's quite persistent, isn't she?" Ted said.

"I hate to say I told you so," Pete replied, "but I doubted right from the start that the fake auction scheme would keep her off this case."

"My sister said the same thing. All I know is,

it's too bad that those crooks got to Jackie the night of the fashion show. Otherwise, I might never have had to introduce myself to Nancy as Chris Chavez."

"What exactly happened?" Pete asked.

"Well, one of these guys told Jackie that they had kidnapped me, and they'd let me go if she agreed not to be in the fashion show. They knew I was after a story involving them and that she was supposed to model clothes they intended to steal.

"Jackie, of course, is no idiot. She insisted they let her see me before she would make such an agreement. So they told her to go to some building and the next thing she knew, she was blindfolded and pushed into somebody's basement."

"Obviously, she got out unharmed," Pete commented.

"Obviously, but not before I turned up at the fashion show and discovered Nancy Drew in her place. Of course, I didn't know who she was at first. I even thought she might have been planted by the crooks. So I asked her to dance, hoping to ingratiate myself enough to keep tabs on her in the future."

Pete laughed. "Not an easy thing to do with Nancy."

"Exactly. When I realized who she was, I knew I had to do more than that. A meddlesome teenager would not help my investigation."

"And so you sent her off on a wild-goose chase."

"That's right," Ted concluded.

Back at the pier, the young detectives had managed to restrain Rosalind, but now they heard their captors' voices outside the small room. Even though the men did not know what had happened, they were cutting off the girls' escape route!

"I wish Rozzie would get over here to help us count this stuff," Frank grumbled. "Without some assistance, we'll be here all night!"

"Last time I saw her, she was going to check on Nancy Drew. Why don't you see what's holding her up?"

Frank approached the door, but suddenly stopped dead in his tracks as police sirens sounded outside.

"The cops!" he yelled. "Let's get out of here! Roz, are you in there?" he shouted toward the room. When he received no answer, he ran to the door and locked it. Then he darted after his companion.

Everything was quiet for a few minutes until

Bess spoke up. "I don't hear the sirens anymore, and the police haven't come into the building, either. Do you think they just happened to drive by?"

George shrugged. "Could be. There's a phone on the wall over there. Why don't we call the precinct?"

Nancy instantly picked up the receiver, but the line was dead. Fighting a wave of panic, she realized they were locked up in an abandoned warehouse and might not be found for days!

"How about these?" Bess asked, handing Nancy a pair of scissors.

She attempted to free the lock with them, but had no luck.

"Let's try to break the door," she suggested, forcing herself to stay calm.

Nancy and the cousins threw their weight against the wood several times, but it wouldn't even crack. Finally they stopped, rubbing their bruises and taking deep breaths.

"What are we going to do?" Bess moaned.

"I suppose we'll have to wait for someone to find us," Nancy said. "I—" She stopped suddenly, sniffing the air. Smoke was seeping in under the door!

"The building's on fire!" Nancy cried out.

20

The Last Twist

Rosalind made noises through her gag, trying to indicate a spot on the wall where several overalls hung on a hook. Nancy removed the garments, and found a key hanging behind them.

With shaking hands, she inserted it into the lock. To her great relief, it worked!

Instantly, the girls pulled Rosalind to her feet, took the gag out, and dragged her along out the door. Tongues of fire were lapping over the racks of clothing, spreading quickly and threatening the group's escape.

Nevertheless, they hurried on bravely. The young detectives covered their mouths and kept their heads low. Rosalind, however, allowed the rising heat to bite her face and the

smoke to settle in her throat as they ran toward the entrance.

Flames had torn through the door by now and the girl could not get out without being injured. Nancy looked for another exit, but none seemed to exist!

Would they all be consumed by the fire?

As the frightening thought occurred to everyone, a blast of water suddenly shot through the door. Then another blast, and another!

The girls quickly ducked out of range, knowing the pressure of the deluge could sweep them back into the raging flames.

"Are you all right?" Nancy asked Rosalind, whose eyes were flooded with tears.

The woman gulped back the smoke in her mouth, coughing hard, and nodded.

Then a man kicked in the door and called for them to come out.

Nancy's eyes were smarting, but she clearly saw Ted Henri near a fire truck. He and Pete Grover were talking to police officers who had laid handcuffs on Woody, Frank, Belini, and another man whose back was to Nancy.

When she stepped in front of him, she gasped. "Mr. Iannone!" she cried.

"He was the go-between at the Millington Company," the reporter explained as someone slipped Nancy's cloak over her shoulders.

She looked at him with narrowed eyes. "And what were you, Mr. Ted Henri, alias Chris Chavez?"

"Then you knew—"

"Of course! I admit I didn't figure out the ruse right away, but when I ran into the real Chris Chavez, and Bess and George overheard your conversation with Jacqueline, not to mention the one I overheard between you and Belini, I figured it all out."

"Including the Galen Kaiser story?"

"That's right. My friends went to check the mug shots for the man who turned out to be the real Russell Kaiser, and found instead a picture of your friend Pete Grover over here!"

"Pete Grover?" Ted stared at Nancy, then at his companion.

"I do look like him, don't I?" the man asked with a grin.

"Are you telling me you're not Pete Grover, who's wanted for check forgery in California?"

"No. That's my cousin. I'm Alan Grover, and I work in the garment industry. That's why Ted asked me to help him on this case. He needed an inside man."

"Oh, I'm sorry," Nancy apologized.

"That's all right." Grover smiled. "A pretty

girl like you can make a crook out of me any day."

"How did you know about Galen Kaiser?" Nancy asked quickly, hiding her embarrassment.

"Oh, I read his obituary. Then, when the real Russell Kaiser started to bid on the medallion that had belonged to his uncle, I put in a counterbid to attract your attention. I figured he really wanted the piece, and I wouldn't be taking too much of a risk competing for it."

Nancy chuckled. "That's what I thought, until I almost had to part with several hundred dollars!"

George and Bess, who had been explaining to the police about Rosalind's capture, now came up to the group.

"It wasn't very nice to send us on a wild-goose chase," George said to Ted, drawing a sigh from the man.

"I know. I'm sorry, really I am," he replied, and dug his heels into the gravelly soil. "If it weren't for you, Nancy, I might never have wound up this story."

The girl bit her lips in a smile.

"The fact is," Ted continued, "I heard about your visit to the Millington office."

"Am I right that Rosalind went to work there

after she left Reese Associates, then quit Millington, along with Mr. Iannone?"

"Yes. She was afraid you'd find out too much too soon. Obviously, she didn't want you to poke around Millington, figuring you would discover information about her deal with Iannone."

"I gather that they were using this pier building as a drop for clothes—smuggled imports, mostly—which would be sold to a dress house like Millington. Since they were smuggled, there were no export taxes to pay." Nancy laughed. "So they were priced lower than clothes made by manufacturers in the States."

"You really do amaze me, Nancy," Ted said admiringly. "Anything else I ought to know?"

"Just that I heard a boat outside the building, and I have a hunch that the two guys who tied me up inside the warehouse are on it."

"We saw the boat," Bess put in quickly. "It headed out into the river."

Nancy advised her and George to report their observations to the police while Ted Henri nodded his head.

"As much as I hate to admit it," he said, "I think all the accolades belong to you, Nancy."

"Well, I still haven't figured out everything," she said, striding toward the prisoners who were about to depart in two patrol cars.

At the same moment, she noticed a man emerge from a darkened taxi several yards away.

"The meter's still running," he said, "and nobody's even thanked me."

"For what?" Nancy asked.

"For calling the police," he replied. "Your friends stayed in that building a bit too long to suit me. I was too chicken to go in after them myself, so I buzzed my radio and somebody sent the cops. Good thing, too, 'cause they swarmed on those guys just as they started to set the fire."

"Well, we all thank you," Nancy said, giving the man a big smile. She then turned to Rosalind who was seated next to Belini in the back of the police car. "I have only one question," she said. "If you had such a good thing going with sales of cheaper merchandise, why did you steal Mr. Reese's designs and gowns? It seems to me you were trying to ruin his business."

"I was." Rosalind sneered. "He was so terrible to my sister, Paula Jenner. She had worked for him for years and then—poof—he fired her. She needed that salary badly and he took it away for no reason at all."

"But you know the man has a volatile temper," Nancy said in Reese's defense.

"Even so, I was determined to get back at him. He has made life miserable for a lot of people, including me."

Nancy recalled how the woman had cried openly when the designer had screamed at her the night of the fashion show.

"Did you sell any of his designs to Chalmers?" the girl questioned.

"Yes. Arnaud Hans agreed to use them. But he modified them a lot. There's such jealousy and competition between the men that, as much as it pleased him to scoop the designs, he wanted to change them."

As the woman revealed her story, Nancy felt pity for her and Arnaud Hans who, despite his natural talent, would lose the esteem he had earned over the years simply because of envy and greed.

The patrol cars began to move forward, and Ted Henri turned to Nancy. "Would you and your friends like a lift home?"

Bess and George accepted gratefully, while Nancy chuckled. "Are you going to figure out a way to get rid of us again?"

"Don't tell me you don't trust me." The reporter grinned. "After all, how could I share my by-line in the newspaper with you if you were to disappear? I do mean to give you the credit you deserve, Nancy Drew!"

Before they left the area, Bess and George had offered to pay the taxi driver several times the amount on the meter, but he refused.

"This trip was on me, girls," he said. "I'm just happy that you're all safe. Here's my card," he added, "in case you need another ride some day."

George laughed. "We promise it won't be anything like this one!" she exclaimed, running to Ted's car.

On the way back to Aunt Eloise's apartment, Bess mentioned Jacqueline. That prompted Ted to explain the events of the first night he had met Nancy. When she heard that he had suspected her of being planted by the crooks, she laughed.

"This sure is an initiation for me," she said.

"Into what?" asked Al Grover, who sat next to her.

"Into the inner workings of a New York reporter's mind!"

Aunt Eloise was asleep when the girls arrived, and they waited until morning before they told her about their adventures at the West Side pier.

"Oh, how awful!" Miss Drew exclaimed when she heard everything. "Your father will never forgive me, Nancy!"

"Maybe I'd better call him," Nancy said with a chuckle. "I don't want him to read about it in the newspaper!"

Before she had a chance to dial, however, the police captain phoned to inform her that the men on the boat had been caught. "That winds up the case, Nancy," he concluded. "You did a wonderful job. Your dad will be proud of you."

Nancy giggled. "He doesn't know what happened yet. I was just about to call him."

Mr. Drew was amazed by his daughter's story. When she finished speaking, he said, "You'd be interested to know that the name Kaiser appeared in a news article today."

"Russell Kaiser?" she asked, surprised.

"Yes. Seems to me it was in a syndicated column, so you'll find it in the New York papers. I have to hurry for an appointment, so we'll talk about it later."

"Thanks, Dad!"

When her father hung up, Nancy asked Aunt Eloise for the morning newspaper. She scanned it and quickly discovered a small headline, which read, KAISER GETS THE LION'S SHARE!

Excited, Nancy read the story out loud:

"'An unusual medallion was acquired by Russell Kaiser during an auction of Speers, Limited. It came from the estate of Russell's uncle, Galen Kaiser, and bore the family crest—a lion.

"'The medallion appeared to have no great value, but Russell Kaiser, who had been out of the country when the estate was turned over to the auction house, remembered a story his uncle once told him.

"'Galen Kaiser had bought a magnificent black opal during his world travels. Later he was told that opals were known to bring bad luck and that they should never belong to anyone not born in the month of October since its lucky gemstone is the opal. After some misfortune, Galen Kaiser hid the stone and did not look at it again. When he died without a will, no one in the family found the opal.'"

"Because it was hidden in the medallion!" Aunt Eloise broke in gaily.

"That's right," Nancy said. "'And it was only when Russell Kaiser went to the preview exhibit at Speers and saw the medallion with a small, boxlike clasp on the back of it that he realized the stone might be concealed inside.'"

"No wonder he kept bidding!" George said.

"And to think Nancy almost won it," Bess said, a bit dejected.

"I'm not disappointed at all." Nancy smiled. "We couldn't have afforded any bad luck on this mystery!"

When Mr. Reese heard the girls' story later, he couldn't have agreed more. "You all deserve medals of honor," he declared, "and a special celebration!"

"Even though your dresses were ruined last night?" Nancy replied. "You know, Rosalind made me put on an old cotton one so she could take the one you gave me to wear, but it was destroyed, too."

"My dear," the designer said, "what's a little silk and taffeta worth compared to your well-being and that of your friends? I owe so much to each of you and hope you will never ever have such a dangerous experience again!"

He did not realize, of course, that Nancy would soon begin a treacherous hunt through Europe in search of the *Captive Witness*.

"On the contrary." Nancy giggled. "My goal is to be a *model* detective!"

Nancy Drew® in

The Captive Witness

The Captive Witness was first published
in the UK in a single volume in 1982 by
Angus & Robertson (UK) Ltd.

Contents

1

Airport Trouble

Nancy Drew brushed a strand of titian hair out of her eyes and patted it back into place as she stood in the Munich, Germany, airline terminal reading a cablegram.

NANCY DREW
C/O EMERSON COLLEGE AUSTRIAN TOUR
PAN AMERICAN AIRWAYS
MUNICH.
DEAR NANCY:
HAVE INTERESTING AND URGENT CASE RE FILM STOLEN FROM VIENNA FESTIVAL OFFICE. CALL ME IMMEDIATELY.

LOVE,
DAD

As he had so often, Carson Drew was calling on the detective skills of his eighteen-year-old daughter on behalf of one of his legal clients. This time, by coincidence, the mystery involved the final destination of Nancy's tour group, the city of Vienna.

The trip was being sponsored by Emerson College which her special friend, Ned Nickerson, attended along with two other freshmen who frequently dated Nancy's closest companions, Bess Marvin and George Fayne. As soon as the girls heard about the Austrian tour, they arranged to join it.

"I hope you're holding good news," Ned said, as he joined Nancy on the edge of a crowd of happy students milling around Professor Raymond Bagley, the college tour leader.

Ned was Nancy's most ardent admirer and she couldn't resist teasing in reply. "Well, I don't know if you'll think it's good news or not, but Dad's just assigned me to another case and I may have to leave the tour for a few days."

Ned groaned. "Not another mystery?" Then he brightened. "On the other hand, maybe I can go with you on this one?"

Before Nancy could answer, Dr. Bagley's voice was heard. "All right. Everybody here? Anybody missing, speak up." The professor with his shock of unruly brown hair and his oversize, brown-rimmed

200

glasses gave the appearance of a happy owl.

He had no trouble seeing everyone in his group since he was almost six feet, six inches tall, though slightly stooped from more than twenty years spent leaning down trying to hear what was going on in his classroom.

Nancy waved to get Professor Bagley's attention. "Two of them are missing, sir, as usual," she called, her blue eyes twinkling.

"Oh, no, not again!" moaned her girlfriend, slim, attractive George Fayne. She clutched her short, dark hair in mock despair. "Wait. Don't tell me," she said. "Let me guess. I see it all in my crystal ball. There's this couple. It's—" She covered her eyes with one hand and waved the fingers of the other hand in pretended excitement. "It's Bess Marvin! And Dave Evans! They are entering a snack bar. They have disappeared into a snack bar. They won't come out!"

"Correct." The girl detective laughed. "Your pretty cousin with the weakness for food, and her constant companion with a weakness for Bess."

"All right," called the professor, "let's all grab our bags and those of our two missing friends and we'll find the bus. It should be in this area over here."

But before Dr. Bagley could move, he was confronted by a big, hard-faced man in a porter's uniform. He bowed, clicked his heels, and picked up the tour leader's suitcases and his small musette bag which still bore the government initials, very faintly—u.s.

"Permit me, sir," the porter said with a slight accent. "Permit me, Herr Professor Bagley."

The professor adjusted his glasses and stared.

Ned Nickerson smiled. "Well, Professor Bagley," he said, "we all knew you had an outstanding international reputation as an art and music expert but here's the proof. Everybody knows you."

But the usually affable teacher didn't smile. Instead, he took a step toward the porter and extended his long arms. "See here," he said sharply. "Give me that luggage. I thank you for your courtesy but I'll carry my own bags, if you don't mind."

The porter attempted to smile reassuringly but his hard features couldn't make the effort. Instead, he took a few steps back, bowed, and clicked his heels again. "*Nein, nein,*" he protested. "I'll take care of everything." He walked away very rapidly toward the door leading to the taxis.

"Come back here," called the professor.

"*Ja*, I will meet you on the other side," the porter shouted over his shoulder as he threw the bags on a hand truck and began pushing it away at a fast trot.

Professor Bagley waved his arms. "What does he mean, 'the other side'? The tour bus area is in the *opposite* direction. What is he doing?"

"I think, sir," said Nancy, moving quickly to Professor Bagley's side, "that he's stealing your bags."

"Oh, no," Ned declared. "He just *thinks* he's stealing them. Burt!" He motioned to the short, but powerfully built, Burt Eddleton who was George's beau. Both boys were on the Emerson College football team and their quick reactions showed why. They zigzagged their way through the crowd, streaking after the rapidly disappearing porter.

Both Nancy and George were close on the boys' heels—too close for George because as Ned and Burt left the ground and attempted to hurdle a pile of suitcases, they became entangled and went flying over the luggage with George sailing right over the top of them.

Nancy, narrowly averting the pileup, saw the porter dash out the doors toward the lines of taxis, buses, and private cars. As luck would have it, he collided with another hand truck which delayed him long enough for Nancy to veer off and go through a set of doors that brought her out on the sidewalk a hundred feet ahead of him.

As the man ran toward her, pushing the truck, he suddenly looked stunned and angry to find Nancy blocking his path.

"Get out of the way, girl, or I'll hurt you!" he snarled.

Nancy did not budge, though. "Just drop those

suitcases," she said evenly. "Drop them on the ground and I'll let you go."

The man, who was well over six feet tall, heavyset with large, muscular arms, couldn't believe his ears. "*You?*" he sputtered. "*You* will let *me* go? You insignificant little creature. You stupid girl. I will crush you like a bug!"

Without further warning, he charged at the girl detective, the angle of his attack leaving her little choice but to outrun him or jump into the speeding traffic.

Instinctively, Nancy made her move. She leaped high, grabbed a projecting pipe, swung her feet up and over the oncoming car and dropped them solidly on the man's right shoulder.

The impact broke her hold and she was thrown to the ground but managed to scramble quickly to her feet. Her opponent wasn't as lucky or skilled, much less prepared for an eighteen-year-old girl capable of such acrobatic feats of strength. As a result, when Nancy's feet hit his shoulder he tripped off balance. The force of the impact spun him around. He lost his hold on the cart and went crashing into the wall.

Nancy quickly grabbed the professor's bags, threw them behind her and assumed a defensive judo position. The porter, bleeding from a cut on the head, struggled to his feet and was about to attack when he heard the cries of Nancy's friends in hot pursuit.

Realizing he could not win, he pointed a thick finger at the girl detective. "You get in our way again, Nancy Drew, and I promise you, I will get you. I will take care of you, *myself!*"

Suddenly, the man was gone. He had vaulted a railing and leaped into a black sedan which moved off so quickly that Nancy had no time to check the license plate.

Ned ran up, limping from his fall, and took her by the shoulders. "Are you all right, Nancy?"

She looked up at him, smiling, but still panting from her struggle with the "porter." She nodded, "Oh, sure, Ned. I'm okay. But he *escaped*." Her voice was filled with disappointment.

"It's just as well," George gasped. "He looked as if it would take an army to capture him. Good riddance."

Ned and Burt took the suitcases and they all walked back toward the waiting room. Professor Bagley, who could not move too fast because of a leg wound received during his army service, came up to them, casual and smiling.

"I can't thank you enough," he said, when told of Nancy's successful confrontation with the would-be thief. "You're a wonder, Nancy. Do you think he had time to open the bags and take anything?"

"Impossible," she said. "I had my eyes on him every inch of the way and, as you can see, the straps are all in place."

But Nancy's detective instincts were beginning to stir as she watched Professor Bagley's almost too casual attitude toward the threatened theft. "What in the world did that man think you were carrying in your luggage?" Nancy asked.

The professor simply laughed. "Beats me. Maybe he wears size fourteen double A, too. I heard there were one or two other people in the world with feet that size."

For the first time since she had known Professor Bagley, the girl detective realized he was skirting the truth. He wasn't lying. He just wasn't saying much. There is something special in his luggage, she decided—something he doesn't want anyone to know about. Yet how could he be so calm when it was almost stolen?

Once aboard the tour bus, however, the attempted theft was pushed into the back of Nancy's mind. She stopped at the wheelchair which occupied a special area in the front of the bus and spoke with the occupant, a handsome young man named Eric Nagy. Eric was an Emerson student who, though in his early twenties, had just entered college. Months before the tour, he had been involved in an auto accident which left him paralyzed from the waist down. He was blond, with a wide jaw, prominent cheekbones, and soft hazel eyes which Bess called "hauntingly poetic." Eric's parents had come from Hungary but he had been born in River Heights.

"Hi, everybody! Did you miss us?" Bess grinned. A chorus of shouts, groans, and whistles greeted the arrival of the pretty, blond girl and her friend, Dave Evans.

Nancy quickly motioned for Bess to sit beside her. "You missed all the excitement," Nancy told her as the bus started off. She recounted the attempted theft of the professor's bags.

"Wow!" Bess exclaimed, "and the guy really said he was going to get you?"

"Oh," Nancy scoffed, "I'm not worried about myself."

"But what about Professor Bagley?" Bess answered. "He may be famous, but he's not rich. Why would a thief single him out?"

"I don't know," Nancy said. "I do have this gnawing feeling, though, that the professor is in danger."

"Oh, I hope not." Bess sighed. "I mean, what's going to happen to our beautiful, peaceful trip? After all the plans we've made and—"

"Shhh," Nancy said. "Did you hear that?"

They both listened. A strange thumping and bumping noise seemed to be coming from the bottom of the bus. It continued for five minutes. Finally, Bess said, "I'm going to tell the driver." Marching up to the front of the bus, she reported the noise, listened to his explanation, and returned to her seat.

"He said it was nothing," Bess informed her friend.

"Nothing? It sounded as if the bus were ready to fall apart."

"Well, I don't hear it now," Bess said. Suddenly, however, the noise erupted again. "This is ridiculous," she remarked. "Nancy, why don't you talk to the driver this time since I couldn't get anywhere?"

Nancy got up and confronted the man. His manner was short, rude, and irritated.

"It is nothing but a loose tool bouncing around in the luggage compartment. If the *Fräuleins* ever expect to get to Salzburg, they must stop annoying me with such stupid questions."

Nancy returned and looked at Bess. "There is no noise. Or, if there is, it is just a loose tool bouncing around in the luggage. Also, the *Fräuleins* have to stop annoying the bus driver, he says."

"What a grouch," Bess said. "Never mind. Look, we're pulling off the road for a rest stop."

When the bus rolled to a halt, everyone, except Nancy, exited toward the restaurant. She had felt her left shoelace snap and by the time she had fixed it, found herself alone. "I knew I should have worn loafers," she grumbled, leaving the bus to join the others. Then she stopped.

Thinking no one was watching, the driver had raised the hood of the engine and was disconnecting a large part. He looked around furtively, then threw the part behind some nearby bushes, closed the hood, and headed for the restaurant.

Nancy felt her heartbeat step up. Their own driver was sabotaging the tour bus! Why?

2

The Shaking Bus

The driver, who was a wiry, sallow-faced man with pitted skin and dark eyes, wore a black cap to cover his almost totally bald head.

"Attention," he called in a rasping, somewhat high voice, as he came through the restaurant door. "Attention. I'm afraid there will be a little delay. The bus has broken down. They will have to send a new part out from Munich."

"How long will that take?" Professor Bagley asked.

"Not long," the driver said. "You can find accommodations at the hotel next door for the night. The part should be here by noon tomorrow."

"Tomorrow!" the professor cried. "Oh, see here,

211

that will throw our schedule off completely. What's wrong with the bus? Several of our students are excellent mechanics. Why not let them take a look?"

"No!" the driver shouted, his face suddenly burning with anger. "They cannot fix it. I myself am an expert mechanic. I know what I'm talking about. These are mere boys. They know nothing."

"Do you suppose this would help you repair your bus, Mr. Expert Mechanic?"

The bus driver whirled to see Nancy standing in the doorway holding an automobile part at eye level. The driver turned pale.

"I don't need a woman's help," he blustered. "The part will be here in the morning."

"What is it exactly?" Professor Bagley said, adjusting his spectacles and peering hard at the object in Nancy's hand.

"It's a distributor cap, sir," Nancy told him. "If you remove it from an engine, there's no way for the electricity to flow to the spark plugs. I just saw our driver take this distributor cap off the engine and throw it into the bushes."

"In that case, we'd better call the police," Professor Bagley said coldly, advancing toward the culprit. The driver, cornered, took a step toward the door, but Ned, Dave, and Burt were already blocking it. Before anyone could stop him, the man turned and dived through a window!

He hit the ground, rolled, and came up running.

"After him! Get him!" the professor cried as the students burst out the door to chase the man. Ned had almost caught up and was ready to make a flying tackle when he heard warning shouts and screams behind him. He turned just in time to see an ominous black sedan bearing down on him in almost complete silence.

The young collegian had stopped for only a fraction of a second, but the danger of his situation made everything suddenly appear to move in slow motion. He felt his leg muscles contract and expand as his body leaned and he threw his arms up and out in a spread-eagle dive, feeling the wind rush beneath him. The car barely missed him, and Ned crashed into a ditch where he rolled over twice before coming to a sitting position.

He was just in time to see the car slow down, the door on the passenger side swing open, and the bus driver leap in. The door closed silently and the phantom car disappeared swiftly over the horizon of a hill.

"Boy, oh, boy!" Dave yelled as he led the charge of young people forward to see if their friend was all right. "I thought he was going to hit you for sure, Ned."

Ned got up, limping and massaging his left knee. "Twice in one day on that leg." He groaned. "Once in the airport and now here." He flexed his leg and then grinned. "It's okay. But did you hear that car?"

"No," Nancy said. "I couldn't hear anything."

"That's what I mean. No sound! The driver had to be going at least sixty when he passed me. Then he stopped about twenty feet away. And when that little rat-faced guy jumped in, that car zoomed off without so much as a whisper."

"Well, it's custom-made," Nancy commented. "It looked like a Daimler, a Mercedes, and half a dozen other cars combined."

"Anybody see the driver?" Bess asked.

"I did," Nancy said. "And guess who? The porter who tried to steal the luggage. I'll never forget that face."

As soon as she could, Nancy cornered the professor alone. "Dr. Bagley, do you know something that maybe I should know? I realize we're all your students right now, but I'm also a pretty good detective. How about it? What's going on?"

The professor studied his pipe, which had gone out as usual, and then he motioned her to come with him. "Let's go get some lunch, and I'll try to explain."

But once they were seated at the neat red-and-white checkered table in the rear, Dr. Bagley spun the conversation out slowly. Nancy waited, conquering her inner impatience while the professor ordered them both a light lunch and exchanged small talk with the waitress dressed Bavarian peasant-style.

When the waitress finally left, Professor Bagley cleared his throat, hunched his shoulders, and peered down at Nancy with his friendly, educated-owl expression. "Nancy, what I'm going to tell you must be kept in the strictest confidence. The safety of ten helpless children depends on your silence."

The girl detective nodded, feeling the hairs along the back of her neck prickle.

"I'm very much afraid," the man began with a sigh, "that in trying to do a good turn for a band of unfortunate little orphans I have placed my entire student tour in the most awful danger."

Nancy waited to hear more but the professor lapsed into silence, thinking. The tension built quickly inside her, forcing her to speak. "What kind of danger, sir?"

The professor brought both hands down on the table in an expression of frustration. "That's the maddening part of it," he snorted. "I don't know! I don't know how desperate these people may be or what they may do. Right now they seem to be doing nothing more than delaying us. But as the zero hour draws nearer, who knows to what extremes of violence they may be driven?"

Once again the man became quiet, causing Nancy

to burst with curiosity. "Professor Bagley," she said, gathering courage, "do you realize you've told me absolutely nothing except that you have to help ten children and that our tour may be in danger?" Her eyes twinkled at him. "Believe it or not, I guessed that last part."

The tour leader stared at her, then broke into his characteristic soft chuckle. He shook his head. "The absentminded professor," he said. He ran his hand through his unruly hair. "You know, Nancy, you have the most charming way of telling a boring old teacher that he's being—well, boring!"

Nancy started to protest. "Oh, no, sir. I didn't mean that."

But Dr. Bagley waved his hand and smiled. "No, no, no. I understand. Of course, you didn't. All right, let me get to the point. I'll start at the beginning."

He cleared his throat. "I trust that you will keep what I'm about to tell you completely confidential."

"Of course," Nancy assured him.

"From time to time, I work for our intelligence unit."

"You mean you're a secret agent for the United States?" the young detective asked, prompting a nod from the professor.

"About a month ago, I was approached to help a refugee repatriation group. These people take care

216

of anyone needing their assistance to leave any of the oppressed countries of Eastern Europe and come to the West, that is, to Western Europe and America.

"They asked me to use this tour as a cover to help them bring across the Austrian border ten orphaned children whose closest relatives have already defected. Most of them are living in France, England, or America.

"The children range in age from six to thirteen. Unfortunately, the communist government of their homeland refuses to see this as a nonpolitical undertaking to reunite orphans with their families. Instead, they say that the government will take care of the children, and any attempt to bring the orphans out of Eastern Europe will be viewed as kidnapping."

"If the government won't let them go," Nancy said, "what can you or the refugee group do?"

"Ah," said the professor, arching his brows and holding up one long forefinger as he so often did when teaching, "that's the catch. The children are somewhere in Hungary. They are being kept in hiding by an organization of dedicated people who have sworn to get them safely across the border into Austria."

"How?"

"Somehow. I don't know and I won't until I get to

Vienna. Then I'll be told how they plan to use me and Eric to get the job done."

"Eric?" repeated the young sleuth, incredulous. "You mean Eric Nagy?"

The tour leader nodded, then motioned to Eric who was seated several tables away. As the smiling young man rolled his wheelchair forward, the professor said, "Eric, I've let Nancy in on our mission. I'm sure you won't mind because she could be of great help to us. Anyway, she's such a good sleuth with a nose for clues that she would have figured it out all by herself within a day, at most."

"Oh, wait a minute, Dr. Bagley," Nancy said, blushing. "Nobody is that astute."

"I'm delighted to be associated with the beautiful Miss Drew," said Eric, smiling and looking very intently at Nancy, so intently that she felt herself blush more deeply and observed Ned, watching from across the room, shift uncomfortably in his chair.

The professor nodded and grinned. "Yes," he said, "I knew, somehow, you'd feel that way. But back to business. Nancy, Eric got into this because his parents were born in Hungary. His family has always been very active in helping others escape from behind the Iron Curtain. Eric is now carrying on the tradition."

As Dr. Bagley talked, Nancy's mind raced over

the possibilities, wondering how a middle-aged professor with a leg wounded in the war and a young man confined to a wheelchair could possibly help refugees escape. Didn't such attempts always involve a great deal of running, jumping, and physical exertion? But it would be bad manners to ask and realizing she didn't have all the facts, the girl listened and said nothing.

"It so happens," the professor continued, "that this particular mission involves someone very close to Eric—a thirteen-year-old cousin who is one of those ten children."

"Excuse me." They looked up and saw Ned standing uncomfortably, trying to smile. "I just wanted to say that we're running pretty late and we don't have a bus driver anymore and I'd like to volunteer to drive everyone to Salzburg." Ned's eyes flicked from Nancy to Eric and back to the professor.

Dr. Bagley smiled. "I appreciate your concern for the tour, Ned. Thank you. I'll accept your kind offer. And please pardon our rudeness in excluding everyone but I've got to discuss something confidential with Nancy."

Ned nodded and moved off uneasily, allowing Professor Bagley to return to their main subject.

"Now," he said, as he finished his coffee and started to prepare one of his numerous pipes which he could never keep lit, "I'd like to explain about the porter who tried to steal my luggage. You see, it was a ruse that backfired on me. I knew somebody was going to try stealing the luggage and I *wanted* him to."

"What?" Nancy gasped. But before the professor could elaborate, Bess Marvin burst in the door, her eyes almost popping with excitement.

"Nancy! Dr. Bagley! Hurry! The bus! The bus! Something's happening to it. I think it's going to explode!"

3

The Mozart Lecture

For the second time since their arrival at the rest area, the tour group rushed out of the restaurant in response to an emergency. They ran to within fifty feet of the bus where they stopped as the professor warned urgently: "Stand back!" From the interior of the bus they could hear a series of noises, a fierce crashing and banging.

"It sounds like some kind of animal is in there," Burt said.

"I think it's going to explode!" Bess cried, wringing her hands. "It is, isn't it? It's going to explode and nobody wants to tell me."

"Explode?" repeated the professor. "Why in the world would it explode?"

"Because maybe there's a bomb inside," Bess said, clutching the professor's arm. "Maybe that crazy bus driver planted a bomb. Maybe—"

Suddenly, Nancy and her friends found themselves alone as the rest of the tour dived for cover inside the restaurant as they took in Bess's words.

"Now look what you've done, Bess," George teased. "You'll have everybody climbing trees in a minute. Will you stop talking about bombs?"

"I can't help it if I'm allergic to things that blow up," Bess replied.

"Nothing's going to blow up." George sighed. "Except maybe my head. You've given me a terrible headache."

"What do you think, Nancy?" the professor cut in, as the onlookers continued to stare at the bus which was starting to rock slightly from whatever was causing the uproar inside.

A smile broke over the young detective's face. "No," she said, "I don't think it's a bomb or anything dangerous. Stay here a minute. I believe we can solve this mystery very simply."

Nancy ran to the bus, opened the front door and reached inside to grab a large key dangling from the steering column. Immediately, she hurried to the luggage doors and unlocked them. As they fell open, everyone gasped with relief and surprise.

Inside, tangled up with the baggage, was a man in

222

long red underwear. He was bound hand and foot with his own belt and tie, and judging from the color of his face and the muffled sounds coming through the gag in his mouth, he was furious.

"Some bomb," George said.

"Well, who is he?" Bess asked, beginning to calm down from her fright.

"I wager he's the real bus driver," George offered.

"You're right," Nancy said, as the man's gag was removed and, in a torrent of surprisingly good English, he let everyone within 500 yards know who he was. How dare they let a helpless man bounce around in a luggage compartment for almost two hours while a thief drove his bus! he exclaimed.

"But we didn't know," Bess protested. "Honestly. We heard a noise but—"

"You heard a noise! You heard a noise!" the indignant man repeated as he wrapped himself in a blanket provided by the restaurant owner. "Of course you heard a noise!"

"Well," Bess said, backing away defensively, "we told the driver and he said you were just a bunch of loose tools bouncing around. I mean, not that *you* were loose tools but that's what the noise was. Oh, I can't explain. Nancy, help me," the girl wailed.

"Loose tools!" screamed the little bus driver, now almost dancing with frustration. "You should have realized that he wasn't telling the truth," he added, grinding his teeth. "Did he look like a bus driver? No! Now *I* look like a bus driver."

As everyone gaped at him, his eyes traveled down his body, which was wrapped in the blanket with his bare feet sticking out. Again his face turned red, and he angrily shouted once more. "That's right, stare at me. Embarrass me. Get me my clothes!"

Ned moved in to assist. "I'll take him inside," he said, "and I'll see if the people here have some spare clothes to lend him. I'll be back." He put his arm consolingly around the man's shoulders. "Sir," he said, "you have been through a terrible ordeal. We are very sorry. Let me help you. Come with me and we'll get some clothes for you and some lunch."

"Don't touch the bus," the driver cried, waving a warning finger at the others as Ned led him away. "I will assume command again when I return."

When he and Ned finally disappeared into the restaurant, the whole group broke out laughing.

"Don't touch his bus!" George smirked.

Bess, completely recovered now, resumed her old, humorous ways. "Hey, George, didn't I tell you there was a *bomb* in that bus?"

Again the young people laughed.

"You were right," Eric said. "If that wasn't an explosion I don't know what to call it. But seriously, it must have been pretty frightening being tied up and gagged like that, worrying what was going to happen to you."

Bess, who was standing close to Nancy, whispered, "You see what I mean. He's really a very sensitive boy—and you know what?"

"What?" said Nancy.

"I think he's developing a crush on you."

"Oh, Bess, stop it." The young sleuth chuckled.

Their joking, however, was interrupted by Professor Bagley who said he wanted to talk to Nancy. They strolled together along a grassy path.

"I'm glad you remember that we never did finish our conversation," Nancy said. She smiled eagerly. "You left me hanging back there when Bess came running in shouting about the bus. The last thing you told me was that you wanted them to steal your luggage."

"Can you guess why?"

"Yep." Nancy grinned. "I think so."

"Okay." The professor laughed. "Let's hear it."

"Well," Nancy said, "my guess is that someplace in your luggage was something you wanted them to find, that would throw them off the track of the ten children."

"Bull's-eye," Dr. Bagley said softly. "Absolutely on target. What I did, purposely, of course, was to let them watch me slip a sealed envelope into my musette bag, that over-the-shoulder bag I've carried ever since army days. It's army issue, you know. Anyway, that envelope contains very authentic-looking documents which give all the wrong information about where the children are, how many there are, and most important of all, the wrong time and place at which they will cross the border."

"And they fell for it," Nancy said.

"Sure. I wasn't too obvious about planting it in the bag. What I did was to go in the men's room at Kennedy Airport in New York, carrying the envelope and my bag. When I came out, I only had the bag. I looked like a typical, clumsy amateur attempting to conceal something."

Nancy covered her eyes with both hands and pretended to wail. "Oh, I really did it, didn't I? You had them set up so nicely and then I and my friends came along and ruined the whole thing."

The professor shook his head. "No, no, no. They'll try again, so don't worry. I'll make the phony information available for them again—not too available, though. I'm willing to bet that within two days they will have found it. In fact, next time I'll give them time to read it, replace it, and make it look as if nothing had been touched."

Nancy nodded. "That's very clever, Professor. You must have been a good spy during the war."

He shook his head. "Actually, I was a very bad spy. People who are six feet six and need glasses can't exactly fade into the scenery. Sometimes I wonder how I came through it all without getting caught."

Strolling back to the hotel, they found the driver outfitted in a set of oversize clothing provided by the innkeeper. With a full stomach and lavish praise from everyone, the driver soon became very talkative and friendly.

As he headed the bus once again down the highway toward Salzburg, he entertained the group with a nonstop monologue about the beauties of the south German and Austrian countryside, the glorious musical traditions of the city of Salzburg, and most important, the life of the driver's personal hero, the great composer Wolfgang Amadeus Mozart.

"He was born in Salzburg, you know," the driver called out so that all could hear. "Born in that beautiful little city on January 27, 1756. He was a genius! A genius! I tell you!

"He played the harpsichord by the time he was four, composed music at the age of five, performed before the empress at the court in Vienna when he was six.

"He never went to school. Imagine that! *Never went to school*. His entire life was music. He performed as a child prodigy in concert tours throughout Europe.

"But as he grew older, the novelty wore off. Though he was composing the greatest music ever heard, no one seemed to care because by then, he was a grown-up."

The driver was now building himself up to a fever pitch similar to his mood when he was released from the luggage compartment. His knuckles gripped the wheel tightly, and he was starting to run off the road occasionally as he waved first one and then both hands in the air.

"He tried to seek his fortune in Vienna, got married and had children, but could not get a regular job. Will you believe that, young people? The most gifted composer the world has ever known—a superb performer as well—and the world ignored him. They ignored the man who composed *Don Giovanni!* The man who composed *The Magic Flute!* Forty symphonies. More than six hundred works in all!

"And they did not give him enough to support his family. He died in poverty at the age of thirty-five!"

The little man turned completely around and shouted the words, running off the road once more and causing an intake of breath by everyone on board.

"In poverty!" the driver bellowed, once he had the bus back on the road again.

"Oh, Nancy," George whispered. "In a way, I wish we had the other driver back. I wish he'd steal the bus."

"At the age of thirty-five!" the driver exclaimed.

"And they buried him in potter's field in a pauper's grave with no marker so that to this day," and he turned again to shout the words, "to this day no one knows where his body lies! The greatest composer of all time and one of the ten greatest men who ever lived! Wolfgang Amadeus Mozart! When you go to Salzburg to the cathedral, bow your heads and say a little prayer for the souls of those who denied him fame and fortune while he lived!"

Suddenly, the man lapsed into a brooding silence and said no more all the way to Salzburg. The passengers, who had been tense, braced for an accident, suddenly felt themselves go limp with relief.

Bess spoke first. "You know," she told Nancy, "he scared me to death and I wouldn't want to go through it again but I have to admire his passion for Mozart. I didn't know those things about him."

Nancy smiled. "Neither did I. I guess that's the first bit of education we're going to get on this tour."

"I suppose so," Bess said, "but I hope the rest of it moves at a slower pace."

Gradually, conversation picked up and the rest of the trip into Salzburg was spent talking, singing, and admiring the countryside. When they pulled into the ancient town, they headed immediately for their hotel and disembarked, somewhat tired but looking forward to baths and a good dinner.

As the driver and porters were unloading the luggage, the professor went inside to register the group. In five minutes he reappeared, clearly irritated.

"Attention! I have some unfortunate news. The hotel says that they received a call about four hours ago canceling our reservations. We have no rooms for tonight!"

4

Mysterious Interference

For a moment, the group stood stunned by the professor's announcement. Then everyone tried to talk at once.

"No rooms? How are we going to brush our teeth?"

"Or take a bath?"

"Or do my nails?"

"Or sleep?"

"Wait! Wait! Wait!" Dr. Bagley called. He held up his hands, quieting them down. "The hotel manager has assured me that he will make every attempt to see that we get proper accommodations at another hotel. He understands that we're the victims of practical jokers. Now if we will keep our heads, we can muddle through. So let's go back inside and splash some water on our faces in the lobby rest rooms and freshen up a bit. We'll be able to have a lovely dinner while the hotel stores our baggage and makes other arrangements."

"Excuse me, Herr Professor." The speaker was a rather stout man with a huge, black mustache and an easy, smiling manner. "Excuse me. Professor Bagley? I couldn't help overhear your conversation with the desk clerk when you checked in. Permit me to introduce myself. I am Herr Adolph Gutterman. I think I may be able to help you."

Hesitantly, the professor extended his hand. "Pleased to meet you, I'm sure. But I think we're being taken care of quite adequately."

Herr Gutterman looked doleful. "Oh, Professor, excuse me, but I don't think that's true. Of course, the hotel will try. But this is the height of the tourist season. Every hotel is booked to overflowing!" He laughed and made a sweeping gesture. "The hotel will not be able to help you. But I can."

Dr. Bagley was obviously becoming annoyed by Herr Gutterman's insistent manner. "Well, perhaps so," he said, a little coolly, "but let's give the hotel a chance. Now, if you'll excuse me, my people are famished. We must go in to dinner."

Moving right in step with the professor, Herr Gutterman was not to be put off. "Excellent idea," he cried, thumping him on the back. "I'm hungry, too. I'll join you and explain how I can assist you."

Resigned to his fate, the professor forced a smile and nodded, being too well mannered to be rude even though Herr Gutterman was obviously proving himself a pest.

As they passed the desk, Herr Gutterman received a look of irritation from the manager. The fat man returned it with a wide smile and said, in a booming voice, "Yes, it's a shame that we have hotels in Salzburg that fail to honor their reservations, but there are always a few rotten apples in every barrel."

The manager, watching Herr Gutterman virtually take charge of Professor Bagley's group, snapped his pencil in anger.

Once in the dining room, Herr Gutterman proceeded to explain what he was offering without anyone having asked him to do so.

"I am in real estate," he announced, "and I deal in properties all over Austria. It so happens that I know a very nice, small hotel just a few blocks from here. I had reserved a large number of rooms, more than twenty, for another group that canceled out just this morning. I am offering you these rooms."

The offer was tempting, but the professor, completely put off by the loud, aggressive manner of the real estate man, refused to commit himself. "As I

234

said before," he repeated politely, "we'll wait to see what the hotel can do for us."

"Suit yourself, Herr Professor, suit yourself," boomed the realtor, again slapping the professor on the back.

George leaned over and whispered to Nancy, "I think if he whacks the professor once more there's going to be violence."

Nancy nodded. "You know, George, I think I've seen Herr Gutterman before, but I don't know where."

George looked at the realtor. "Hmm. If *I* had ever seen a two-hundred-fifty-pound, six-foot man with a big, black mustache and a loud voice like his, I think I'd remember where."

As they talked, Herr Gutterman kept up a running fire of conversation—or, rather, a monologue—as he told poor jokes, provided most of the laughter, then complained about the bad service and bragged about his vast wealth. By the time dinner was over, everyone was thoroughly sick of him.

To their astonishment, however, he picked up the check for the group and paid for it before anyone knew what he was doing. He then led the unwilling students out of the restaurant and back to the hotel manager's desk where he loudly banged on the bell despite the fact that the manager was standing less than three feet away.

"A little service, please," he rumbled.

"What is it, Herr Gutterman," the manager inquired icily.

"I wanted to know if you have obtained rooms for my friends on Professor Bagley's tour. If not, I shall escort these unfortunate people to my hotel and see that they are treated as all guests in Salzburg *should* be treated. I tell you, Herr Schoenburg, your hotel is a disgrace to the nation. A disgrace!"

"Weasel!" hissed the hotel manager. "How dare you come in here and behave this way. Bruckner! Bruckner!" A tall, strong young porter came striding across the room. "Escort Herr Gutterman out of the hotel."

Herr Gutterman, flashing his fat smile, held up both hands. "That won't be necessary. I am leaving. But you, my friends," he said, turning to Professor Bagley and his group, "can meet me on the sidewalk after this incompetent gives you his bad news."

With a flourish, Herr Gutterman waddled away through the doors and into the street. The manager, flushed with embarrassment, turned to the professor.

"Sir, I am chagrined to have to tell you that I cannot find you accommodations. Believe me, if I could do anything to make up for this terrible mistake, I would."

The professor nodded and rubbed his chin.

"What do you suggest we do? We must sleep. To-morrow we begin our tour here in this city."

The manager passed one hand over his eyes. "Much as it pains me," he said, "I think you had better accept Herr Gutterman's offer."

Reluctantly, the professor agreed and the forlorn group filed out onto the sidewalk where Herr Gutterman, completely unperturbed by his recent dismissal from the hotel, was waiting with a smile and a bear hug for the professor.

"Now," he rumbled, "you come with me and you will be treated as honored guests." Subdued, the group followed Herr Gutterman down the street, instructing the bus driver to bring their bags as soon as possible.

To their surprise, the hotel, though small, was clean, neat, and pleasant in appearance. Nancy, Bess, and George were assigned a large room with bunk beds. Their bags arrived as they were testing the mattresses and checking whether the water faucets worked.

Leaving the other girls to unpack, Nancy went downstairs to make her long-delayed call to her father. But when she reached the phones in the lobby, she found they were in use and would be for some time since there was a long waiting line ahead of her.

The clerk on duty motioned her to come over to

the desk and told her that if she was in a hurry she could use the pay phone on the street half a block away. Nancy thanked him and hurried out the door, turning left and walking along the quiet, dimly lit street until she saw the booth. It was on the opposite side built against a high stone wall. Nancy entered, fumbled for her Austrian coins, and then dialed the number of her home in River Heights.

"Hello!" It was the cheerful, deep voice of her father, Carson Drew.

"Hi, Dad!"

"And who might this be?"

"Very funny. Who else calls you Dad?"

The lawyer laughed. "How are you, dear? How do you like Austria?"

"Beautiful. But so far our bus driver was kidnapped, a car almost ran over Ned, a man tried to steal the professor's luggage, and somebody canceled our hotel reservations."

Her father groaned. "Well, it sounds like a typical trip for my Nancy. Do you know why all these things have been happening?"

Nancy hesitated. Dr. Bagley had sworn her to secrecy about the orphans, and she couldn't violate her promise. "Well," she said, "let's say I'm working on it, Dad. But tell me about Vienna and the stolen film. It sounds fascinating."

Carson Drew proceeded to outline the case. Kurt Kessler, a noted film director from an Eastern European country, had defected to America more than a year before. He had managed to smuggle out several valuable reels of film, which he had since edited into a documentary condemning the oppression of human rights in his native land. The film was entered in a very important film festival to be held in Vienna during the coming week.

"This morning," Carson Drew said, "Kessler received a call from the festival authorities. His film has been stolen. Unless he can recover it by Wednesday morning, the world will not see or hear his story."

"But why can't he get another print made from the negative and rush that to Vienna?" the girl detective asked.

"He thought of that, of course," her father said. "Unfortunately somebody on the other side thought of it, too. Kessler made the mistake of leaving his negative at a laboratory for printing. He should have stayed with it to protect it. But he didn't, and an hour later the laboratory burned to the ground. The negative was destroyed. The stolen film, if it still exists, is the only copy of Kurt Kessler's *Captive Witness*."

Nancy whistled. "But if government enemies stole it," she said, "don't you think they destroyed it right away or at least took it out of Austria? After all, that fire in the lab was probably a case of arson."

"Right," Mr. Drew said.

"So we're probably on a wild-goose chase," Nancy said, somewhat crestfallen.

"No, I don't think so. I have reason to believe that Kessler's enemies will take good care of the film because they want to trade it for something even more valuable to them."

"But what?"

"That," the lawyer said, "is what my beautiful, talented daughter is going to have to figure out."

"I appreciate the compliment, Dad, but what I need are some solid leads."

Carson Drew sighed. "Well, I wish I had some. The best I can offer is one contact. His name is Richard Ernst and he's the official at the film festival who can tell you the details about the theft. Contact him at the festival office. That's about all I can tell you. Oh, except for one thing. Be careful and watch out for two enemy operatives. One is tall, heavy-featured, with blond hair and blue eyes. The other is shorter, wiry. He has a bad complexion. Pitted skin."

Nancy almost dropped the phone. "Oh, Dad, say no more. I think I know the fun-loving pair personally."

"You do!"

"Yes. I wish I could explain on the phone but—" Nancy stopped. "Dad! Dad, did you hear that? It sounded as if someone were tapping this line."

There was a long pause and then her father's voice came through. "That's not possible on this end, Nancy. Remember we had our phone system constructed to make taps impossible? And at great expense, I might add." There was another pause. "Nancy, be careful. If there is a tap, it's on your end."

A chill ran up the girl's spine. She wondered how it could have been done so quickly. No one knew she was calling from a public phone booth. Then she remembered how the hotel clerk had specifically beckoned her to the desk and told her about the pay phone. It had been a setup!

"Dad," she said. "Dad?" There was no answer. She jiggled the hook. "Dad, can you hear me? Dad?" After a few seconds, she gave up and tried to dial again but the line was completely dead now.

As she hung up, something banged and scraped violently across the top of the phone booth and the light went out. Suddenly, Nancy found herself alone on the almost completely darkened street as the figure of a tall man moved slowly, purposefully, toward her.

5

An Unpleasant Invitation

"Nancy Drew! What are you doing standing in a dark phone booth at this hour of the night?" The threatening, tall figure peered into the booth, and much to Nancy's relief, she realized it was Dr. Bagley.

"That's a good question." The young sleuth sighed. "I was talking to my dad back in River Heights. Then I thought I heard a tap on the line. But he reminded me that our house has special equipment to prevent tapping at his end, so it must've been on mine.

"But look." She pointed up at the line running from the booth. "I don't see any taps. And anyway, right after that, the line went dead, the light switched off, and I heard a crash on top of the booth."

The professor peered up. "It was just the branch scraping across that broke the light wire. I don't see any phone lines so they're probably all underground, which rules out a wiretap. I think you're just a little edgy about everything that's happened."

Nancy bit her lip, concentrating hard. "You're right," she acknowledged, "but what were you doing walking out here alone?"

"I was going to use the telephone."

"Why didn't you use one in the hotel?"

"Well, there were too many people waiting."

"And did the desk clerk call you over and tell you to use the pay phone down the street?"

"Yes. Did he tell you, too?"

"Uh-huh. Isn't that odd?"

The professor thought for a moment. "Yes, it is. But not as odd as the question of why they would tap a pay phone when they could so easily tap the phone in the hotel."

"You've got me. I'm dizzy thinking about it, Professor. Let's say it was all my imagination and we can both go to bed early and get some sleep."

The professor escorted Nancy back to the hotel. When she opened the door to her room, she found Bess and George both sound asleep. Very quietly, so as not to wake them, she got out her pajamas and toilet articles and prepared for bed. But when she lay down, she couldn't go to sleep right away. The tangled events of the day kept marching through her mind. She hadn't bothered to unpack because she knew that first thing in the morning she had to make plans to leave the tour and drive to Vienna. Then she could try to locate Kurt Kessler's missing film before the Wednesday deadline.

On the other hand, she thought, I feel bad about leaving Dr. Bagley when the tour is being harassed and he still hasn't figured out how to get those poor kids across the border.

Tossing and turning, the girl detective finally drifted off to sleep, exhausted by the events of the day.

The next morning, she was awakened by Bess's exuberant bubbling about Salzburg. "Nancy, are you still asleep? Listen, I don't want to miss anything! The cathedral. The puppet shows. The palace. The concerts. And Mozart's home. Oh, I couldn't miss *that!*"

"I agree," Nancy moaned sleepily. "If you did, our little bus driver would probably drive us all the way to Vienna screaming out another lecture about his hero."

"Right," Bess agreed. "Now, when are you two getting up? It's eight o'clock already."

"Eight o'clock?" came an agonized cry from under a pillow hiding George's head. "In the morning?

Oh, no! Nancy, do something. Stop her. She's killing us."

But Nancy, struggling to a sitting position, yawned and shook her head. "You can stay in bed, George, but I've got to get up."

"Great," Bess said. "Where do you want to go first, Nancy?"

"Vienna."

"Vienna?" the cousins chorused as George emerged out of the covers. "What do you mean Vienna?" she asked. "We're not due there until—when?"

"Sunday," Bess put in.

"And this is only Friday," George said.

"I know, I know," their friend said, heading for the bathroom. "Do you mind if I take my shower first? I really have to rush."

"Oh, no, you don't." Bess laughed, barring the bathroom door. "Not until you tell us about this Vienna stuff."

"Nancy Drew," George said slowly, pointing a forefinger at the young detective, "are you going off to solve another mystery and leave us alone on this tour?"

"Well . . ." Nancy said.

"That's it," George said. "I knew it. And I suppose you can't talk about it."

"Only a little bit. Somebody stole a film from the festival that opens in Vienna Wednesday and I'm trying to find it. There. No secrets. Okay?"

"Humph," Bess said. "And all those huddles—
you and the professor and—and handsome, young
Eric. What were they all about?"

Nancy raised her nose in the air, pretending total
bewilderment. "I'm sure I don't know what you
may be referring to," she said with a theatrical swirl
of her robe, and disappeared into the bathroom to
the echoes of her friends' laughter.

After breakfast, Nancy began phoning car rental
agencies and to her chagrin, found that there wasn't
a single car available.

She came back and joined her friends in the restaurant. "No luck," she said. "This is really awful. I
don't know how I'm going to get to Vienna unless I
take a bus."

"Would that be so terrible?" George asked.

"No. It's just that when I arrive in Vienna I'll
probably need a car to get around."

"You could not get on a bus," came a booming
voice they all recognized. It was Herr Gutterman
struggling up out of the depths of an armchair that
had concealed even his massive bulk. He waddled
over to their table and, making an elaborate, somewhat comic bow, he said good morning.

"May I sit down with you lovely ladies?" he
asked, and then pulled out a chair before anyone
could reply. "Ah, I thank you. Now, Miss Drew,
you must not think of taking a bus to Vienna. You

246

have no idea how crowded they are at this time. Probably you would have to stand, and who wants to stand when they are on their vacation, *ja?*"

Nancy smiled sweetly. "I don't think I have much choice."

"Ah, but you do, beautiful lady! I myself will see that you get to Vienna in the perfect safety and comfort of my own automobile driven by my own chauffeur."

At this point, Ned Nickerson strode into the dining room. The sound of the boorish Herr Gutterman offering Nancy a ride to Vienna made him almost trip and spill the cup of coffee he was carrying.

Continuing to smile sweetly at Herr Gutterman and looking over his shoulder directly at Ned, Nancy said, "Herr Gutterman, that is extremely nice of you. I accept your offer if we can leave within the next hour or two."

Both Bess and George had to struggle hard not to say something, and Nancy felt George's foot nudge her own under the table.

"Excellent, excellent," Herr Gutterman bellowed as he heaved himself to his feet. "I will make arrangements immediately and we shall leave—at noon?"

"That would be wonderful," Nancy said. "Thank you so very much."

Rubbing his hands with pleasure, Herr Gutterman left the hotel while Ned rushed over and sank down in the vacated seat.

"Nancy," he said, his eyes filled with disbelief, "*you* are going to accept a ride to Vienna with *that man?*"

"Yes," Nancy replied, her eyes twinkling. "What's so upsetting about that?"

Ned began to feel hot under the collar. "You and that two-ton creep?" he asked again, his voice rising. "Wait a minute. Let's back up. Why *are* you going to Vienna today? Another detective assignment?"

Nancy nodded.

"In the middle of our tour? Oh, now, Nancy." Then he remembered his original objection. "And you're going with Gutterman?"

Nancy couldn't contain her laughter any longer and she doubled up.

"What's so funny?" Ned cried, genuinely upset.

"Nothing, nothing." She giggled. "And don't get all strung out. Here's the joke on Herr Gutterman. I want *you* to go with me to Vienna! Just imagine Gutterman's face when he sees both you and me waiting for him! You will come, won't you?"

6

Kidnapped!

Ned's face changed from a look of intense anxiety to one of such unrestrained happiness that all three girls began laughing.

"Very funny, Nancy Drew," said Ned. "Very funny. You are the worst tease I ever met. Now what would you do if I said no?"

Nancy wrinkled her nose at him. "I suppose I'd have to drop into a hole in the earth when Herr Gutterman came to pick me up. You wouldn't let that happen, would you?"

"Of course he wouldn't," George said. "He would follow you to the ends of the earth."

"To Vienna, anyway," Ned declared.

The young people split up, Nancy and Ned making their good-byes and explaining to Professor Bagley that they would meet him and the tour in Vienna on Sunday. At noon, they were both standing in front of the hotel with their bags.

Within a few minutes, a beautiful brown sedan pulled up with Herr Gutterman at the wheel. He was beaming happily as he fought his way out from under the steering wheel which pressed against his bulging stomach.

Hurrying around the car, he picked up Nancy's bags and placed them in the trunk. As he did so, Nancy glanced around for Ned. He was gone! And Herr Gutterman was opening the rear door and gesturing for her to enter and be seated.

"Oh," Nancy said, "could you wait a moment, please? I've forgotten something." Turning, she dashed back into the hotel where Bess and George were watching the scene through a window.

"Did you lose something, Nancy?" Bess giggled.

"Where is Ned?" Nancy cried.

"Oh, Ned!" Bess said. "You're looking for Ned?"

"Come on, you two, what are you doing to me?" She stopped. "Oh, I get it. He's getting even for my teasing this morning. Okay, I apologize. Now please tell me where he is."

Ned appeared, almost magically, at Nancy's elbow. "Oh, Nancy, I'm so sorry." He grinned. "I just wanted to make sure you really wanted me to go."

"Oh, you!" Nancy laughed.

The two young people hurried outside where Herr Gutterman waited impatiently. Nancy smiled at him. "Herr Gutterman, I hope you won't mind, but my friend Ned Nickerson also has to go to Vienna. I thought that with so much room in your big car perhaps you wouldn't mind giving him a lift, too."

"I'd very much appreciate it," Ned said, using his most humble tone.

The barest flicker of annoyance passed over Herr Gutterman's face, but he quickly covered it by laughing loudly, assuring Ned he was delighted. For good measure, he slapped him on the back—a bit harder than necessary.

With great ceremony, he ushered them into the back seat, then trotted around front and squeezed himself into the driver's seat. He called through the speaking tube into the rear seat. "You will pardon me if I do the driving myself until we pick up my chauffeur. He is on the other side of town."

"Perfectly all right," Nancy called, settling back in the plush interior. "What a beautiful car," she said. "I see that it's been freshly painted." Some of the paint had come off on Nancy's finger as she touched the door.

"Yes," Herr Gutterman replied, "I try to keep my cars looking new."

"Hmm," Ned said, "a refrigerator, a telephone, a television set. Herr Gutterman, you travel in style."

Nancy noted a clicking sound. Herr Gutterman

had locked all the doors electronically. Well, thought Nancy, nothing unusual about that. Dad's car operates that way. Even so, the gesture made her uneasy.

As they crossed Salzburg and slowed down to enter an alley adjoining an old building, a warning sounded in her brain. A freshly painted car. Why? A ride to Vienna. Why? Hotel rooms just when they needed them. Why was this seemingly innocuous pest so solicitous of the Americans?

Nancy felt a shiver as Ned said, "Nancy, do you hear the engine of this car?"

"No."

They both realized, simultaneously, what this meant. "Like the black car," Ned whispered. "The same silent engine."

"It's the same car, Ned. They painted it yesterday. The paint is still wet—and the doors are locked."

Who was this Gutterman?

As Nancy asked the question, the car pulled up to a doorway and a man dashed out. Gutterman squeezed out from behind the driver's seat and the chauffeur slid in, turning to stare at Nancy and Ned. They gasped as they realized he was the short, wiry man with the pitted face—the man who had stolen the bus in Munich.

Now the fat man began to take off his coat. Underneath he wore great pads that, as he slipped them off, made him lose seventy-five pounds in appearance. Next he removed his wig and began tugging at his mustache. With blond hair, no mustache, and considerably lighter in weight, he was the same man who had attempted the luggage theft at the Munich airport.

"I can't believe it," Ned murmured.

"Well, we saw it with our own eyes," Nancy said. "And I thought I was so clever to get Herr Gutterman to drive us to Vienna."

"Yeah," Ned said. "Now what?"

"Relax, I guess," the girl detective said, "while we try to figure a way out."

"But there is nothing you can do, Nancy Drew," came Gutterman's voice through the communications system. "The doors are locked. The windows are tinted so that you can see out but no one can see into the rear compartment. I can see you by switching on a secret electrical impulse which clears the window separating us. All I have to do is press the button."

"Don't worry, Nancy," Ned whispered, "we've got to stop sometime, and there are bound to be cars nearby. Then we'll yell our heads off. Someone will notice us."

Nancy nodded and then, as luck would have it, they found themselves side by side with a police car at a red light. Instantly, the two young people set up the loudest racket they could.

"Help us!" Ned cried. "Help! Help!"

"We're being kidnapped," Nancy yelled.

But the more they shouted the less effect it seemed to have. The policemen sat, talking casually to each other. Not once did they turn in the right direction. At last, the police car drove away and Herr Gutterman's annoying voice broke in on them again.

"You shouldn't shout like that." Gutterman laughed. "You'll ruin your voices. It's futile, because the rear compartment is completely soundproofed. I guess I forgot to tell you that. In fact, it is airtight. If air were not pumped in to you constantly, you could not breathe."

"What do you intend to do with us, Herr Gutterman—or whatever your name is?" Nancy questioned, looking at him, her blue eyes now like ice.

"Herr Gutterman is as good a name as any," their captor said. "My chauffeur is Herr Burger. As to what we will do with you, well, we will take you to a place where you will not be able to meddle in matters that don't concern you. Whether you ever come back, I have not yet decided."

7

Hazardous Ride

Resigned to the fact that they could do nothing until their captors, at some point, opened the doors, Nancy and Ned did their best to relax as the silent brown car headed south and began climbing higher and higher into the magnificent Austrian Alps.

Since every word could be monitored by Herr Gutterman, the couple talked of trivial matters while at the same time writing surreptitious notes on the pad Nancy kept in her bag.

"Lovely weather, isn't it?" Nancy asked as she scrawled a note.

"Charming," Ned replied as he watched Nancy's words form on the page. "Charming. And with such delightful traveling companions."

Ned, Nancy had written, *they must stop eventually if only to stretch their legs. When they do, let's remember that I have this.* Nancy pointed to a small, innocent-looking book with a blue cover which she held in her lap. She turned it slightly and Ned saw that along the spine, in the middle of the title, there were actually small holes cut out of the center of two *o*'s. The title made Ned grin: *Noodles*.

Ned took the pad from Nancy, very casually, and scribbled his reply. *Haven't read the book. But I loved the movie. Why the holes?*

Nancy took back the pad and wrote two words: *Tear gas.* Reading them, Ned could hardly restrain himself. He wanted to shout but refrained. Instead, he wrote on the pad, *Cleverest girl in River Heights. When the time comes, try to spray the big guy. I'll jump the little fellow.*

My hero, Nancy wrote, stifling a giggle. *Why don't you jump the big one?*

"Beautiful scenery," Ned said aloud. "Do you suppose Herr Gutterman and Herr Burger appreciate it?"

"Why, of course," Nancy said, adding, "I bet that before this trip is over, you'll find tears in their eyes."

Herr Gutterman, who could hear everything they said, guffawed. "Enjoy the view, little ones," he called out. "Enjoy it while you can."

"Is that a threat?" Nancy asked coolly.

"Oh, let's say, a final warning," Gutterman rasped.

"A warning about what?" Nancy asked, baiting the man. "What were we doing that could ever justify our abduction?"

"Abduction? Oh, my, my, my, what a harsh word."

"That's what the police would call it," Ned chimed in.

"The police! The police are so stupid and slow. You and I, Nancy Drew, are much quicker than the police. Much brighter."

"Very flattering," Nancy said, "but I know too many policemen who catch too many people like you, so I can't buy that line."

Gutterman laughed. "Like the ones in the police car a little while ago?" He roared again. "We don't worry about the police, but we do worry about people who have big ideas."

"Big ideas about what?" Nancy persisted, trying to find out just how much Gutterman knew of her activities. What, if anything, did he know about the mission to save the orphans; and did he also know about Nancy's personal mission to find the stolen documentary, *Captive Witness*? Or was it possible that he was involved in some unknown project that concerned neither the orphans nor the film?

Whatever the answers, Herr Gutterman remained silent, refusing to be drawn out on the subject. He sat sideways, keeping his eyes riveted on them, his mouth twisted in a mysterious, sardonic grin.

As the car climbed higher, the road became more dangerous. They began traveling along two lines cut out of the mountainside with sheer cliffs falling away into beautiful, lush, green valleys across which wandered lovely, clear streams fed by the melting glaciers and snows of the Austrian Alps.

Traffic was sparse with no cars traveling in their direction and only an occasional car or truck coming the other way. The open road made Herr Burger feel slightly exhilarated.

"I'm a bit bored with this slow driving," he called back to them. "I think I'll show you how experienced Alpine drivers take these roads."

"Here we go." Ned groaned. "A Saturday night cowboy. They've got them all over the world, I guess."

"Just hang on," Nancy said. "No matter what Herr Burger does, I'm sure he wants to stay alive just as much as we do."

Within the next few minutes, the couple began to doubt whether that was true. Herr Burger speeded up until he had the beautiful car careening around turns, spraying dust, pebbles, and bits of tire rubber into the air. Then, roaring down a relatively straight stretch of road, he threw the car into a skidding loop that took them within six inches of a cliff edge where there was no guardrail. Herr Gutterman's only response was a bemused look and a question thrown over his shoulder at his captives.

"Do you enjoy this, Miss Drew? Your friend seems a little blue around the lips."

"Sorry about that," Ned said. "I always turn blue when I'm happy."

"Is this fast enough for you, Miss Drew, or would you like Herr Burger to speed up? Are you frightened, Miss Drew? We wouldn't want to frighten you."

Nancy looked at Ned. "He's unbelievable," she said. "He's like some childish villain out of a bad movie."

"Miss Drew? You're not frightened, are you?" The noise of the squealing brakes and the flying gravel were making it difficult for Gutterman to hear them up front where the windows were open. He was gazing back at her, smiling cruelly.

"No, no, I'm not frightened," Nancy said, swinging wildly and hanging on to the strap. "Mr. Nickerson and I are terribly impressed, as a matter of fact."

Gutterman's face flushed beet-red. "Oh, is that so?" he snarled. "We'll see how impressed you are when we start questioning you."

"Oh, please don't question us," Ned cried mockingly.

Gutterman grew extremely angry at his prisoners'

refusal to show fear. His anger finally intensified to the breaking point when Herr Burger, negotiating another dangerous, screaming turn, caused Herr Gutterman to bang his head sharply against the window.

The big man let fly a stream of German invective mixed with French and German phrases that gave Nancy the impression that Gutterman was calling Burger a lunatic and moron. Burger was so upset, he wound up swerving into the opposite lane where the car faced a huge truck coming the other way.

For a split second, it appeared the two vehicles would collide but at the last moment both drivers veered sharply and barely missed each other. The danger of a head-on smash, however, was avoided at the price of a worse possibility. Herr Burger, completely rattled, was now driving straight toward the edge of a cliff!

"Look out!" Nancy and Ned cried with one voice as they both dropped down to the floor and covered their heads to minimize injuries in an accident.

As they crouched there, doubled over, they felt the car veer violently again, and heard a splintering, crunching sound. The car stopped, and there was silence.

Nancy was the first to bring her head slowly up to look out the window. "Oh, Ned," she gasped quietly, "We'd better start praying. Look where we are."

8

Danger in the Alps

"Don't move!" It was Gutterman's voice, trembling and filled with fear. "Don't even breathe."

All four passengers had good reason to obey the order because the car had gone partially through the guardrail and was teetering over the ·cliff. It's right rear wheel hung out in space and the left one was poised on the very edge.

"Let's get out of here," Burger cried, starting to climb out on his side, which was safely on the road.

Gutterman stopped him with a snarl. "If you lay one foot on the ground, I'll make you wish you were never born!"

"But what can we do?" Burger whined.

Gutterman pondered the question carefully. "It

seems to me that you and I can't get out because the weight of our friends in back will then topple the car right over the edge."

"You could open the back door on your side, Herr Burger. Just push the switch and unlock it, and Ned and I will get out slowly. Then you can get out, too," Nancy said steadily.

"No, you don't," Gutterman responded. "You two might make it and Burger could jump. With all the motion, the car would go over and take me with it."

"Well, you can't get out your side," Nancy pointed out. "You'd step into space, just as I would."

"No," Gutterman decided. "This is what we will do. Both of you should move as far over to the left as you can. I will climb over Burger and stand on the running board. Then, Burger, you start it up and see if the four-wheel drive can pull us out of this."

"Wait a minute," Ned protested. "If that doesn't work, you and Burger can jump free, but Nancy and I will go over the edge with the car."

"How clever you are," Gutterman sneered. "You do catch on quickly. That should make you both want to hug the left side of the car with all your might."

With no other choice, Nancy and Ned flattened themselves against the left side. The car tilted and rocked slightly.

"The worst is yet to come," Nancy breathed through her almost clenched teeth, "when that big galumph Gutterman tries to crawl over Burger. If he makes one slip, we'll really rock!"

"Don't think about it," Ned said. "Just squeeze yourself against this door."

Holding their breath, they froze as Gutterman, with surprising grace, managed to climb over Burger and out onto the left running board of the car. He hung off as far as he could, bearing his weight down fully, then told Burger to put the car in gear.

Burger did as he was ordered. Slowly, almost imperceptibly, the big, brown car began to move, its left rear wheel sending some gravel and rocks into the valley as it slipped slightly. The whole car tilted and, with a soft lunge, pulled up until the right rear wheel spun into contact with the ground and rolled to safety.

"Masterful driving," Gutterman said, patting his henchman on the shoulder. From the back seat, neither Ned nor Nancy let up on their tormentors.

"Oh, masterful," Nancy said. "Wasn't it, Ned?"

"Wonderful. Almost as good as the way he was driving when he went through the guardrail."

The two young people strived to make their captors so angry that they would open the back door to get at them. Nancy's plan could then be activated. While Ned attacked, she would fire her tear-gas "book" and perhaps they could finally escape.

But Gutterman and Burger were in a self-congratulatory mood. They even began singing as Burger continued to take the car higher into the mountains, this time at a more reasonable speed.

After several hours of driving, however, Burger pulled the car off on a dirt road and drove to what appeared to be a shepherd's hut. He stopped about a hundred feet away and turned around, almost backing over an extremely steep gorge in the process.

Nancy gulped again. "I don't know what they're going to do to us, Ned, but whatever it is, it has to be better than being locked in a high-powered automobile driven by Herr Burger."

"Absolutely," Ned concurred. "But what do you suppose they have in mind?"

The young couple soon found out as both Burger and Gutterman got out and walked around to the right-hand back door. "Now," Gutterman rasped as he unlocked the door with one hand while keeping the other thrust threatingly in his coat pocket, "you get out, Miss Drew. And you, Mr. Nickerson, you stay far over on the other side of the car if you know what's good for you."

Ned glanced down at Gutterman's pocket. Was there a gun inside? he wondered. Reading Ned's mind, the girl detective cautioned him.

"Don't do anything, Ned, please."

"Where are you taking her?" the young man demanded.

Gutterman flashed his evil smile, but said nothing. When Nancy got out, the door was shut and locked. Ned was left alone, helplessly watching the two men lead Nancy toward the shack.

But as she entered what appeared to be a crude building, she was amazed to find it beautifully cozy with sparkling, waxed floors, a cheery fireplace, a pretty rug, and upholstered furniture.

"Being a shepherd must pay very well," Nancy murmured, gesturing at the expensive furnishings. "But the shepherd doesn't own this anymore, does he?" she added, looking hard at Gutterman. "The wolves have taken over."

Gutterman shrugged. "Wolves. Sheep. I have no time for your small talk, Miss Drew. Let's get down to business."

"Excuse me," Nancy said, "but it was a long drive up here. Do you have a powder room where I could freshen up a bit?"

Gutterman pointed to a door at the far end of the room and, with an expansive bow, indicated that Nancy would find what she wanted there.

Will there be a window? she wondered. If so, will it be big enough for me to squeeze through? Her experienced eyes roved over every inch of the cottage searching for something, anything, that might produce a way out of the trap.

Once inside the bathroom, she saw there was no lock on the door. Obviously, Herr Gutterman had used this building for previous interrogations and didn't want his prisoners to lock themselves in while they plotted their next move.

Glancing swiftly around, she discovered a window but, unfortunately, it was high up and much too small even for a willowy eighteen-year-old.

After splashing water on her face, she dried off with a towel and looked in the mirror.

"Think, Nancy," she hissed. "Think. Don't just stand there."

Back outside in the living room, she found Herr Burger busily making coffee while Herr Gutterman lounged in a chair near the door. Apparently, Ned was still left behind in the car. Nancy noted quickly that the three windows in the room were all barred on the inside. Escape that way was impossible. Then she brightened. If escape through the window was impossible, then pursuit would be impossible, too. If only she could slip outside and lock the door behind her! Gutterman and Burger would be trapped!

Herr Gutterman was talking, babbling really, about his cleverness, and Nancy only half listened as she concentrated on escape.

The door to the room was made of solid oak, but Nancy had noticed a peculiar feature. On the outside walls were two metal slots like those found on cattle cars. They were used to hold a two-by-four or other heavy piece of timber across the door. Normally, such a crude but effective lock would be put inside a door to prevent forced entry. But obviously Herr Gutterman found himself constantly in need of locking people in, not keeping them out. Hence, the door to the building opened outward and could be blocked easily by dropping a piece of timber in the slots.

Instantly, Nancy flicked her eyes about the room looking for the timber to do the job. She saw it leaning against the doorjamb.

All she had to do was rise from her chair, pass Gutterman, grab the timber, open the door, slam it, and then throw the timber into place across the door.

She groaned inwardly. I'll never make it, she thought. But then Herr Gutterman said something that made her sit up straight.

"Of course," the man purred, "it would be advisable for you to answer my questions very quickly and correctly. You see, we left the engine of the car turned off. Therefore, no air will be fed into the back seat. Poor Mr. Nickerson. Who can say how long he will last?"

9

The Alpine Prison

Nancy quickly recovered and concealed her fright from Gutterman by flattering him. "Herr Gutterman," she said, "I don't know what line of business you are in, but I know you are much too cultured and urbane a gentleman to let an innocent person be injured. Why can't Ned be brought in here? You could tie him up. You don't have to hurt him."

Gutterman smiled. "You are a very clever girl, Nancy Drew. You know how to get your way. But this time, things will go better for you if we talk first. Besides, I'm sure Mr. Nickerson can last at least fifteen minutes. Now then, why are you mixed up in this ridiculous attempt to kidnap ten little children from Eastern Europe?"

"I don't know what you're talking about, Herr Gutterman; I'm not mixed up in anything."

"Your whole tour group is under suspicion," Gutterman continued. "Every one of you. But you most of all, because it would make sense for them to hire you for this job. If worse comes to worst, the charming Nancy Drew might charm the children across the border and charm the guards and charm everyone else."

Nancy continued to look calm but inside she was broiling. By the time this long-winded man finished asking three or four questions, Ned would be in real trouble, unable to breathe.

Her eyes, which had been trained on Gutterman's, now followed his hand down as he stubbed out his newly lit cigarette. It was then that she saw the car keys, lying on the table within easy reach. Fearing she would lose her courage if she hesitated, she took a deep breath and went into action.

Herr Burger had just put some iced coffee on the table in front of her and had gone back into the kitchen. With one swoop, Nancy grabbed the keys, flung her iced coffee into Herr Gutterman's face, and made a run for the door.

Gutterman was already on his feet and in pursuit. But then fate intervened as Herr Burger, hearing the glass shatter, rushed into the room, straight into the arms of Herr Gutterman. As they teetered, grunted, and crashed to the floor together, Nancy grabbed the timber and raced out the door. She had just enough time to slip the bar into place before she heard Gutterman smash against the solid oak, screaming.

To her relief, Ned was not only alive but yelling, trying to indicate that it was getting stuffy in his airless compartment.

She slammed the door and turned on the intercom. "Hang on, Ned, I'm looking for the ignition switch," she said.

Nancy began running her finger rapidly over the whole confusing array of switches and buttons. Finally, she found the starter, inserted the key, and pumped the accelerator. Nothing happened.

"Maybe it's flooded," Ned suggested.

"Oh," Nancy said in exasperation, "why does everyone always say that when you can't start a car?"

"Because that's generally what's wrong."

From the hut, Nancy could now hear noises which sounded like wild beasts fighting to claw and push their way out of captivity.

She laughed in spite of herself. "Apparently they don't like being locked up."

"I'll say," Ned shouted. "Look at that." As they watched the sturdy oak door, they saw a fist suddenly push right through it, shattering a plank completely. "Did you see that?" Ned asked. "And he's just warming up! Nancy, let's get out of here!"

"I'm trying." Again, the girl detective pressed on

the gas pedal and turned the key. Then a thought struck her. Some custom cars had a double ignition. One would have to be unlocked before the other one could work.

"Uh-oh," Ned said. "Look who's coming."

Nancy glanced up to see the enraged face of Herr Gutterman and the narrow, ratlike face of Herr Burger peering through the shattered door as Gutterman reached out to remove the timber blocking their exit.

"Nancy, what are we going to do? Listen, let me out!"

"That would be crazy!" Nancy cried. "No, I'll lock all the windows and doors. Then, at least, they can't get in."

The girl detective managed to hit the lock switches just in time.

Gutterman promptly threw a tantrum, pounding his fists, and finally his head, on the side of the car.

"You might as well give up," Nancy called. "You can't get in. Eventually, I'll get this started and when I do, it'll be bye-bye, Herr Gutterman."

Suddenly, Gutterman looked up. His hair was in disarray. His eyes were wild and red-rimmed. His tie was hanging down and his shirt was disheveled. But he let fly a cry of triumph.

"Aha," he shouted. "I'm not beaten yet." He darted in front of the car and lay down directly in its path. "Now try to get away!" he exclaimed. "You'll kill me, if you do, and you're too much of a lady to do that, aren't you, Miss Drew? Yes, I know you are. Your moral code wouldn't allow you to do something that might result in death or even bodily injury to another person, even to save your own life.

"That is why my kind wins and your kind loses these little battles, Miss Drew." Gutterman continued his lecture as his partner stared at him, unbelieving.

"Have you lost your mind?" Burger cried. "You *will* be killed, you maniac."

Nancy heard Gutterman, though neither she nor Ned could see him. "Not crazy," he bellowed. "You'll see."

But Herr Gutterman didn't know about the girl detective's superb driving skills and quick reflexes. While Gutterman was raving, Nancy found the second ignition. It was hidden behind a false cigarette lighter. She turned it quickly and then, quietly, slipped the key into the ignition itself.

"Ned," she whispered. "I've got it. Hold on, I'm going to start the car and back up like a rocket, then swing to the right."

"Got it," Ned replied softly. "Let's do it! I need air!"

In one swift and easy motion, Nancy started the engine, slammed the car into reverse, and went spinning back a dozen feet as soft pine needles slipped and churned under the wheels. Suddenly, the car slid downward as if on ice.

"It's the pine needles!" Ned shouted. "Quick, put it into first gear and the four-wheel drive will pull us out."

Smoothly, Nancy reversed the gears. The car shot forward and made a wide circle to the right, leaving the stricken Gutterman and Burger wailing in loud, shrill voices.

Out on the highway, Nancy pressed the big car to just under the speed limit and headed back for Vienna. From the back seat, she could hear Ned's voice. "Oh, that was tremendous! Tremendous! Let's go back and do it again, now that I can breathe. I want to see the looks on their faces."

"Once was enough." Nancy laughed as she pulled to the side of the road, unlocked the door switches, and made room for Ned in the front seat.

"Boy," Ned said, settling down, "it feels good to be out of the old cell, doesn't it? Well, anyway, now our worries are over."

"I don't know about that," Nancy said.

"Sure they are," Ned insisted. "We've got a nice car, we're headed for Vienna, we know that the people who are threatening the professor and the tour are really a bunch of muscleheads. They're not too smart, even if they do have beautiful cars and instant hotel reservations.

"By the way, why are they threatening the professor, and why are you going to Vienna? Do you realize I'm just stringing along with you, good old faithful Ned, and I don't even know what I'm getting myself into?"

"And I owe it to you to tell you," Nancy replied. As briefly as possible, she filled him in on the details of both the rescue effort involving the ten children and the mystery of the stolen film.

"Well, you'll figure everything out, Nancy. You always do. I have faith in you. If you need any heavy muscle work done, just call on your obedient slave."

"Thanks," Nancy said. "But right now, we're in trouble."

"What kind of trouble?"

"Well, just for starters, how about car theft?"

"Car theft? Those guys kidnapped us."

"Sure. But do we have any witnesses? Gutterman and Burger can claim they were nice enough to give us a ride and we took their car."

"But why would they want to draw attention to themselves?"

Nancy pondered the idea. "I suppose you're right, but even so, I don't want to be found with this car. I think we'll have to run the risk of leaving it someplace inconvenient."

"Gee, I hate to give up this beautiful buggy. Why don't we take our chances and explain it to the police if we have to? We'd be telling the truth."

275

Nancy shook her head. "We can't take any chances on this mission," she replied. "So this is where we get off."

"In the middle of nowhere? In the Austrian Alps?"

"Trust me," Nancy said.

10

Amphibian on Wheels

Nancy slowed down the big, brown car and at a small, almost hidden side road she pulled off. In a few moments, the car was lost from sight in the forest.

"Do you have any idea where we're going?" Ned asked.

"Not really," Nancy said, "but as we know, this car has four-wheel drive. It's obviously waterproof as well as soundproof and it's built high, providing a lot of space between the bottom of the car and the roadbed. That means we can drive it almost anywhere."

"Maybe even across a lake!" Ned chuckled.

"Don't laugh," Nancy said. "It could be amphibious and able to travel on water just like a boat!"

"In that case, did you pack an extra snorkel for me?" Ned teased.

"Not only that," Nancy said with a giggle, "but a set of flippers too!"

"Uh-oh, I'm beginning to think you're serious," Ned continued.

"I wish I were."

"Then I suggest we try hunting for another good road to Vienna," Ned said, "before we wind up in the drink!"

"Don't tell me you don't trust me, Ned," the young detective replied, eliciting no response from the boy.

They drove for almost an hour over the side road, which was little more than a pair of dusty ruts. It ended in a small stream about two feet wide.

"Now what?" Ned asked.

"We follow the stream," Nancy said. "Why?"

"Because streams always lead to people and houses, and anyone who gets lost in the woods should remember that." Ned laughed. "Oh, remember how they used to drill that into you at summer camp?"

"Yes," Nancy said, "and it happens to be absolutely true."

As the car bucked and lunged along the now grassy, now muddy streambed, Ned brought up the possibility of discovering a river large enough to float down. He had no sooner said it when they heard a rush of water and saw the little brook feed into a much larger stream, almost forty feet across.

"Well," said Ned, "here's where we find out whether we're riding in an amphibian."

"See those knobs and instructions?" Nancy asked. "This activates air pontoon sacks on the side, and this converts the engine power into a propeller drive shaft, which drops down when you push this button."

To their amazement, it all worked and they found themselves sailing grandly through the Austrian Alps in Herr Gutterman's beautiful automobile-boat. The thought made Nancy almost wistful.

"Ah, dear Herr Gutterman. What a trick we've played on him."

"It can't be helped," Ned said. "He really has to learn that he kidnapped the wrong people. He really—!"

"Shhh! Ned!"

The boy listened and gulped. "Is that sound what I think it is?"

Nancy nodded as the noise of raging water grew louder. "And I hope it isn't one of those two-hundred-foot Alpine monsters."

"Did you have to say that?" Ned asked worriedly. Suddenly, they tipped over the edge of a short fall that exploded into fast-moving rapids, which twist-

ed and turned the car so quickly that Nancy had all she could do to keep the nose pointed downstream.

"Is it leaking?" she yelled.

"I don't think so," Ned shouted. "Just some spray coming in the windows."

After a few minutes of quick contortions, they found themselves in a placid stretch of water. But rounding a bend they saw what was obviously one of the huge waterfalls they feared. Half a mile ahead, the stream simply dropped out of sight and they had a clear view down a wide, beautiful valley.

"We've got to get ashore somehow," Nancy called, and she aimed toward the right bank. The water was shallow, but unfortunately there was no place to drive the car completely out of the river and continue overland. The valley walls fell too sharply. The best the travelers could do was to drive it up on a narrow ledge four inches above the water.

"Well, this is it," Nancy said. "Good-bye, good old quiet brown car. We'll have to leave you here."

Ned started to laugh. "This is really terrible, you know. Do you realize how long it's going to be before Herr Gutterman finds his car?"

"Oh, he'll pop up again and we can give him directions," Nancy said, her eyes twinkling.

"We can give him directions, all right, but how will he ever get it out of here?"

"By helicopter," Nancy replied. "A helicopter

could pull him out, and speaking of a helicopter, we could sure use one ourselves."

Night was coming on, and with no way out except straight up the steep side of the valley, the two young people began to lose their jocular mood. The higher they climbed, the more rugged the terrain, and their breathing and luggage became heavier.

At last, after what seemed an interminable length of time, they started downhill again, discovered a path, then a road, and finally a town. As luck would have it, a bus destined for Vienna was due, and ten minutes later, they were standing in the aisle, clinging to the luggage racks for support.

"Look at us," Ned said. "Our feet and our shoes and socks are soaked. We've got mud on our clothes. We've had no lunch or dinner and we have to stand up all the way to Vienna."

But as Ned spoke, two people sitting nearby prepared to get off the bus at the next stop. With relief and soft cries of thanks, the two exhausted young people sank into the empty seats.

"Safe at last," Nancy said.

Suddenly, there was a commotion ahead in the road. "Wait, wait!" came the cry in German. "Wait for us."

Realizing it was Gutterman's voice, Nancy's blood froze. She grabbed Ned's hand and squeezed. "Be quiet," she whispered, hastily pulling two large scarves out of the bag lying at her feet. Quickly, she tied one around her head. "Do you have a hat?" she whispered.

"Yes, my old crushable Irish tweed. Got it in my pocket."

"Put it on your head. I know it's not good manners, but this is an emergency."

Nancy then handed him the second scarf to tie around his neck. She pulled his hat low and adjusted the scarf before they both eased down in their seats, pretending to sleep.

Gutterman and Burger clambered aboard and made their way down the aisle to take positions directly next to the couple.

Gutterman was still in a temper. Burger was sullen. He said nothing while Gutterman sputtered low, threatening sounds, all in German. Nancy, from her limited knowledge of the language, was able to pick out the essence of Herr Gutterman's bitterness. Burger, he said, was to blame for everything. If he had not made iced coffee back in the shepherd's hut, Nancy Drew could never have thrown it in his face and distracted him enough to get out the door.

Then, when he, Herr Gutterman, had bravely put his fist through the door and lain down in front of the wheels, Burger had not had the presence of mind to lie down in back of the wheels, preventing the escape.

And so it went as Nancy listened, her heart beating for fear they would be detected. Still, she could not help but be amused by Herr Gutterman's obvious frustrations. Eventually, Gutterman and Burger obtained seats directly in front of Nancy and Ned, and the two young people sat quietly until they arrived in Vienna. Cautious, they waited for their former captors to disembark before the couple took off their scarves, grabbed their luggage, and caught a taxi for their hotel.

Rooms were waiting for them and because they both felt exhausted, they decided to say good night immediately. Nancy ran a hot tub and was already soaking when she heard the phone ring. Stumbling out of the tub, she wrapped herself in one of the huge European hotel towels and lifted the receiver. It was Ned.

"Nancy!" he cried. "I was watching television, and guess what? We made the headlines! We've been listed as missing. They found the car."

"What?"

"Someone found the car and there are pictures on TV showing it being airlifted by helicopter. Authorities haven't figured out whom it belongs to yet."

"Just wait till they do," Nancy said. "When Gutterman finds out what happened to his car, he'll explode like a volcano!"

"We'd better call Dr. Bagley to tell him we're all right," Ned suggested.

Nancy placed the call to Salzburg instantly. "Professor," she said, "this is Nancy."

There was a stunned silence and then shouts of joy. "Nancy! It's Nancy. Are you all right? Is Ned there? What in the world is going on?"

Quickly, Nancy recounted the kidnapping, the escape, and the crazy fate of Herr Gutterman's car. Professor Bagley agreed that from now on, the tour had to keep close track of everyone.

The professor then filled her in on the group's activities—including the trip to Mozart's birthplace, where the little bus driver was barred from entering. "The authorities there said he always makes a scene and contradicts the guides constantly." The professor laughed.

"Oh, and one other funny thing happened," he added. "Eric left his wheelchair outside the men's room because it wouldn't fit through the door. We lifted him inside and when we came out, he noticed there was a different wheelchair in place of his. Another young man had taken Eric's by mistake, but Eric managed to catch him. For a minute, the other fellow was wheeling his chair like mad, trying to get away because he thought Eric was a little crazy chasing him yelling at the top of his lungs."

Nancy laughed. "That's all we need," she said, "a stolen wheelchair." As she hung up the receiver, she heard a noise that made her whirl around. An envelope suddenly appeared beneath her door. She stepped toward it, feeling her pulse quicken. The envelope was addressed to NANCY DREW, CAR THIEF.

11

Wild-Goose Chase

Without waiting to read the message inside the envelope, Nancy dashed impulsively to the door and flung it wide as she stepped out to see if she could catch a glimpse of the messenger. The corridor was empty.

She smacked her forehead lightly with the palm of her hand. "Oh, that could have been Gutterman," she muttered. "Of course, it was Gutterman. And I opened the door and ran out."

Quickly, she tore open the envelope and read the message written in old-fashioned script.

Dear Nancy Drew,
You are to cease all independent efforts to
kidnap the children and to find the film

Captive Witness. *If you persist, you will be hurt. If the price is right, however, it may be possible for you to obtain both the children and the film. Be in the hotel lobby at 9 P.M. tomorrow. Come alone. I will take you to see the film to prove I have it. You have my word of honor that you will not be harmed. You will be returned safely. Afterward, we can talk about what I really seek from you people.*

G.

So Gutterman does know I'm looking for the film! Nancy said to herself.

Although she had half suspected it, this was the first time he had given any indication of such knowledge, and Nancy concluded that he must have discovered her connection with *Captive Witness* fairly recently. Otherwise, she was sure he would have spoken to her about it long before.

But how did he find out? If her phone call home wasn't tapped, then, Nancy concluded, there must be a spy in the film festival's office who overheard a conversation between Richard Ernst and her father!

The prospects of her meeting with Gutterman churned in her mind as she flopped into bed and fell asleep uneasily.

When she saw Ned the next morning, she said nothing about Gutterman's note or about the invitation to meet him alone that night to see the documentary. It bothered her to keep it secret from Ned, but she believed that the fate of the children and the film hinged on a risk that was solely hers—finding out what Gutterman wanted!

First, she must learn all she could about the stolen film. After brunch, she telephoned the festival office and spoke to Richard Ernst, who her father had said would be her best source of information.

They found the festival offices just off the Ringstrasse, the great band of streets enclosing downtown Vienna which once marked the outer walls where the Turkish invasions had stopped in the sixteenth and again in the seventeenth century.

"Do you know," Nancy asked Ned as their taxi made its way through the crowded streets, "that those sieges of Vienna gave us two things we now eat for breakfast?"

Ned shook his head.

"Well, it was during the first Turkish siege that the bakers of Vienna invented the Vienna roll. And it was the Turks who brought coffee to Central Europe. Can you imagine Europe today without its coffeehouses?"

"And with that colorful information," Ned said, "we find ourselves in front of the film festival offices."

Richard Ernst, the festival representative, was a

meticulously dressed, polite, and proper Austrian who kissed Nancy's hand and offered coffee and delicious pastries. When Nancy asked for milk instead, he smilingly obliged.

But soon his face became serious. "Last Wednesday," Mr. Ernst said, "a man appeared with a letter written on Kurt Kessler's stationery and bearing Mr. Kessler's signature. It instructed festival authorities to give the messenger the copy of *Captive Witness* in our possession and to accept in exchange a revised copy that the messenger handed us."

"I'm surprised there was no more formal procedure involved," Nancy said.

"Well, we winged it, as you Americans say, because it was the first time anything like that had ever happened to us. We're a fairly new festival and, I suppose, a bit naive."

"So you simply gave the man the original film?" Nancy continued.

"No, I left the room to ask my associate, Mr. Etienne, what he thought, and when I came back, I discovered that the messenger had taken our copy and left the so-called revision. It turned out to be a completely blank reel. As I told your father, Miss Drew, we accept full responsibility and we will pay all damages, but I'm sure that money is not the real issue. For Mr. Kessler, it is the heartbreak of losing a vast piece of his lifework."

"Would you describe the man who took the film,"

Nancy requested. "On the other hand, let me. He was short, wiry, with pitted, rather sallow skin. He's almost bald, but not at all well mannered so he probably never removed his hat. He has a kind of ratlike face and beady eyes."

Mr. Ernst gasped. "That's amazing. Miss Drew, I must say I suddenly have enormous respect for your detective abilities."

"I must confess," Nancy replied, "that we've been tangled up with a couple of bad characters for the past few days. The one I described played the role of a bus driver, so why not a messenger, too?"

Nancy paused for a moment, letting her eyes gaze off into space, her brow slightly furrowed. "May I see the can that the film was in when the messenger brought it?"

"The can?" Mr. Ernst asked. "Why, yes, I suppose so."

He rummaged through files and produced a metal can, considerably battered, with some labels still attached. Nancy checked each label. The can had travelled all over Europe: Warsaw, Paris, Berlin, Rome. But there was only one label from Vienna, which she examined closely with her pocket-size magnifying glass.

"This is it! Thank you very much, Mr.—er, Herr Ernst. Come on, Ned."

"Nancy, where are we going? What do you mean, 'this is it'? Will you slow down? Nancy!"

But the girl detective was running now, down the steps, out into the street, signaling for a taxi. Ned caught up in time to open the door for her. When they were both inside, Nancy gave the driver an address she had scribbled down.

The driver glanced back at the two of them. "Are you sure you young people want to go there?" he said in a deep, resonant voice.

"Yes, yes," Nancy said, "and hurry, please."

"Nancy," Ned persisted, "what did you see on that film can?"

"An address of a film company here in Vienna. Chances are that that was the place the blank reel came from and probably the same place where Kessler's copy of *Captive Witness* was taken. Understand?"

"Interesting idea," Ned said, "but it seems a little thin."

"I've had thinner clues," Nancy remarked, settling back to watch the scenery. That proved to be a grim experience, however, as the buildings and the people began to look more disreputable. The road became bumpier, too, more pitted with holes, and littered with debris.

To make matters worse, the afternoon skies had darkened and droplets of rain splashed against the windows. As they passed one corner, a group of street urchins threw stones at the cab.

"Charming section," Nancy told the driver. "I'm

hoping it ends before we reach the company office we want. It's called Ciné-Ouest."

When they found Ciné-Ouest, however, it was in a wreck of a building set back from the road and almost concealed by weeds and high bushes. No one seemed to be around. Ned asked the driver to wait.

"Wait? Not a chance. You two young people would be smart to return immediately to your hotel. They'll steal the fillings from your teeth out here."

"We'll be all right," Ned insisted halfheartedly, as they paid the man and stepped out for a look at their target. Wasting no time, the driver locked all the doors, made a U-turn, and sped away in a shower of mud.

Together Nancy and Ned made their way to the front door of Ciné-Ouest. It was locked.

"That figures," Nancy said. "It's Saturday and the employees probably work a five-day week. Let's see if someone left a window open."

"That's burglary, technically speaking, of course."

"I know. But so long as we don't take anything, it's only trespassing," Nancy rationalized. "Besides, if we do find *Captive Witness*, it's our right to take it because it was stolen from our side in the first place."

"Okay, you convinced me." Ned sighed. "Let me try this window."

To his surprise, it opened easily. Both he and

Nancy slipped through onto the first floor, which was surprisingly neat, clean, and well painted. They found themselves in a room with racks and racks of films.

"It'll take hours to go through all this stuff," Ned moaned. "Wouldn't we do better to come back with a court order and some policemen?"

"Uh-uh," Nancy said. "The spy network over here would know in a minute. They'd move the film for sure. No, we just have to start looking."

But before taking another step, they were halted in their tracks by a low, menacing growl. A giant Doberman pinscher guard dog stood thirty feet away with his snout poised low and his lips drawn back exposing great, slashing teeth. He stared at them, ready to pounce.

Almost simultaneously, Nancy and Ned said the identical words: "Don't move and don't breathe."

"Don't look him in the eye, either," Nancy added. "The dog will think you're challenging him and will attack."

"You're probably right," Ned said, "but I have a hunch this guy means to jump us no matter what we do. What about those stacks? Do you think we can climb them fast enough to get away?"

"Yes, but then we'd be stuck there until Monday morning."

"What about your trusty tear-gas book?" Ned asked.

"I have it, but it only works up to about six feet."

"Well, once he's that close, he'll go all the way. Still, give me the book."

"Oh, no," Nancy said. "It's mine. I can handle this as well as you can."

"Maybe so," Ned went on, "but I happen to be standing about two feet in front of you and that means he is going to deal with me first. Please give me the book, Nancy."

"All right, but—"

"Uh-oh!" Ned broke in, snapping up the book. "Here he comes!"

With a savage roar, the giant dog flew across the room in three huge bounds. Nancy was just about to leap toward the window as the dog landed, preparing to spring in a final lunge. Ned, however, sprayed his eyes with tear gas at point-blank range, slightly from the side.

The animal yelped, making Nancy wince as she hurried outside. But she knew that the Doberman, whining now and pawing at his eyes, would not suffer any permanent damage. He would regain full sight within a day.

Meanwhile, Ned had climbed through the window, too. He grabbed Nancy's hand and led her running up the road away from Ciné-Ouest.

After a block, they slowed to a walk. They trudged through the drenching rain for what seemed like hours before finding a cab, and arrived back at the hotel, mud-splattered, soaked to the skin, and exhausted.

"That was wonderful fun." Ned grinned at Nancy. "And we've never looked lovelier. Now, master detective, do you have any more excursions planned for me tonight?"

She was about to say no when nervous thoughts about her nine o'clock meeting with Gutterman began to plague her. Should she tell Ned so that he could shadow her and call in the police if necessary? Or would Ned, in his eagerness to protect her, be discovered? If so, the young detective could lose her only chance to free the children and find the valuable film!

12

Captive Witness

Despite the risk, Nancy decided she had to carry out the mission by herself. She thanked Ned, and with the promise to be up bright and early for breakfast, she parted from him and returned to her room to repair some of the damage to her mud-spattered clothes.

After a hot bath and a hasty manicure, she dressed in a simple navy-blue skirt and white blouse with a powder-blue cardigan.

Gutterman arrived promptly at nine. Burger, of course, was with him, driving a rather battered and old-looking automobile.

"I must apologize for the homely nature of my car, Miss Drew," Herr Gutterman said, "but it seems that magnificent ones attract strange people who borrow and dump them in unlikely places."

Nancy felt her jaw tighten, but she refrained from answering.

"But let bygones be bygones, at least for now," Gutterman said. He smiled thinly. "Would you be so kind as to sit in the back seat with me while Mr. Burger drives? For security reasons, of course."

Nancy nodded. "Do you want to blindfold me, too?"

Gutterman clapped his hands together in an expression of rapture. "How wonderful to do business with a professional! Of course, we must keep the location of this film a secret. *Ja?*"

"*Ja!*" Nancy declared.

Gutterman tied a large, clean white handkerchief around her head. "And now, Miss Drew, I'm sure you are going to try memorizing the sequence of every turn we make. I advise you to save your energy. You'll only get terribly frustrated."

Despite the warning, Nancy tried to note all turns and stops, but the constant twisting made the route nearly impossible to follow.

When the car came to a final halt, Gutterman helped her out and escorted her up a flight of twelve very low steps, leading her through a heavy door that squeaked badly on its hinges. Once inside, they turned right down a short hall and right again through a door that Gutterman closed and locked.

He sat Nancy in a chair and removed her blindfold. They were in a dimly lit room with a film pro-
jector behind her and a blank white screen in front
of her. Without a word of explanation, Gutterman
hit the projection switch, turned off the lights and
for one hour, Nancy watched the first part of Kurt
Kessler's film, *Captive Witness*.

What passed across the screen was a documentary film of life inside Kessler's homeland. Leading
intellectuals, most of them with their backs to the
camera, spoke against cruelty and oppression.
There were segments showing beatings on the
street by police and other unpleasant scenes that
created a harrowing image for the oppressed countries of Eastern Europe.

When the reel finished, Gutterman flicked off the
switch and turned on the lights. "There is one more
piece of film," he said, "but it's a waste of my time
to keep watching this drivel. Have you seen
enough?"

Nancy, who was greatly moved by what she had
seen, looked scornfully at the man. "Yes, thank you.
Besides, I'll see the whole thing at the festival."

Gutterman laughed raucously. "You have a delicious sense of humor, Miss Drew. Also a ridiculous
sense of honor that actually led you to believe no
harm would befall you tonight."

Nancy flashed her eyes. "What?"

"Now, don't get so upset. No harm will come to you tonight, but what astonishes me is that you actually did trust me. Nine times out of ten you would have been wrong."

"Can we get to the point?"

"Oh, by all means. Let's start with my proposition."

"Excuse me," Nancy said. "Let's start with mine. The fact is that none of your people know where the children are. You're bluffing."

A glimmer of annoyance crossed Gutterman's face. He waggled one thick forefinger at Nancy. "Don't get cute with me, Miss Drew. We not only know where they are but who kidnapped them from us as well as the precise date and time they will try to escape.

"We will be there to intercept all of them, unless, of course, you are reasonable." Gutterman rubbed his hands together and walked away a few paces, glancing back at Nancy dramatically. "All we want is the arch traitor, Kurt Kessler! The man who turned on his own country and who now desires to show this treacherous film about his own people! It's a lie—all of it!"

Nancy flared up. "Kurt Kessler happens to be one of the most respected film directors in the entire world. I'm sure he must be telling the truth, and if he isn't, then why doesn't your government refute

300

him with facts and logic instead of punishing helpless children?"

A small smile played around Gutterman's lips.
"Did you say *my* government? Miss Drew, I have
no ideology. I am a patriot who pledges allegiance
to whoever pays me the most. If, after you give me
Kurt Kessler, your country wishes to buy my ser-
vices, I might even steal him back for you!"

"I don't think we'd ever sink that low!" Nancy replied scathingly.

Gutterman waved his hand, carelessly dismissing
the insult. "You can't hurt my feelings, Miss Drew.
I abandoned them years ago. Now, what have you
decided? Will you persuade Kessler to appear at the
border crossing and give himself up? As I said, you
can have the children and even this silly film, because they will make him renounce it. He will say
the Americans made him do it."

Nancy tried to conceal her revulsion, knowing
that the success of her mission relied partly on Gutterman.

"You mean," she said, her voice trembling with
outrage, "that you will torture him until he denies
everything he believes in? Haven't you done
enough to him already? You made him spend nine
years in labor camps and four years under house ar-
rest, and what about all the other years when his
work was confiscated or destroyed?"

"I've no time for your nonsense," Gutterman

said, replacing her blindfold. "I want you to contact Kessler. Let him make his own decision. You have until noon tomorrow."

In a dazzling series of twists and turns, the young detective was returned to the hotel. She immediately went to a pay phone and called her father, relating Gutterman's offer. Mr. Drew put her on hold while he contacted Kessler and then came back to Nancy with the answer.

"Of course," Carson Drew said, his voice crackling with anger, "I knew what Kurt would say. He's a hero, and heroes automatically do things like this. You tell your contact that Mr. Kessler will fly to Vienna tomorrow. He will do as they request on a guarantee there will be no tricks, Nancy."

As her father finished speaking, tears flowed down Nancy's cheeks, and she had a hard time keeping her voice from breaking. "Okay, Dad. No tricks, and tell Mr. Kessler we all love him."

Nancy went to her room, changed out of her clothes into a nightgown and stared dazedly in a mirror as she brushed her hair. The sorrow over Kessler's probable fate, however, soon replaced itself with anger.

"Wait a minute," Nancy murmured out loud. "If only I could retrace the route to the building where *Captive Witness* was stored!"

She knew she couldn't possibly recall the twisting, winding way but there were other things that came to mind. The sounds, for example. She had heard trains coupling and uncoupling and there had been the shriek of a train whistle. From somewhere, too, had come the music of a merry-go-round. Where in all Vienna would that be? She had less than two days to find out!

For several moments, too, the young detective thought of the ten children in hiding. How much longer would they remain safe from the other side?

13

The Stricken Messenger

After a full night's sleep, Nancy bounced out of bed filled with energy. She couldn't be sure of the route Gutterman's car had taken her, but she had jotted down everything she could remember.

She dialed Ned's room number and was greeted by his sleepy voice. "Come on, Ned. Get up and get dressed. Meet me right way. We've no time to lose. Today is the big day! Breakfast in ten minutes."

Half an hour later, Ned, still bleary-eyed, wandered into the hotel restaurant and slid into the seat opposite Nancy. "I can't believe it." He yawned. "You look radiant and I look like a sack of wet laundry. How do you do it, Nancy?"

Nancy waved her hand impatiently and grinned.

"Now stop flattering me and be serious. Look." She pushed a map of Vienna toward him. It was cross-hatched with lines of purple, green, and red.

"What is this?" Ned mumbled, taking a swig of orange juice.

"It's the route to the film," Nancy said.

"Which film? Our film—*Captive Witness?*"

"Yes, yes, yes. I saw part of it last night."

Ned was completely confused. "Last night?"

The girl shook her head. "I saw it with Gutter-man."

"Gutterman!" Ned exclaimed.

"I wish you'd stop repeating everything I say." Nancy laughed.

"Well, everything you say is so fascinating I just can't help myself."

"Let me explain," Nancy said, and told her friend the entire story of her meeting with the man.

"That's really terrific," Ned said when she had finished. "I came along to protect you and what do you do? Play right into the hands of that crook."

"But I had to. Don't you see? If I had told you, they might have found out and canceled the whole thing. I'm sorry. Forgive me. But please hurry. I need you to rent and drive a car so we can retrace the route Gutterman took me on last night."

Ned looked at her ruefully for a moment, then smiled. "Okay. Let's go."

Once they had secured a car and were on their way, Nancy spread the map on her lap. "I think it was somewhere around here."

Ned paused to follow her finger. "You realize, of course, you're pointing to half of Vienna," he said.

"I know." Nancy sighed. "Well, let's start with the red line, and keep our speed at twenty miles per hour."

For more than four hours, they cruised up one street and down another with no success. At last, Nancy folded up the map and put it in the glove compartment.

"I give up," she said.

"Oh, don't do that," Ned replied.

"But it's hopeless. I didn't see any building with a flight of twelve very low steps leading up to the front door."

"Shall we go back then?"

Nancy nodded grimly.

"Look, it isn't worth fretting over. You did better today than yesterday. At least, this time we didn't get chased by a hungry Doberman."

"Thanks for the consolation," Nancy said, half-smiling.

They returned to the hotel in time to meet Professor Bagley and their friends who were arriving on the tour bus. The first voice they heard was that of the little bus driver. It was loud and strident, commanding the attention of everyone within a block.

"Strauss! Oh yes, he was so-so. He wrote pretty music—*The Blue Danube* and *Tales from the Vienna Woods*. But what is that compared to Mozart?"

Suddenly, Bess and George spotted Nancy coming toward them. "Nancy!" the cousins chimed simultaneously and raced toward her.

"I see our bus driver is still at it." Nancy grinned.

"All the way from Salzburg." George groaned.

"Did he run off the road again?"

"Not once but many times," Bess said. "It was awful. Once he got so angry because someone compared Beethoven to Mozart that he actually stopped the bus, ran outside, and shouted into the valley, 'Beethoven is a bore. Mozart is sublime.' Over and over. The professor had to go out and drag him back into the bus."

As soon as Nancy had seen Bess and George off to their rooms, she turned to Professor Bagley and the ever-present Eric Nagy. They went to a nearby sidewalk café, and after ordering hot chocolate and croissants with butter and jam, Nancy related her recent experiences, including the fact that Kessler would probably agree to trade himself for the ten children.

Dr. Bagley's face drained white. "We can't let that happen," he said angrily. "Kessler can't go back."

"I know," Nancy said under her breath. "Have

you received your final instructions regarding the time and place of the crossing?"

"Not a word, but I expect to receive information today. I've been told to stay around the hotel and keep myself visible. By the way, the cat burglar struck at last."

Nancy's eyes twinkled with excitement. "You mean they took the bait?"

"They certainly did. Last night, I left the false document in a sealed envelope at the bottom of my musette bag. I had folded the message twice and dropped a few grains of salt in the middle of it. This morning, I opened the envelope and the salt was gone. Someone did an excellent job of unsealing the envelope, reading the contents, and resealing it perfectly, but didn't notice the salt."

"Well, I must say that was a bit more subtle than the business at Munich airport," Nancy remarked. "Of course, I suppose if the theft had worked there, you probably would've found the bag later, thrown away somewhere, with certain things missing but the envelope left intact just to make it look like a regular robbery."

"Good deduction, but that would have been equally clumsy of them. Anyway, now that they have the information, all we have to do is wait for our contact to surface with the correct details."

Ned, who had gone to his room, returned shortly

308

to join them, engaging in banter with Eric as they vied for Nancy's attention. Dr. Bagley watched in amusement wearing his owl look.

Suddenly, Nancy heard a man's voice coming from the table directly behind the professor. "Don't turn around, Dr. Bagley," he said softly, but urgently. "Pretend I'm not here. I am your contact. Listen carefully. We are now free to tell you where you will find the true instructions regarding the rendezvous with the children. Look—"

The voice stopped, choking in a half-strangled sound. Nancy whirled out of her chair to see the man fall in the throes of a heart seizure. She took the initiative, helping Ned and the professor roll the man on his back and loosen his clothes. Leaning on her extensive training in first aid and paramedic techniques, she took his pulse and bent to listen for his heartbeat.

"I don't hear anything," she cried.

Quickly, she assumed the correct position for mouth-to-mouth resuscitation while Ned, who had assisted Nancy in similar emergencies, administered chest pounding.

In seconds, the man was breathing again and his heart began to beat. "Keep him warm," Nancy ordered as some hotel employees appeared with a blanket. "I hope that someone has called an ambulance."

Indeed, someone had, and as they waited for its arrival, the victim began to regain consciousness though he was paralyzed on the left side of his body.

He tried to speak but could make only indistinct, gurgling sounds. Nancy tried to quiet him, but his eyes rolled wildly toward Eric Nagy.

"What's he trying to tell us?" Dr. Bagley said anxiously.

But the man's words were so garbled, neither Nancy, Ned, Eric, nor the professor could decipher them.

"It's a shame," Nancy said as the ambulance came. The man tried to raise himself, pointing at Eric before falling back on the stretcher, exhausted. "I know he's trying to tell us something about Eric, but what?" the girl muttered.

"I have no idea," Dr. Bagley whispered back, "but it's impossible to discuss secret business with fifty people gaping over our shoulders."

"Someone ought to stay with him every single minute until he's able to communicate," Nancy remarked.

"I agree, but I don't think—" the professor started to say as the doctor in charge interrupted the conversation.

He complimented Nancy and her friends for saving the man's life while attendants carefully placed the patient in the ambulance.

"Thank you," Nancy said. "I'm his niece and I would like to accompany him if I may."

Ned gasped and the professor looked up, somewhat less startled.

"I'll call you from the hospital," the young detective told her companions as the ambulance doors closed and the vehicle moved off.

What no one had noticed, however, was the small, black car that had pulled away from the curb and followed the ambulance. In the front seat with evil grins on their faces were Herr Gutterman and Herr Burger.

14

The Terrible Truth

In the ambulance, Nancy looked through the man's wallet for some clue regarding his identity, so that should he die, contact might be made with the people who had sent him. His name was Robert Haberman and his address was in West Berlin. That was the only information Nancy found.

At the hospital, after a prolonged examination, the doctors told Nancy that Herr Haberman was doing fine, that the paralysis was only temporary and he would soon recover.

Nancy begged to stay at his bedside because it was important for her to speak with him, if only for a few seconds, when he regained his speech or could hold a pencil to write a message. The doctor agreed, and Nancy sat quietly next to Herr Haberman's bed.

"I admire you, Herr Robert Haberman," Nancy said softly. "But how I wish you would wake up soon."

Remembering her promise to call Professor Bagley and Ned, she stepped into the corridor but froze instantly at the sight of Herr Gutterman arguing with a hospital guard.

"But he is my brother," Gutterman was pleading.

Nancy hesitated. "That man is not related to us at all," she declared, hurrying forward to confront Gutterman.

"*Related to us?*" Gutterman bellowed. "See here, my good fellow, this woman is not related to that patient at all!"

"I bet he can't tell you his brother's name," Nancy said quickly, watching Gutterman flounder.

"All right," the guard said, "what is his name?"

"He uses many names," Gutterman went on. "His real name is Gutterman, of course."

"That's enough," the guard replied, taking Herr Gutterman by the arm and twisting his wrist just enough to keep him under control. "Now, please leave this hospital."

With Gutterman out of the way, at least for the moment, Nancy dashed to a public phone and called the professor's room. Ned answered.

"We're all sitting here trying to figure out what to do. Did our friend revive?"

"No," Nancy said, "but he'll be all right, thank goodness. I'm afraid, though, he might not be able to talk to us for days, and we don't have that much time. Also, Gutterman's been trying to force his way in here. I got rid of him for a little while but I wouldn't be surprised if he doesn't blow everything for us."

"Well, something's got to give. Wait. The professor wants to talk with you."

"Hello, Nancy,"

"Hello, Dr. Bagley. Do you have any ideas what we should do next?"

"Not really. I was hoping our contact man had a backup who would fill in for him in case something unexpected like this happened. No luck, though. We did have another strange incident, too. Somebody went off with Eric's wheelchair. This time it wasn't by mistake. He actually tried to steal it."

"What?"

"It's true. Somebody grabbed it and tried to get out the front door with it, but the doorman's pretty tough. When he went after the thief, well, the fellow let go of the chair and just ran."

"Did you see him?"

"No. And the doorman couldn't give much of a description either."

Suddenly, bells began tripping off in Nancy's head. Eric's wheelchair! When Herr Haberman suffered his attack, he kept looking at Eric, trying to point to him, to say something. But what?

"Ned!" Nancy cried. "Go straight to Eric. Guard him. Guard that wheelchair—with your life if necessary. Forget about sending anybody to this hospital to relieve me. I'm coming right back."

She raced past the friendly guard, almost knocking him down in her haste and calling an apology at the same time, and headed outside. She leaped into a cab and begged the driver to take her to the hotel as fast as the speed limit allowed. Once there, she ignored the stately, lumbering elevators and flew up the three flights of stairs to the professor's door.

Ned called out. "Who's there?"

"Me!" she panted. "Let me in, please."

As soon as she was inside, she rushed toward Eric. "Please, can you get out of your wheelchair and sit on the bed for a while?" Nancy requested.

When the young man complied, she asked Ned to find some tools, including a screwdriver, pliers, and a hammer. "Oh, yes, and order another wheelchair right away."

"Nancy," Dr. Bagley said, moving toward her, "you're going too fast for all of us. Slow down, and tell us what you're up to."

Nancy pointed to Eric's chair eagerly. "The message must be hidden in there—all the instructions for rescuing the children. We've been carrying the information ever since we left the States, but they didn't want us or the enemy to know."

As the young detective's revelation settled on everyone, all three men responded with equal excitement. Tools and a substitute wheelchair were ordered promptly, and the professor and Eric began fiddling with the metal frame, trying to unscrew the bolts with their bare hands.

Within ten minutes, the entire chair had been stripped down to its components. Even the rubber had been removed from the wheels on the chance the instructions were concealed underneath. But they weren't. Despite all their efforts, there was no trace of anything.

Nancy clapped her hands to her forehead, holding them there in frustration. "Oh, I feel so foolish, and I was so positive!"

"Don't blame yourself, Nancy," Dr. Bagley comforted her. "We all thought you were on the right track."

"But now poor Mr.—I mean, Herr—Haberman is still the only one who can help us. Somebody should go back and stand guard again."

"I'll do it," Ned offered.

"Just a minute, Ned," Eric said, clearing his throat. "I've been thinking about the wheelchair seat. I noticed a little while ago that it's slightly un-comfortable. As a matter of fact, there's a tiny lump in it."

He pointed to the leather seat, which had been cut off the chair but otherwise lay intact on the floor.

"The seat!" Nancy cried. "Oh, of course! I could kiss you, Eric!"

"Better not," Ned replied in a half-kidding tone. "But somebody had better open that seat. Here, let me."

Taking out his penknife, Ned inserted the blade in the leather seam, slitting the stitches holding the two pieces together. Out fell a small, thick brown envelope.

Nancy tore open the flap and then quickly hand-ed the packet to the professor. Dr. Bagley adjusted his glasses and started to read. He became so en-grossed in the message that he forgot to read it aloud. Instead, he stood there, mumbling softly un-der his breath, making little exclamations while the three young people swelled with curiosity.

Suddenly, Dr. Bagley looked up, aware of his oversight, and apologized profusely. "Oh, I'm terri-bly sorry. This is so fascinating," he said. "The plan is to let our enemies think the crossing will be made on the Czech frontier while in fact the children will be escaping over the Hungarian border.

"There is a small, detailed map here that indicates the exact place between Austria and Hungary where the children will be brought and from which the final move will be accomplished."

Everyone was jubilant. "If we can just get those kids out safely," Ned said, "it will be worth the whole expedition. Of course, it would be super if Nancy could find the *Captive Witness* film, too. But the main issue is those kids and saving Mr. Kessler from a fate worse than death."

Nancy remained quiet on the subject, though deep down it saddened her to think she might fail to recover the film. After all, it represented something very important to its creator.

As she pondered the idea, a knock on the door interrupted. It was a soft, insistent knock that somehow made everyone feel there was something urgent waiting on the other side.

Professor Bagley opened the door and found himself looking down at a short, frightened-looking man. He stood alone with his hat held diffidently in his hand.

"You are Dr. Bagley?" the visitor said softly, taking a quick glance down the corridor to make sure no one had followed him.

The professor nodded.

"May I come in? I have very important news. Terrible news."

319

Hurriedly, the professor ushered him in and then closed and locked the door. The stranger stood uncomfortably in the middle of the room. He was obviously poor and bedraggled but had done his best to make himself presentable enough to enter the hotel. His graying hair had been combed into place, but his pants bagged and his old coat was shiny with the memory of such hard use.

Even though he's bone dry, Nancy thought, he looks like a shivering puppy.

The man sat down gently as though fearful he would break something. He looked from one to another seeking permission to speak further. Nancy nodded her head encouragingly and he began.

"My name is Emile Popov. We had hoped to bring ten children out through Hungary with six adults posing as three married couples traveling with their children. We picked Hungary because it is so much easier to cross the border there. The Hungarians and Austrians are on good terms unless, of course, an alert is sounded.

"Of course, with our enemies looking for the children, we have to expect the Hungarians to tighten their security, too.

"Even so, we thought we could do it until two of our couples were arrested while traveling from East Germany. My wife and I managed to escape, thank goodness. We have all the children and we arrived this morning at a little hut. It's almost a dugout, hidden in the brush about a mile from the border in the swampy section of the lake.

"But we now have no way to get across. We can't try to go through the regular checkpoint with ten children. We can't expect to climb the fence at some other point along the border. Our organization has been disrupted. Almost everyone has been arrested or gone into hiding."

"Mr. Popov," Professor Bagley said, "what do you propose we do?"

"With God's help, Professor Bagley," the man said, "you must find a way to sneak some people across the border, pick up our children, and come back here with them. We have no one left to do the job."

15

Perilous Plan

As Professor Bagley heard the little man's words, he shook his head. "I think," he said, "I'd better sit down." He sank heavily into a great brown armchair and stared at the floor.

Nancy, on the other hand, decided that their visitor needed some cheering up. "Well, Mr. Popov, how would you like something to eat? It's time to relax a bit, and when we're all done talking, you should have a bath and then a bed because I can see that you've had to do some crawling and hiding to get here. Am I right?"

Mr. Popov nodded somberly. He looked down at his hands, which Nancy had noticed were badly scratched, with flakes of dirt around the nails. His shoes were muddy, too.

"With your permission, dear lady," he said, "I gratefully accept the offer. Food and a bath would be wonderful. But first, let me at least wash my hands and face."

He disappeared into the bathroom while Nancy phoned room service and the young men donated slacks, a shirt, and a jacket to replace Mr. Popov's tattered clothing.

Professor Bagley stared at Nancy, still perplexed. "I didn't expect this at all. Really I didn't. We're not equipped to go into Hungary. I don't know how we would start. The refugee organization shouldn't leave us hanging this way. I mean, I know we have to do something, but—"

Nancy patted his arm. "Why don't we have a long talk with Mr. Popov and try to find out as much about the operation as possible."

"Let's call the refugee organization, too," Dr. Bagley said, brightening at the idea. "You never lose your optimism, do you?"

"Not if I can possibly help it," the girl said.

Professor Bagley dialed the contact for the refugee organization and talked for nearly five minutes.

"There's a storm watch here," he said into the phone. "The wind could start whipping up in a few hours, you know."

Nancy had overheard the tail end of the conversation and was bewildered by the strange talk about bad weather.

"I heard we're due to have clear skies tomorrow," she commented when the professor hung up.

"Storm watch means time is running out," he replied grimly, explaining that he frequently used weather terms as a code. "We can never be sure if someone is listening in on a conversation."

He paused sadly, then added, "They say they're a small group and everyone who works with them is completely committed to two other operations tomorrow. One is on the East German border and the other on the Romanian border. There isn't a person to spare. If only we could hold off our rescue for a week. Let's see what Mr. Popov thinks."

When the man emerged, face and hands now shining, he was overwhelmed by the gifts of clothes laid out for him and the dinner that room service wheeled in moments later. As he ate, Nancy and the professor carefully learned as much as they could about the children, their exact location, their individual ages, and their ability to remain silent when necessary.

"They must keep quiet when they pass close to the Hungarian border guards," the professor told Popov.

"Of course. No question about that, and they will," the man replied. "They understand the seriousness of all this, and they dearly want to be with their families again."

The conversation then shifted to the choice of time selected for the border crossing. It was to have been just before midnight when the guards would be awaiting relief, and when they were apt to be most careless, tired, and eager to get home.

"They would not search so thoroughly then as they would at the beginning of their watch," Mr. Popov said. "But why are we even talking about such things? They are no longer important since there is no way to bring the children out now through a border checkpoint."

"What about the possibility of cutting through the fence?" Ned asked.

Nancy shook her head. "It's probably wired."

"You mean it will electrocute on contact," Ned commented.

"I don't know about that, but I imagine it must be connected to an alarm," Nancy replied.

"How about digging under the fence then?" Eric questioned.

"Friends." Mr. Popov held up his hands to interrupt the discussion. "You can cut the fence. You can dig under. But the risk is so terribly great that the guards would catch you. Remember, with ten children you cannot move very quickly. No, we must think of something completely different."

There was silence until Ned snapped his fingers. "I've heard of people escaping by balloon," he said eagerly, but seeing the frowning faces of his listeners, he dropped the idea. "Where are we going to get a balloon anyhow?"

Nancy studied Mr. Popov for a moment. She was startled to see tears in his eyes. She hurried to his side and put her arm around his thin shoulders. "I am so afraid," Mr. Popov said, half choking, "that I will never see my wife or the children again. It is only a matter of days, perhaps hours, before they find us."

Nancy felt tears spring to her own eyes as she hugged the man encouragingly. "Mr. Popov, you are one of the bravest people I've ever known because you are afraid, but you do what you have to anyway. You have to fight twice—once against your fear and once against your enemy. You are a remarkable man, and we are proud to help you."

Mr. Popov squared his shoulders and said in his still-choking voice, "Thank you, Miss Drew. Thank you."

"And don't worry," Nancy continued, "because we will be there to get you—all of you—tomorrow night."

Professor Bagley gulped. "Ah, Nancy, I'm not sure we should make such a flat promise like that one. We might find it too hard to keep."

"Trust me, Dr. Bagley," the young detective said. "I have a plan. It's not complete yet. But I know it will work." She looked at him imploringly.

326

At last the professor gave way, and she smiled a little.

"Who can resist you, Nancy? Okay, let's give your plan a chance—particularly since I don't have one of my own."

The girl inhaled deeply. "So far," she said, "only the four of us know about the children. Right?"

"Right," Eric replied.

"Well, we're going to need assistance. We have to bring in Bess, George, Dave, and Burt."

Nancy ran her hand through her hair and paced back and forth. "For now, Mr. Popov, you stay here in this room and we'll ask the hotel to bring in a cot. Okay, Dr. Bagley and Eric?"

They nodded.

"Thank you," Mr. Popov replied. "I am very tired, but I must be up by two A.M. and on my way back so that I can cross before daylight."

"That's fine," Nancy said. "We'll send you along with a duck call. Ned, we must find a duck call."

"A duck call?" the young man said in amazement. "What in the world are you going to do with that?"

"We'll use it for a signal. Get two duck calls. Tomorrow night Mr. Popov will listen for it. When he hears it, he'll answer us. Just three short bursts. Quack! Quack! Quack! That's all. It will be a new moon and black as pitch so it's the only way we'll be able to find one another."

"Besides, it's a natural sound and won't arouse

suspicion," Professor Bagley remarked.

"Or not much, I hope," Nancy said.

"The call's a good idea," Mr. Popov concurred. "The place we're staying in isn't a house. It isn't even a hovel. Just a hut. And we have no lights. Even if we did, we couldn't show them."

"Wait a minute, Nancy," the professor interjected. "We have to start thinking about what is physically possible. Now, you know I can't really run. My left leg has been stiff ever since they flattened me for doing that column of music criticism for the River Heights newspaper."

The young people laughed at the professor's habit of making a joke about the wound he had received in combat.

"So," Dr. Bagley continued, "that means I'm going to be kind of a fifth wheel in this operation."

"Not really," Nancy replied. "You are the most visible one. You are the person the other side has been watching most. That could prove to be a very valuable asset."

"You mean I could be your decoy."

"Yes, you and Eric could draw attention away from the real rescue attempt while the rest of us waltz across the border with the Popovs and the children."

Professor Bagley pulled his ear thoughtfully. "Well," he said, "I wouldn't include Eric as a decoy.

In fact, my boy, I think it's time to say something, don't you?"

"Guess so." The young man smiled from his position on bed where he'd been sitting ever since his wheelchair was destroyed. "You and Ned had better sit down when I tell you this, or rather when I show you this."

Nancy furrowed her brow slightly. "Have you some secret weapon that will help us save the children?"

"Oh, just a small one. Here—watch."

The handsome young man stood up and walked across the room in front of the onlookers. For a moment, everyone was speechless, and then recovering, they cried out almost in unison:

"Eric! You can walk!"

16

The Shoppers' Ploy

"Eric!" Nancy cried happily, "you can walk! How wonderful!" And impulsively, she gave him a hug. Ned, too, leaped up and grabbed the boy in a bear hug, slapping him on the back.

"You rascal!" the young collegian said. "You had me fooled, that's for sure."

"Me, too," Nancy said, her eyes sparkling like blue diamonds. "He really is an actor. All I can say is congratulations on your amazing recovery. No doubt you'll have to do a lot more acting if we're going to transport those children safely into Austria. I guess we all will."

"I'm really sorry to have deceived everyone," Eric said, chuckling a little, "but you can see the advantage of my being in a wheelchair. A man who can't walk wouldn't be of much help to anyone trying to escape enemy territory."

"So our opponents don't regard you as a threat," Nancy said.

"And the idea of using the wheelchair to deliver the final, secret instructions was a stroke of genius," Dr. Bagley remarked. "The papers were probably slipped into the chair that time we lost sight of it in the hotel."

Once the effect of the surprise had died down, Nancy and the professor began the complicated work of organizing a job for each person. First, Nancy telephoned Bess, George, Burt, and Dave and asked them to join the group.

"Wow, look at that wheelchair," Dave said. "Did a truck run over it?"

"What on earth happened?" Bess chimed in.

"Everybody sit down and listen," Dr. Bagley told them. "Please keep your voices down because what you are about to learn has already set off one explosion in this room. It's amazing all of Vienna didn't hear it."

In a few sentences, the professor revealed that Eric could, indeed, walk and the entire group had to collaborate in an effort to help ten children escape from Eastern Europe. Nancy then filled in about the missing film and how the enemy had offered to trade it and the children in return for Kurt Kessler's surrender.

"What?" George said. "That's downright outrageous!"

"I'll say it is!" Bess exclaimed.

Burt and Dave also expressed anger when they heard Nancy's final piece of information.

"Please, please," Dr. Bagley said, quieting the group. "I know how you all must feel but we must keep cool."

"Or we'll ruin everything," Nancy added.

George's eyes flashed fire. "I'll fight them myself," she muttered evenly.

"You bet—me, too," Bess added.

Everyone smiled at this unexpected sign of pugnacity from the usually timid girl.

"Don't look at me that way. I'm an absolute terror when I get angry."

With the preliminary talk behind them, Nancy cleared a large table, spread out a map of the border area, and began marking the points gleaned from the small map found in the wheelchair. She circled the general border area and with Mr. Popov's aid, located the exact spot where the children and Mrs. Popov were hidden.

"It's so close to the border," the man said, "that we thought of making a run for it in the dark, but that would be too much for the smaller children. We'd be sure to make some noise and be discovered in no time."

His listeners fell silent as they considered alternatives. Finally, Nancy tapped her finger on the map and spoke musingly.

"I think I know how to make this whole thing work. Ned, you organize the gang to buy the things I'm going to write down on this list. Then give me some time to make a few phones calls from the booth in the lobby so they can't be traced. We'll meet here in this room at eight o'clock tonight. In the meantime, Mr. Popov, you go to bed and get some sleep."

Nancy's friends read her shopping list with amusement and numerous wisecracks. The list included the following items:

Eleven inner tubes
One small tank of compressed air
Black greasepaint
Theatrical makeup kit
One ball gown circa 1880 with hat to match
One titian wig (long hair)
Six assorted pairs of sunglasses
A limousine, but no driver, to be ready at 7 A.M. the next day
A rental car large enough for six people also ready at 7 A.M.
Two duck calls

Two rubber scuba suits
Detailed maps of the Czech and Hungar-
*   ian borders*
A chauffeur's uniform to fit Eric
A baseball hat to fit Dave

"Sounds wonderful, but where am I going to find a baseball hat in Vienna?" Dave asked.

"And the titian wig," George said. "Are we going into our sister routine, Nancy?"

"I like the eleven inner tubes and the duck calls." Ned laughed. "Can you fathom what'll happen to me when I stroll into an Austrian department store and ask for eleven inner tubes, two duck calls, and six pairs of sunglasses? They'll haul out a straitjacket!"

"I'll take full responsibility if they do!" Nancy giggled.

"You will?" Ned smiled.

"Of course. Now hurry and try to be back here by eight P.M. for a briefing."

As the group started to leave, Ned halted them. "Hold it a minute. Nancy, come here. Look, quick!"

Nancy ran to the window and peered through the draperies. Below, parked on the other side of the street, was a large, light-blue car.

The girl stared inquiringly at Ned. "What am I supposed to be looking at?"

"In the car," Ned said. "In the passenger seat in front. Do you see him?"

Nancy glanced again. This time she felt a lump in her throat. Herr Gutterman, dressed in a suit that matched the color of the car, had curled his lips into an evil smile and was blowing kisses toward the window.

17

Freedom Props

"Well," Nancy said, "it's Herr Gutterman, but what else is new except the pretty paint job on his sedan?"

"He obviously doesn't care if we see him," Ned said.

"No," Nancy replied, "but that's because he must have a lot of his people staked out around here ready to trail us wherever we go. You realize what that means."

"As we go shopping, we'll have to break up. Each of us will have to head for a different store," Ned said.

"Try to lose them and don't let them see what you're buying. That's important."

The group split up as directed and Nancy retired

336

to the lobby phone booth with a handful of coins. In quick succession, she called her father, the River Heights Footlighters Club, which was a little theater group, and finally, an old friend of Mr. Drew's, a prominent and wealthy Austrian.

When Nancy emerged from the booth almost an hour later, she was amused by the sight of a somewhat nervous man with square features and thinning hair who pretended to read a newspaper. It took little imagination to see that he was one of Gutterman's henchmen.

Unable to resist the temptation to create some mischief for her enemy's benefit, Nancy ducked back into the phone booth where she hunted for odd telephone numbers. They included the Animal Rescue League, an insect exterminating company, the backstage number of the Opera House, a plumbing supply store, and finally some random names and numbers picked from the directory.

She wrote them down with great care, then crumpled the paper and stuffed it into the top of her bag, allowing it to protrude. Then she stepped out of the phone booth, and walking fast, brushed against a palm branch which caused the paper to rustle to the floor.

As she reached the elevator, she took out her makeup mirror and, pretending to arrange her hair, watched the man with the square face quickly snatch up the paper.

Nancy smiled. That would keep him occupied for most of the afternoon. He'll drive himself crazy looking for the significance behind that jumble of totally meaningless numbers, she mused.

By eight o'clock, most of the group had reassembled in Dr. Bagley's room and Mr. Popov was emerging from a nap, shower, and shave. The luxury of wearing clean clothes added a flush of happiness to his face.

The last of the team to arrive was Bess. She was gasping for breath and dragging a large box. "Never," she said, exaggerating her breathing for comic effect, "never send a girl out to buy an 1880 ball gown in Vienna. Do you know how much it cost? Even to rent? Do you know how much it weighs? I'll tell you. Five hundred pounds, minimum. Feel this thing."

She heaved the large box up on the bed and Nancy, opening the package, held up a long, beautiful red gown.

"Perfect," she said. "Beautiful. Well done, Private Marvin. We might promote you to corporal for this."

"Don't do me any favors," Bess said, laughing, "unless you assign a captain to go with me next time to carry the heavy stuff."

Nancy ran a check on all the items she had requested. With only a few substitutions, her friends had produced everything.

"All right, Nancy," Dr. Bagley said, "we've followed your instructions. Now we're eager to hear what you have in mind. Obviously, water is involved. But how?"

"Let's take it step by step," Nancy said. "Professor Bagley will lead the first platoon north, here." She pointed to the map. "This is the Czech border, the place the children are supposed to cross according to the phony documents the enemy has already seen."

"So you think that's where Gutterman's gang will be," Ned said.

"I'd like to believe that, but they may not be there. After all, they were trying awfully hard to get a look at Eric's wheelchair also. They were probably the ones who tried to switch his wheelchair for another one. Who knows what they know by now."

"My group is the decoy, right?" Dr. Bagley said.

"Yes. You will leave in the big rental car pretty early and head for the Czech border, the point I still have my finger on. Don't hurry, though. I think it would be fun if you were to drive all over Vienna first. Do some sightseeing, visit the Vienna Woods, have lunch, and generally drive Gutterman's men crazy. They will never be able to figure out what you're doing. Sound reasonable?"

"Uh-huh," Ned said. "But what about the wig, the inner tubes, and the makeup?"

"Aha," Nancy cried, "that's still a secret. Now,

the new wheelchair will be occupied not by Mr. Nagy, but by Mr. Eddleton."

"Me?" Burt gulped. "Why me?"

Nancy grinned. "You're about the same build, almost the same height. You don't really look alike, but you have the same coloring. Now, why don't you try out the chair for size and comfort?"

She led the boy to it, stuck sunglasses on him as well as the baseball cap. Burt smiled broadly.

"How do I look?" he asked.

"Just like a revised edition of Eric Nagy!"

"Ah, please don't praise me too much or it will go to my head."

"So long as you don't lose it," George muttered under her breath.

"Now, George." Nancy smiled. "For one day only, you will be Nancy Drew!"

"Not the famous detective?" Her friend gasped in pretended surprise.

"You will wear this titian wig after we shape it a little bit to look more like my hair."

"Do I get to wear sunglasses, too?" George inquired.

"Of course, and this beautiful, floppy straw hat that will hide most of your face."

"Fantastic," George replied. "And, of course, I will also get to wear your gorgeous white dress. But suppose it doesn't turn out to be a sunny day? Suppose we go mushing up to the Czechoslovakian border and it's raining cats and dogs, and you can hardly see your hand in front of your face. Do we still keep wearing our sunglasses?"

"Mm-hmm. Besides, it won't matter very much," Nancy said, tapping George's head affectionately, "because no one will see you that close up."

"Only when Nancy and I get cornered by a Doberman pinscher," Ned said.

"And Mr. Nickerson," Nancy continued. "How would you like to accompany George in your most attentive manner. You know, stick close and block the enemy's view as much as possible?"

"Oh, so I get to wear sunglasses, too," the boy responded.

"Now let's get down to serious business," Nancy said.

"What about us?" Bess asked, referring to herself and Dave. "Do we turn into wallflowers for the day?"

"Most definitely not. You go along with the gang to the Czech border. Just be your own sweet selves. No disguises necessary."

"Oh, phooey," Bess said, "and I wanted to dress up."

"Why don't you give her an inner tube and some sunglasses, Nancy?" Ned laughed, prompting Nancy to throw a wad of paper at him.

"I'd like to remind everyone that another person will be making the trip to the Czech border and unless our mission succeeds, he won't be coming back."

"You're speaking of Kurt Kessler," Eric said softly.

A hush fell over the group and all joking stopped.

"We have to think of him and those kids at all times," Nancy said. "There's a heavy responsibility weighing on all of us."

"You've explained the decoy operation adequately," the professor said. "But what about the actual rescue of the children? No one has been left unaccounted for except you and Eric."

"And we're the ones who will have to get the children out," Nancy declared.

"Nancy," Ned said with alarm in his voice, "you can't do this by yourselves. You'll need help."

Of course, it wasn't only the awareness of impending danger that had prompted the remark. Ned was also cognizant of his handsome young rival who would be working closely with Nancy.

"On the contrary," she said, "in order to rescue those kids we need the least number of people involved. The less noise we make, the less visible we are, the more successful we'll be."

Ned swung his head back, hurling a sigh in Eric's direction.

"For the decoy operation," Nancy said, "we can hold a big parade, send lots of people to attract attention. So long as Gutterman thinks that Dr. Bagley, Eric, you, and I are up there, he'll be completely fooled."

"I hope so," Ned said. "But why Eric? Why not me?"

Nancy walked over to him, laying her hand gently on his arm. Then, quietly and sweetly, enunciating each word, she said, "Because Eric can speak Hungarian, German, Czech, Russian, Polish, and even some Romanian. That's why."

Hesitating a moment, Ned smiled at Eric. "Hey, good luck. I do and don't envy you."

Eric merely smiled, allowing Dr. Bagley to resume questioning. "Well, we know who is going to try to bring the children out. I'd still like to know how."

"Oh, I forgot to tell you," Nancy said.

"Can you beat that?" Bess put in. "She forgot!"

"Gather round the map," the young detective said. "This," she went on, indicating a long body of water slightly pinched in the middle, "is a lake or *See* as the Austrians call it. It separates Hungary from Austria at this point, and the boundary line runs right through the middle. It is a popular resort area for the Austrians, though the Hungarian end of the lake is not so well developed and has miles of

343

marshes and wetlands. This is the westernmost part of the famous steppe lakes that dot the Hungarian plain."

Nancy went on to explain that an oddity of this body of water, called the *Neusiedler See*, was its extreme shallowness, much like the lakes of Florida, with a depth averaging only four feet and with few points deeper than six feet.

"How did you find all of this out?" Ned asked.

"From an Austrian friend of my father's whom I called. He's well acquainted with the area and helped me make certain necessary arrangements there."

Nancy did not reveal what they were, however. "Anyway," she said, "we'll be able to slip into the water on the Austrian side, walk and wade south across the border, and come up on the shore within a few hundred yards of where the children and the Popovs are hiding. That's when we'll use the duck calls to communicate with them."

"That's fine," Professor Bagley said. "Ingenious, Nancy, really. But some of these children are only six years old. We don't know how many of them can swim. How—oh, of course, the inner tubes."

"That's right," Nancy said. "We'll blow them up in the water using the compressed-air tank, just before we cross the border."

"Why inner tubes?" Bess asked. "Why not the

kind of life jackets they have on airplanes?"

"Because they're bright yellow and it would be a job dying them black. Those jackets are made to be seen. Black inner tubes seemed to be the only answer for us. We'll lash them together and go wading and paddling into Hungary."

"Past the patrol boats. Past the mines. Past whatever protective barriers they may have put in the water," the professor stressed.

Nancy swallowed hard. "Well, we can't prepare for everything on such short notice. If there are boats, mines, barriers, we'll just have to pray we can dodge them and get through. There is always risk in everything that's worthwhile."

"I hate to throw more cold water on it," Dr. Bagley went on, "but one more question. How and where are you planning to go into the water? It stays light until about eleven o'clock in the evening this far north in August. Also, I seem to recall that the lakeshore is a resort area."

"So it's well populated," Ned added.

"That's right," the professor said. "You might have trouble slipping into the lake unnoticed. You'll probably have to cut through someone's property in order to get into the lake."

Nancy could hardly suppress her eagerness. "Oh, Dr. Bagley, I would love to tell you how we're going to make our entry into the water, but I can't. I want

345

it to be a big surprise when we reconvene here at the hotel on Wednesday morning with all those children safe and sound."

"Can't you even give us a hint?" George asked.

"Well, I can say this. I will begin by arriving at the lake in a limousine with Eric posing as my chauffeur. I'll be wearing thick theatrical makeup and that gorgeous ball gown!"

The professor cast his eyes upward as Nancy threw her arms over her head, joyously watching the astonishment on her friends' faces.

"You're right, Nancy." Dr. Bagley chuckled. "It's better to keep it a secret. I don't think my heart could withstand another revelation."

18

A Hero Arrives

When Nancy arrived back at her room, she saw that the message light was blinking on her telephone. She called the front desk and the clerk promptly read her a cablegram from her father confirming that Kurt Kessler would arrive in Vienna that night via a connecting flight from London.

Nancy had barely enough time to phone Professor Bagley and arrange to drive with him to the airport and pick up the film director.

"You know, Dr. Bagley," Nancy said when they were finally on the way, "it's hard for me to remember any mystery I've ever worked on where I had so much responsibility for the lives of other people."

"I know how you feel," the professor replied. "I have very mixed feelings about meeting this extremely talented man. Tonight and tomorrow may be his last free hours unless we succeed."

Despite their trepidations, both Nancy and Dr. Bagley maintained happy expressions as they watched the director cross the terminal from the customs area.

"Mr. Kessler," Nancy said, walking toward him with her hand outstretched, "I was sure I'd recognize you right away."

The man smiled. "And I would know you anywhere, Miss Drew, since I have spent so many hours in your father's office surrounded by your photographs dating back to childhood days."

Nancy blushed crimson. "Oh," she said, "Mr. Kessler, may I present Professor Bagley, the man who was given the job of transferring the children and who asked me to help."

As the director and the professor exchanged greetings, Nancy studied Mr. Kessler's face. She was saddened to see how very old he seemed.

Early newspaper photographs revealed him to have been extremely handsome as a young man. Now, though he was only middle-aged, his good looks had been replaced by deep lines etched by pain on weather-beaten skin. His eyes, which were naturally deep-set, were even more sunken; and his hair was grayish-white and quite thin.

He did all he could, however, to conceal his painful memories. He spoke with enthusiasm, and the soft, sad eyes were still capable of flashing with humor. As they walked back to the car, Nancy listened to his conversation with Dr. Bagley, thinking of Kurt Kessler weeping, when he was alone, for the things he had shown in *Captive Witness*.

I just have to find his film, she thought.

As the threesome rode back to the hotel, Nancy felt compelled to tell Mr. Kessler, "I'm the one who's guilty for getting you involved in all of this. If we fail to bring those children out and you are forced to go back across that border, I don't know what I'll—"

The director interrupted quickly. "No, Nancy. Never blame yourself. With or without you, the same things would have happened. The only difference now is I have you on my side."

"What bothers me," Dr. Bagley said, "is that even if we do manage to free the children, what's to prevent your enemies from trying to stop other people who want to leave and demanding you in exchange?"

"Look, anything is possible," Kessler replied, "but I think this is a single attempt. If they get me, they win; but if we get the orphans instead, there will be so much publicity that no one would dare trouble me again. By then, they will have been exposed and who would believe otherwise?"

"They want the world to see Kurt Kessler crossing the border voluntarily," the professor muttered.

"Of course," the director said. "They will probably have a crew there to film it, and with such a film, they can issue all kinds of propaganda—how the Americans forced me to make *Captive Witness*, how it is nothing but lies."

"So you don't think they intend to kidnap you?" Dr. Bagley asked.

Kessler shook his head. "No. Kidnapping me would serve no purpose. They want me to give up freely."

"It's so unfair and cruel," Nancy commented.

"On the contrary, Nancy," the film director said, "it's insane." Then his voice dropped. "What I dread most is that if I cross the border, I will find that my film has been destroyed."

He lapsed into a brooding silence which remained unbroken until the professor spoke.

"Mr. Kessler, I promise you that under the plan we've worked out there would be no way for them to get you across the frontier unless the film and the children are turned over."

"Besides," Nancy added, "we already know they don't have the orphans because just this evening we met Emile Popov, the man who is hiding them in Hungary."

Kurt Kessler sighed happily. "There are so many

exceptional people in this world. America has produced you and Dr. Bagley, and now you tell me about this Popov."

The discussion faded as the hotel came in sight. Nancy persuaded room service to serve a late snack in the professor's room where introductions were made to Eric and Mr. Popov. They excused themselves quickly and went to Ned's room next door, leaving the trio to talk alone for another hour. Nancy outlined the plan involving the decoy group and a strike team to accomplish the final mission.

"You are a marvel," Kessler said admiringly, "and if we all survive tomorrow, I am going to make a film about Nancy Drew."

The young detective floundered for an answer. "You may change your mind after you see me in action," she said, then realizing that wasn't quite what she meant, added quickly, "Of course, I do feel confident about—"

"I know you do," Mr. Kessler interposed gently, "and I am very grateful to you."

Without any further discussion, Nancy said good night and went to her room. At eleven the next morning, she heard a knock at the door. It was George wearing the titian wig, Nancy's dress, and the floppy straw hat. Standing right next to her was Ned. Their hands were clasped and they were gazing deeply into each other's eyes—or as deeply as they possibly could through their enormous sunglasses.

Nancy had to put her hand over her mouth to stifle her amusement. Then she hissed at him, "Stop that! You'll give us all away! Now scoot!"

Blowing kisses, Ned and George disappeared down the hall. Nancy went to the window, certain it was under surveillance, and peeked out to observe the rest of the decoy team stepping into the big rental car.

Burt, disguised as Eric, was being helped out of his wheelchair and into the front seat. Bess, Dave, and the professor were there, as was Kurt Kessler. Presently, Ned and George joined the group.

As their car pulled away, Nancy searched in vain for some sign of Gutterman's powder-blue car. It was nowhere in sight. A black Mercedes, however, containing two of the men she had seen skulking in the lobby, shot out from the curb and began shadowing the professors's vehicle.

Where was Gutterman, though? Nancy wondered.

Either he had already gone to Czechoslovakia and would greet the professor's team at the border, or he was lurking somewhere else.

What also vaguely worried her was how Gutterman expected to persuade Kessler into surrendering if Gutterman did not produce the children. Did he know where they were? Had he already swooped down on them in Hungary and transported them to the Czech border?

Nancy could imagine his cruel laughter as she and Eric plunged through the dark waters of the lake, sending out their duck-call signal in vain!

Then another chilling thought occurred to her. Suppose ten other children had been assembled at the Czech border, pretending that they were the orphans? Who would know the difference? Only Eric, whose thirteen-year-old cousin was among them, and Eric would be far away on the Hungarian frontier.

Oh, why didn't I ask Dr. Bagley if he had any way of confirming the children's identity? Nancy chided herself.

She puffed her cheeks and blew out the air in a great sigh of frustration. She had missed checking out one very important detail, so it would have to be left to fate!

Going to her dressing table, she opened the theatrical makeup kit and for the next hour, worked to transform herself from a fresh-faced young woman into a nineteenth-century lady at least ten years older, complete with a black beauty mark on her cheek.

Then she wriggled into the tight confines of the beautiful, glittering red ball gown. A glossy brunette wig with long, soft curls topped the disguise.

Although she wasn't sure if the wig style was typical of the late 1800s, she decided it complimented the outfit perfectly.

At four o'clock, Eric telephoned. "Your car awaits, madam," he said.

"Thank you, Otto," Nancy said. "I shall be down immediately."

Making no attempt to slip out quietly, Nancy swept down the main staircase into the lobby. Onlookers stared at her incredulously as she waltzed to the door where Eric, in a black wig and large black mustache, took her arm and led her to the rented limousine.

Nancy was completely aware that she had stepped past at least two of Gutterman's men but felt confident that they hadn't recognized her.

As the limousine drove off slowly, the assembled doorman, porters, guests, and passersby issued a round of applause. Nancy waved graciously.

"Who is that?" an American woman inquired upon entering the hotel.

"Oh," said the doorman, not wishing to appear ignorant of the hotel's guests, "she's a very famous actress. She stays here all the time."

All the way out of Vienna, Eric kept checking his rearview mirror to see if anyone was following them. Half an hour later, he said with a tone of caution, "I think we're in the clear, Nancy."

"I hope so, but keep an eye on that mirror. By the

way, Eric, you make a lovely chauffeur. And that mustache!"

"You like it?"

"It's beautiful."

"And may I compliment you, madam. You look wonderful. A little overdone for daytime perhaps, but so what?"

"Do you know the route by heart?" Nancy asked.

"Every inch including side roads. We are presently on Route 16 south. We will turn east on 304 through Eisenstadt. Then to Schützen, and after that I have to wind down some smaller roads until we reach Mörbisch."

"When we get there, I'll take over."

"I can't wait to find out why you are dressed that way." Eric laughed.

"You will—soon." Nancy giggled.

But their good humor was dampened when Eric, looking in his mirror, noticed a car following them. He alerted Nancy who, peering through her binoculars, picked up the powder-blue sedan with Gutterman and Burger inside.

"Ooh!" Nancy said in exasperation. "How—how? Gutterman seems so dumb sometimes but he isn't. He must have extrasensory perception or something close to it."

"I can try to lose them on a side road," Eric volunteered, frowning.

"No, we'd only wind up in trouble for breaking the speed limit. Do me a favor, though. Pull into the next service area and look for a spot where we can't be observed too easily."

Within a few minutes, Eric found the right place and brought the big limousine to a halt. Gutterman and Burger drove by trying to appear disinterested.

"Doesn't he realize we'd spot that blue car a mile away?" Nancy muttered. "I don't understand that man at all."

Hurriedly, they bought several cans of motor oil. Nancy climbed into the trunk, carefully protecting her voluminous dress. Eric propped the trunk lid so that it stayed open about eight inches and handed Nancy the oilcans and an opener.

They soon overtook Gutterman and Burger who had pulled over to wait at a roadside stand. As soon as the limousine went past, the evil duo started trailing them again. Nancy, feeling the car round a big bend, punched holes in two of the cans and began pouring the oil on the road. She quickly opened two more cans and repeated the process.

Gutterman and Burger, who were several hundred yards to the rear, could not see this until it was too late. As their car hit the slippery fluid, it went into a long skid, sending it off the road, down a ravine, and into a swamp where it settled in mud.

Eric stopped the limousine at a stand, and quickly notified the police of an oil slick so that other motorists would be alerted. Then, with Nancy rejoining him, they resumed their ride.

"Gutterman will be steaming now," the young detective said, her blue eyes dancing, "but I had no choice."

Inwardly, though, she was beginning to worry. Gutterman had probably guessed where she was going. He must have known she was heading for the outdoor theater on the lake at Mörbisch. Otherwise, why would she be wearing theatrical attire?

Nancy now revealed her complete plan to Eric. She would join the chorus in *The Merry Widow,* an operetta being performed at Mörbisch. The theater was one of Austria's most popular tourist attractions. Since Nancy had played in the Footlighters' production of the same operetta, she was capable of singing the entire score. She had arranged to become a member of the Mörbisch chorus for one night only.

"But what does all this have to do with rescuing ten children?" Eric questioned.

"Everything," Nancy said. "Remember, the professor said we might have trouble getting into the water without being seen? Well, the theater is built out over the lake. When the show finishes, the sun will have set and we'll be able to slip into the water behind the building, inflate our inner tubes, and sail for Hungary."

Eric whistled in admiration. "What an idea! Pure genius!"

"I wouldn't go that far." Nancy grinned as they pulled up to the theater.

"Tell me, how did you manage to talk your way into the theatrical company?"

"That was easy," Nancy said, shaking her brown wig. "Oh, and there's the man who worked me into the company. Let me introduce you."

Nancy rushed toward him, hugging the tall, white-haired man as he stood in front. His name was Georg Waldheim, a dear friend of her father's. He was a patron of the arts, and knew many people connected with the theater, so it was simple enough for him to gain permission for Nancy to sing.

Saying good-bye to Herr Waldheim, who whispered good luck to her in her mission, Nancy led Eric backstage. He was carrying the suitcase filled with the inner tubes, the small air tank, and the rubber suits. Eric was to remain there throughout the performance. He sat quietly, waiting for the dressing rooms to empty, then scurried out a window and climbed down on the pilings with the suitcase. He set up camp where no one could see him sitting on the wooden supports.

Nancy went onstage and sang her heart out as night began to fall. Eric, meanwhile, inflated the tubes, donned his rubber suit, and applied black greasepaint to his skin in order to stay better hidden in the dark.

But toward the end of the last act, as Nancy was caught up in the swell of lush melodies, she happened to glance out into the audience. There with his opera glasses trained on the performers was Herr Gutterman!

19

Across the Frontier

The girl detective had to conquer the urge to crouch down or hide behind the other singers. Any movement she made would make her stand out immediately, and Gutterman would be sure to identify her.

So, instead, she continued to sing to the very last note. But the minute the lights were dimmed for curtain calls, she broke out of the line and raced toward the dressing rooms. Quickly, she wriggled out of her dress into her bathing attire, and again slipped the gown over her head.

Before the rest of the cast had left the stage, Nancy was out a side door and approaching the water. It was almost as dark as the night itself, and not until she reached the protective shadows of the trees did she dare to remove the dress covering her scuba suit.

She joined Eric on the pilings where the inflated inner tubes lay lashed together with cord. Nancy covered her hands and face with the remaining greasepaint and waited with Eric for the cast and crew to leave the theater.

Above them they could hear conversation mixed with laughter and footsteps. Then a voice cut through the noise. "Nancy Drew! Has anyone seen her? I have an urgent message for her."

Nancy and Eric exchanged glances. "I know it's Gutterman. He has an uncanny ability to alter his voice and appearance, but I'm positive it's he."

Her companion nodded as the voice called out again.

"What does he expect me to do? Rush right out and say 'Here I am'?" Nancy said.

"More likely, he's hoping somebody else will spot you and say 'There she is!' " Eric replied. "On the other hand, what if Dr. Bagley is trying to reach us?"

"No chance," Nancy said brightly.

"Why not?"

"Because he doesn't know where we are, remember?"

Eric grinned. "You're right."

"I only kept this part of the plan a secret to surprise everybody later. Now it's working to our advantage."

Although it seemed like hours, probably no more than twenty minutes passed until everyone had left and the theater lights were extinguished. There was silence except for the night sounds of the lake and the chirping and shrill of insects and night birds. Then Eric groaned.

"What's the matter, Eric?"

"The car. It's still there. I left it in plain sight. Gutterman will see it. He knows we drove down in a limousine so he'll know you're still in the area."

"And he'll go right to the closest Hungarian border crossing and alert the guards. The whole frontier force will be onto us!" Nancy cried. "We have to move fast!"

Slipping into the water and pushing the raft of inner tubes ahead of them, they began moving south as fast as they could without making splashing sounds.

"I can't see you," Nancy whispered back. "Everything is black on black."

"Maybe we should hold hands," the young man suggested.

"Well," Nancy said, smiling to herself, "we can always hang onto the string of tubes. As long as we don't lose them, we'll always be together."

It was Eric's turn to smile, his white teeth gleaming in the night. "We could," he said, "but it'd be nicer the other way."

"Eric," Nancy said, "no offense but you'll have to keep your mouth closed because your beautiful white teeth shine like a beacon."

He chuckled. "Okay, let's go. No more small talk."

Half wading and half swimming, they made good time. Nancy estimated their speed at about one and a half miles per hour or, roughly speaking, half the speed of walking. Therefore, it would take them approximately an hour to reach the point where they expected to find the Popovs and the children.

Occasionally, they stumbled into holes but soon learned to glide with their feet just grazing the bottom.

The shoreline became increasingly swamplike as they moved into Hungarian territory, and there were few lights to show them where land was. Since it was now close to midnight, most house lights had been extinguished. For a while, the two young people lost their bearings and were forced to stop.

"What I wouldn't give for one burst of moonlight," Nancy said.

She had no sooner spoken when a tremendous flash of light zigzagged across the sky followed by a clap of thunder. In the glow that spread over the whole lake, they could see clearly that they weren't far from the twisted tree that Popov had said was near his hiding place.

"Are you all right, Nancy?" Eric asked.

"Yes, but scared. I thought they were shooting artillery at us."

"Give them the signal," Eric went on.

Taking out her duck call, Nancy blew three short, sharp quacks. There was no answer. She tried again, but still no reply.

"Should we go up onshore?" Eric asked.

Nancy was about to say yes when they heard the answering cry of Popov's duck call. Moments later, faint shadows bulked out of the night and Nancy and Eric waded ashore to meet them.

Emile Popov was carrying one child, a six-year-old. "He can sleep through anything," he said, handing the boy to Eric. "Be careful when you put him in the tube. The water will wake him and we don't want him to cry out."

Nancy and Mrs. Popov took the other two six-year-olds. The older children gathered around Emile Popov, holding onto a rope he carried to keep them together.

Eric began speaking softly to the children, paying special attention to the thirteen-year-old boy who was his cousin. In spite of their joyous reunion, the two kept their voices low.

Nancy now took charge of painting everyone's

faces black, but as she finished, Eric whispered nervously.

"Listen! Everyone be still."

The group froze at the sound of several automobiles approaching.

"Trouble," Mr. Popov said. "They're coming. No one else would be coming at this hour. Quickly! Quickly!"

Shoving off and keeping low behind the high reeds that covered the inshore waters, the little convoy began moving north again toward the Austrian border.

Car doors opened and closed now and the loud voices of Hungarian police guards drifted across the lake. They trained their flashlights on the hut where the refugees had hidden, then swung the lights toward the shore.

Did they suspect that the escape was being made by water? Would they send out boats? Nancy knew that the Hungarians had small patrol craft as did the Austrians, but since this was a relatively peaceful border, she hadn't worried about them.

The urgency of the situation prompted all of the children, except the smallest, to slip out of the tubes and help push. Each of the older ones stayed close to a younger one, using a buddy system they had devised over months of hiding throughout Eastern Europe.

The searchers, running now along the shore, shone their lights out across the water.

"Stop," Nancy whispered.

Everyone halted instantly. The flashlight beams played over and around them, but the darkness of their attire and the cover of tall reeds kept them from being seen.

If only it would rain to block their vision, Nancy thought.

But the rain didn't come and the flashlights continued to sweep across the lake. Then, after ten minutes, drops began to dot the water. Within another minute, a full-scale storm was raging, and the curtains of water made the flashlights useless.

Jubilantly, the convoy started moving again. Pushing and swimming as hard as they could, they approached the Austrian border. The flashlights, now dim blobs, receded toward the direction from which they had come.

"Only two hundred yards to go," Eric whispered over his shoulder.

"Look!" Nancy exclaimed suddenly.

Lying directly in front of them was a powerful light that attempted to cut through the heavy rain. It was mounted on a small patrol boat.

For the first time since their mission began, Nancy wanted to cry. There was no way to tell if it was a Hungarian or Austrian craft in the dark. They were

367

so close to freedom, and the children were so cold from the lake water that they struggled to keep their teeth from chattering.

Oh, please help us, Nancy prayed as Eric moved to her side.

"I've got an idea," he whispered. "I'm going to swim out toward the center of the lake, a few hundred yards or so, then cross to the Austrian side. Then I'll start shouting and screaming like a maniac. The patrol is sure to be distracted enough so you can scoot through with the kids."

"Oh, Eric, am I glad you dreamed that one up. I just ran out of ideas. Be careful, though."

"I will."

It took the young man fifteen minutes to position himself. By then, the rain had slackened and the light from the boat was scanning the area with such intensity that the little group was forced to wade far back into the reeds and crouch low.

Suddenly, Nancy heard Eric. He was whooping and yelling like an Indian tribal attack on a frontier fort. The men in the patrol boat reacted instantly and cruised toward the uproar.

Pushing out of the reeds once again, Nancy and the Popovs covered the final distance of the border in five minutes. They didn't stop until they reached the theater. Coming out of the water into the chill night air, some of the children at last began to whimper. The Popovs went from one to the other, murmuring words of comfort for they were now safe on Austrian soil.

While the couple led the children to the limousine where warm blankets awaited them, Nancy observed an Austrian patrol boat pull ashore with Eric and two Austrian policeman. They wanted to see for themselves if the young man's tale about the refugees was true. Discovering that it was, they saluted and left.

Of course, jamming so many people into one automobile, even though it was large and ten of the occupants small, was no easy task. But nothing could dampen anyone's spirits. Within half an hour, most of the children had fallen asleep. Nancy was surrounded by four of the smallest ones in the front seat.

"Are you happy, Eric?" she asked.

"It's a dream come true," he said, "and may I add that you were fantastic."

"Oh, I don't know about that," she said with a lilt in her voice. "You're the one who really wins the honors. If you hadn't pulled that stunt, we never would have made it."

"Aw, shucks," Eric said, imitating the twang of Old West movie heroes. "It weren't nothin'."

Nancy laughed, but a sobering thought stopped her. Everything except recovering Kurt Kessler's

369

film had been accomplished. He had risked his life to help save the children, but the young detective's personal assignment to find *Captive Witness* had failed.

For the rest of the trip back to the hotel, she racked her brain. Was there no way to recover that film?

20

Herr Gutterman Unmasked

When they finally reached the hotel, the Popovs and the children were met by members of the refugee organization. It would arrange their transportation to relatives and friends in England and America.

Professor Bagley then related the events at the Czechoslovakian border. "They tried to fool us by showing up with ten other children who had been trained to lie about their identities. Fortunately, I had been given photographs of the real orphans. How the Hungarians carried on, screaming and threatening!"

"George took off her wig and waved it at them." Bess giggled. "That really infuriated them."

"Then Burt got out of the wheelchair and started dancing with her." Dave laughed. "The commissar or whoever he was turned purple!"

"On the whole, it has been a huge success." Dr. Bagley smiled. "Thanks largely to Nancy."

"You are much too kind, sir," she said. "Everyone did his or her part beautifully. The only thing that has me down is the fact I can't find *Captive Witness*.

Kurt Kessler, who was enjoying a cup of coffee and chatting with Ned, turned to reassure Nancy again. "Yes, I wish I had my film back, but I'll make other films—better ones, too. Please don't worry so."

Nancy explained, though, that it was irritating to have seen half of it yet to be unable to locate the place where it had been shown.

"You actually saw it?" the director cried, causing Nancy to reveal the incident of her meeting with Gutterman.

"Unfortunately, Vienna has no grid system of streets like other cities," Nancy said, "so the twists and turns we took really confused me." She paused a second. "I did hear certain sounds, though."

"What were they?" Kurt Kessler inquired with mounting eagerness.

"Well, trains. A train yard, to be exact, and a merry-go-round."

The film director furrowed his brow for a few moments, absentmindedly pulling at his shirt cuffs. Suddenly, he stopped and gripped the table with both hands. "Wait a minute!" he exclaimed. "I stayed in Vienna for a time before going to America, and I think I know where you were."

Nancy and the director dashed down the three flights of stairs, found the rental car and, with Mr. Kessler at the wheel, they headed north.

"You were somewhere between the great railroad yards up ahead and the Prater amusement park on the right. The building with its twelve steps has to be around here."

Completely elated, Nancy shone her flashlight on the buildings as her companion drove the car up and down the streets in the area. They found nothing, though.

"Let's not give up yet," Nancy said, causing him to speed the vehicle in another direction. Silently, they rode down a series of side streets lined with more old, run-down buildings. Then Kurt Kessler turned a sharp corner, and Nancy gasped in excitement. "There—down that side street. The second building! It has twelve steps!"

Kessler counted them and accelerated the gas pedal. When he finally halted the car, they stepped out fast and hurried up to the front door. It was locked, but it took the director only a few seconds to

373

open the lock with a tiny metal pick.

"Someday I'll have to tell you how I escaped out of Hungary," he said to Nancy who was grinning almost as broadly as he was.

Once inside, the young detective closed her eyes, recalling how she had been turned when taken there by Gutterman. She indicated the door to the director. He motioned her to stand back as he listened carefully.

"Someone is in there," he said softly. Then, without another word, he put his shoulder to the door and burst through. Nancy was right on his heels.

"Good evening," came a voice from a chair that swiveled to face the two visitors.

It was Adolph Gutterman! In one hand, he was holding the film *Captive Witness* and in the other, a flaming cigarette lighter. His eyes seemed glazed as if he were entranced by the fire.

Kessler moved forward, slowly, staring into them. "Hagedorn?" he said softly. "Heinrich Hagedorn?"

Gutterman did not reply. The lighter was flaming wildly now, threatening to singe the man's finger. Gently, Kessler took the lighter and then the film. He placed it in its tin container.

"You know him?" Nancy asked in bewilderment, adding, "I don't understand—he just let you take the film right out of his hand without a protest."

Kessler lowered his eyes toward Hagedorn's trembling fingers as they covered his face, muffling a deep cry.

"We were in the film business together when we were young," Kessler murmured. "He was a good director. A great actor. A master of disguises, voice changes. One of the best in the world."

"How did he come to be a spy then?" Nancy asked.

As she spoke, the man slumped back in his chair, frozen in shock.

"It's a long story," the director continued. "I don't even know it all. He lost both parents in Nazi concentration camps. Those who took control, fed him, educated him, trained him to act and direct. But he was too wild, too creative. He wanted to do things his own way.

"He made a short film that was the most devastating attack on political oppression I have ever seen."

"More devastating than *Captive Witness?*" Nancy asked.

"Much more. He went to prison for years because of it. Then suddenly, he was released on condition that he make propaganda films for his country. What he really was being trained for was a future in espionage. He became a spy in order to keep his wife and children fed."

Now Kessler's voice began to waver. "He had

compromised everything for the people he cared about most—"

"I still don't understand, though, why he just let you take that film right out of his hand," Nancy interrupted quietly.

Kessler took a deep breath before going on. "Because of our friendship, I suppose," he said.

"He and I were in prison at the same time. When he finally managed to get out, he helped me escape. I remember he said it was more important for my film work to be seen than his.

"Unfortunately, neither Heinrich nor I realized that our captors would pin my escape on him. The next thing I learned was that his wife and children had been killed in an automobile accident."

"How terrible!" Nancy gasped.

She gazed at the man in the chair whose eyes were now pinched shut. No wonder he had behaved so erratically, appearing brilliant one moment and childlike another. He was only playing the role of someone who wouldn't permit himself to be hurt again. Seeing Kurt Kessler, however, had revived those feelings he had attempted, perhaps unsuccessfully, to abandon.

After Kessler had placed a call to the police, Nancy told him thoughtfully, "I've learned a lot from this experience, mostly that you can't understand what other people have to endure unless you put yourself in their shoes."

Of course, she had no idea that she would soon face another, similar challenge when she solved *The Gondolier's Secret*.

"That's why I make movies," the film director said. "I made *Captive Witness* to show the world how the other half is forced to live."

Nancy's eyes flashed to the tin container Kessler had held tightly since he took it from his old friend. "And I guarantee that everyone who sees this picture will be a captive audience!" she exclaimed.

A few days later, when the young detective and her traveling companions were gathered at the Vienna Film Festival awards ceremony, they listened intently to the names of those recommended as producer of the Best Foreign Documentary. Kurt Kessler was one of five nominees, all of whom had done outstanding film work.

"I'll be so disappointed if he doesn't win," Bess confided to Nancy as someone on stage opened an envelope.

Kessler, who sat on the other side of the girl, murmured under his breath during the endless wait, then gasped as his name was called. A huge round of applause went up from the audience.

"Oh, I'm so happy for you," Nancy told him, letting him step quickly into the aisle.

When he reached the microphone, everyone was still clapping loudly and he quieted them with his hands. "Please, please. You are all too kind," he said. "I cannot accept this award alone. I must share it with someone without whose courageous help I would not be standing here now."

A murmur rose among his listeners, as he paused before going on. "Nancy Drew, will you please join me here?"

"Me?" Nancy said quietly.

"Yes, you!" her other friends whispered from behind, coaxing her out of her seat. "You deserve it, Nancy!"

Nancy Drew® in

The Mystery of the Winged Lion

The Mystery of the Winged Lion was first published
in the UK in a single volume in 1983 by
Angus & Robertson (UK) Ltd.

Contents

1

Crash in the Night

"Isn't Venice romantic?" Bess Marvin sighed dreamily. Her eyes drifted from the hotel terrace where she and her cousin George Fayne were sitting to the moonlit canal that barely rippled under the oar of a passing gondola.

"Oh, it's okay," the pretty, dark-haired girl said, mildly enthusiastic.

"Is that all you can say?" Bess replied. "I'm sure if Burt were here, you'd feel different. I mean, just imagine if he and Dave were—"

"And don't forget Ned," Nancy Drew interrupted as she walked toward the table.

Ned Nickerson, Dave Evans, and Burt Eddleton were special friends of the girls.

"Nancy!" Bess exclaimed, a bit startled. "What happened to you? We were beginning to think you were kidnapped by the hotel concierge!"

Despite the smile the blond girl thought she would elicit, she noticed a grimness in Nancy's face that hadn't been there earlier when they arrived in Italy.

"Something's wrong, isn't it?" George said, making the same observation.

"I'm afraid so."

"Don't tell me there's a mystery in the Venetian air?" Bess put in. She rested her chin in one hand. "I mean, we *are* going to finish our vacation in peace, aren't we, Nancy? Please tell me we are."

"I wish I could," the young, titian-haired detective answered.

Her blue eyes traveled to the darkened windows of the great domed church across the Grand Canal, the largest course of water dividing the city. "If I live to be as old as that basilica, Santa Maria della Salute, I will never understand how this happened."

"How what happened? What are you trying to tell us?" Bess pressed the girl. Nancy drew in a deep breath.

"Ned, Burt, and Dave are in jail," she said.

"What?" her listeners cried aloud.

"Sh-sh. Keep your voices down," Nancy cautioned. "We just received a message—"

"From the boys?" Bess interrupted. "Where are they?"

"Here."

"Here—in Venice?"

"Let Nancy talk," George rebuked her cousin, but found it difficult to follow her own advice. "I thought they were flying directly back to New York after the Emerson College tour ended."

"That's what I thought," Nancy replied. "But now I have a hunch they were planning to surprise us."

"So they're in Venice!" Bess exclaimed.

She was ready to ask several more questions but Nancy quickly intervened. "The fact is I don't know any of the details—least of all, why they're in jail. Ned apparently phoned here. The message was brief and there was a phone number, which I tried calling. Unfortunately, I couldn't find anyone who spoke English.

"I finally asked the concierge to get on the line. He said something in Italian, mentioned Ned's name, and from that point on, all he kept saying was '*Si . . . si . . . si.*' When he hung up, he told me that the boys were in jail, and we would have to go there if we wanted to know more."

"Incredible," Bess said, pushing her chair back from the table.

"Where are you going?" George asked.

"To the jail, where else?"

"But it's after ten," Nancy said, "and according to the concierge, we must wait until morning when we can bring a suitable interpreter with us. He promised to get one."

"Gee, I hate to leave the guys stuck in that place overnight," Bess objected.

"We all do," George said, "but I doubt we could get them out without the help of a lawyer and maybe even the American Embassy."

Nancy now revealed that she had placed a telephone call to her father in River Heights. He was a distinguished attorney whose international connections might prove instrumental in freeing the three young collegians.

"There's a six-hour difference between Italy and the States," Nancy said, "so it's almost four-thirty at home. Dad's probably still in the office. At least, I hope so." She glanced at her watch. "Let's go back to our room. That call should be coming through soon."

Bess took one final glance at the glint of light dancing on the black water. It filtered out of several windows opposite the Gritti Palace Hotel where the girls were staying, including those of a large store displaying two fully lit crystal chandeliers and other glassware. Above the store was an elegant apartment framed in arches that curved roundly to an inverted V.

Suddenly, however, the chandeliers were turned off and there was a faint shatter of glass.

"One of the chandeliers must've fallen!" Bess cried out, causing Nancy and George to stop in their tracks.

"Well, I'm sure it didn't drop all by itself," Nancy said. "Maybe there's a thief in the store! Come on, we'd better investigate!"

"What about your father's phone call?" Bess asked as the young detective hurried ahead of her.

"I'll leave a message with the concierge to tell Dad I'll call him when we get back," Nancy said. After stopping in the hotel lobby for a moment, the three friends darted outside to the gondola station, where the gondoliers were talking animatedly. Apparently, they were unaware of what had happened across the way.

In the few Italian words she knew, Nancy persuaded one of them, a man with a full black beard and a deep crust of wrinkle over his eyes, to take her and the cousins to the other side of the canal. She told him what they had witnessed.

"Oh, I heard crash," the gondolier said in halting English. "But did not know where come from."

"The thief's probably gone by now," Bess announced as the boat pushed off.

"I'm not sure of that," Nancy said. "There's an awful lot of crystal in that place."

The ride took less than five minutes, and Nancy requested the gondolier to wait for them while they ran down the alley that led to the front entrance of the store. Upon reaching the building, they paused indecisively.

"There's nobody here now!" Bess whispered hoarsely.

"Sh!" George said, as footsteps sounded inside.

"He's coming out," Nancy murmured, pulling

her friends into an adjoining doorway.

"What if he's bigger than we are?" Bess went on, but neither of her friends answered.

The door was opening slowly, almost too slowly to suit Nancy. Then it closed again.

Oh, why doesn't the thief come out? Nancy wondered, her eyes suddenly lowering to the pavement.

The angle of a nearby street lamp had caught the girls' figures in its glow and threw their shadows in front of the store!

"Look!" she whispered to her friends, pointing to the shadows. "He's seen us."

"Let's get out of here," Bess pleaded.

"Just a minute," George said. "The door's opening again."

She felt the muscles in her throat tighten as the entrance remained ajar. No one emerged, however. Then, on impulse, Nancy surged forward, peering inside.

"Oh, Nancy, please don't," Bess begged as the young detective stepped into the store.

"Come on, there's no one here now," Nancy urged.

Reluctantly, Bess and George followed. They

tiptoed through one room into another, until they came to an open back door that led to the canal.

"He's gone!" Nancy exclaimed in disgust, staring at a speedboat that was just leaving.

"And we ought to go, too," Bess murmured.

Just then, as the boat passed the large window facing the canal, the intruder threw a heavy stone. It shattered the window instantly, setting off a shrill alarm.

"Come on, now we have to get out of here!" Nancy exclaimed, and rushed her friends to the front entrance. They ran into the street and down the alley into the waiting gondola.

"Hurry, please hurry!" Bess told the man.

The ear-piercing shrill of the alarm made him hesitate only a moment before he pushed off again across the black water. When they reached the dock, he helped the girls out of the boat, accepting several bills from Nancy.

"*Grazie*," she said, thanking him and darting toward the hotel without turning back to catch the look of puzzlement in the man's face.

To her dismay, there was no message from her father; and as they took the elevator upstairs, Bess added another note of concern.

"You realize, of course, that the gondolier thinks we broke into the store," she said.

"Well, we didn't," George said. "The door was wide open, if you remember."

"Try explaining that to the *polizia*," Nancy said. "I know we didn't do anything wrong, but somehow I do feel very guilty about it."

Once they were in their room, she swung back the shutters that overlooked the street entrance to the hotel. She saw their gondolier talking with someone who wore a hotel uniform, and motioned the cousins to the window.

Bess moaned. "He's probably turning us in."

"Maybe we ought to call the police before they do," George agreed.

"I suggest you learn a few words in Italian first," Nancy said. "Like 'I am not a thief.'"

"Very funny," Bess said.

"I'm dead serious," Nancy replied, as the jingle of the phone suddenly broke the conversation.

"There they are. The police. They've come to take us away." Bess groaned. "Well, at least the boys will have company in jail."

To Nancy's relief, however, the call was from

her father's office. "It's Dad," she announced happily, her expression quickly fading when his secretary spoke.

Miss Hanson explained that Mr. Drew had left town on business and was not expected back until the next evening.

"Oh, I see," Nancy said. "Well, would you please ask him to call us at the Gritti Palace Hotel in Venice as soon as you hear from him? Also, please call our housekeeper, Hannah Gruen, in case Dad checks in at home. It's very important."

"I'll be glad to, Nancy," the woman replied as the young detective said good-bye and hung up.

The girls spoke little while they readied for bed, taking turns in the shower and slipping into nightgowns before they slid under the covers. They had no sooner switched off the lamps, when a heavy rap on the door startled them.

"Don't answer it," Bess said fearfully, but Nancy had already turned the lights back on.

"What? And pretend we're not here?" George said, shaking her head. Nancy scrambled out of bed.

"Who's there?" she asked, throwing on a robe.

Surprisingly, no one answered but there was a second, more insistent knock.

"Who is it?" Nancy asked again. She stepped closer to the door.

This time a voice responded, but the words unraveled so quickly, the girl did not catch all of them. One, however, was painfully clear—*polizia*! The police!

2

Ned's Story

While Nancy reached for the door handle, Bess and George leaped out of bed and pulled on their robes.

"Oh, Nancy." Bess shivered nervously. She imagined that on the other side of the door was a big, burly police officer holding very large handcuffs.

To her amazement, though, it was only the night clerk. He smiled in a perfunctory manner.

"I am sorry to disturb you," he said in a heavy Italian accent, "but it seems that Andreoli, the gondolier—well, he told me you girls may be in some trouble."

He searched Nancy's face, then glanced at

the others, waiting patiently for an answer.

"You're right," Bess said impulsively, and felt a sharp nudge from her cousin.

"On the contrary," George said, "someone else is going to be in trouble as soon as we find out who he is."

"I'm sorry. I don't understand," the clerk replied.

"It's very simple," Nancy said and explained the details of what had just happened.

When she finished, the man released a long sigh. "I think perhaps it would be wiser if you told all of this to the police. Do you not agree?"

"Yes, I do. In fact, I plan to tell them everything tomorrow when we have an interpreter with us. The concierge said he would locate one to help us on another matter."

"I see. Very well, then. Good night."

As the clerk walked away, Nancy noticed that the bottoms of his pants legs were wet. Since it had not been raining, that seemed odd, and she mentioned her observation to the others.

"Maybe he fell into the canal." Bess giggled, feeling greatly relieved that her imaginary policeman had proved otherwise.

Nancy rolled her eyes in mock disgust. "Let's

go to sleep," she said. "Tomorrow's going to be a full day."

In the morning, the three girls awoke to a steady downbeat of rain. They dressed more warmly than usual, putting light slickers over their clothes, then headed for the terrace where they seated themselves under the protective tarpaulin cover. Immediately, they noticed the name of the glass showroom that bore a large crack in its front window.

"*Artistico Vetro*," Nancy said, translating the words. "Artistic glass. I wonder who owns it."

"Probably an old Venetian family," George replied, shifting her glance to the menu in front of her. "Prosciutto and melon. That sounds good."

Bess wrinkled her nose. "I'd rather have yogurt," she said, "with honey, of course."

"For a minute there, I thought you had finally decided to go on a diet!" her slim, athletic cousin teased, then turned to Nancy. "What about you? What are you going to have this fine, misty morning?"

"I don't know yet. I've been studying that store across the canal."

"Well, other than that hole in the window,"

Bess commented, "I don't see anything of interest."

"Even so, I'd still like to investigate further," Nancy countered.

"If you want my advice, I think we should stay as far away from that place as possible, especially since we're under suspicion for breaking into it!" Bess declared. "Besides, we have to see the boys."

"We have to do more than that," George said glumly. "We have to *free* them, and that's not going to be easy."

Nancy concurred with a deep, impatient sigh as their waiter handed her an envelope. She opened it hastily, then let out a cry of disappointment. The message inside had almost been entirely obliterated by the rain!

"I can barely read it." The girl detective moaned, passing it to her companions. "See if you can do any better."

But they were just as stymied. They hurried through the meal, finishing it with an inquiry.

"Who gave you this note?" Nancy asked the waiter.

"The concierge."

Questioning the concierge, however, provided no additional information.

"All I can tell you, Miss Drew, is that the envelope was here at the desk when I returned from the back office," he said. "Now let me introduce you to your interpreter."

He motioned to a young man who was seated on a bench opposite them.

"Antonio, these are the American ladies who require your assistance today," he said. "They need to go to the *Questura Centrale.*"

"*Si,*" the young man said with an engaging smile.

"Antonio is a student at the university," the concierge continued. "I think he will prove most helpful."

When the young man heard about the Emerson boys' predicament, he nodded sympathetically. "I will take you to police headquarters right away," he said. "Perhaps we can straighten things out. Follow me."

He led them out of the hotel and through a maze of small streets called *calli,* whisking the girls to the Rialto Bridge and finally, the police station. There in the lobby stood a high desk flanked by smaller tables. A captain in uniform looked up and greeted them very pleasantly in Italian.

Antonio spoke to him briefly, then the group

was ushered to a room at the end of a narrow corridor. Except for a table and a few chairs, it was empty.

"Please sit down," Antonio said, as the captain disappeared to get the prisoners.

None of the girls spoke, listening instead to the echo of their companion's foot tapping on the tile floor.

"How much longer do we have to wait?" Bess asked, but a minute later the Emerson students were brought into the room.

Instantly, it was filled with chatter and a deluge of questions from both sides that prompted the accompanying guard to clap his hands sternly. Antonio helped quiet the group, whispering to the officer who nodded back.

"You only have a little bit of time to talk," Antonio informed the Americans.

"In that case," Nancy said, "Ned, please repeat what you just told me. I especially want Antonio to hear this since he is going to help us get you out of here."

Ned, whose clothes were rumpled from sleeping in them all night, smiled gratefully at the young man. "If the police hadn't confiscated everything we brought with us, I could show you what they found," he said.

"Dave says you were stopped at Marco Polo Airport here in Venice," Bess interjected.

"That's right," Ned replied. "We stepped off the plane, went to the baggage area, picked up our luggage, and went to the customs officer. He made us open everything. That surprised me because I've always gone through foreign check-ins very quickly. Not this time, though.

"When the guy looked in my small suitcase, I almost flipped. There was the most beautiful glass artpiece inside—"

"What was it?" Bess interrupted, curiously.

"It was an abstract figure of a horse with hooves shod in gold. The customs officer started to examine it. He called somebody else over as well. I tried to tell them it wasn't mine, but nothing registered."

"The fact is," Dave said, "that neither of the men spoke much English."

"I told them I was traveling with friends," Ned said.

"And the minute he introduced us," Burt replied, "Dave and I were goners, too."

"Look, we'll figure out where that piece of glass came from," Bess declared, "and send it back where it belongs."

"That's just the problem," Nancy told her

friend, prompting Ned to finish his story.

"It broke into lots of little pieces," he said.

"What?" George gasped. "But how?"

"When the customs people kept turning it, it slipped through their hands—"

"And *splat*," Burt said.

"Oh, how terrible!" Bess cried, suddenly leaping out of her chair. "Well, then there's no case, no evidence, no nothing."

"On the contrary," Nancy said, "there's a lot of circumstantial evidence."

The guard who had been standing near the door now moved forward, signaling the end of the discussion. But before they left, the young detectives promised to do all they could to help the boys.

"Dad's due back this evening," Nancy said, "so I'm going to call home very soon."

"Sorry I messed up your trip," Ned answered bleakly.

"Don't be silly. I'm happy you're here—even if it is under lock and key!" There was a trace of laughter in her voice that barely masked her concern. "See you later," Nancy said.

When the girls reached the lobby again, she asked Antonio to request a look at the evidence.

He spoke to the police captain for a moment but to Nancy's chagrin, the officer was unwilling to show it to them.

"Tell him I'm a detective, Antonio," Nancy said.

"Your name?" the captain replied.

"Nancy Drew."

"Ah!" he said, adding something in Italian and finally the name of the Gritti Palace Hotel. Nancy also thought she heard him refer to the gondolier, Andreoli.

I should have told the police what happened at the glass showroom the minute we arrived here, Nancy chided herself. She watched the captain study her and the other girls closely.

"*Signorina,*" he said in a tone that forecast imminent doom, "I'm afraid you and these young ladies are also in trouble."

3

D. D. MYSTERY

The word "trouble" was enough to send Bess reeling.

"We haven't done anything wrong," she blurted out before anyone could stop her.

"Bess!" George hushed her, allowing Nancy to talk instead.

As concisely as possible, the girl detective told about the previous night's events. Antonio translated whenever necessary.

"I don't think the captain believes her," Bess whispered to her cousin.

"Listen, they're not going to throw us in jail," George said under her breath.

"Don't count on it. Especially when—uh-oh—wait till you see who's here."

"Who?" George asked, turning around sharply.

Amazingly, it was the gondolier who had ferried them across the canal the previous night. It seemed he had been summoned by the police to give an account of the girls' behavior.

We never should've run away like scared rabbits, Nancy thought, listening to the drone of the gondolier's words. He spoke in Italian, but too rapidly for her to understand everything. She looked questioningly at Antonio, who held up a hand to keep her quiet.

It was only when Andreoli finished talking that the girls' interpreter spoke. "The gondolier says you and the others insisted he take you to the glass shop last night," Antonio began.

"That's because we heard a crash and concluded there was a thief inside," Nancy said. "You see, the lights went out suddenly and we figured one of the chandeliers fell—"

Antonio smiled. "Andreoli says he heard the crash but did not know what happened because he was not looking in that direction. The police investigated and indeed, found a broken chandelier. They are still trying to discover whether anything is missing from the store."

"Then—they don't think we're thieves?" Bess stammered in relief.

"Are they going to let us go?" George added.

Antonio nodded. "But you must not leave Venice without telling the police, since the case has not been cleared up yet. Also, Captain Donatone says you must do no more investigating from now on. It will only get you into trouble. You understand?"

Bess giggled when they all left the police station. "You heard the man, Nancy. No more detective work. That means we're about to take an enforced vacation—a dream come true!"

"Oh, so you intend to leave poor Dave in jail!" George exclaimed.

"Hardly!" Bess grimaced. "But once the boys are out, we'll have no choice but to spend every moment lolling in the sun. Aah!"

"Well, it's still too early for me to call Dad," Nancy said, fumbling for the envelope in her pocket. "Antonio, I have something else to show you. Let's get out of this crowd first."

The rain had slackened to a fine drizzle, causing the girls to push back the hoods of their slickers as they cut away from the swarming tourists and headed for the Piazza San Marco.

"We'll have some cappuccino, if you like," their guide suggested.

"Oh, I like," Bess said gaily, following him to an empty table at Florian's.

It was one of several cafés where small orchestras played almost continuously in the shelter of the square's unending arcade, its stony gray facade now lightening under the passing raincloud.

Awestruck by the majesty of the cathedral opposite, Nancy temporarily forgot the reason she had hurried everyone away from police headquarters. The basilica, she concluded, was like a tapestry woven in mosaics and colored marble with figures of angels and saints standing guard over the huge gray domes.

"That was the church of the Doge, you know," the young man said, giving their order to the waiter. "He presided over the government of Venice—all one hundred seventeen islands that make up the city—and all official ceremonies were held there, not the least of which was the Doge's election."

As the observers noticed that only one of the famous *Quadriga*, the four stately bronze horses, remained above the central archway, George asked, "Where are the rest of the horses?"

"They are being restored," Antonio said, smiling. "After all, they've been here since the thirteenth century!"

Suddenly Nancy recalled Ned's description of the glass artpiece that had landed him in jail. It was an abstract horse shod in gold. Could it possibly be a modern version of this ancient statue? The idea penetrated her mind as Antonio continued to speak.

"It was the Doge—Enrico Dandolo, at the time—who brought the horses from Constantinople," he said. "To this day, though, nobody knows where they came from originally. Some believe Emperor Constantine took them from the Greek island, Chios. Others believe they used to decorate a Roman arch. But—"

"Yes?" George said as he hesitated.

"That's the mystery. Because, you see, no horses exist in Greek or Roman art that resemble our Venetian beauties."

"Speaking of mysteries," Nancy said, showing Antonio the message, "what do you make of this?"

He pondered it carefully while the waiter placed a cup of cappuccino in front of each person. The girls swallowed the frothy hot beverage in small sips, waiting for Antonio's reaction.

"Are you sure this was intended for you and not the police?" he asked.

"The envelope has my name on it," Nancy replied. "Why?"

"Well, because it seems to be a plea for help from someone who lives on the Grand Canal. That's about all I can make out, though. The person's name has all but washed away in the rain." He steadied his glance on the missing letters. "There is a capital *D* followed by a small *o* or *u*, I'm not sure which. Then, there is another capital *D* followed by a small *a*."

"Maybe it's from a *dogaressa*," George suggested, drawing a grin from the young man.

"I doubt it," he said. "They all died centuries ago. But it could be from a *duchessa* or a *duchessina*—"

"Who lives in a *palazzo*," Bess said eagerly. "Oh, Nancy, let's try to find her!"

411

"No police work, remember?" George needled back.

"Who says this is police work?" Her cousin chuckled. "If someone asks us for help, we can't very well deny it, can we?" She gulped the last bit of liquid out of her cup. "Come on, troops!"

"Unfortunately, I won't be able to go with you," Antonio said, "I have a class—a special summer course I just signed up for. But, please, if you need me later, call me. Here's my telephone number."

"You've already been a great help to us," Nancy said gratefully, promising to contact him if necessary.

Then, taking the lead, she and George left the café with Bess trailing behind. The latter had slipped under the arcade, pausing only a second in front of a shop window filled with glittering jewelry, much of it enamel.

But seeing her friends dart through the *sottoportego*, the passageway that ran beneath the buildings, she called out, "Hey, wait for me!"

"You must've found something you want to

buy," George said when her cousin caught up to them finally.

"I sure did. The most exquisite butterfly pin ever. You should see that place," Bess went on eagerly.

"Maybe tomorrow," Nancy said.

"I agree," George added. "We can't waste the afternoon shopping. There's too much to do."

Consequently, Bess carefully avoided looking in any other display windows along the streets that ran behind the square and the trio reached their hotel in less than five minutes.

"I hope Dad's home by now," Nancy remarked, putting the key in their door.

Her phone call proved fruitless, though. Hannah Gruen had not heard from Mr. Drew but she promised to have him return Nancy's call the minute he arrived.

"Thanks a lot," the girl said, and hung up the receiver in disappointment.

Then she hunted for the local telephone directory under the night table and scanned all the listings under D.

"Looking for a *duchessa*?" George inquired.

"No. Just someone whose initials are D. D.," Nancy replied. "After all, there's no reason to think the message came from royalty."

"That's true," Bess said, but a glance at the listings told her that if Nancy were right, the search could easily consume the rest of their stay in Venice.

Nancy came to the same conclusion and shut the book.

"No luck, huh?" George said, shifting some clothes out of her suitcase into an empty drawer.

The young detective did not answer. She was staring at the message again, concentrating hard on it, when suddenly a vivid image of the elegant apartment across the canal flashed into her mind.

Had the person who lived there seen her and her companions take the gondola back and forth from the Gritti? Had he or she somehow learned who they were and hoped to contact them?

Nancy mentioned the possibility to her roommates.

"Even though the police captain told us to stay away from *Artistico Vetro*, he didn't say anything about the occupants above it," she added with a grin. "Also, I don't see why we can't inquire about other residents in the area while we're there."

Bess pinched her eyes in a tight frown. "I think that's asking for trouble," she said.

"Well, we'll go even if you don't want to," George declared.

"I wouldn't think of letting you go without me." Bess smiled.

When they went downstairs again, however, they were disappointed to find all of the gondolas had left the station.

"We'll have to take the *vaporetto*," Nancy said, referring to the large water-bus that traveled regularly up and down the canal.

She inquired about the nearest landing stage, then led the way through a small street that fed into a second one ending at the water's edge. The boat was already there filled with passengers, but the young detectives managed to get on and squeeze through to the guard chain on the opposite side.

They stood close to it, watching drops of sunlight on the small ripples as the *vaporetto* pulled away from the float, churning its engine loudly.

Unexpectedly, a stranger stumbled roughly

into Nancy, forcing her to move forward.

Now she was poised at the very edge of the vessel with nothing but the chain between her and the water. She tried to step back, but the crowd behind her would not budge.

Suddenly the stranger thrust his hands onto her shoulders, pushing her down hard. Nancy slipped and fell against the metal links, sliding under it before anyone could catch her!

4

The Duchessa's *Secret*

As Nancy slid forward, the passengers gasped
in horror. Luckily, however, the girl had managed to grab the chain, keeping herself from
falling into the canal!

"Nancy!" Bess cried, she and her cousin div-
ing to help her. The stranger, meanwhile, had
edged past them and lost himself in the crowd
of onlookers.

"Just pull me," Nancy said hoarsely. "I can
make it."

But her fingers were bone-white and
threatening to give way any second.

"Lean back as far as you can," George told

her, putting her arms under Nancy's and tugging her upward.

"That's it. More, more," Bess urged. She watched the girl's feet grope for a toehold.

The ticket collector, who had been at one end of the *vaporetto*, now hurried forward muttering in Italian.

"*Che cosa sta succedendo qui?* What's going on here?" he asked as the young detective finally managed to swing her weight onto the boat and stood up.

"Someone pushed me," she said.

"*Non capisco. Che cosa dice?* I don't understand. What is she saying?" the young man replied. He looked at George for an explanation.

"My friend says someone pushed her," Bess answered. "Like this." She motioned with her hands. "You understand now?"

But the ticket man shook his head.

"Give up. Obviously, no one saw it because it's so crowded in here," Nancy said to the girls as the boat approached its first stop. She glanced through the passengers, most of whom where local people who spoke little or no English and quickly lost interest in the rescue once it was over. Which one of them, she wondered, had tried to push her overboard and why?

No answer came, though, as everyone hurried onto the landing stage.

"Do you suppose it was deliberate?" Bess asked Nancy after they debarked. "It seems to me there was very little standing room and someone could have bumped against you accidentally."

"It was deliberate all right," Nancy said, describing precisely what had happened.

"But who would want to hurt you?"

"And for what reason I'd like to know?" George added.

"That's what I keep saying to myself," Nancy remarked, as they ducked down an alley and walked to the *fondamenta*, the street that ran parallel with the canal.

When they reached the glass shop, however, they were surprised to find a sign on the door.

"'*Chiuso*,'" Nancy said. "How do you like that? It's closed."

She peered inside at the array of stemware glistening on the shelves that swept past elaborate mirrors to the chandeliers in the back.

Suddenly, Nancy's eyes fastened on someone's reflection in a mirror.

"Look!" she said, but Bess and George had already seen him. "It's Andreoli!"

Nancy tapped on the window, hoping the gondolier would respond, but he had already slipped out of sight.

"This is getting to be very frustrating," Bess said as an overhead window slid open.

"*Prego*. Can you come up?" A voice drifted down, causing the girls to step back from the building. The handsome elderly woman who had addressed them was probably in her seventies.

"Who are you?" Nancy asked.

"I will tell you when you come upstairs. There is a door to the right."

Without giving the girls another chance to speak, she closed the window.

"I wonder why she wants to see us," Bess said, following Nancy and her cousin to the second-floor apartment.

"She probably wants to kidnap us." George laughed, as the door swung open.

"Please come in, young ladies," the woman said graciously.

She gestured to a beautiful silk sofa that sprawled in front of a marble fireplace in the living room.

"I am the Duchessa Maria Dandolo. Perhaps you have heard of the Doge, Enrico Dandolo. I am a distant relative."

Nancy gulped excitedly, as she remembered Antonio's story about the Doge who had brought the bronze horses from Constantinople. "Did you, by any chance, send a message to me—Nancy Drew—this morning?" she asked.

"Yes, I did."

"But how did you know who Nancy was?" Bess inquired, incredulous.

"A friend of mine told me. Professor Bagley. He called to say hello before his college tour left Europe. When I told him I had a problem, he informed me that a very bright young detective was on her way to Venice. 'She's the person to help you,' he said."

"Oh, my goodness," Nancy responded, flattered by the professor's glowing recommendation.

"He also mentioned your friends, George Fayne and Bess Marvin," the woman con-

tinued, lighting her eyes on them. "He described you all so vividly that I immediately
recognized you when I saw you standing
downstairs. So . . . I take it you received my little note?"

"We did, but we could hardly read it," Nancy
said. "It was washed out by the rain."

"Then, how did you know where to find
me?"

"As you said, *Duchessa*, Nancy's a first-rate
detective," George said, chuckling.

With that, there was a knock at the door, and
the woman rose to answer it. To the girls' astonishment, it was Andreoli.

"You almost got us into a heap of trouble!"
George accused him. "If you hadn't told the
night clerk about our trip across the canal, we
wouldn't have had to explain ourselves to the
police, who, by the way, warned us not to do
any more detective work!"

The gondolier looked crestfallen. "I not
know who you were then," he said haltingly.

"Poor Andreoli. Don't be so hard on him," the
duchessa said in his defense. "He told me
about your conversation with Captain Donatone. I believe his restrictions concern only

police matters. I am asking you as a private citizen to help me on a matter in which I do not wish to involve the authorities."

"Yes?" Nancy asked, her curiosity rising.

"I have a nephew who is quite brilliant, an artist like his father, and he—" She paused as if unsure whether to continue.

"And he?" George prompted her.

"Well, he has been kidnapped—taken away from Venice, his family, his work, everything."

"Why didn't you tell the police?" Bess asked.

"Because I did not want the publicity. If I reported the kidnapping, there would be stories in the newspaper. My family would be very upset."

Gazing at the elegant appointments in the room, the fine brocade, the crystal and marble, the girls concluded there was great wealth hidden between the lines of Maria Dandolo's story. Throughout, Andreoli had remained quiet.

"I want you to find my nephew," the woman went on. "I will pay you well."

"I never take money, and I am not sure I can accept the assignment anyway," Nancy said, surprising her companions.

"That's the first time I've ever heard Nancy

Drew turn down a chance to solve a mystery!" Bess exclaimed.

"Well, as Andreoli knows," the girl replied, "our friends are in trouble."

"They're in jail," George stated flatly.

"Yes, I know all about it," the *duchessa* said, "but what does that—"

"I'm afraid I have to devote my time to them until they are free. I'm sure you can understand that."

"Of course, but perhaps I can help you in that regard," Nancy's listener replied, causing a flutter of excitement among the girls. "I cannot promise, but I can certainly try."

She said something in Italian to Andreoli whose head bobbed up and down at every syllable. "*Si, si,*" he replied.

"But *signora*," Nancy started to say.

"*Duchessa,*" the woman corrected her.

"Then, *duchessa,*" Nancy continued, "please tell me how it is you can help my American friends when you fear going to the police about your own relative?"

"That is an easy question to answer. You see, I have many friends in high government positions who can—how you say—move things along for you. But Filippo. Well, he would be in even greater danger if I revealed his disappearance to them. I do not trust anyone now—except you."

The woman lowered her eyes, tracing a thin crack in a black marble table. "It's pathetic how old things break and fall apart with time," she said. "I'm trying hard not to let it happen to me, especially now. Please, you must find Filippo. It is your duty as a detective!"

5

Revelations

Nancy was thunderstruck by the woman's pronouncement and if it were not for her curiosity about the artist's disappearance, she might have politely excused herself.

The twinge of uncertainty in the girl's face was very evident. "Please, forgive me for talking as I do," the *duchessa* said softly. "I cannot force you to help me. I—I'm not myself these days."

"I understand," Nancy said. "Why don't you tell us more about Filippo. When was he kidnapped?"

"Less than three days ago while he was making some deliveries to our factory in Murano."

427

"Are his captors demanding money from you?" George asked.

"No. Not money."

"What do they want then?" Nancy asked.

Maria Dandolo gave a long, arduous sigh. "I cannot give you any more information until you say yes, you will help the Dandolo family."

"I will," Nancy said, "once the charges are dropped against my friends. They are completely innocent, you know."

"Fair enough," the *duchessa* said, smiling. *"Uno momento."* She excused herself to a nearby telephone while Andreoli rose from his chair.

"Scusi, signorine," he said. He spoke to the woman in Italian, nodded at the girls, and left immediately.

"Strange, very strange," Bess commented to her friends. "I mean what does a gondolier have to do with a duchess?"

"Maybe he's her private chauffeur or runs errands for her," Nancy said. "What intrigues me more is, what was he doing in the store below?"

When the woman finished making her call, she informed the young detectives of her success. It would take no more than two hours to clear the Emerson boys, she said. "You can pick them up about four o'clock," she added, sitting down again.

"Now I must confess something else to you," she continued. "I'm partly responsible for your friends' trouble."

"But how?" Bess asked, dumbfounded.

"My family has been in the glassmaking business for generations," the *duchessa* explained. "We own a factory in Murano and have several stores throughout Italy, including the one downstairs."

"Oh, then that explains why we saw Andreoli in the window before," Nancy interrupted.

The woman nodded. "Yes. He helps me with many things. But what I want to talk about is the particular glass sculpture that was found in Mr. Nickerson's luggage. It was one of the most beautiful things Filippo ever designed," she said sadly. "Ever since he was a small boy he's been fascinated by the *Quadriga*, the magnificent bronze horses atop the Basilica San Marco."

So I was right, Nancy thought. The glass statue was modeled after them! "Was Filippo carrying the piece when he was kidnapped?" she asked aloud.

"No. As a matter of fact, it had disappeared from our showroom in Murano a few days earlier. I reported the theft, and the police alerted customs officials throughout Europe to be on the lookout for it."

"So the chances are, if we find the thief, we may also find the person who framed Ned," George concluded.

"No doubt," the *duchessa* said. "I was afraid the sculpture would be taken out of the country, and apparently it was. But why it was planted in your friend's suitcase is still a mystery."

"Well, it's quite possible the burglary in your showroom last night was done by the same people who captured your nephew," Nancy offered. "What was actually stolen?"

"Nothing, or so it seems," the woman replied. "And the police have no idea why the chandelier fell. It is all so very strange."

She stood up and went to a writing desk from where she removed a piece of paper and handed it to Nancy. On it was a winged lion with a small Bible next to it and underneath, a

430

few words in Italian. Translated, they said, "Peace to you, Saint Mark, my evangelist."

"Does this mean anything to you?" Nancy questioned.

"It does indeed. The winged lion and open Bible are the symbol of Venice. So are the words," Maria Dandolo answered. "Our patron saint is the Evangelist St. Mark. Filippo uses the symbol as a signature on his work."

"Then, are you saying that your nephew sent this to you?" Bess asked.

"Someone left it in my mailbox two days ago. You see, it has my address on the reverse side. Unfortunately, I don't know who brought it here. But it's unmistakably Filippo's handwriting."

"Perhaps he wasn't kidnapped," George spoke up. "Since no one has asked you for ransom, perhaps he just went away for a few days."

"No. There was a telephone call from someone—a man with a very deep, husky voice. He told me they had taken my nephew somewhere and said, 'You may not see him again unless—'"

"Unless what?" Nancy prompted her.

"'Unless you give us the formula that your brother, Filippo's father, uses to make glass with.'"

"Is Signore Dandolo the only one who has the formula?" Bess inquired.

"No, I think I have a copy somewhere among my papers."

"Why didn't they kidnap your brother?" Nancy volleyed another question.

"Apparently they couldn't find him at the time," the *duchessa* said. "So instead they took his most precious possession—his son."

"Where *is* Filippo's father?" the young detective asked.

"After my nephew's disappearance, he went into hiding, and I assure you, no one will ever find him."

The statement drew a long pause from the girls until Nancy spoke. "I see now why you don't want any unnecessary publicity," she said. "Not only because you might be risking further harm to your nephew, but also to his father. Have you no idea where they could have taken Filippo?"

"No, no idea at all." Maria Dandolo's eyes blinked sleepily as she finished speaking. "I am very tired now. I have not slept too well since all of this happened. Please forgive me. I must ask you to leave."

"We can talk later," Nancy said. "Perhaps we will have a chance to meet your brother as well."

"Perhaps. We will see."

In the meantime, Nancy and the cousins intended to contact police headquarters about the release of their friends.

"She seems to be holding something back from us," George said as they boarded the *vaporetto* for the return ride.

"She's just being cautious," Bess declared. "Don't you agree, Nancy?"

"I don't know quite what to think—yet. But I'm hoping the brains of Emerson College will come up with something."

"I'm sure they will!" Bess gleamed brightly. "Just think if we hadn't met the *duchessa*, Dave might have been forced to spend the rest of his days in a Venetian prison—"

"Pining away for his beloved Bess." Her cousin chortled.

"It isn't funny, George Fayne, is it, Nancy?" the girl said.

But the Drew girl wasn't paying much attention to the familiar, teasing banter between the two. She was thinking instead of the magnificent church built by the Doge Contarini for Venice's patron saint. It dominated the main piazza and its immensity was staggering. Undoubtedly there were numerous rooms inside and, behind the chapels, dark, unthought-of corners where someone could hide or be secreted away from the world.

Filippo's intriguing signature might, in fact, be a clue to his whereabouts! Nancy deduced. So the cathedral, the monument to the Evangelist Saint Mark, was the next logical place to search for the *duchessa*'s nephew.

6

Captured!

When the three girls finally debarked from the *vaporetto*, they returned to their hotel at once. To Nancy's disappointment, she discovered that she had missed the long-awaited call from her father by only a few minutes.

"I'd better try to reach him right away," she said. "I don't want him to worry."

So the instant the girls were in their room, Nancy dialed the operator who, unlike previous occasions, was able to place the call immediately.

"Dad, is that you?" Nancy said when the man's resonant hello crackled over the line.

"Nancy?"

"Yes, Dad. Oh, I'm so glad I finally got hold of you."

She explained the trouble that Ned and the other two boys had gotten into, quickly adding, "But we met a *duchessa*—"

"Who has connections in high places?" Mr. Drew chuckled.

"Exactly," Nancy said, smiling to herself.

She revealed the details of what had occurred, finishing in a cheerful tone. "So that's the story. No assignment for Dad this time!" she declared.

"Maybe you'll find one before I arrive, though," he replied.

"Before you arrive?" Nancy asked excitedly. "Are you coming to Italy?"

"Day after tomorrow. Believe me, it's as much a surprise to me as you. I have to help out a client in Rome. He was planning to consolidate his business with an Italian company that wants to expand to the States. But a problem came up, and I've been handling one end of it while his lawyer in Rome was supposedly taking care of the other."

"What do you mean 'supposedly'?" Nancy inquired.

"Well, it seems that the lawyer hasn't been pushing things along fast enough to suit my client. Anyway, I don't intend to spoil your fun with all of this dreary business."

"It's not dreary," Nancy insisted. "I just hope you find time to enjoy yourself while you're here. You are coming to Venice, aren't you?"

There was some hesitation in her father's voice before he answered. "If I can manage it—I'll call you as soon as I get into the hotel in Rome. I'll be staying at the Grand."

The conversation ended shortly, and Bess let out a long sigh. "I'm tired," she said.

"But it's not even three o'clock," George remarked, giving an involuntary yawn.

"See what I mean?" Bess said. She stretched out on the bed, shutting her eyes for a moment while Nancy spoke.

"It'll be another hour before we can pick up the boys at the police station," she said. "I'd like to visit the basilica on the way. Anybody want to join me?"

"Sure," George responded, but the gentle snore that dissolved in Bess's pillow proved she had already fallen fast asleep. "We can leave her a message."

"Good idea," Nancy said and scribbled something on a piece of hotel stationery. "I'll tell her to meet us in front of the central arch in forty-five minutes."

"What if she doesn't wake up in time?"

"Then we'll go on to headquarters without her."

Wasting no more discussion on the subject, the girls left the hotel for the piazza, which was now filled with pigeons and a long line of tourists in front of the basilica.

"It's really awesome," George said, following Nancy inside, and fastening her eyes on the colored mosaics and marble which were no less splendid than the arrangement of domes and arches.

Although Nancy had told George her idea that Filippo might be held captive in the building, both girls now tended to dismiss the idea, seeing the number of people who poured endlessly through the cathedral.

Nevertheless, they stayed in the line of visitors until they found themselves on the steps of the presbytery, the space around the main altar, gazing at a magnificent block of fine, hammered gold composed of enamels and precious stones.

"It's beautiful," Nancy murmured, pulling back to get a broad view of it along with several other visitors who were taking pictures.

George, at the same time, had moved down the marble steps, closer to the panel and away from Nancy. She was suddenly surprised when the young detective darted toward her and tugged on her arm urgently.

"Come on," Nancy said.

"What's the hurry?"

"I'll explain later."

But as the young detectives pushed their way to the far side of the cathedral, the twilight glow from the overhead windows was swept into darkness.

"Can't you tell me where we're going?" George asked her companion.

"I'm looking for someone—a man who came up behind me while I was standing at the altar. Unfortunately, he ran off toward the north transept. I didn't get a good look at him before he fled."

"Did he talk to you?" George asked.

"Yes. He—he—warned me to stay away from the Dandolo family. Otherwise—"

"Otherwise what?"

"He said I'd end up like the Doge Dandolo himself."

"He's buried in a crypt below here," George said, her throat catching on the words.

"I know."

"Maybe we ought to go back to the hotel."

"Are you kidding? No, sir."

Undaunted by the mysterious threat, Nancy pressed deeper into the arm of the transept, discovering a small, empty chapel at the end. The scent of burning tallow was unusually strong, suggesting that someone had recently doused candles near a door hidden in the shadows. Curious, the girls walked toward it, wondering whether the man had used it to escape.

For a fleeting moment, they imagined footsteps running in their direction and turned sharply. Then, unexpectedly, the door flung open and four strong arms reached out and grabbed them.

"Let g—" George cried, her words garbled

quickly by the hand that dragged her through the doorway.

Nancy also tried to shriek but to no avail as a gag was quickly drawn over her mouth and she was thrown face down alongside George on something soft and tufted like a quilt. The girls' wrists and ankles were tied next. Then the men left, closing the door after them and locking it.

Question after question tripped through Nancy's mind as she wondered who the men were and what they intended to do with their captives. Were they connected with Filippo's abduction? If so, might they not keep Nancy and George prisoners until they had finished with the Dandolo family?

We could be trapped here forever! Nancy concluded.

A similar fear had also occurred to George and she made a futile attempt to roll over but found herself pinned next to a wall. It felt cold and damp as her fingers brushed against a thin opening that seemed to run up and down in a straight line. George grunted into her gag, trying to tell Nancy she had discovered another door, maybe one that was unlocked!

Nancy understood instantly and looked up and down the crevice, searching for a doorknob but none was apparent in the darkness. So, with a hopeless sigh, she lay back on the blanket, breathing in its dank, musty odor.

Bess, on the other hand, had awakened out of her deep sleep and upon discovery of Nancy's message, she had quickly freshened up. She took the elevator to the lobby and strode toward the door, stopping midway when the night clerk greeted her.

"Where are you going in such a hurry?" he said, flashing a smile as he approached the girl. "You must slow down. Enjoy yourself." He added something in Italian that Bess did not understand.

"I have to meet my friends in front of St. Mark's," she told him.

"Well, perhaps I will go with you."

Bess looked at him quizzically and although she didn't wish to offend the man, she said abruptly, "I'm sure I can find the piazza without assistance."

"I'm sure you can, but I would like to come anyway. We go."

So rather than discuss it further and lose more time, Bess let him follow her outside.

"Shouldn't you be working?" she asked him.

"Not till later," he said. "Now tell me about you and your friends. Do you plan to stay in Venice a long time?"

"Not really. Just a week. Of course—"

"Of course, what?"

By now, the two had passed over a small bridge leading to a string of *calli* that fed into the square, and Bess tried to avoid giving an answer.

"Thank you very much for accompanying me," she said pleasantly, hoping at last to part company as the basilica loomed into view.

But the man pretended not to hear the remark and picked up his pace as they crossed under the arcade. When they reached the main portal of the church, however, Bess was disappointed to find her friends weren't there.

"I don't see them anywhere," she said anxiously.

"Perhaps they are inside."

"Perhaps," Bess replied. A glance at her watch told her she was only a few minutes late, so it was quite possible that the young detectives had not yet left for headquarters.

"Follow me, please," the man said in a tone of authority. "We'll find them."

"But—" Bess tried to protest, thinking she would miss the girls if they stepped outside while she went in. Even so, she tagged close to her guide, concluding that Nancy and George might, by chance, wait for her.

Once inside the building, however, Bess almost lost sight of the man as he dived between the huge marble columns leading to the north transept. Before taking another step, she glanced through the crowd, but not seeing Nancy or George, she darted ahead, following the clerk a few feet. Then she stopped, suddenly aware that he had drawn her away from the rest of the tourists.

Instinct told her to turn back, but the man's voice echoed out of the shadows, halting her.

"They're here," he called, and drew the unwitting girl forward.

7

Reverse Approach

Bess eased through the darkened chapel, which now carried only a faint scent of candles. "Where are you?" she asked, failing to conceal her nervousness.

"Over here."

But in the bleak emptiness of the room, the man's reply seemed to come from different directions.

"Where? I can't see you," Bess cried.

He struck a match and lit one of the candles, casting an eerie glow on the far door and sending a shiver of fear through Bess. She started to turn away, but it was too late. A thick, woven scarf billowed over her head and was pulled

446

back tight between her lips, preventing her from screaming. She stumbled forward, trying to wrest herself from her attackers, but it was no use. They shoved her through the open door, and in her blindness, she tripped over her friends and fell between them, eliciting loud moans. Instantly, her wrists and ankles were tied like theirs. Then, the door clicked shut and the men departed.

Until that moment, Nancy and George had remained hopeful that Bess would be the one to rescue them. Somehow, though, she too had been tricked. Now they wondered if anyone, even the Emerson boys, would ever find them!

Despite the *duchessa*'s promise, it was almost eight before Ned, Dave, and Burt were permitted to leave police headquarters. At the Gritti Palace, they registered and went to their room quickly, then dialed their friends on the next floor. To the boys' surprise, the girls weren't there.

"Very strange," Ned said. "I wonder why Nancy didn't leave a message for me."

"Maybe they got tied up somewhere," Burt answered, unaware of the truth in his comment.

"But it's so unlike her," the boy continued, feeling strangely uneasy. He spoke to the night clerk again. "Are you sure you have no idea where Miss Drew, Miss Fayne, and Miss Marvin went?" Ned inquired, observing beads of perspiration along the man's forehead.

"I'm quite sure, but—ah, come to think of it, they did mention going to the Lido."

"That's the beach." Dave laughed. "I doubt they'd get much of a tan in the Venetian moonlight."

"As a matter of fact—" The man bristled. "There is quite a bit of night life over there. Perhaps your friends found some charming escorts."

The remark nettled Dave since he was positive the girls would not succumb to casual dates with strangers. If anything, they were probably on the trail of a dangerous criminal!

"Listen," Ned went on, "how do we get to the Lido?"

"By the hotel boat. Or," he added quickly, "if you don't care to wait for the next one, which is due here in an hour, I can arrange for a water taxi."

The boys quickly looked at each other, agreeing to the latter suggestion immediately.

"Just go through that door," the clerk instructed, nodding past the newcomers. "And welcome again to the Gritti."

"Thanks," Ned said. He stepped outside, but realized a moment later that he had left his wallet in the boys' hotel room and excused himself. "Don't leave without me, okay?"

"Don't worry!" Dave and Burt called back as he darted into the lobby a second time.

Now asking for his room key once more, Ned flew to the elevator and took it one flight up to Room 124, but when he tried to open the door, it wouldn't budge. Again and again he jiggled the lock without success, then gave up and returned to the lobby only to discover that the clerk had left the desk unattended.

Now what? the boy wondered as a voice from behind pulled him toward an adjoining office. There, he found a man in a hotel blazer talking animatedly on the telephone. He glanced at Ned, but made no effort to end his conversation.

"Ned!" Dave shouted through the door off the landing-stage. "Taxi's waiting!"

"Okay, okay," his friend answered, dropping

the key on the front desk. "I just hope you guys have enough lira for all of us tonight."

He quickly explained what had transpired, causing Burt's and Dave's eyebrows to lift. "Maybe we'll wind up sleeping on some baroque sofa in the lounge," Burt groaned as the trio climbed into the boat.

Ned let the comment pass, speaking to the driver instead. "Lido," the boy said briefly just to confirm their destination.

"*Si. Capito*," the man replied, sending the boat through the inky-black water toward the lagoon where a cruise ship lay anchored in a brilliant dazzle of lights.

"I guess he understands," Dave commented, descending to the cabin below.

Ned and Burt, however, chose to remain outside. They were fascinated by the foamy trail of whitecaps that curled in the wake of their boat as it streaked along a channel of log markers flanking the course to the Lido. As it came into view, Burt pulled out a map of the beach resort, noting the main hotels offering musical entertainment. One of them was the Excelsior where they seemed to be heading.

"It sure is dark around here," Dave said,

sticking his head out of the cabin to feel the cool settling of air as the boat slackened its speed.

"I'll say," Burt remarked.

"And you and I had better duck before we get our heads knocked off by that bridge coming up," Ned told him.

The driver had already motioned them down. Keeping his eyes fixed straight ahead, he cut the engine and allowed the boat to glide slowly between the brick walls until it cleared the low, stony arch.

At the same time, Ned noticed the dark figure of a man on the other side of the bridge. He had lowered himself with a rope and was dangling to the right of the arch, holding himself with one hand while the other swung out, sending a small shapeless object in their direction.

"Watch out!" Ned cried to the boatman who instantly shifted the gear into reverse and stopped. The mysterious object fell a few yards short of its target and sank into the water.

"What was that?" Burt asked, mystified.

"Well, I don't think he would've climbed down a rope just to throw a stone at us," Ned said soberly.

"You're right. It was probably a bomb of some sort," Dave grumbled.

"Good thing it didn't hit the boat and go off. We'd be a plate of spaghetti by now," Burt said.

The driver, meanwhile, had continued backing away from the bridge, and Ned stepped quickly toward him. "We must keep going," he said. "*Prego.* Please. We have to go to the Hotel Excelsior!"

But the boatman shouted back in Italian, refusing to shift forward again.

"He's scared," Burt said. "He knows it was an attack, not just some kid's prank."

"At the rate we're going," Dave said, worried, "we might not get another taxi for hours. I think this calls for drastic measures."

"Like what?" the other boy replied, watching his friend's eyes travel to the murky, black water.

"I'll show him it's safe," Dave said, stripping down to his shorts. "Follow me!" he yelled to the helmsman.

"Dave? Are you crazy?" Ned called out but his words faded under the shouts of the driver, as the boy dived in.

"Now he's really in a tailspin," Burt whispered, watching the man angrily shift the boat forward.

"Have to admit it worked, though," Ned said.

Dave had succeeded in swimming several yards beyond them before the boat caught up to him, and he was reluctant to come aboard again. Apart from a possibly heated confrontation with the driver, he feared that the man might turn back. But the boys insisted that Dave had had enough exercise and pulled him out of the water.

The driver merely glared at him as Dave spoke, shivering, "It's freezing down there."

"Here. Dry yourself off, good buddy," Burt said and handed him a towel from the cabin.

"For this, you deserve a big dish of pasta on me!" Ned chuckled. "Too bad I don't have my wallet."

The remark drew a good-natured frown from his companion, who put his suit on quickly. "I can always take a raincheck," he said as the boat swung under a second bridge and finally pulled up to the hotel float.

He paid the driver, who offered a grim steely grunt in return, and then followed his friends into the hotel and down a long carpeted hallway. From the second floor, they heard a drum-beat and leaped up the stairway two steps at a time, hurrying past guests in glittering evening attire. The boys paused, however, when they reached the noisy room above.

"There she is! That's Nancy!" Dave gasped, directing Ned's attention to an attractive, titian-haired girl in a green silk dress. She moved off the dance floor with her date behind her and sat down at an empty table for six.

Soon a shock of wavy blond hair resembling Bess's also bobbed into view.

"See?" Burt said. "They did find dates and came here to dance."

"Hmph. It would serve them right if we left Italy without even telling them," Dave said, pursing his lips.

"I have a better idea," Burt replied, an air of mischief in his voice.

8

The Cap Clue

While the boys stood gaping at the crowd of dancers, Nancy, Bess, and George lay bound and gagged in their dark prison, their skin prickling with its damp chilliness. The hours had slipped away, and they wondered if their captors intended to abandon them forever!

I've got to get us out of here, Nancy said to herself, feeling the rope on her wrists cut deeper as she tried to work it loose.

Her companions shifted into slightly more comfortable positions: Bess sat against one wall and George leaned against the other with the mysterious opening in it. If only she could get to her feet to explore the rest of it!

She pressed her shoulders back and dug her toes into the floor beneath the blanket, pushing her weight upward. She made small progress before sliding down again, then repeated the exercise, getting no further than before.

Come on, George Fayne, where are those old judo muscles? she prodded herself.

She continued her attempts to stand up until the ache around her bound ankles became unbearable and she was forced to stop. Bess, on the other hand, had discovered a rough projection of wood at the base of the wall. She rubbed her wrist binding against it, snapping a few of the rope threads, and pressing hard to break the rest.

Although the girls' captors had buried them in impenetrable darkness, they hadn't taken away their ability to hear; and the sound of rope splitting over something sharp gave renewed hope for escape.

Nancy pulled herself next to George, groping for a nail or a piece of chipped wood, anything to help cut her bindings. George did the same but, finding nothing, determined to make one last attempt to get up.

She rapped her knuckles against the wall and hoped Nancy would understand that she needed her assistance.

She wants me to help anchor her, Nancy concluded, swinging her legs against George's feet.

That's it. Good, the other girl thought and pushed back and up again, allowing her toes to press into Nancy's tightening muscle. Inch by inch she moved until at last she felt a latch.

She's found something—a door handle perhaps! Nancy gasped excitedly. She dared not budge, however, waiting for the next signal.

George slid her body to one side and continued to hop back on her feet until she was able to stand, using the wall as her support. The latch, she soon discovered, was a few inches out of reach and she sighed unhappily. Nonetheless, the bindings on her ankles had loosened a little and she decided her exercise hadn't been entirely in vain.

Bess, meanwhile, had tired of her own labor and gave Nancy a turn at the piece of wood. The young detective ran her rope cuff over it in a sawing motion, stopping only once when a twinge of pain shot through her arm. No doubt she would find deep welts in her wrists she decided, but put the thought out of her mind as the rope started to snap. Just like Bess's, the threads broke a few at a time, then more, but the remaining ones were stubborn. They held fast like steel; and suddenly the young detective realized that only part of the cuff was rope. The rest was wire!

Now, for one of the few times in her life, Nancy felt beaten. She could never break wire over wood. She needed something stronger, like metal, and yet there was no way to communicate her discovery to George or Bess who had met the same obstacle.

Unaware of their friends' predicament, the Emerson boys had ventured across the dance floor at the Hotel Excelsior. Ned in particular kept his eyes on the table where the titian-haired girl had recently sat down.

"All set?" Burt asked his two companions.

He had noticed an attractive group of three girls, who seemed to be together, and walked toward them.

"American by any chance?" Burt inquired, drawing giggles from two of them.

"Not quite," the third one answered a bit disdainfully. "I'm from London, and they're from Austria."

"Well," Burt went on clearing his throat. "I'd like to introduce myself and my friends."

"We're very happy to meet you," the blondest girl replied. "My name is Helga Doleschal and this is Elke Schneider."

"I'm Christine Mott," the Londoner said.

As the boys told about their recent trip through Vienna, the conversation rippled with laughter until everyone rose to dance. Ned swung his partner toward the end of the room hoping to catch Nancy's eyes, but at the same instant, he realized that her table was now empty! He scanned the dancers, but she wasn't among them.

"Is something wrong?" Christine asked.

"Huh? Oh, no," Ned answered in the midst of his distraction. He wondered, though, how he and the other boys could have missed seeing Nancy and the cousins leave; and when the music finally stopped, he whispered to Burt and Dave.

"Obviously they're gone. Maybe we ought to go too," Ned said. "I'm bushed, anyway."

"Me too," Dave said. He muffled a yawn. "It's not everyday in the year I get to swim in a canal!"

"You—swim in canal?" Helga asked. "I did not think you were permitted to do such a thing."

"You're not," Burt laughed, "but he doesn't understand Italian warning signs."

"Tsk, tsk, tsk," the girl replied in mock disapproval. "Perhaps you will have to stay in Venice until you learn. We'll be here at least through Saturday."

"So if we need a few lessons in Italian, can we depend on you to teach us?" Dave grinned.

"*Senza dubbio.* By all means."

The young men offered a few more pleasantries, then waved good-bye, wondering if their American girl friends had already returned to the Gritti Palace. Considering the lateness of the hour, it seemed more than likely.

"Shall we call them when we get in?" Burt asked.

"Why not?" Dave said, while Ned reserved his answer until they were down the corridor.

"Actually, I'd like to check out that bridge," he said.

"The one where the bomb came from?" Dave replied.

"Yup."

"But I thought you were tired."

"Well, let's say the brisk night air just woke me up."

As a matter of fact, Ned had been itching to investigate the area but had decided not to until he had tracked down Nancy. Now he was ready to begin again, and led his two companions out of the hotel to the street.

He tore down a flight of steps and cut through clumps of oleander into an empty garden that trailed along the small canal.

"Suppose we get arrested for trespassing?" Dave asked Ned.

"Suppose we do?" Burt said. "It's better than being accused of theft."

Ned chuckled. "I hope you both realize you're beginning to make me feel guilty over absolutely nothing," he went on, and pushed beyond the dimness of a few lamp posts.

The threesome now walked evenly toward the bridge, looking for any evidence of the person who had thrown the explosive.

"I'm sure it was homemade," Ned murmured.

"Lucky for us it wasn't designed to go off in water," said Burt, when he spotted a dark felt cap on the ground.

He dived for it, noticing footprints as well. They were fairly small and close together, which implied they belonged to someone shorter than either of the boys.

"Let me see the cap," Ned requested, peering at a well-worn label inside. "Didn't we pass a store with this name?"

He held it in front of Dave and Burt.

"Yes, on the way to the Gritti, I think," Dave replied, "but there are probably hundreds of people who own hats like this one."

"And I'm sure the proprietor won't remember who bought it," Burt concurred.

"Even so, I'm going to hang onto it," Ned remarked. "One thing Nancy taught me is never take any clue for granted."

"I'm not convinced that bomb was strictly intended for us," Burt said.

"Well, if it wasn't, then who was it meant for?" Dave asked.

"Maybe our boat driver," Burt suggested.

"I doubt it," Ned said.

"But why would anybody want to hurt us?" Burt asked.

"I don't know," Dave replied. "Perhaps it's all tied in with the trouble over that glass statue."

"True," Ned said, "and I'd sure like to find out who masterminded *that* little frame-up."

"Wouldn't we all," Burt declared, as the putting sound of a boat approached from the hotel. "Uh-oh, I think we just missed our ride back."

He and Dave had observed the boat schedule on the canal entrance to the Excelsior, and cast frowns at each other.

"There'll be another one," Ned said confidently.

"No, there won't," Dave answered. "Not until tomorrow morning."

"Are you positive?"

"Positive."

"Oh, well, considering all that's happened tonight—" Ned sighed. "I guess we ought to be glad it isn't raining, too."

With that, a flash of lightning cracked through the sky and small bullets of water trickled down the boys' faces.

"See what I mean?" the Emerson boy said, tossing his shoulders in disgust. "That takes care of our detective work!"

9

Thwarted Search

As rain heaved itself in waves across the canal, Ned and the other boys ran back toward the hotel from where the last boat of the evening had just left. They tried to attract the driver's attention but it was no use. The rain was beating harder now and blurred their vision.

"Hurry," Ned said in a panting voice. "Maybe the guy at the dock can radio the boat back."

But when they reached the man in uniform, he was huddled behind the door talking to someone else.

"Scusi," Burt said, attempting unsuccessfully to cut into the conversation. Dave cast an impatient glance at Ned who was equally dismayed.

At last, however, the man turned to them, and, hearing their predicament, said he would call a water-taxi as soon as the storm lifted.

"That could take hours," Dave said pessimistically.

"Boy, I hope not," Ned replied. "I'm exhausted—"

The rest of his comment faded quickly, though, as a young, titian-haired woman in a green silk dress trailed down the stairway carrying a large umbrella. She paused briefly at a display of clothing in a window, then turned, aware of Ned staring at her.

"Look," he whispered to his friends, "that's the girl we saw upstairs."

"And it isn't Nancy," Dave remarked sheepishly. "Now what?"

"Well, before we do anything else, let's call the Gritti and see if the girls are back."

"Good idea," Burt agreed, following the other two to the main lobby.

After a brief explanation to the concierge, Ned was offered the use of a nearby phone. The call went through immediately despite an interruption of static, but to his disappointment, the answer was the same as before. His American friends had not returned.

"Oh, but—yes—wait a moment," the night clerk said. "There is a message here for you. Shall I read it?"

"Yes, please," Ned answered, waiting anxiously while paper rustled out of an envelope at the other end.

"It says— Are you listening?" the clerk inquired.

"Yes, yes, I'm here," Ned said. "Go on."

"It says, 'Sorry we weren't able to see you today. Something unexpected came up and we had to leave Venice. We'll try to be back by tomorrow, but if we can't, we'll see you at home.' It is signed, 'Your friend, Nancy Drew.' "

"That's all?" Ned asked.

"*Si.*"

"Please put it in our box then," he said. "We'll pick it up when we return."

"As you wish."

With that, Ned hung up the receiver. He was troubled as well as mystified by the contents of the letter, which he related to Burt and Dave.

"It's not only the formality of the signature," he stated.

"You can say that again," Dave interposed. "At least, Bess would've signed 'Love, Bess.' I mean, does Nancy always add her last name?"

"No, never. But what bothers me more is the fact she didn't say where they all went."

"Obviously, they're on a secret mission," Burt concluded.

"Hmph. Since when is a secret mission a secret from us?" Dave answered, eliciting a nod from Burt.

"And what's all this business about seeing us at home if they don't get back to Venice?" Ned added in a tone of disbelief.

"That is a bit much," Burt agreed, "but I guess we'll have to take a look at the handwriting to make sure it's from Nancy—"

Another crash of thunder ended the discussion, however, and the threesome returned downstairs, determined to press the man on duty for a taxi. But he remained adamant.

"I am sorry," he said. "I cannot do anything for you. No one will come."

"But what if it was an emergency?" Dave asked.

"What can I say? Look at the rain now. It's worse than ever."

As he spoke, gusts of wind spilled angrily across the canal, churning the water into high waves.

"Too dangerous, too dangerous," the man repeated. "You sit, or go upstairs and dance. Enjoy yourselves—inside!"

If only the boys could, but they felt trapped and helpless, wondering where Nancy, Bess, and George had disappeared to.

The time passed slowly as the threesome wandered through the hotel again, looking in display windows that lined the corridors while hoping for a letup in the weather.

"Hey, check this out," Dave said, drawing his friends' attention.

"What is it?" Ned replied absently, then focused on a shelf of crystal. These things look very similar to the piece the customs man found in my suitcase!"

"Don't they, though?"

The boys noted the signature under the manufacturer's sign. It was an unusual design of the famed winged lion followed by the name Filippo.

"He sure makes some beautiful stuff," Burt commented, "and judging from the fact there aren't any prices on it, I bet it's pretty expensive, too."

Although they anticipated finding more samples of the artist's work, they didn't and finally gave up their search.

"I was just thinking," Dave said. "Suppose Nancy's note isn't legitimate? The night clerk told us they mentioned going to the Lido. What if they're still here?"

"Well, I'm sure they wouldn't have missed the last boat back to the Gritti," Burt said.

"Unless they did by accident or were forced to," Ned replied. "Weather permitting, we can still make a search of the beach and every hotel."

But there had only been a temporary break in the storm, which now grew stronger than ever.

"It looks as if we'll have to book ourselves in here for the night," Ned continued, "and postpone our investigation until tomorrow."

"That's fine with me," Burt said, glancing at Dave who nodded also.

Despite the fact that it was peak season at the beach hotel, the boys were able to obtain a room. It was considerably more expensive than they had counted on, but they took it anyway.

"What's a few lira more or less when our friends may be in danger?" Dave said as they registered their names.

"Exactly," Ned agreed. "But remember, I don't have a wallet."

The other boy smiled limply. "In that case—" he sighed—"I guess we'll have to settle for cold rolls in the morning."

"Could be worse," Burt said, as they followed the porter to the elevator and their room, which proved to be a small suite.

"Maybe we ought to stay up to really appreciate all this," Dave quipped, gazing at the velvet furnishings and tasseled drapes.

"You go right ahead," Burt said, "but I'm going to bed—immediately."

A deep yawn emphasized his intention.

"Me, too," Ned added, collapsing against his pillow. Dave followed suit, but only after one more sweeping glance.

With the steady downpour of rain thudding against the windows, he barely imagined next morning's sunlight.

But the next day, it burst across the boys in a blaze of warmth, jolting them awake.

"Close the drapes," Dave mumbled as he pulled the sheet over his head.

Ned had already dived into the shower, leaving Burt to pry Dave out of bed.

"Get up," he said. "It's after nine."

"Okay, okay," Dave answered but made no attempt to move.

"Don't you want to find Bess?" Burt went on, stretching to his full frame.

"Sure, sure. Just give me five more minutes."

However, by the time they all reached the dining room, it was well past ten o'clock. Ned had made one final call to the Gritti to see if there was any further message from Nancy; but as he suspected, there was none.

During the course of the night, the girl detectives had been carried to another room within the basilica. It had happened while they were sleeping. Their gags had been doused with something sweet, to assure their abductors there would be no struggle. When the prisoners awoke, they felt light-headed, aware of the sickening odor that still clung to their nostrils.

They must've drugged us, Nancy surmised. But why?

She stretched her legs out groping for the familiar wall but it wasn't there, and the young sleuth realized they had been moved. No doubt they had been secreted away in a room where there was no chance of anyone finding them!

Her only consolation, though, was that Ned and the other Emerson boys were probably out of jail by now.

When they don't find us at the hotel, they'll know something happened, Nancy thought, and they'll start searching right away!

10

Troublesome Discovery

Nancy's other hope was that her father would be arriving in Italy, too; and he would join in the search, unless, of course, he became immersed in his own case and did not try to call Nancy until later in the week!

As these troublesome thoughts continued to plague her mind, she dragged herself backward, bumping into George and Bess who also realized they were in a new location. They, like their companion, had begun to explore it. But Nancy was the first to discover an old radiator with a thin metal pipe that jutted out from the base.

She slipped her wire cuff over it and rubbed

back and forth until her bonds snapped in half, freeing her hands at long last! Then she reached for the gag around her mouth, removing it just as quickly.

"The wire's off," she told her friends happily, "and I'll get rid of the ankle rope any minute. Just be patient."

But her words fell short as footsteps in the distance echoed along the marble floor.

"Someone's coming. Uh-oh," she said, putting back her gag.

The footsteps stopped momentarily, and the young detective wondered if the person was one of their captors. But before she could think about it further, she heard men's voices, muttering Italian in low, growling tones. Still, Nancy understood a few of the words, among them the name Dandolo!

Filippo's kidnappers! she gasped. But what are they saying about him?

Instantly, she freed herself and her friends, signaling them to remain quiet as she peered through the door lock. But a lug was in it and she could not see the men.

"What if they find us like this?" Bess whispered nervously.

"Sh," George warned her. "Nancy's trying to listen."

But the girl detective was not having much success. She strained to hear the words passing between the two, catching only a few that made no sense to her at all.

"What are they saying?" Bess asked.

"Be-ess," George chided her again.

"I'm not sure. Something about 'Roma' and 'Murano,'" Nancy replied.

"Rome and Murano—hmph," George repeated. "I wonder—"

The sound of footsteps interrupted again, and Nancy slid away from the door.

"Quick! Put everything back on," she warned. Fast as lightning, the girls obeyed, holding their breath as the shuffle of feet stopped on the other side of the wall. The men spoke again, but in low, indistinct voices that faded as their steps unexpectedly changed direction.

"Whew!" Nancy sighed moments later when it was clear the men had left.

She tried pushing the lug out of the lock but it wouldn't give.

"Now what will we do?" Bess asked, showing the same fearful expression that usually drew a word of comfort from her friends.

This time, however, George said, "I'm not sure."

"Neither am I, but—" Nancy started to say.

"But what?"

"Well, it seems to me we have two choices. We can either wait here like three sitting ducks or try to get out."

"But we already tried," Bess countered.

"Oh, I know, but I have another idea."

While the young detective revealed her plan of escape, the Emerson boys were working on their own investigation. They had checked out of the Hotel Excelsior and walked up the beach, observing the long rows of cabanas that obscured their occupants from view.

"Maybe we ought to ask if the girls signed up for one," Ned suggested.

"Just lead the way," Burt said, leaping down the terrace steps to a small entranceway.

There they found several guests from the Gritti Palace who had arrived only minutes before. They were eagerly awaiting the cabana assignments listed on a large sheet of paper bearing columns of names.

"That's what we want to see," Dave whispered to his friends.

Although they were impatient, they waited politely for the other people to finish and leave, then made their inquiry. Unfortunately, it led to a negative response.

"Of course, they could be using a cabana at another hotel," Burt offered.

"Not if they're guests of the Gritti," Ned replied. "It has a reciprocal arrangement with the Excelsior regarding cabanas. Come on, let's go."

The boys continued their walk, pausing briefly to admire the deep azure water that lapped in gentle waves against the shoreline.

"It'd be nice just to lie out there and bake." Dave sighed, turning his face up to the sun.

"Okay, beach boy, that's all the tan you're going to get today," Burt teased, picking up his pace. "It's hard to believe there was a storm last night, isn't it?"

Upon closer observation, though, he realized it had done more than leaf damage to the trees. A telephone line had come down, along with a traffic light that lay splintered in the road.

"How far do you want to go?" Dave asked Ned.

"Just up to the Hotel Des Bains. I figure if the girls got stuck here overnight they'd probably want to get back to the Gritti to change, and they'd have to take the boat from the Excelsior."

"What if they were on the trail of something important?" Burt asked. "You still think they'd rush back to the Gritti?"

"Let's put it this way," Ned said. "We haven't passed them yet, so there's a chance we may."

But the trip to the Des Bains proved as fruitless as everything else, and the boys decided to take the next boat back to the Gritti. As soon as they arrived, they requested to see Nancy's message.

To their amazement, it wasn't in their mailbox.

"But the night clerk said he was going to leave it for us," Ned insisted.

"You will have to ask him, then," said the man behind the desk. "I know absolutely nothing about it."

"Well, perhaps you can send someone up to open the door to 124," the boy went on, glancing at the key in front of him. "This didn't work for me last evening."

A look of puzzlement greeted the statement. "Then how did you get in?" the man inquired.

"We didn't," Dave said. "We got stuck in the storm at the Lido."

"Oh, I see. Well, just a moment. Let me call someone to help you."

The clerk disappeared into a back office and a porter soon picked up the troublesome key. The boys followed him upstairs, and stood watching as he inserted it into the lock, turning it gently until it clicked open.

"Now how is that possible?" Ned said, utterly astonished, as the porter nodded and left. "Maybe I dreamed I—"

"Old cheapo here thought he'd save a few lira by leaving his wallet behind." Dave laughed teasingly.

"That's me, all right." Ned grinned and opened a dresser drawer, pulling out the wallet and a few coins inside. "Here you are."

"Huh?" the other boy replied in bewilderment. "I mean, what's this for?" he said, as Ned dropped the coins in his palm.

"I think it's important to keep one's reputation intact," the boy said briefly, allowing a long silence before he broke into laughter. "If you could only see the look on your face!"

"Mine?" Dave gulped, catching a glace in the mirror. "Hey, what's that?"

He pointed to a thin crack along the bottom of the glass.

"I wonder how that happened," Burt said. "It looks as if someone threw something at it."

"Like this, perhaps?" Ned said, holding up his penknife which he had picked up from the floor. "It was in the top drawer."

He pulled open the drawer, the contents of which were in complete disarray.

"Somebody's been in this room, all right!" Ned declared. "Check the other drawers and your luggage."

The boys wasted no time examining their things.

"All my stuff is here," Dave announced shortly.

"Mine too," Burt added.

481

"Well, I'm not missing anything either," Ned said, staring at the mirror crack. "It seems to me someone must've been awfully frustrated to do that—just because he didn't get what he was looking for."

"Maybe, or else he was in a big hurry. He started throwing things out of your drawer and the penknife hit the mirror."

"But if that's the case, then why isn't everything else all messed up?" Ned asked. "It just doesn't make any sense unless—he was here when I came back for my wallet, stopped his search, and shoved the stuff into the drawer."

"But why go to all that trouble?" Burt commented. "It seems to me that regardless of his habits, a stranger who was caught in this room by you or any of the hotel staff wouldn't have much of a defense."

"True—but suppose he *was* one of the hotel staff?" Ned proposed, letting the full weight of his deduction sink in.

"Okay, Nancy Drew," Dave said with a smirk, "who's your suspect?"

11

Undeserved Accusation

"The night clerk, of course!" Ned declared, proud of his deduction.

"The night clerk?" Burt repeated, admitting his bewilderment. "I don't understand. Why him?"

"Because when I realized I couldn't get into the room last night, I went back to the lobby and he wasn't around," Ned said.

"But that doesn't mean he was in our room," Dave pointed out.

"True, but then what about Nancy's message—the one he read over the phone? Where is it? We already agreed that it didn't sound like something she would write."

"Are you suggesting that the clerk made it up?" Burt asked, causing Ned to set his jaw firmly.

"Yes, I think so."

"And he sent us to the Lido even though he probably knew the girls weren't there," Dave put in. "Then he contacted a friend and asked him to blow up our boat!"

"Well, in that case, all we have to do is wait for him to come on duty," Dave said. "We'll take him by force, if necessary."

"Oh, sure," Burt replied, "right in the middle of the hotel lobby."

Ned noted the hour, saying that it was still early and they had plenty of time left to plan their strategy. Meanwhile, they had no other clues to where their friends were.

"All I know is, if I'm right about the clerk," Ned said, "he's probably hoping we'll book a flight home very soon. Actually, that might not be a bad idea."

"To go home and leave the girls stranded?" Dave said, incredulous.

"No, no, no. We'll just pretend we're leaving," Ned assured him.

"But how can you make believe you're leaving and not really leave?"

"By checking out of here and going to another hotel."

"I don't think it's that simple," Burt said, "because in order to make our departure look realistic, we'd have to take the hotel boat to the airport, then sneak back."

"Are you sure you want to go through all that?" Dave asked. "I mean, wouldn't it be just as easy to take our bags and walk out the door?"

"Hardly," his friends chorused.

"We can't take the chance. One of the other staff members might mention it to the night clerk," Ned pointed out, "and then we'd really be sunk."

So it was jointly decided that they would switch hotels.

"I wonder if we can find out where the clerk lives," Burt said.

"Probably not without drawing suspicion on ourselves," Ned replied.

"I don't even know his name," Dave commented. "Do either of you?"

Both boys shook their heads. "I'm sure we

can find out, though," Ned said, opening his suitcase to repack it.

Burt, meanwhile, telephoned the desk to announce their departure for the airport, prompting Dave to hunt through his guidebook for the name of another hotel.

"How about the Danielli?" he suggested.

"How about setting up a tent in the square?" Burt answered with one eyebrow raised.

"In other words, the Danielli's out," Dave said. He leafed through a few pages. "Now, here's something. The Pensione Seguso. 'Its furniture is elegantly old-fashioned and Venetian. The sitting room and dining rooms have antique, embroidered red-silk wall coverings.'"

"Well, I wouldn't consider any place that didn't have red-silk wall coverings," Burt crooned in a high-pitched voice.

"My point is, we could probably stay there without being discovered by the night clerk."

"You're right," Burt answered. "Is there a phone number for the pensione?"

Dave nodded as he dialed, and inquired about reservations. "We'll need a large room for three," he said into the receiver, then hung up. "You know, something just occurred to me.

What if the girls come back to the Gritti after we leave? We should tell them where they can find us."

"And risk having somebody open the letter?" Ned asked. "Uh-uh. We'll call them later."

"Okay, whatever you say," Dave replied, allowing the discussion to end as they got ready to leave the hotel. By the time they checked out and started for the airport as part of their ploy, it was well into the afternoon.

Nancy, Bess, and George had determined the steps they would take should their abductors return. Hoping it would be soon, they waited in the unbroken silence of their prison.

Then, several hours later, they heard the familiar clatter of shoes on the cold marble floor outside.

"Get ready," Nancy whispered to her friends.

George immediately felt her muscles tighten while Bess, quivering slightly, tried to quell her nervousness. The footsteps halted just outside the door, and someone began to push the handle, at the same time muttering in Italian. Nancy laid her hand on Bess's signaling her to remain quiet.

"Che cosa c'é che non funziona con questa porta? What's the matter with this door?" he said as the handle jiggled from side to side, convincing the young detective that it was not one of their captors. If it were, he would know there was a lug in the lock.

"It's stuck!" she called out.

"Chi c'é lí? Who's there?" the man replied, letting the knob go and causing Nancy to strain for the little Italian she knew.

"Siamo in tre. Bloccatio. Per favore aiuteteci," she said haltingly. "Three of us. Locked up. Please help."

"Where'd he go?" Bess asked as the man left in silence.

"I hope he went to get help," George answered, but to the girls' chagrin, it seemed to take forever before the stranger returned.

His voice, now low and indistinct, rose only once as someone else, probably a locksmith or a maintenance person, tried to remove the lug. After several attempts, all of them unsuccessful, he began to drill around it.

"I don't believe it," Bess said. "We're really going to get out of here."

But her optimism faded quickly as the work

on the door came to an unexpected end and the men departed.

"What's the matter? Why did they stop?" George asked, no less agitated than her two companions.

"I don't know, but I hope they come back before our captors do," Nancy said.

"Oh, Nancy, you're right," Bess replied. "What'll we do—"

"Look, let's not get ourselves upset before it happens," George interrupted, trying to relax.

But it was not until the work on the lock started again that the trio felt another glimmer of hope, and it was not until the door stood open that they believed they were free.

"*Grazie, grazie,*" the girls said over and over to their rescuers, one of whom proved to be a priest.

He smiled through his owl-eyed glasses, nodding as he stepped past Nancy to look into the room. Upon sight of the rope and the gags, he gasped in horror, pointing them out to the other man in workclothes who stood behind him. Nancy showed them the deep, red impressions that circled her wrists, then indicated Bess's and George's, too.

Exclamations of horror sputtered from the priest as he took Nancy's hand and led her forward. Bess and George followed, leaving the workman behind to pick up his tools and the evidence of the girls' imprisonment. Soon they found themselves in an office at one end of the basilica, where the priest made a phone call to police headquarters.

"Here we go again," Bess murmured hopelessly, while Nancy drew the priest's attention to Antonio's card, which she had removed from her pocket. She motioned to the telephone.

"*Prego*. Go right ahead," he said, nodding.

It was nearly half an hour later when Antonio arrived on the heels of two policemen, one of whom was Captain Donatone. As quickly as she could, Nancy explained what had happened to her and her friends, and Bess described how the hotel clerk had lured her into the trap.

Antonio translated the story into Italian, drawing deep, confused frowns from his listeners.

"He says it's impossible," the young interpreter told the girls. "The priest says it is unthinkable that anyone would use the basilica as a prison."

"It may be unthinkable," George said, "but it

happened. Just look at our arms and legs."

"He does not say you are lying. Only that he cannot imagine such a thing."

"Maybe our abductors were dressed like priests," Bess offered.

There were nods of consideration followed by a loud, unconvinced sigh from Captain Donatone. He said something to the girls' interpreter that Antonio hesitated to repeat.

"What is it, Antonio?" Nancy asked.

"He says—you like this detective business too much. Maybe you like to play tricks on the police."

"What?" George replied, indignantly. "That's crazy!"

"Look, all we have to do is show him the door, the lock, and the lug," Nancy said quietly. "Besides, the priest is a witness."

But when Antonio conveyed all of this to the men, the priest suggested fetching the workman. He appeared shortly and after several minutes of conversation between himself and the police, most of which the girls did not understand, Antonio cleared his throat.

"Well?" Bess asked, hoping they had finally been vindicated.

"Well," Antonio said, "according to this man

491

the lug could have been put into the door from either side."

"That's preposterous!" George exclaimed.

"Calm down," Nancy told her, turning to Antonio again. "You believe us, don't you?"

"Of course."

"Then why don't the police?"

"It's not a matter of what they believe or don't believe, Miss Drew. They just think you are—how you say—meddlesome."

Nancy lowered her eyes for a second, replying in her steadiest voice, "I'd like to make an official report at headquarters anyway."

"That is your privilege," Antonio said as the girl's lips trembled, not so much from fear as determination to prove herself.

12

New Developments

The police offered to take Nancy and her friends to headquarters at once.

"I just hope they don't try to keep us there," Bess confided to her cousin as they walked toward the Rialto with Antonio.

"How could they?" George replied.

"I don't know. But I'm sure they'd figure out a way if they wanted to."

"Bess," Nancy interrupted, "do you think that you would be willing to interview the night clerk for us?"

"The night clerk—me? And wind up in another closet? Uh-uh. No thanks."

Even George looked askance at the idea.

493

"What makes you think he'll show up for work—especially when he finds out we escaped?" she asked.

"Well, it's only a hunch, mind you," Nancy said, "but according to my watch, he ought to be going on duty soon, in which case there'd be very little time for anyone to have reported our escape."

By now, the group had reached the familiar iron door of the police station, and the girls wasted no more conversation on the current topic. Instead, with Antonio's help, they gave a report of what had happened to them, supplying as many details as they could, including a description of the night clerk.

"I hope you realize you are making a very serious charge against this man," Antonio translated on behalf of the captain. "Perhaps you should think about it again. After all, it's possible he was simply trying to get to know you, miss, and became an innocent victim of circumstances?"

Bess shook her head resolutely. "No, Captain," she said, "I was the victim of circumstances."

"If you say so—but you have yet to tell me

why anyone would want to hold all of you prisoners."

That was Nancy's opportunity to reveal the conversation she had overheard in which the name Dandolo was mentioned, but she didn't say anything, honoring her promise to the *duchessa*. No one knew about Filippo's disappearance, and Nancy vowed she would not let the information slip out now.

"*Molto bene*. Very well then," Captain Donatone said, filling in the silence. "We will look into the matter further, but I cannot promise what we can do about it. I suggest, however, that you return to the States."

"We will consider it," Nancy answered politely, then asked about her Emerson friends.

Hearing they had been released the previous day, the young detectives were both elated and eager to see them.

"Can you imagine how worried they must be about us?" Bess said as they hurried back to the Gritti Palace Hotel accompanied by Antonio. "Oh, we'll have to go out for a big reunion dinner tonight! I'm absolutely famished!"

George tossed her gaze to a sign that said DO FORNI. "Then that's the restaurant for you," she announced. "Two ovens for a double-sized stomach!"

"Very funny, George," her cousin replied. Despite the grimace on her face, however, she felt a modicum of delight at being the butt of George's teasing again, which she had sorely missed during the past twenty-four hours. "You don't still want me to talk to the night clerk, do you, Nancy?" she inquired.

"It all depends. Let's see if he's around first," the girl detective said. "Actually, I'm hoping we can get to our room before he turns up—*if* he turns up." She gave a sidelong glance to George that did not pass unnoticed by Antonio.

"Perhaps it is not wise for you to stay at the Gritti," Antonio suggested.

"But it's so beautiful," Bess commented. "Oh no, we wouldn't want to stay anywhere else in Venice."

The young man smiled, spiraling his gaze toward the sky that now flushed pink in the setting sun. "Well, then, you had better run if you want to catch the view on the canal," he said. "It should be spectacular."

"'Bye, Antonio," the girls said in unison.

"We'll be sure to call if we need you," Nancy added cheerfully.

When they reached the Gritti, however, the girls' spirits sank considerably. Their friends from Emerson College had not only checked out of the hotel. They had left for home!

"I just don't believe this is happening to me," Bess groaned.

"To you?" George asked. "What about the rest of us?"

"Well, you know what I mean," Bess said, collapsing on her bed to stare at the ceiling. "First, our beautiful vacation turns into a nightmare and then Dave takes off."

"He wasn't alone, either," Nancy put in. "It just doesn't make sense. It's so unlike Ned."

"And Burt," George added, sitting in the chair by the window. "By the way, did anybody notice the night clerk lurking around?"

"No," Nancy said in a faraway voice, now feeling an uncontrollable desire to sleep.

Perhaps it was due to the stress of recent harrowing events and the fact that since the girls' arrival in Venice, they had spent little time relaxing. Whatever the reason, Nancy sank deeply into her pillow; and it wasn't until the phone rang some forty minutes later that she and the other girls awoke.

"Hello," she said, stifling a yawn as she listened to the voice at the other end. "Ned! Where are you?"

"Are they all still in Italy?" Bess asked eagerly.

Nancy motioned her to be quiet, and when she finished speaking on the phone, she said, "The boys are here, but Ned wouldn't tell me where they're staying. We'll meet them later under the belltower in the square."

"Next to the basilica?" George asked warily.

"You're sure you were talking to Ned and not somebody who sounded like him?" Bess put in quickly. "I'd hate to walk into another trap."

"If you're really worried about it," Nancy said softly, "I can see the fellows alone."

That was more than enough to spur Bess to her feet. "I wouldn't think of it. George, please hand me my cosmetic bag," she said and flew into the bathroom, poking her head out of the door for a second. "How would Dave feel if I didn't show up?"

"Beats me," George said, doing all she could to refrain from giggling at her cousin's newfound energy.

When Bess finally reappeared again, her hair was swept back in a crown of waves, but instead of asking for the girls' opinion as she usually did, she leaped to the closet.

"Guess it's my turn," George went on. "What are you wearing tonight, Bess?"

"Oh, something exotic. My silk dress perhaps," she said, referring to a cream-colored outfit that complemented her fair skin. "Of course, I was hoping to have a tan by now, but . . ."

Her words faded as she rumbled through her shoes, while Nancy made her own selection of clothes, a pretty ruffled skirt with a blouse to match and low-heeled sandals. Those, she concluded, were not only comfortable for walking but perfect for chasing any would-be assailant!

"Speaking of kidnappers—" Nancy said offhandedly.

"Oh, do we have to?" Bess put in, as she buttoned a cuff.

"It is a dreary subject," Nancy agreed, "but unfortunately it's also a reality for us. I'm sure the *duchessa* is wondering why she hasn't heard from us."

"And I'm wondering if she's been contacted again," George said. "Do you suppose we should also try seeing *her* later?"

."That's a thought," Nancy said. She picked up the phone, ready to dial the woman's private number but changed her mind. "We can call from the restaurant."

"Whew!" Bess grinned. "For a minute there, I expected you to cancel out on dinner."

Nancy grinned back. "Come on, everybody. Let's go."

When they reached the downstairs lobby, they glanced at the registration desk looking for the night clerk but he wasn't there, and Nancy inquired about him.

"Erminio Scarpa is on vacation, *signorina*," his replacement informed her. "Perhaps I can help you."

The young detective hesitated, then continued.

"Could you, by any chance, give me his home address?" Nancy asked, causing the man's face to become animated.

"As a rule, we do not—" he started to say.

"The police are looking for him," Nancy interrupted boldly.

"He tried to kidnap us," Bess blurted.

"What?" their listener answered, shaking his head in puzzlement. "That's the craziest thing I ever heard. Not only that, it's quite impossible, too. As I said, Mr. Scarpa is on vacation."

"Well, perhaps we aren't talking about the same person," Nancy said. "The man we have in mind has thick black hair that sits like a cap over his ears. He's about your height—"

"I tell you he hasn't been here," the clerk insisted, admitting that the description fit Mr. Scarpa. "Perhaps you have him mixed up with someone else."

"May we have his address, please?" George cut in.

"I'm sorry. It's against our policy. Now if you will excuse me."

The man turned on his heel, leaving the girls utterly stunned by his lack of sympathy.

"He's covering up, that's all," Bess told her friends as they headed for the piazza. "We'll just have to track Scarpa down on our own."

"That's the old spirit," George said. "Got any brilliant ideas how to do it?"

"We can start with the telephone directory," Nancy replied, "and if that fails, we'll speak to our hotel manager in the morning."

Soon the trio arrived at the belltower. The boys were there already, and Ned and his two friends hugged the girls joyfully.

"Are you ready to eat?" Burt asked. "We're starved."

"So are we," the girls replied in unison and Nancy mentioned Do Forni.

"It's supposed to have wonderful risotto," she said gleefully.

"Then let's go!" Ned exclaimed, taking her arm.

Once they were there, however, they spent less time on the meal and more on news of the past twenty-four hours. When the boys heard what had happened to their friends, they were shocked and angry.

"We tried to find you at the Lido," Ned said. "The night clerk told us that's where you went."

"That figures!" Bess groaned.

"He sent us on a wild-goose chase," Ned said, "and then told one of his buddies to sink our boat."

"There was this creep hanging from a rope," Burt muttered. "Too bad he didn't fall into the drink—"

"But we found a clue!" Dave cut in. "Ned, show Nancy the cap."

The girl looked it over carefully. "Someday

I'll find out whom this belongs to," she vowed. "But now tell us why you were thinking of flying home? Did you really believe we had left Venice?"

"Of course not," Ned said. "As a matter of fact, we—" He stopped speaking instantly as three pretty girls emerged from the restaurant doorway.

Burt and Dave had seen them too, but pretended not to, downing large helpings of the creamy rice dish in front of them. "You were right, Nancy. This risotto is spectacular," Burt said, steering George's gaze away from the threesome they had met at the Hotel Excelsior.

But upon seeing the boys, the girls waved and came forward. "Don't forget," Christine said to Dave, "we'll be here until Saturday."

As she spoke, Bess smiled pleasantly. "That's nice," she said. "We're leaving tomorrow."

"We are?" Dave coughed, gulping on his glass of water.

"Yes, if you make a date with her!" Bess giggled under her breath.

13

An Inescapable Snare

As the blush of embarrassment faded from Dave's face, Christine and the Austrian girls strode to the far end of the restaurant, leaving Ned and the other boys to explain how they had met.

"It all started with a mistaken identity," Ned said, telling about the titian-haired girl who closely resembled Nancy.

"Of course, we soon discovered she wasn't you," Burt piped up, "and we took up the hunt all over again."

"Oh, we knew you wouldn't abandon us," George said, smiling.

"And now that we're all together, we can

really help the *duchessa!*" Nancy exclaimed.

"A real *duchessa?*" Burt asked.

"Mm-hmm. She lives on San Gregorio opposite the Gritti," Bess offered, "and she wants us to find—"

The sting of her cousin's eyes caused her to stop mid-sentence. "Don't talk too loudly," George said, so Nancy could continue.

"Maybe we ought to let the *duchessa* tell you the story herself. I did promise we wouldn't discuss it with anyone."

"Including me?" Ned chuckled.

"I'm afraid so," his friend said. "But you'll hear all the details very soon." She excused herself momentarily, fishing a *gettone*, or token, out of her purse to use in the public telephone that stood near the door. "I'll only be a minute. Order me a *mascarpone* for dessert!"

"Now look who's being extravagant!" Bess laughed. "Make that *due*—two!"

When Nancy rejoined the group, she seemed less jovial; and the elegant dish in front of her registered only mild satisfaction on her face.

"Is something wrong?" Ned asked immediately.

"I'm not sure," she said. "I started to tell the

duchessa that we wanted to bring you and Burt and Dave over to meet her and she cut me off before I could finish. She said she had no need to talk to me again."

"What?" Bess replied in astonishment.

"Maybe she just isn't up to having visitors," George remarked.

"I don't think that's it," Nancy said. "She sounded perfectly fine, not at all tired, but something was definitely wrong. I wish I knew what it was."

She took one spoonful of dessert, then let the utensil fall on the dish, a spark of sudden awareness in her eyes.

"She said, 'Do not come now. I do not need only you,'" Nancy repeated. "The way she spoke sounded so awkward."

"Maybe she was trying to tell you just the opposite of what she meant," George said.

"Exactly," Nancy replied, as Ned asked the waiter for the bill.

"How do we get to San Gregorio?" the boy said shortly.

"By *vaporetto*, *motoscafo*, or—how about taking a *traghetto*?" Bess grinned.

"Since when did you learn so much Italian?"

George asked her cousin teasingly, "and what on earth is a *traghetto*?"

"It's a short ride in a gondola from one side of the canal to the other. Is there anything else you'd like to know?" Bess continued, laughing lightly as the group left the restaurant.

"Not just now, thank you," her cousin said, and hurried ahead with Burt, who was aiming for a fleet of gondolas parked behind the restaurant.

"I gather we're going to take a *traghetto*," Bess called out breathlessly. She stopped to adjust the strap on her shoe, but Dave grabbed her hand before she could do so.

"Come, Miss Italy. The boat's going to leave without us!" he exclaimed.

"Oh, it is not," she said. Nevertheless, she picked up her pace, soon finding herself and her friends in one of several gondolas, all of them filled with eager tourists whose voices barely tittered under the booming shouts of the gondoliers.

"Isn't this fun?" Bess said. She leaned against her seat to watch the lead boat with its jaunty pilot.

He had begun to serenade his passengers,

singing a familiar tune to the black silky sky that loomed fuller as they glided down the narrow canal.

"I have a feeling we should have gone to the gondola station on the square," Nancy murmured impatiently.

"We'll make it," Ned assured her, touching her hand. Burt, however, made a different observation.

"I'd say we're in for a traffic jam," he said, as the oars stopped turning and the gondolas came to a halt just at the edge of the Grand Canal.

Shouts relayed from one gondolier to another, and Ned turned to theirs, asking what the trouble was, but the man did not hear him as he yelled out to no one in particular. Then, as if by magic, the gondolas began to move again. Just before they slid under a low bridge, Nancy detected a pair of green fiery eyes staring down at her from a first-floor window of a building on the canal.

"Oh, Ned, look," she said. "Have you ever seen such a big black cat?"

"I hope it's not an omen for the future," the boy said, laughing, but his comment slipped past Nancy as she noticed a man's profile in the same window.

His hair, thick and black, lay caplike over his ear!

"That's the night clerk from the hotel!" she exclaimed, drawing the others' attention to the window. But it was empty now and the gondola had swept away too quickly, leaving in its wake only a vague impression of the window's location.

"At least, we know he's still in Venice," Nancy said. "I intend to come back here tomorrow and check out that building."

As she spoke, the gondolas, still hugging together, turned up the canal, and George asked if anyone had bothered to tell the gondolier where they wanted to be taken.

"I didn't," Burt said.

"Neither did I," Ned chimed in. "I thought you did."

"Don't look at me," Dave said, causing Nancy to motion to the oarsman.

"We—want—to—go—over—there," she said. *"Prego."*

But the man shook his head, and she wasn't

sure if that meant no or he didn't understand.

"*Prego*," she began again, pointing toward the building in the near distance where a lamp shone in the *duchessa*'s apartment.

Still the man didn't respond, and the lead gondolier began to sing, drawing the whole flotilla in line with each other and letting Nancy's words fade under the applause.

"You know what?" Bess whispered to the young detective.

"What?" she said, already suspecting the answer.

"I think we're part of a tour group."

George groaned disgustedly. "This could take hours!"

"And by then who knows what may have happened to the *duchessa*?" Nancy said anxiously. "Oh, Ned, this is terrible. We have to do something."

The only idea that occurred to him had worked once before; but the question was, would it work now?

"Ned, please!" Nancy persisted as she watched the gondolier dip and turn the oars again.

It was almost unbearable to feel the craft surging forward, away from the troubled woman's home; and the painful look in Nancy's eyes was all it took to send the boy into action.

14

Strange Behavior

Ned leaped to his feet, causing the gondola to tilt sideways while he removed his jacket.

"What are you doing, Ned?" Nancy cried while their gondolier poured out a warning.

"Sit down, sit down," he shouted in Italian.

"Ned, please," Nancy added.

"But you—" her friend started to say, prompting the girl to repeat her plea.

"I didn't mean for you to swim to our destination," she said, relieved when he was seated once again. "As for the *duchessa* ... well, I'll just say a prayer for her that she's all right."

By now they had drifted further up the Grand Canal, passing graceful palaces built from the twelfth century to the present, their unlit facades a sad reminder of the powerful men and women and great artists who no longer lived there.

"I wouldn't mind having my own personal palazzo," Dave remarked.

"Then, how about that one?" Nancy asked pointing to a building with festive gold-trimmed poles in front of it. But when she saw that it was a museum, she retracted her suggestion. "I'm afraid the Guggenheim isn't for sale." She laughed.

"I wonder if they still keep a lion in the garden," Ned put in.

"A what?" Nancy asked.

"A lion. The Guggenheim was originally called the Palazzo Venier Dei Leoni because, according to tradition, the Veniers had a pet lion."

"Now I've heard everything," George commented, watching a preoccupied look slowly blossom in Nancy's face.

The young detective had tried hard not to think about her awkward conversation with the *duchessa*, but it continued to haunt her. And if it weren't for George's sudden canting interruption, Nancy would not have hesitated to voice her thoughts aloud.

"'And there afloat on the placid sea . . . lay a great city,'" George said, recalling a passage from a book she had once read. "'Gondolas were gliding swiftly hither and thither. Everywhere there was a hush.'"

"Bravo. Thank you," Bess cheered. "That was beautiful."

"Well, don't thank me. Thank Mark Twain." George dimpled her cheeks in a smile. "He came to Venice sometime in the 1860s and wrote about it in *Innocents Abroad*."

"You know," Nancy said, joining in the conversation, "according to tradition, the gondola evolved when the first people who lived on the lagoon got caught in high tide and had to paddle with their hands!"

I hope we won't have to do that!" Bess exclaimed.

"Don't worry, silly," George chided her. "This gondola is perfectly balanced, isn't it, Nancy?"

"Yes, they're all built to very specific dimensions. Not only that, but the boat is made up of some two hundred and eighty pieces of wood. Altogether, they weigh over a thousand pounds!"

"In other words, banish your fears, Bess." Burt chortled. "Besides, see that iron piece on the prow? On top of those six teeth is the Doge's hat. He'll watch over you."

"I'd rather Dave," the girl replied, mockingly defiant, as she coaxed his arm around her.

When the tour finally ended, the young people walked to the Gritti and Nancy called the Dandolo residence again. This time there was no answer.

"She must have gone out," Nancy said, worried.

"Or to bed," George pointed out. "It is late, you know."

The young people managed to find a gondolier to take them across the canal. When they arrived at the *duchessa*'s apartment, however, the door was securely locked and no one answered their insistent rings.

"She could be out. She could be sleeping, or she could be in trouble," Nancy concluded in distress.

"Personally, I think that you're letting your

imagination run away with you," Bess said. "I mean even though the phone message was a bit strange, it wasn't a desperate cry for help either."

"I agree," George said. "Anyway, it seems to me you ought to wait until morning and try to contact her again."

Nancy did not answer, but hesitantly, she examined the lock.

"You can't just break into someone's apartment," Ned said, pulling her away.

"Okay. You're right. Let's go back to the Gritti," the girl sighed. "I just hope the *duchessa* will be able to tell me tomorrow what she was trying to say tonight."

"How about coming to our *pensione* for breakfast?" Ned suggested when they reached the other side of the canal. "It isn't the Gritti, but it's very comfortable and the food is quite good."

"Sounds great!" Bess said, accepting the invitation for everyone. "'Bye!"

The girls awoke early, and Nancy made a notation to leave a message for her father should he call from Rome while she was out.

"Dad's due in tonight," she told her friends,

"and I'm sure he'll phone the minute he arrives."

As she spoke, she picked up the receiver to dial the Dandolo residence. There were four long rings before anyone answered, then came a hello that temporarily startled the girl.

"Andreoli?" she said, recognizing the deep-chested voice.

"*Si.*"

"This is Nancy Drew. Is the *duchessa* there?"

"*No. No . . . arrivederci.*"

"Wait . . . Andreoli," Nancy said, but the man had already clicked off the line. "I have to go over there right away," she announced immediately.

"What about breakfast?" Bess asked. "Can't you—"

"You go ahead without me," Nancy replied. "I'll join you as soon as I can."

"I'm coming with you," George decided. "Bess, how about you going to meet the boys?"

"Sure," Bess said. "But, are you sure you two will be all right?"

"Don't worry," Nancy said. "We'll be fine."

Since Ned hadn't called yet, Nancy gave Bess

517

the *pensione*'s address and the trio parted company. Nancy and George said nothing, however, until they reached their destination. Then they knocked fiercely on the downstairs door.

"Hello! Anybody there?" Nancy called out. To her relief, it finally opened, revealing Andreoli, the gondolier. His face was very pale, almost sickly, and there was no smile of greeting.

"The *duchessa*, where is she?" Nancy asked.

"Not here," the man replied crisply before lapsing into Italian and making the girls' eyebrows furrow quizzically.

The only word they understood was Murano, the largest island in the Venetian lagoon and the site of several glass-making factories, among them Artistico Vetro! Had the *duchessa* gone to visit Filippo's father?

She must have, Nancy decided, but why so suddenly?

Unable to communicate her questions to Andreoli, she sensed an unexplained nervousness about him, possibly the result of his concern for the woman's whereabouts. Whatever the reason, though, he pushed the door forward, indicating he had no more to say. But Nancy poised her hand against it.

"May we go upstairs?" she asked on impulse. How do I say it in Italian? "Andreoli, *di sopra*."

The gondolier hesitated, holding the door in place, then pulled it back slowly with great reluctance. He led the way up the wooden flight and stopped a few steps before the landing as if he had changed his mind. The girls, however, had already glimpsed the unexpected scene beyond the half-open door at the top. The drawers of the desk stood open, their contents strewn on the floor!

"What happened?" Nancy asked, leaping past the gondolier.

He hurried after her and shook his head, spilling out an answer, which trailed after her as she darted from room to room to see if anything else was out of order. Satisfied that nothing was, she figured the intruder had found what he was looking for and departed quickly.

Knowing just how secretive the *duchessa* had been about her nephew's disappearance, Nancy now understood Andreoli's reluctance to show her the living room.

He's probably afraid I'll report the intrusion to the police, the girl decided, trying to assure the gondolier otherwise. But discussion with him proved hopeless, prompting her and

George to say good-bye quickly. They had not asked their boatman to wait for them so they headed for the landing-stage up the street.

Unlike previous sojourns on the *vaporetto*, there were fewer passengers onboard this time. Their eyes were attracted to the dappling of sunlight on the water while Nancy's were only vaguely fixed. What had the intruder been searching for? she wondered, then the most obvious answer struck. A copy of the glass formula!

Of course! Why didn't I think of that right away? Nancy thought as she and George hurried to the Pensione Seguso.

When they finally arrived, Ned asked them what had taken so long. "We were beginning to get worried," he said.

Nancy gulped in a deep breath and took the seat opposite him. "I'm sorry . . . really," she replied as a waiter quickly introduced the menu to her. Food, however, was the last thing on her mind; she ordered only one poached egg.

"Is that all you want?" George asked, offering her the basket of rolls.

"I'm not very hungry this morning," Nancy

said, and proceeded to tell about her visit with Andreoli. "It's too bad Antonio wasn't with us."

"Who's Antonio?" Burt inquired, drawing a quick reminder from George about the student who had accompanied the girls on their visits to police headquarters.

"Oh . . . sorry for the interruption, Nancy. Please go on," the boy said. When she finished speaking, he and his Emerson friends exchanged glances.

"Do we foresee an unexpected trip to Murano?" Ned asked.

"Yes, most definitely," Nancy answered. "It occurred to me that the *duchessa* might have followed the intruder there, but somehow I just can't imagine it. She's not exactly feeble, yet I would have thought Andreoli would have taken her."

"Do you think she was kidnapped, too?" Bess asked.

"Possibly."

"Well, I suppose that we'll be able to find a boat to take us to Murano right now, if you like," Ned said, but Nancy's mind was on the night clerk whom she had seen in the window the previous evening.

"I have to make one small investigation first," she remarked with a glance at her watch. "I'm going to visit Scarpa's apartment. Do you all want to wait for me here or shall I meet you somewhere?"

"Why don't we go with you?" Ned suggested.

"A whole group might be too conspicuous. It's better if I go alone. I won't be long," Nancy said, pausing. "How about meeting at one o'clock under the clock tower? You could line up a boat for Murano in the meantime."

Before anyone could object, the girl stood up, kissed Ned lightly on the cheek, and dashed out of the dining room.

Using the restaurant Do Forni as her starting point, she wandered along the street looking at the names above the residents' doorbells. To her chagrin, Scarpa was not among them.

"I'll never find the building this way," she muttered to herself and went back to the gondolas stationed behind the restaurant.

Before stepping into one of them, she instructed the gondolier to take her through the narrow canal only. "Grand Canal—no," she added firmly.

"*Si, signorina.* No Grand Canal."

Somehow, perhaps because of the lazy feeling created by the warmth of the day, the ride seemed particularly long to Nancy. They floated past a row of peeling brick buildings that melted into one another without distinction. But as the gondolier dug his oar under the bridge, two tigerish eyes sprang into view behind the elusive half-open window; and Nancy felt her blood race.

15

Sisterly Protection

At the sight of the familiar black cat in the window, Nancy gasped, holding her breath for a second and wondering if its master was there too. She signaled the gondolier to stop at a small landing-stage up ahead where she stepped off and hurried down the short alleyway next to the building.

Suddenly, from an iron balcony neatly lined with small pots of red geraniums, the young detective heard a distinct meow as two of the pots suddenly fell against the grating and the feline flew to the ground in a single leap, landing on all fours. Nancy froze, glancing upward just in time to see the window click shut.

Someone is up there, she decided and quickly sidestepped the animal.

As she suspected, there was no name on the front door but to her surprise it was open. She entered cautiously, not seeing the figure above her who spoke shortly.

"Who are you?" the woman asked.

Nancy felt a disquieting tremor pass through her body as she gazed at the crippled form above her.

"I am a guest at the Gritti Palace Hotel," she replied, not wishing to reveal her name, "and I am looking for a Mr. Erminio Scarpa. I thought he lived here."

"Come up, please," the woman replied. She dragged her legs away from the door, relying on two canes for support.

"I hope I'm not disturbing you," Nancy commented, climbing the wooden stairs.

"Not at all," her listener said and indicated a comfortable chair in the living room, which the girl took. "It is my pleasure."

Nancy noticed the simple yet tasteful furnishings in the apartment, along with a small collection of photographs on a corner table. One in particular drew her attention, but she waited for the woman to speak before inquiring about it.

The woman politely introduced herself as Lucia, and then came abruptly to the point.

"Why are you looking for my brother?" she asked and laid her canes down by her chair, causing Nancy to reconsider her approach.

Did she dare reveal all her suspicions to the man's sister? It stood to reason she would be protective of him, and would she not learn more from Nancy than the young detective wanted her to know? Nevertheless, Nancy proceeded with her questioning.

"I am a detective—"

"You?" the woman said in surprise. "But you are so young."

Nancy smiled. "I'm just an amateur detective," she explained, adding that she had been asked to investigate a matter that had recently occurred at the Gritti Palace Hotel.

"How recently?" her listener inquired.

"Within the past few days."

"Well, I doubt that Erminio could be of much help to you. He's on vacation, you know."

"Have you not seen him then?"

"No—not since last week."

"And you have been in this apartment all this time?" Nancy replied.

The woman seemed hesitant to answer. "No,

527

but what does that have to do with my brother?" she asked.

Although Nancy had carefully avoided making accusations against the man, it was evident that Lucia was uneasy, as if she also had some hidden anxiety about him.

"I thought I saw him last evening," Nancy said finally.

"Impossible," the woman snapped back. "Besides, what do you want with him?"

"I'm afraid I will have to talk to him directly."

As she talked, her eyes darted to a photograph on the table. In it were four people, including Lucia and Erminio. The third person was a pretty, dark-haired woman who bore a slight resemblance to them and next to her was a handsome young man. It was his face that had caught Nancy's attention.

"Is this a family picture by any chance?" the girl inquired, rising from her seat to look at it more closely.

"Yes and no," Lucia said. "That is my younger sister. She is presently in Switzerland, visiting friends."

"And the young man—is he a younger brother?" Nancy continued.

In the short silence that ensued, she found herself staring at the features of the young man in the photo. Although the gap in their ages was considerable, the comely expression was the same. Yes, indeed, he looked very much like the *duchessa* herself!

"No," Lucia said faintly, "he was a friend of my sister's." She did not volunteer any other information about him. "I am sorry my brother is not here to talk to you, but I will tell him you came."

"When do you expect to see him again?" Nancy asked.

"Oh, not for some time yet."

Not surprised by the answer, the young detective thanked the woman for her help and left. In a strange way, her visit had proved successful. She secreted her discoveries in the back of her mind, hopeful she would soon figure out the Scarpa connection with the Dandolo family.

Noting the time as she walked toward the piazza, Nancy quickened her steps. It was well past one o'clock, and she knew that her friends would probably be worried. As she turned the corner, she heard footfalls running in her direction from behind, then an arm grabbed hers.

"Ned! Where'd you come from?" Nancy said in amazement.

"Some detective you are," he teased. "Didn't even know I followed you from the *pensione*, did you?"

"Nope."

"Well, I thought you might have needed some unexpected assistance."

"That's really nice of you," the young detective said, admitting some slight trepidation about meeting Scarpa face to face. "As it turned out, though, I met his sister instead."

"Hm-mm," Ned replied. "You'll have to tell us all about it on the way to Murano."

"We have a boat, then?" Nancy asked.

"As you requested, *signorina*," the boy said, taking her hand and running across the square.

Having told the others of his plan to track after Nancy, Ned had asked Burt and Dave to arrange for the outing and shifted the meeting place from the clock tower to the nearby dock.

"How does it feel to have your very own shadow?" George quipped as Nancy and Ned stepped aboard the launch.

"It feels great." Nancy smiled. She waited

until they were underway, however, before she told about her encounter with Lucia Scarpa.

"Do you suppose the guy in that photograph is Filippo Dandolo?" Bess asked eagerly. "I mean, he could be another relative of the *duchessa*'s."

"That's true," Nancy said, "but I have a strong hunch it is Filippo. Now I'm more curious than ever about all of this business. We just have to find his aunt."

By the time the group finished talking, they were halfway to Murano, having cut through the lagoon past several smaller islands toward a gate of open waters.

"Isn't it wonderful?" Bess crooned, as the boat picked up speed, sending a fine, briny spray over her.

Dave coughed lightly. "If you don't mind taking a shower in the middle of the ocean!" he exclaimed.

"Oh, you. You're so unromantic," the girl said.

The island loomed closer now, and the driver throttled the engine, letting the boat chug into shore the last few yards.

"It's not exactly a tropical paradise," Ned

whispered to Nancy, who had made a similar observation.

Even so, the immediate view was of the factory, Artistico Vetro, and that satisfied her more than enough. She ran down the paved walkway to an entrance that led into a room filled with several kilns and supply shelves. She approached a man in gloves and work apron who was firing something in one of the ovens.

"I'm looking for Signore Dandolo," Nancy said.

The man shrugged. "Not here."

"Where is he?"

"Do not know."

"What about the *duchessa*?" the young detective persisted. "Has she been here?"

"No. She never come."

As he answered, he punctuated the remark by twirling his stick of white-hot glass for the last time. Nancy, at the same time, was alerted to someone moving about in an enclosed room several yards away. The door was closed, but the small window facing the ovens revealed a woman with gray hair.

But she slipped out of sight so quickly the girl could not see her features. Still, Nancy was almost positive it was Maria Dandolo!

16

Inquiries

"Who—who was that in there?" Nancy asked the glassmaker.

"Nothing in there—storeroom," he replied in a casual tone. "No one there."

Instantly, Nancy ran to the door and tried to open it, but to her dismay, it was locked.

"*Duchessa*! It's me, Nancy Drew!" she called out, "and I brought my friends with me!"

The girl stopped, however, when she realized that there was no one behind the window, only sacks of supplies.

"She's gone!" Nancy said, concluding there must be another door to the storage room although it was not immediately visible.

For a moment, she glanced back at the

glassmaker whose concentration on his work had begun to falter. He volleyed a warning in Italian, telling the visitors to leave or else. Nancy, however, was determined to pursue her investigation.

"Is there a showroom?" she asked the man, undaunted by his blazing eyes.

"*Si*, but it is closed."

Despite the pronouncement, the young detectives hurried out of the factory and down the pavement once more, quickly discovering an adjoining building. To their delight, the entrance was open and they sped up the carpeted stairway with its steel railing glistening brightly under a magnificent handcrafted chandelier.

"Someone has to be here," Nancy said, darting into a room filled with shelves of stemware.

The lights were on and a recent order lay next to a pen on a table that Nancy focused on briefly. She was struck by the design on the paper. It was Filippo's well-known signature, the lion of Venice!

"Look, everybody!" she exclaimed, pointing to it as someone paused behind them in the doorway.

"May I help you?" the man inquired.

"I hope so," Nancy said. "Are you Signore Dandolo, by any chance?" she asked.

The man pressed his lips into a broad smile, showing an overlap of teeth that detracted from his otherwise rugged face. "No, I am not Signore Dandolo. I am Mr. Chiais, the new manager here," he said. "The *signore* has retired."

"He has?" Ned spoke up.

"Yes, now, may I show you something? Some fine glasses like these perhaps." He took a pair of exquisite goblets from a shelf and held them toward the light, revealing tiny flecks of gold leaf in the ball of the stem. "These are the most beautiful of all."

"Oh, they are," Bess commented.

But Nancy still had her thoughts on the storeroom. "Of course, you know the *duchessa*," she went on.

"Of course," the manager said.

"Well, have you seen her recently?" Nancy asked coyly, watching his eyes roam from the shelf to the table, where he had placed the two glasses.

"No, she never comes here."

"Nancy thinks she saw her, though," Bess challenged in reply.

"Oh, really. Not around here, I don't imagine," Mr. Chiais answered, as the girl fell silent under her cousin's gaze of warning.

"As a matter of fact, I did," Nancy admitted.

The manager let out a nervous laugh, saying, "I'm sure it is a case of mistaken identity. She is too old to take boat trips to Murano."

"Mr. Chiais," Nancy interposed, "how long have you been in charge here?"

"A few weeks or so. Now—are you interested in any of these glasses?" he continued, taking two more off the shelf.

"Not really," the girl replied, "but I would like to see the factory storage room."

"That is out of the question," the man said. "Only the Dandolo family is permitted inside."

"Even though Signore Dandolo is retired and the *duchessa* never comes here?" Nancy asked.

"Look, *signorina*," he went on, fiercely defensive, "I cannot—it is not within my power to show you something that is quite frankly none of your business."

Nancy stiffened, feeling Ned's consoling hand on her shoulder. "I suppose we ought to be going then," she said, much to the surprise of her friends, who deduced she was already on the verge of a new plan.

She turned on her heel, letting George march

out first. But as they stood at the edge of the stairway ready to descend, Nancy's eyes fastened on the crystal pieces in the opposite room. They included sculptures and glass etchings, all of them exquisite.

"You take the same door to leave please," Mr. Chiais called as the group stepped into the second room. "We are closing now," he noted sternly, but not before Nancy had observed Filippo's distinctive signature on several pieces.

"We'll be back," the young detective said with a courteous smile and followed her companions outside.

"Let's pretend we're leaving and go to the landing stage," she said. "Then we'll circle back and watch the factory. It should be shutting down soon, and I want to see if the *duchessa* comes out."

"Good idea," Dave said. "We can hide behind the bushes across the way."

Within a few minutes, everyone had stationed themselves accordingly. The wait, however, proved longer than they anticipated. It was almost an hour before the last workman left.

Then, suddenly, a gray-haired woman in a

fashionable suit emerged. She walked out of sight with almost imperious steps.

"Nancy, maybe that's the person you saw," George remarked under her breath. "She could pass for the *du..he*ssa from a distance. Only this woman's a lot younger."

Ruefully, Nancy had to admit George was right. Still, the young detectives waited for the manager to leave as well.

As soon as he locked the door behind him, Burt said, "I guess that's it for tonight. Everybody has gone home."

Nancy agreed. "Let's go, too."

"What's next on the agenda?" Ned asked.

"How about dinner?" Bess declared, suggesting the girls return to the Gritti to freshen up first. "We can meet at the belltower again."

Everyone adopted the idea instantly. But when Nancy, Bess, and George arrived in their hotel room, the phone was already ringing.

"Maybe it's your father, Nancy," George said.

The look on Nancy's face as she answered it suggested otherwise.

"Oh—*Duchessa*, I'm so glad you called!" she exclaimed. "Are you home now?"

There was a long pause, increasing the cousins' suspense and prompting them to gaze searchingly at their companion.

"What is she saying?" Bess whispered eagerly as the conversation continued.

"Oh, I see," Nancy said into the receiver. "Well—perhaps. Just a minute." She held the phone away, pondering her reply, then spoke to the woman again. "Yes, I'll be glad to come. Besides, I have a lot to report. Yes, I will. *Arrivederci!*

"The *duchessa* wants to see me," the girl went on after she hung up. "At the showroom in Murano."

"So she *is* there," George murmured, overlooking the perplexity in her friend's voice.

"Then why didn't she speak to you when you saw her?" Bess inquired.

"It was probably the other woman I saw," Nancy replied. "The *duchessa* didn't mention knowing we were there—if in fact that really was the *duchessa* who called."

"So are you going back to Murano?" George asked tensely.

"Tonight at ten."

"Not alone I hope."

"Well, she stressed that I ought to."

"Uh-uh," Bess commented. "I wouldn't do that if I were you. You could be sailing right into a big Venetian trap!"

The identical thought had occurred to Nancy, and she dived into her closet, removing a dark, ankle-length skirt from a hanger along with a high-collared silk blouse. Then she hunted for her small disguise kit that she always carried when she traveled.

Realizing what their detective friend was up to, Bess puffed her cheeks anxiously. "George and I absolutely refuse to allow you to do this," she declared. "It's too dangerous!"

"Not if she has her own personal chauffeur and judo expert!" George exclaimed, donning the souvenir gondolier's hat she had purchased earlier. "At your service, *Duchessa!*"

17

Cagey Calls

As George finished her statement with a deep bow, Nancy shook her head. "I thought of masquerading as the *duchessa*, but that could be just as dangerous as showing up as Nancy Drew," she said.

"So maybe you ought to pick a disguise somewhere in between," Bess suggested.

"Precisely," Nancy went on. "Dark hair, different style, a few lines on the face, and—"

"*Voilà!* You're thirty years older!" Her friend giggled. "Brilliant, my dear detective!"

"I don't know how brilliant it is, but I hope it helps me past the guards if there are any; and even if that phone call from the *duchessa* was on the up-and-up, I'm sure she won't mind my little charade."

"You know, I'm beginning to think you'd be safer with a football captain at your side than with me!" George exclaimed.

"We all ought to go along," Bess said. "There's greater safety in numbers."

"I don't agree," Nancy said. "I'm sure two can investigate more efficiently and secretively than six. I'll call Ned to see what he says."

The boy concurred fully with his friend's plan. "Just don't disguise yourself before we have dinner," Ned said in a teasing voice.

"Don't worry. I won't change one strand of hair until afterwards."

When the group was all together, though, Ned's bantering tone faded. "Maybe we ought to go armed with the local police force," he told Nancy.

"We can't," she said, keeping her voice barely above a whisper. "The *duchessa* would have a fit if she thought I had told you all about Filippo's kidnapping—never mind the police!"

"But what if the same thing happened to her?" Burt supported Ned.

"I still can't take the risk of telling the police

anything," Nancy said. "She made me promise."

"Okay, okay," Dave acknowledged, "but you shouldn't refuse a back-up team—"

"In case you both get stuck for some reason," Bess joined in.

"I'm hoping we won't, but if we do, I'd feel better knowing the rest of you are safe on Venetian soil and can send reinforcements, if need be."

"That's a good point," Dave admitted. "But how will we know what you've found or didn't find?"

"And how will we know you're all right?" George asked.

"There are phones everywhere at the factory," Nancy pointed out. "We'll call you the minute we arrive."

"But the switchboard probably shuts down after hours," Bess retorted.

"Then . . ." Nancy laughed, snapping her fingers. "I'll send a seagull with a message!"

Although her lighthearted response did not bring a smile to anyone's face, Ned was finally convinced that they should proceed as planned. The others would be certain to alert the police if they didn't hear from the couple by morning.

"Besides," Nancy said, "what if something turns up while we're gone that requires the attention of four skilled detectives?"

The question, however, went unanswered as they left the restaurant. Ned and Nancy made arrangements to meet at the dock from where they had taken the boat to Murano.

"See you in an hour," the boy said, as they left in separate directions.

But when Nancy and the girls reached their hotel room again, she was unprepared for the message waiting for her.

"It's from Andreoli," the girl told her friends. "He is going to call me at eight-thirty."

"Aren't you supposed to meet Ned then?" George responded.

"Yes, but it's only a five-minute walk to the square," Nancy replied. "Besides, Andreoli doesn't speak much English so I'm sure I won't be on the phone long."

She stuck her head out the window, glancing toward the empty gondola station, then drew the curtains and disappeared into the bathroom carrying the disguise kit. When she emerged a while later, the girls were duly impressed by the remarkable transformation that had occurred.

"Well?" Nancy asked, smoothing her hair. "What do you think?"

"If I didn't know better," George said, "I'd say you were a middle-aged dowager!" Bess crowed.

Nancy's usually soft reddish-blond hair was now quite brown and pressed back into an elegant knot. Her face had also been powdered to look wan and, using an eyebrow pencil, she had created lines under her eyes and across her forehead.

"Who's Ned going as? Father Time?" Bess quipped.

"I don't look that ancient, do I?" Nancy asked, chuckling. "Maybe George will lend him her gondolier's hat."

"Why not?" the girl said. "Just make sure you don't get caught, that's all. I want my hat back!"

Before Nancy had the opportunity to comment, however, Andreoli's call interrupted unexpectedly early. To Nancy's astonishment, he suddenly seemed to have acquired greater fluency in English.

"Miss Drew," he began, "I have heard from

545

the *duchessa*. She told me to tell you she has found her nephew. There is no more for you to do."

As the words rang in her ears, Nancy caught herself questioning the identity of the caller. The voice was familiar and at first she believed it belonged to Andreoli; but when she finally put down the receiver, having only said a brief good-bye, she gaped at her friends.

"What's the matter?" George asked, watching Nancy's pallid face turn crimson.

"That was Erminio Scarpa!" she announced.

"Huh?" Bess replied in utter amazement.

"I'm positive," Nancy said. "He called himself Andreoli, but his English was too good."

"Oh, Nancy," Bess said, her anxiety blossoming again, "please don't go to Murano!"

"I have to. Suppose the *duchessa* is being held a prisoner there?"

"In her own factory?" George asked.

Without defending the point further, the young detective took off her robe and put on the blouse and skirt she had chosen for the occasion.

"How about wearing this too?" Bess said, offering Nancy her evening shawl.

"Oh, that's perfect," the girl said. She checked her watch. "It's eight-thirty. I wonder if the message we received really was from Andreoli or Scarpa?"

"Why don't you wait five more minutes just to be sure?" Bess suggested.

"Okay."

But no other call came, and Nancy finally left her companions. When she was gone, they confessed to a mutual feeling of uneasiness. Should they abide by Nancy's request and not follow her, or ignore the young detective's instructions entirely?"

"Let's discuss it with Burt and Dave," Bess suggested. "I don't trust myself to make this sort of decision, do you?"

"No, ma'am," her cousin replied. "Besides, what if we do something against Nancy's wishes and it backfires?"

Bess breathed heavily, whistling a sigh. "We're really on the spot, aren't we?"

18

Unexpected Arrival

The two remaining couples had telephoned and decided to meet at the entrance to a park not far from dockside after Nancy and Ned were safely on their way to Murano. Bess and George, however, had lingered in their hotel room until after nine o'clock, thinking that Mr. Drew might call, and that would be their opportunity to ask his advice as well.

"Burt and Dave will be wondering where we are," George finally said. "We'd better go."

"I guess so," Bess said uneasily, following her to the elevator.

When they reached the lobby, though, they saw a porter carrying in a suitcase from the hotel float. Directly behind him was Nancy's father!

"Mr. Drew!" Bess and George cried out.

"Why, hello, girls!" he replied, looking beyond them for a sign of his daughter.

"Nancy isn't here," George whispered out of earshot of anyone else.

The secrecy in her voice carved a frown on the attorney's face, and he registered as quickly as he could, following the porter to his room. Then he hurried back to the lobby where the cousins waited for him.

"Now will you please tell me what happened?" he asked.

George explained that they were already late for their date with Burt and Dave and suggested they head for the park.

"You know, it's funny how I had to shift my plans around," Mr. Drew told the girls on the way, "only to discover Nancy is missing."

"Oh, she's not missing," Bess reassured him.

"Well, I'm glad to hear that, at least," the man said, walking briskly toward the square.

"We didn't know you were coming to Venice today," she continued.

"I didn't either," Mr. Drew replied. "My

flight was changed because of a last-minute call from my client, and I had to make a stopover in London on the way. As it is, I don't have to go to Rome until the day after tomorrow, so I thought I'd surprise Nancy by coming here first."

"Believe me, we couldn't be happier," George said.

She smiled affectionately at the man as she and Bess caught sight of the Emerson boys standing near the park wall. Upon seeing the girls and Mr. Drew, they darted forward.

"Mr. Drew!" Dave shouted loudly, causing Bess to raise a finger to her lips. George motioned everyone toward some benches away from strolling passers-by.

"Nancy told us you were going to Rome, Mr. Drew," Burt said, ferreting out the same explanation the lawyer had given the cousins.

"What's happened to Nancy? I assume Ned's with her," the man said.

"You're right," Bess replied and revealed his daughter's plan, which, in view of her past ploys to uncover secret information, did not seem too extraordinary.

"Sounds pretty clever to me," Mr. Drew remarked, "but I can't say I'm happy that she and Ned went to Murano alone."

"That's what worries us," George admitted. "As a matter of fact, Bess and I were wondering if we shouldn't take a boat out there ourselves."

As she said this, Nancy and Ned were watching the night lamps around the factory penetrate the mist that had crawled over the island.

"It's not exactly the warmest night of the year either," Nancy said, pulling her shawl closer, as their boat driver put on one final burst of speed. "Ned, please ask him to shut off his lights."

"Will do," the boy replied, and within seconds the driver cut his engine, letting the boat idle forward in the darkness.

Upon reaching the landing stage, Ned paid him the round-trip fare and asked him to wait. Then, he strode with Nancy to the factory.

To their delight, no one was on guard to scrutinize them at close range and perhaps send them back to Venice. On the other hand, there was an iron grating across the factory door that bore a large padlock.

"Well, we knew it wouldn't be easy to get

inside," Nancy murmured, moving along the building to a closed window.

Despite the chill in the air, the girl dismantled her shawl, throwing it over Ned's shoulder while he lifted her up to push the frame.

"It's locked," Nancy said when it refused to budge. "Now what?" she sighed, sliding down again.

"This way," Ned directed. He had observed a second door hidden in the shadows of a vine trellis. They walked toward it, discovering it was open! "Come on," the boy whispered and started to go in.

But Nancy quickly pulled him back, cautioning him to wait while she pressed her ear to the door. Hearing nothing, though, she pushed it back gently and took one step, then another until she was satisfied no one was behind it.

Suddenly, a light flickered in the adjoining building that housed the showroom, and Ned jumped, startling his companion.

"That must be your appointment," he said.

"I know," Nancy replied.

But she was determined to investigate the factory before making an appearance. She hurried on tiptoe toward the storage room, trying the door without success and digging into her purse for a hairpin.

"How about this?" Ned asked, producing his small penknife and pushing one of its multiple blades into the hole.

He turned it back and forth gently. For a moment he thought he heard a click, but realized it was only his imagination.

"Let me try it, Ned," Nancy said, slipping the hairpin in next, then dropping it in favor of a small, stiff postcard she found in her purse. She worked it against the bolt until it snapped! "Follow me," she whispered, pulling out a pocketsized flashlight.

The storeroom, which at first glance seemed to be no more than a small appendage to the factory, proved to be deceivingly large with metal supply shelves against the back wall and sacks of potash and lime under them. But contrary to what she had thought earlier, there was no other door besides the one they had just opened.

"I don't see the *duchessa* anywhere, do you?" Ned said, smiling into the shadows at Nancy.

"She's supposed to be waiting for me in the

showroom. Remember?" Nancy chuckled. She felt her way past a long worktable, saying nothing more until her heel caught the edge of a floorboard.

"Find something?" Ned asked.

"Could be. I'm not sure."

The young detective flashed her light along the wood, stopping on three small hinges and a thick metal bar that stretched across the opposite edge.

"It's a trapdoor! Let's try to open it," the girl urged, while Ned dropped her shawl on the table.

He fell to his knees, pressing his full weight against the bar, rolling it back inch by inch until the flashlight revealed a tiny finger hole. But the boy had no sooner started to lift the secret door when they heard a strange rustling sound outside and Nancy switched off her light.

At this moment, Mr. Drew and Nancy's friends were still talking and had decided, for the time being, not to hire a boat for Murano.

"Did Nancy say how long they expected to be gone?" her father inquired.

"No," George said, "but based on our trip there today, I'd say no more than two or three hours. She asked us not to call the police till morning, though, if we didn't hear from them."

"That's too long to suit me," Mr. Drew said. "But let's wait a bit longer before we plunge ahead. So long as Ned is with Nancy and they have a boat and a driver at their disposal, I'm sure Ned will head her back if the going gets too rough."

Despite all of his assurances, his listeners doubted that Ned could succeed in changing Nancy's mind once she was on the track of something important.

"Sir," Dave said, changing the subject, "you started to tell us about your client. Did you say he's in the glass business?"

"That's right," the man replied, sitting back on the bench and gazing at the lagoon. "But it seems he's gotten mixed up with some unscrupulous people over here who have accused him of stealing their designs. It's absolutely ridiculous—"

"Why do you say that?" Bess asked.

"Because I know my client. He's impulsive and enthusiastic, but he's not a thief." Mr. Drew paused before he continued his story. "On Giorgio's last trip to Rome, the Italians gave him some dishware to show his sales people in the States. He asked me what I thought of his going into partnership with the Italian factory, and I said I wasn't in favor of it, mostly because of his own particular business problems.

"Unfortunately, Giorgio had already made his decision. He had started negotiations anyway, and they fell through. That didn't surprise me completely—"

"But I still don't understand why the factory people say he's a thief," Burt interrupted.

"Well, because in the midst of their talks, the designs started turning up on dishes sold in the States," the lawyer replied grimly.

"Maybe someone who works for him made a dishonest deal for himself," Dave suggested.

"Quite possible," Mr. Drew said, "but I have a hunch that the Italian factory had a hand in it."

"Why would the factory try to frame Giorgio, though?" George asked.

"To take over his business ultimately. They're threatening to sue him for a lot of money—money he doesn't have. It's all tied up in his company."

"How terrible," the cousins murmured almost in unison.

"What are you going to do, Mr. Drew?" Bess added.

"I'm not sure exactly. I'd like to meet Mr. Alberini. He's one of the owners of the Italian firm. If he's not available, I'll try to see Mr. Scarpa."

"Did you say Scarpa?" Bess blurted out. "Is his first name Erminio?"

19

Taking a Risk

Carson Drew stared blankly into the expectant faces of his listeners, wondering why there was so much intense interest in his response. "Erminio Scarpa?" he repeated. "Come to think of it, I don't remember his first name offhand. It's among my papers, I'm sure. But tell me about the man you mentioned."

That was all the prompting Bess needed. She and George described their encounter with the night clerk, mostly emphasizing his insistence about accompanying Bess to the basilica.

"He and his cohorts just wanted to keep Nancy, George, and me out of their hair," Bess concluded.

As the discussion wore on, Nancy's father became increasingly agitated. He asked several questions about the trip to Murano, finally proposing that they acquire a boat. "Or better yet a police escort," he said. "I noticed a phone on the street for just such emergencies, so if you'll excuse me a moment—"

"We'll wait right here," George said, watching him disappear under the arcade toward the darkened street.

"Nancy will have our hides for this," Bess said to the others, even though she was sure their course of action was the right one.

She had no idea that, only minutes before, the young detective and Ned had crawled under the long worktable in the glassmakers' supply room, listening to the rustle of leaves outside in the still night air.

"Someone's out there," Nancy whispered to the boy.

"Maybe more than one person," he added.

The couple lapsed into silence as the factory door swung open, admitting a flash of light that streamed across the floor to the kilns and crates of broken glass where it stopped. Then the light moved again and the two detectives heard more than one pair of footsteps.

"Just as I thought," Ned murmured, while Nancy leaned forward to follow the traveling light through the small window. "They'll see you," her friend warned and drew the girl back.

Now the steps shuffled closer to the storeroom door, and the handle turned back and forth, causing Ned's heart to thump high in his throat.

Good thing I locked it again, Nancy thought. But what if those men have a key?

She held her breath, praying for the handle to stop moving. Then, to her relief, it did; and she felt Ned relax beside her as he put a hand on her arm. The men, moreover, had begun to talk in a normal, conversational tone.

Too bad I didn't take a course in Italian before I came here! Ned chided himself.

Nancy, on the other hand, concentrated hard on the words and, catching a few of them that she understood, was able to construe the discussion.

They don't have a key for the storeroom door, she gathered. Someone else does. Someone named Alberini.

Then, before she could discern the rest of what was said, the men moved toward the window. They peered inside, exploring the table with the flashlight and, in its beam, picked up the hinged side of the trapdoor. The other end, from which the bar had been removed, stayed hidden under the broad darkness of the table.

Thank goodness, Nancy said to herself, now following the cone of light to the sacks of potash that stood nearby. Suddenly, she heard her name.

"Nancy Drew," one man had said unmistakably, among other words spoken in angry tones. A shiver of fright coursed through his listeners as he pounded his fist once on the small window. Had he seen them after all?

No, he's only trying to vent his frustration, the girl concluded, because if he knew for a fact we were in here, he'd break the glass!

That thought, however, had not occurred to Ned, who was prepared to tackle either of the men if they so much as stepped inside the storeroom. But at last they left the factory.

"Come on, Ned," Nancy said, sliding out of their hiding place. "I want to see what's below this floor."

"You know something?" Ned replied with a soft chuckle. "You really are amazing. My heart stopped beating about five minutes ago, and you're ready to plunge right in again."

"And to think I believed your heart never stopped beating for me," the young detective said lightly. "Come on."

She focused the small flashlight on the finger hole that Ned pulled back on. "It's stuck," he said, pretending it wouldn't budge.

"What?" Nancy gasped, disappointed; but seeing the grin on her friend's face, she realized he was only joking.

He swung the panel wide, revealing a ladder that stretched beyond the dimming glow of Nancy's flashlight to a room bathed in blackness.

"I'm afraid the batteries are ready to give out," she admitted sheepishly, "so I'd better try to save them."

She flicked off the light once she had a firm foothold on the ladder and began to descend slowly, causing the boy to follow with equal caution. When they reached the bottom, Nancy turned the light on again, directing it to a full-length mirror that was obviously undergoing restoration.

But besides seeing her image and that of Ned's, she noticed a canvas sack heaped over something. A white lacy collar surfaced in the light. Instantly, the girl detective turned, letting the beam fall directly on the heavy cloth. It was covering the inert form of the *duchessa*!

"Oh!" Nancy cried, running toward the woman, who appeared to be asleep.

"She's alive, isn't she?" Ned asked anxiously while his companion touched the figure. There was no reaction, however.

"Yes, but I think she's been drugged, Ned."

As she spoke, the *duchessa* let out a soft, pitiful cry much like that of a whimpering puppy. Ned lifted her frail body and carried it to the ladder.

Then, sighing, he realized that he would be unable to take the woman upstairs unless he put her over his shoulder, and even that would be risky given the narrowness of the opening overhead.

"I think we have a problem," he told Nancy, and pointed to their escape hatch.

"You're right," she said, but could not come up with a solution.

"Maybe you or I ought to climb up and tell

the boatman to get the police," Ned suggested.

"But what if somebody catches us leaving?" Nancy responded, suddenly aware of the *duchessa*'s eyes, which had begun to open ever so slightly. "Ned, put her down in that chair over there," she said.

He did, and Nancy curled her arm gently around the woman's shoulder. "Who brought you here?" she asked.

Maria Dandolo said something in Italian, then as if suddenly aware she had been addressed in English, she translated her words, weakly but with clarity.

"Two men."

"What are their names?" Nancy pressed her.

"Alberini and—Scarpa."

"Did they tell you where your nephew Filippo is?" the girl continued.

"Oh, no—poor Filippo." The woman moaned and began to weep piteously. "No—don't hurt him," she pleaded.

"*Duchessa*, do you know where he is?" Nancy repeated with an intensity and firmness that ended the crying.

"No. Anyway, I wouldn't believe whatever Mr. Alberini said."

There was another long, intolerable pause that made Nancy wonder if the woman had somehow hidden the answer in the recesses of her mind, vehemently refusing to accept it.

"Oh, please, *Duchessa*, it's very important that you tell me. I want to help you," Nancy said slowly. "I want to find Filippo."

But again the woman moaned uncontrollably.

"It's no use, Ned," Nancy remarked in despair.

"Well, just tell me what you want to do. Other than my original idea, I can't think of a thing."

Nancy, however, began questioning the *duchessa* once more.

"Are the men going to take you to see your nephew?" she asked.

"They promised me they would if—"

"If what?" the young detective prompted her.

"If I give them the formula."

"Is that why you came here to the factory in the first place?"

"Yes."

Nancy then recalled the seeming intrusion at the woman's apartment on San Gregorio. Papers had been pulled from the desk and strewn everywhere. Had Nancy's first deduction been

566

wrong about an intruder? Wasn't it more likely that the *duchessa* had finally succumbed to the kidnappers' threats and searched frantically for her own copy of the formula?

When she didn't find it she came to Murano! Nancy thought. "What happened to your own copy of the formula?" she blurted out to Ned's surprise.

"I don't know. I could not find it in my desk."

"Did you find another copy?" the young detective went on. "Here, in the storage room, I mean."

"No."

Nancy sipped in another long breath. "Did the men say they'd be back to see you?"

"Yes," the *duchessa* said, her voice now almost inaudible. "Then—they made me call you. They said they would harm Filippo if I refused. I'm sorry, Nancy—so—sorry—" With that, she sank back exhausted and inert once again.

"Pretty clever plan," Nancy said. "Our two friends probably expected to catch me on their second visit. Perhaps I shouldn't disappoint them!"

20

Venetian Victory

Ned stared at Nancy in utter surprise. "Are you serious?"

"Yes, I am," the young detective replied. "You see, if I stall them long enough, you'll have time to get help."

"And you expect me to leave.you on this island alone—without me to protect you?"

"Look, Ned, it's our only chance to find out where Filippo is," Nancy insisted. "The minute you get back to Venice—"

"Why don't I stay here," Ned cut in, "and send the boatman for help?"

"I don't know if we can rely on him. Besides

if the police doubt his story, he may not persist enough to convince them."

"What'll we do with the *duchessa*?"

"We'll have to leave her here for the time being. Ned, please, it's the only way. Believe me!" Nancy urged.

"Whatever you say," Ned replied in a quiet voice.

"I'll keep the men talking as long as I can," the girl said, pulling a small brush from her handbag. She worked the dark powder out of her hair and wiped off her makeup with a handkerchief before scurrying up the ladder.

"Be careful," Ned said anxiously.

"I will. I promise. Now please, don't worry."

Easier said than done, the boy thought, but he lay the *duchessa* on the floor again and prepared for his own departure while Nancy slipped out of the building and onto the grassy walkway that led to the showroom. She slowed her pace only a moment when she heard Ned's feet on the pavement going in the opposite direction toward the dock, then sped forward again.

Upon reaching the showroom entrance, however, she did not ring the bell but stepped softly inside, the thick carpet shielding her from detection.

They must be upstairs, she decided and climbed to the landing.

To her surprise, all doors on the second floor were locked. Men's voices, however, came from one room. They were muffled by the separation of the wall, but as the young detective listened, she realized there were four people speaking in English. One of them was an American. The second was the manager of the glass factory, Mr. Chiais, and the third, Erminio Scarpa!

"Now, Erminio, this is Beppe Alberini talking to you as a friend," the American said, but his words were cut short by a disbelieving laugh—Scarpa's, Nancy surmised.

"You have nothing to worry about," Alberini continued. "So long as the other clerk was willing to give you an alibi, no one will believe some stupid amateur detective."

"But her friend—the one I took to the basilica—she can identify me; and Lucia says Nancy Drew knows where we live."

"But you and Francesco will be out of the country before we get caught. We'll see to it."

"That's right," the manager said. "As soon as we get what we want from Signore Dandolo—"

He's talking about the formula, Nancy thought.

"—we'll join you. It's all very simple," Chiais finished. "Don't worry about the girl. She is only a nuisance, nothing more dangerous than that."

Nancy felt her skin tingle in disgust as the conversation continued. The fourth man in the room, she found out, was Scarpa's brother Francesco, who was in business with Alberini; and it was he, Alberini, and Erminio who had tried to kidnap Filippo's father. But when they couldn't find him, they took Filippo instead. Their plan was to ruin the Dandolo business. After that, they would take care of a contact in the United States by the name of Giorgio, a man whom they had induced into partnership.

It sounds as if they want to create their own little monopoly, Nancy thought, and push all the competition out by any means possible.

When the men started to talk about more casual matters that were of no further interest to the young detective, she knocked firmly on the door.

A chair slid back in response, and Beppe Alberini snarled, "Who's there?"

"Nancy Drew," the girl said cheerfully. "I'm looking for the *duchessa*."

"Ah, yes, of course," the man replied and opened the door. He had a round face, balding black hair and a sarcastic smile on his lips as he pulled Nancy inside. "You know these gentlemen, I believe."

Nancy nodded even though she had never met Francesco Scarpa before. "I would like to see the *duchessa*, please."

"In a moment," Alberini said. "First, I'd like to know how much you have been able to figure out about our operation."

The girl's mind raced. Should she tell the men what she knew? Perhaps it was better not to, yet it might be the only way to stall them!

"Well, I know one of you broke into the Artistico Vetro showroom on the night of our arrival in Venice," she began. Then she voiced a hunch she had had all along. "Since nothing was stolen, although a chandelier fell off the ceiling, I suppose your purpose was to bug the *duchessa*'s apartment."

"Brava!" Alberini exclaimed. "You are, indeed, a clever girl."

"Who did it?" Nancy inquired, but when no one responded, she answered her own question. "I would say Erminio Scarpa. Now I'm sure you're wondering how I figured that out."

She watched the men's rapt faces, stringing out her words slowly. "When Mr. Scarpa came to our room later that night, I noticed that the bottoms of his pants legs were wet." Now Nancy turned to the night clerk. "You pulled that little job, didn't you, just before you came on duty at the hotel? Your boat must've been leaking just enough to leave those telltale wet marks on your trousers."

Furious, the man glared at her but did not speak.

"You were probably the one who also tried to push me off the *vaporetto* the next day," Nancy accused him.

Alberini smiled. "A young lady with your brains and good looks would be an asset to our company. Perhaps, when we're all finished here, we'll offer you a job."

"Thank you, but no thanks," Nancy said coldly. She stared at the man with disgust, then let her eyes roam across the room. They settled on a cap hanging on a coatrack. It was similar to the one Ned had found on the bridge near the Hotel Excelsior after the boys' boat had been attacked.

"Who's cap is this?" she asked, walking toward it.

"Mine," Alberini said. "Why?"

It's quite new, isn't it?" Nancy went on. "You bought it after you lost your other one when you did your rope trick at the bridge, trying to sink my friends' boat."

Alberini's lips spread into an evil grin. "So you found my other one, eh? I'll be glad to take it back. I can always use two."

Where you're going you won't need any, Nancy said to herself, adding aloud, "We've also figured out that it was Erminio Scarpa who went through the other hotel room—the one my Emerson friends were staying in."

"Yes, he was looking for something that belonged to us," Alberini admitted.

"Was it a beautiful glass horse, perchance?"

"Obviously. Francesco had flown to Vienna to sell it to a prospective customer, but unfortunately the deal fell through. He couldn't very well leave it aboard his plane but naturally he was afraid to bring it back through customs since he assumed the officials had been alerted. So he planted it in the boy's suitcase."

"He must've overheard Ned say he and his friends planned to stay at the Gritti Palace Hotel," Nancy put in.

"Exactly, Miss Drew. And since Erminio had access to the rooms there, it would be easy enough to retrieve the statue, or so he thought. By the way, what did your friends do with it?"

"The customs people broke it by accident."

"Oh, what a shame, and it was such a lovely piece, worth quite a bit of money, too." Alberini sighed.

"One thing puzzles me," Nancy addressed the hotel clerk. She riveted her eyes on his. "You probably knew the boys had been arrested and you must've realized that the police wouldn't have permitted them to leave with an expensive glass sculpture that they had allegedly smuggled into the country. So—why did you bother looking for it?"

"Because Alberini told me that he had fixed it with the police to let the boys keep the piece. He said he paid off the captain—" Scarpa's words faded as he stared at his accomplice. "Why did you tell me that?"

"I know why," Nancy said. "Because he wanted you to steal the statue from Ned's room and then have *you* arrested for it. It was a frame-up to get you out of the picture. He probably intended to get rid of your brother as well by a similar scheme."

Now it was Francesco Scarpa's turn to glare at Alberini. "Why, you double-crossing—" he roared. "You lied to us!" A string of Italian utterances spewed angrily from his mouth until he swallowed hard and stopped. "Oh, why did we ever listen to you? You even fooled Lucia and Antonella."

Antonella, Nancy thought, must be his younger sister. "I saw Antonella's photograph," she said, hoping to bring the *duchessa*'s nephew back into the conversation. "She was standing next to Filippo Dandolo."

"It was through her that we were able to persuade Filippo to do some designs for us," Erminio Scarpa said. "It was all Beppe's idea. He gave the designs to an American business associate. He wanted to expand his·operation to the United States."

"Shut up!" Alberini hissed, "or we'll all end up in jail. Let's silence this little busybody and get out of here before her friends alert the police!"

But he had barely finished his sentence when a flurry of noise stirred outside. Then the door flung open and a team of uniformed officers, followed by Mr. Drew and Nancy's friends, dashed forward.

"Dad!" the girl cried, running into his arms as Ned and the others circled her. "Oh, I'm so glad to see you!"

"I hope we didn't interrupt an interesting conversation." Her father grinned.

"Not at all. The interesting part just finished. They were about to get rid of me, and I think they meant for good!" Nancy said, as Ned pinched his eyes in worry.

"I knew this plan of yours was risky!" he said.

"But it worked, didn't it?" Nancy exclaimed jubilantly. "I can tell you their entire scheme—everything!"

Mr. Drew, however, held up a hand. "Before you do, there are a few other people who would like to hear it, I'm sure," he said.

A moment later, Andreoli stepped into the room followed by another police officer and the *duchessa*.

"Oh, *Duchessa!*" Nancy exclaimed, hugging her and helping her to a chair.

"I'm afraid I wasn't too coherent before, was I, my dear?"

"Nonsense," the girl said.

"That's kind of you to say," the woman said, sinking back wearily. "But the drugs seem to have worn off now and I should be able to understand everything much better. First, I want to thank you, Nancy. You saved my life, you know!"

Nancy did not reply, however, as she lit on Ned's gaze. "I'm not sure your life really was in danger—"

"But it was," Andreoli insisted in perfect English. "You see, my sister is not very strong, and another night in that awful, damp cellar would have been detrimental to her health."

"Your sister?" Nancy and her friends repeated, gaping at him.

"Yes. You see, I'm Filippo's father."

"What?" Bess cried, as the man pulled off the black beard he had worn, now revealing the

578

distinguished face of a man in his early sixties.

"I put this on so no one would recognize me. Only Maria knew of my disguise."

"But when she asked us to help her, why didn't you tell us?" George inquired.

"I was afraid to. Suppose you had fallen into the hands of our adversaries? They could have pried the information out of you."

"It's not that we didn't trust you," Maria Dandolo interjected. "We simply felt it wasn't essential for you to know where Claudio was, and we wanted to avoid even the slightest slip on anyone's part."

Then, she turned to the manager. "I had no idea, Giuseppe, that you were part of all this. How very sad. How very, very sad indeed."

Her listener merely looked away, unable to respond.

"And now, where is Filippo?" Signore Dandolo asked at last. He fired an angered glare at the men who remained defiantly closemouthed until Erminio Scarpa spoke.

"What's the use?" he said, coughing out the answer. "He's on Torcello, in a room behind the museum there."

"Opposite Santa Maria Assunta? Yes, I know

it well There is a stone on the wall that bears the winged lion. I can still see Filippo's face when I took him to the island as a small boy. He loved it so, and I believe that was what he had in mind when he adopted the symbol as his artist's signature."

Instantly, the police captain ordered some of his men to the island.

"Before we leave," Mr. Drew said, "I have a question for Francesco Scarpa. Just what is your connection with my client, Giorgio?"

The man scowled. "You figure it out."

"I think I already have," the attorney replied. "You planned to push Giorgio out of a very successful business by accusing him of stealing designs that you forced Filippo to create under threats of harm to the rest of his family. You showed the designs to Giorgio and his sales people, then gave them to another American manufacturer who began to mass market them. Correct?"

Erminio's brother did not answer.

"That was all he and Alberini needed to start a lawsuit," Burt added.

"Actually," Mr. Drew continued, "they had no intention of going through with it. That's why I got no action from the lawyer in Rome and why Giorgio sent me over here to look into things."

"But then what were they after if not damages from a lawsuit?" Bess asked.

"A settlement."

"And don't forget Giorgio's business!" Dave concluded.

"With the Dandolo formula in hand, they could double it quickly and successfully all over the world," Nancy observed.

"By the way, where is the formula, *signore*?" Ned asked Filippo's father. "Safe and sound, I hope."

"It's right here," the man said, tapping his forehead. "I destroyed all the written copies, even my sister's, just to make sure no one could possibly get hold of it. Unfortunately, she left for Murano before I could tell her what I had done."

"I—I could not stand the pressure and the threats any longer," the woman admitted. "I feared for Filippo's life, which, for both of us, is worth much more than anything else in the world. You understand that, Claudio, don't you?"

581

"Of course I do," the *signore* said gently.

"Were the men at your apartment when I called you yesterday and you said you needed not only me?" Nancy asked the *duchessa*.

"Yes. That's when I was going through my desk looking for the formula. When I couldn't find it, they brought me here."

"We came to the factory this afternoon," Nancy said. "I saw someone in the inner storeroom who resembled you. Was it you?"

The woman closed her eyes for a moment. "I tried to get to the window to attract your attention, but the men pulled me away and out of sight before I succeeded."

Now, as the prisoners departed, Nancy wondered whether her next mystery would pose as much of a challenge as the one she had encountered in Italy. She would find out very soon when she found herself caught in a *Race Against Time*.

Meanwhile, though, she was more than happy to see Filippo reunited with his family. He proved to be an attractive young man in his thirties with sparkling eyes that betrayed his sense of humor.

Later that evening when everyone gathered for their last dinner in Venice, Nancy presented one question that only Filippo could answer.

"How did you manage to send the note with the winged lion on it to your aunt?" she asked.

"Before they took me away, I heard one of the men say we were going to Torcello," the young man said. "I had a piece of paper in my jacket and I always carry pencils in my shirt pocket. So I quickly scribbled the note and Aunt Maria's address and dropped it on the street. Apparently someone found it and delivered it to the house."

"That was clever of you, Filippo," George complimented him.

"I wanted to write a message, but as you can imagine, I didn't have time. Once I had put down the address and the symbol, I realized the men were watching me. I told them I had an idea for a new design and stuck the paper back in my pocket for a second. Then, when they weren't looking, I pulled it out and dropped it."

"Unfortunately, neither I nor Claudio connected the message with Torcello," the *duchessa* said, chiding herself.

"Now, now," Filippo said, "let's not talk

about all this unpleasantness anymore. Especially since this dinner is really in honor of my favorite detective."

"Only one detective?" his aunt asked brightly. "I count six of them!"

"Well, my dear aunt, I intend to make five more of these, if you'll all accept them?"

"Oh, my goodness. How wonderful!" Bess cried, watching the veil of gauze fall away from a magnificent glass etching.

On it was the artist's famed signature—a large winged lion—and underneath the words, *My most grateful thanks to Nancy Drew*.

"And ours, too," the *duchessa* said on behalf of herself and Filippo's father.

"This really belongs to all of you," Nancy told her friends, rising to accept the gift.

"Don't worry, don't worry! I said I will make more! A hundred of them, if you like!" Filippo exclaimed, bringing a round of applause and laughter.